PRAISE FOR *NA*

"Darrell James makes a smooth debut. *Nazareth Child* successfully captures and sustains interest."—*Tucson Weekly*

"A compelling psychological journey and powerful debut. Filled with strong, realistic characters; biting dialogue; and tense, turbulent action, *Nazareth Child* proves that Darrell James is a unique new voice, and he's here to stay."—Stephen Jay Schwartz, *Los Angeles Times* bestselling author of *Boulevard* and *Beat*

"The fast-flowing story line will engage readers. It's nice to see James present a woman in control in the leading role."—*Kirkus Reviews*

"A great debut novel that will hold you spellbound to its dynamite conclusion."—*Suspense Magazine*

"James cranks up the tension while spinning a classic tale of good versus evil. Here's hoping for lots more from this powerful new voice on the thriller scene."—Paul Levine, author of *Lassiter*

"While Nazareth certainly delivers all the thrills and chills expected of a good suspense novel, its real power lies in its gripping illustration of how a religious charlatan can use his followers' emotional dependence for his own evil ends. A cautionary tale, and a damned good one."—*Mystery Scene*

SONORA
CROSSING

A DEL SHANNON
NOVEL

SONORA CROSSING

DARRELL JAMES

MIDNIGHT INK
WOODBURY, MINNESOTA

FIRST EDITION
First Printing, 2012

Book design by Donna Burch
Cover design by Ellen Lawson
Cover art: Desert sunset: iStockphoto.com/Ken Canning
        Girl: Fuse/PunchStock
Editing by Brett Fechheimer

Midnight Ink, an imprint of Llewellyn Worldwide Ltd.

Library of Congress Cataloging-in-Publication Data
James, Darrell, 1946–
    Sonora crossing : a Del Shannon novel / Darrell James. — 1st ed.
        p.   cm.
    ISBN 978-0-7387-2370-9
    1. Girls—Fiction. 2. Women private investigators—Fiction. 3. Kidnapping—
Fiction. 4. Psychic ability—Fiction. 5. Arizona—Fiction. I. Title.
    PS3610.A429S66 2012
    813'.6—dc23
                            20120106911

Midnight Ink
Llewellyn Worldwide Ltd.
2143 Wooddale Drive
Woodbury, MN 55125-2989
www.midnightinkbooks.com

Printed in the United States of America

DEDICATION

For Diana, still, in memory

ACKNOWLEDGMENTS

Thanks always to Terri Bischoff and all the staff at Midnight Ink,
who work magic every day.

ONE

THROUGH THE WINDSHIELD OF his pickup, Benito Lara saw the trail of dust forming in the distance to the south and got a familiar, sick feeling deep in his gut—a caravan of dark SUVs, moving fast across the desert floor. *Narcotraficantes*. Men sent by his brother-in-law, Santos, with their bricks of black tar, their bundles of white powder.

The girl had seen it, too.

Even before the dust cloud appeared, Aurea's gaze had turned south and held, seeing things, as she seemingly did, long before they had a chance to happen. A slight smile had crossed the knowing calm of her face. Benito observed his daughter on the seat next to him, content with using scissors to clip photos and headlines from newspapers. "Uncle Santos is with them this time?" he asked.

Aurea lifted her eyes to him, long enough for him see the answer. Then she resumed her work with scissors.

Benito felt his gut tighten.

Such a strange *pajarita*, he thought—a *little bird*. Six years old and not yet schooled, she seemed to have the insights of an adult. Yet the girl had never spoken so much as a single word in her entire lifetime. How could it be that she envisioned such things, he wondered? Of course, the pre-dawn skies had been dark beneath cloud cover. And, with the rains yet to come, it would have made for the perfect time to cross the border through one of the narrow washes. Perhaps the girl had simply deduced her uncle's arrival, drawing on recollection from previous times, other overcast mornings the men had come. *Yes, perhaps*, Benito thought. Then he shook his head. She was different, his daughter, he had to concede that much. But it was her mother and her Uncle Santos, the ambitious drug smuggler, who believed the child *gifted*.

———

The vehicles came out of the desert, crossing the border from Mexico into Arizona, and onto Benito's farm. They followed the dirt road between the fields, where the irrigation ditches this morning were dry and hard-caked. Benito waited until they reached the turn-out in front of the barn before stepping out of the pickup. "Stay in the truck," he told his daughter, as the vehicles—four of them—peeled away in pairs and circled the yard in opposite directions before coming to a stop facing back the way they had come. Benito ran a hand across his dry mouth and took time to glance back toward the house, to consider his wife, Yanamaria.

From two of the vehicles, several men deployed to take up guard positions and watch. They were serious looking, dressed in boots and jeans this morning, weapons bulging beneath satin windbreakers. From a third vehicle—a dark blue Chevy Blazer, closest to the barn—two more men appeared. Benito recognized both of them. One was Paco Díaz, the other Ramón Paz—long-time friends of Santos, devoutly dedicated to him.

The one, Paco, crossed to a place near the barn to light a cigarette and stand smoking while the other, Ramón, came around to the back of the vehicle to lean against it, facing Benito, arms crossed.

In the fourth vehicle, behind the wheel, was Mata—Santos' bodyguard and driver. Built like a massive earth mover, he was known to be as violent and reactive as nitroglycerin. Benito felt himself shrink back at the sight of him. A long, heavy moment passed before the rear door of the vehicle opened and Santos stepped out. He was dressed in a tailored silk suit, his eyes hidden behind dark glasses. He moved in calculated motions, first turning to observe the fields behind him, where mounting monsoon winds swept dust between the rows. Then removing the glasses, he slipped them into his breast pocket and turned his gaze to Benito. "I see the melons are small this season."

"Blame it on La Niña," Benito replied, observing the dark clouds gathering above. "The summer rains, they have been slow to come. But soon, God willing."

Santos nodded agreement. "Such is the life of a poor dirt farmer."

Now, he hesitated, craning his neck to peer past the glare of the pickup's windshield. "Is that my niece I see? I was hoping she would be up this morning."

Santos crossed around the front of the pickup to open the passenger door, saying to Benito's daughter, "And how is my little *profeta* today?"

Benito watched as Santos gathered the girl—small for her age—into his arms. Her hands locked around her uncle's neck.

"My favorite person in the whole wide world," Santos teased, nuzzling the girl with his nose.

Her innocent gaze came to meet his as she offered her most recent clipping for his approval.

Santos took the clipping and observed it. "Ah, you make pretty pictures. How very nice." Santos folded the clipping once and tucked it into the girl's clothing. "For safekeeping," he said to her, then carried her back into the yard with him, where Benito waited.

Benito could feel waves of anger course through him. He wanted to reach out and drag his daughter away, but knew this was not the time. And there were things he wanted to say to Santos—tell him that he would soon no longer be available to help with the trafficking. Tell him that, before long, this farm, the land Santos crossed, would be sold. There would be new owners. Tell him that he and his wife and his daughter would soon move far away, leaving Santos to work his trade without their help. He wanted to say, "*Go! My daughter will no longer be available for your attentions!*" Tell Santos that he should let them leave in peace. And that if he did not, he would go to the authorities himself.

Benito wanted with all his heart to say all these things, but instead he bit back his anger and coached himself *be silent*. He said, "We should make this quick, brother-in-law."

"What?" Santos said, bringing his eyes from the girl to rest on Benito. "Am I not allowed to take time for my niece?"

"Aurea is very fond of you, yes," Benito said, giving in. "I was thinking of your time away from the protection of your home."

Santos held Benito's eyes for a moment, then lowered the girl to the ground. Taking her by the hand, he said, "Come, Aurea. Take a walk with Tío Santos."

Benito threw a glance toward the house, saying prayers that Yanamaria, his wife, Santos' own sister, would be watching through the kitchen window, witness his pain, and come to intervene. But, alas, the windows were shaded with glare, and Santos was now leading Aurea off toward the picnic table that sat beneath the tree. Benito watched as Santos lifted the girl to a seat on the table, then climbed through to sit beside her on the wooden bench.

You are weak and gutless, Benito Lara. He cursed himself silently. *Today you will let it pass, because soon … soon we will all be far away from this man.*

————

At the picnic table, Santos observed his niece carefully, then let his gaze drift off toward the horizon south. Out there, some forty kilometers below the border, lay his home, Cotorra. Between here and there lay hard desert caliches, veined by deep washes, and mountains chiseled with secreted canyons. Through them ran the *senderos*, the Sonoran drug corridors. The avenues of trade that were quickly making him wealthy. *He who controls the corridors, moves with impunity; he who moves with impunity, owns the market.* It was Santos' credo. The code on which he based his life.

But it was not an easy life to maintain.

Santos considered this, thinking of his niece once again—her strange abilities and what they could mean to him. *How blessed, this child! How blessed, the Kingdom of God, from which she descended!*

Santos felt the girl's hands on his face, pulling his gaze toward her, imploring him with her eyes.

"Yes, *profeta*, we are going on a little trip today. How did you know?"

The girl held his gaze.

"Of course! You have already seen it here," he said, tapping Aurea's forehead with one finger.

Aurea held his gaze.

"Let me tell you, little one," Santos said, throwing a conspiratorial glance back toward Benito and to the house where the girl's mother remained inside. "Please understand. There are those who wish to take you away from me. I have heard the rumors, seen ads for sale of this property. Tell me if I am wrong, little one, but are the two of us not joined by a divine bond? You understand then why I cannot allow this thing to happen. Tell me you see."

Aurea's eyes leveled on him, sharing emotions that Santos believed only *he* could understand. But if the girl would only speak, he thought, how much clearer would be the actions he must take. Santos dropped his head in sadness, then slowly lifted it. Speaking off toward the horizon, he said, "Your Uncle Santos loves you very much. You know that! Don't you, Aurea?"

———

Benito stood with his head down, shoulders hunched, silently seething as Santos lavished affections on his daughter. They were close, Santos and Aurea—Benito had to admit—sharing some special bond that neither his wife, Yanamaria, nor he had come to understand. It troubled him. Santos was—Mother of God—a man who lived on the edge. The drugs, the money. Violence followed him like a hungry wolf.

Benito turned his gaze from the picnic table where Santos remained in council with his daughter. There was a time, not all that long ago, when Benito had felt close to his brother-in-law. But then had come the offer of financial support in exchange for use of his farm as a distribution point for the drugs. He had resisted at first. He and Yanamaria. But then came two years of drought, when melon output was lacking. Times became difficult, and there was Santos with his money, seeming to *know* exactly the right time to show, exactly when to offer his hand in support.

On the trail of the money came the dangerous men to drop off the drugs. Another arrived from the American side to pick them up. He and his wife were stuck in the very middle, unable to resist, unwilling to deny. They had come to live with the constant threat of violence. And, of course, the threat from authorities if their crimes were ever discovered.

Be patient, Benito reminded himself. All of this would change soon—once the ad drew a buyer, once the farm had sold. There was a better life waiting for them in the rich Central Valley of California. The promise of a good job for him, one that did not stoop his back and make him old before his time. A special school for Aurea in Fresno, one where they understood her special gifts. And support from his family—his brother, sister, sister-in-law, and mother—all working together in union to help them in their cause.

Be patient.

Santos was finishing, now, lifting Aurea from her seat on the table and returning with her in his arms. Benito watched as they crossed, not to him, but to the lead vehicle. He stood in disbelief as Santos handed Aurea off through the open door of the vehicle to his driver, Mata. The man, cruel as razor wire, started the engine as he gathered her onto the seat next to him.

What was happening?

The car door closed, and slowly the vehicle began to move off toward the road between the fields.

Benito stiffened and started after his daughter. From his flank, Ramón came off the vehicle to grab him and wrest him under control. Benito broke free, and started forward again, only to have Ramón grab him once more from behind and grapple him to his knees.

Benito threw an imploring look to the other man, Paco, who now crushed out his cigarette beneath his boot, and crossed to retrieve a shovel that stood leaning against the barn.

"*¡Madre de Dios!*" Benito cried, imploring of Santos. "In the name of the Virgin, what are you doing?"

The seconds that followed seemed to play out in slow motion. Benito saw Santos pace quickly toward him. Saw him reach inside his coat. Saw the gun that he removed. Benito stretched his hands high toward the sky, offering a plea for mercy. He opened his mouth to scream but heard nothing of his own voice, as Santos pointed his weapon at him and squeezed the trigger.

pop ... pop ... pop ... pop ...

Benito felt the force of the slugs punch into him, felt a sudden weakness overcome his legs. He sagged to the ground, as the hands restraining him released their grip. Pitched forward first onto his stomach, then rolled to face upward into the storm-building sky. Instantly, the slow-motion images ceased, and life became real again.

Benito heard the screen door open, as Yanamaria—responding the sound of gunfire—came onto the porch. *"No!"* was all Benito managed to say, as Santos turned the gun on his own sister and fired.

Now his wife was lying at the foot of the porch across from him, Santos standing over her, looking down at her. From the look on his face, Benito thought that Santos might, for a brief moment, be remembering his sister as she had been as a child. Perhaps, seeing the two of them, brother and sister, playing together in the streets of Cotorra.

Then Santos pointed the gun at her once more and pulled the trigger again.

Benito lay staring up into the darkening sky, watching the storm clouds roil. He could feel little of his body. But he could feel his mind, weightless and beginning to float.

Santos crossed to one of the remaining vehicles and slid inside. The guards piled in behind. The drivers urged the gas, and two more of the vehicles moved off down the road between the fields.

Remaining behind was the blue Chevy Blazer, Paco and Ramón. They were standing over Benito, looking down at him now—Paco holding the shovel.

Across the yard from him lay his wife, dead or dying. And out there, swept away on the growing monsoon winds, flew his daughter—his strange but special little bird. Benito felt the wind stir dust through his hair, felt the first small drop of rain glance his cheek.

It was a sign the summer monsoons had finally come to Palo Blanco.

TWO

FROM THE LOUNGE, BEHIND the firing line, Randall Willingham watched his favorite investigator getting ready. She was adorable, this young woman, even in her pain, aiming a nine-millimeter handgun down-range and squeezing the trigger. He could tell she was hurting inside.

She was Del Shannon. Thirty years old. This morning dressed in boots and tight jeans, a denim shirt tucked in at her narrow waistline. She could use a little more meat on her bones—Randall's opinion—and she wore her hair shagged short like a boy's. Still, she was one of the sexiest women he believed he'd ever seen. Randall watched as she worked through her grief by capping-off rounds at the target.

…pop…pop…pop…pop…pop…pop…pop…

The weapon kicked. Brass shell casings ejected from the chamber and collected at her feet. After fifteen rounds, the gun's slide locked open and smoke curled from the chamber. She ejected the magazine and punched another in place.

Randall reminded himself to be patient, waiting as she adjusted her form—a modified police stance, two-handed grip, that profiled the curve of her hip. She began popping off rounds once more.

When the gun ran empty this time, she holstered it, hit the button that carried the paper silhouette down the wire to her, and examined the results—a tight-fisted grouping, thirty rounds, center mass. *Jesus!* Randall swallowed.

Randall was owner of Desert Sands Covert in Tucson, a firm that specialized in finding and recovering missing persons. This good-looking young woman had come to him three years back looking for a job, and his first reaction had been to put her behind the reception desk where he could look at her. But, *huh-uh*. She wanted to be a field investigator—the job dangerous, sometimes requiring covert actions and deadly force to recover victims of kidnapping or foul play.

Now this young woman with the level green eyes had become one of the best investigators in the business. Much better than either Rudy Lawson or James "Willard" Hoffman—the other two field operatives who shared the office bullpen with her. She got her picture in the papers, it seemed, every time she found some missing person or returned a runaway home.

Randall had come to care about her. That's why, watching her, he could feel something of the pain she was feeling. He waited until she'd removed her ear protectors, then said, "The only time I find you at the shooting range is when you're upset."

Del looked over, only mildly surprised to see him there. "I hope that's not leading to a lecture?" She hooked the ear protectors

11

over the peg next to her, crossed with the silhouette in hand, and tossed it on the low table in front of him.

Randall studied the pattern of bullet holes for a moment. Then said, "No, I just came by to see how you were doing and tell you how sorry I am to hear about Ed Jeski."

Del collected her work duffel from the floor next to the chair, set it on the table, and began rummaging inside. "Yeah...well...I guess shit happens."

"You don't have to play the tough girl with me, sweetheart. I know you once cared for the man."

"*Once.*" Del said. "It's been more than three years since Ed and I were together."

"Still, it's got to hurt. The man was murdered."

"He was a cop, Randall. You come to expect these things."

"What I heard, he was gunned down inside a motel room on South Sixth Avenue. Don't you question what he was doing there?"

Her eyes came up quickly. "Goddamn it, Randall! What do you want me to say?"

Randall took his time with her. The Tucson Police Department was calling it a crime of passion. A jealous husband, a love triangle—the things they were considering. He said, "When did you find out?"

"This morning. I've been out in the field all week."

Randall lowered his gaze. "I have a prospective client coming by the office at four this afternoon. They've asked for you personally, but now I'm starting to think..."

"Don't!" Del said, cutting him short.

Randall looked up.

"Don't treat me like I'm made of something breakable. This thing with Ed, sure it hurts. But I'm not going to pull the covers over my head and die."

"See, that's what I wanted to talk to you about. You've been through a lot this past year."

Del said nothing and continued rummaging inside the bag.

It was closing in on two in the afternoon, a Thursday. They were on the far east side of the Tucson valley. A place known as Scotty's Indoor Shooting Range. It was an elongated cinder-block building that sat with its down-range end backed against the mountains. Plain looking. But a place of significance to Del.

Just a little over a year ago, this range had been the site of the culmination of a lifelong quest Del had been on to find her mother. She had gone undercover with an ATF agent working at the direction of the FBI. She'd been urged by the Feds to help with the investigation, and the assignment had required them to infiltrate the religious compound of the infamous faith healer Silas Rule. Del had agreed, mostly, because of evidence that suggested she might find the mother she'd never known living there. They'd done so—she and the agent—ending it here, in a shootout with Silas Rule, the fabled Kentucky faith healer, himself. But by the time all the dust settled, Del had lost both her parents—mother and father. And it left its scars.

What worried Randall so much was that he'd never really seen this girl grieve. Not a minute during all that time. Instead, she'd gone right back to work, pouring herself into the job with an even greater vengeance. He didn't want to get into a big thing with her about it. But here she was again, another tragedy in her life, and she was turning the screws on her heart like it was a grape in a press from which she had to squeeze all the emotional juices.

Randall let his gaze move to the shooting area, to the sound-absorbing panels that separated the firing line into stalls. Down-range, bright floodlights had the target area lit up like a football stadium. Without meeting her eyes, he said, "You ever think about the future, sweetheart?"

"What's that supposed to mean?"

He turned his eyes to hers. "I mean this job… running around with a gun on your hip… playing around in some pretty danger-ous situations. Where's it going to leave you ten years from now?"

"I haven't thought about it."

"Well, maybe you should."

"Is this the 'settle down and have kids' speech? I've heard it."

"It wouldn't hurt you to examine your life a little, all I'm saying. Pay a little attention to the social side of it."

"There's nothing wrong with my social life."

"Yeah? Name me one female friend you can call up and go have a drink with."

"I prefer drinking with men."

"Okay, then name one male companion."

She seemed to give it some thought. "There's Donnie Ray Ewing… gets himself shot out of a cannon over at the Tucson Race-way. He and I hooked up a couple of weeks ago."

Randall gave her a skeptical look. "Del, honey, it takes more than a night of sweaty passion to call it a relationship. I'm sorry to be so blunt."

"Then let it go, Randall. Call it love on the run, but it's all I've got time for right now."

He was being the father, Randall realized. "All right," he said, shaking his head. "But I'm telling you, you need to take a good look at what you're doing. It affects your judgment on the job."

She continued to rummage inside the bag, the effort purposefully exaggerated. It was her way of telling him to drop the subject.

"Okay," he said. "The client will be coming by the office at four, and they'll be expecting you. But there is one more thing I need to tell you that's not job-related."

"What's that?" Del said, not looking up.

"Marla Jeski came by the office earlier."

This news brought Del's eyes around to him. "Ed's wife?"

Randall nodded.

"What did she want?"

"She wants to talk."

"To me? I don't understand. Why?"

"I didn't get into details," Randall said. "She told me to tell you she would be at the Congress Hotel, in the bar, around three. She said to tell you she hoped that you would come."

Randall watched Del's gaze move off someplace beyond the walls. Ed Jeski had been Del's lover—an affair that had lasted for more than a year. Marla was Ed's wife—now the grieving widow. Randall knew the affair with Ed had been pretty serious—the only lengthy relationship he knew her to ever have. There were promises of marriage, promises of a future together. That was, until Marla announced herself as Ed's wife and broke things up.

That had been a few months or so before Del came to work at Desert Sands. The situation had been pretty ugly from what Randall knew of it—Del finding out about the existence of a wife the way she did. Having him inform her with a phone call, the morning after, that he'd made the decision to go back to his wife and try to make a go of their marriage. Randall believed it had left Del with scars. Now the wife was back, three days after her husband's death, asking for a meeting. Even Randall was curious *why*.

Randall studied Del. He was aware of his feelings for her—times like this, watching her. Something akin to lust, but over-layered with fatherly concern. It made him conscious of his age. Conscious of his thinning hair, his gut lapping over his belt. He said, "So, you gonna meet with her?"

Del nodded once. "I guess."

And that was all there was left to the conversation. He watched her gather her equipment duffel over her shoulder and head off.

"Call me if you need anything!" he said to her departing back-side. And as she stepped through the exit into bright sunlight, more quietly, he said, "*Call me.*"

———

The Congress Hotel was located only three blocks from the Talbot Building, where Desert Sands Covert had its offices. It was late October, seasonably warm, the slight Thursday-afternoon breeze out of the south pleasant. Del parked her Wrangler at the curb near the office and walked the short distance to the hotel. The bar inside was dark and dreary. There were mixed food smells left over from the noon lunch crowd. Marla Jeski sat alone in a booth in the far back corner, head lowered. She hadn't seen Del come in.

Del observed her from a distance for a moment—seeing a woman in her mid-forties, nicely dressed, attractive in a polished-hardwood sort of way. She had lots of jewelry and parlor-done platinum hair. She had a drink in front of her, both hands cupped around the glass.

The last time Del had seen this woman was in a motel room on the west side of town—one she and Ed were about to share. Marla, filled with rage, fists banging on the door, had brought the sheets to Del's chin, and Ed out of bed and quickly into his boxers.

On their frequent dates, Ed would take her home to an apartment he claimed was his. She'd later found out it belonged to one of his cop buddies. Other times, they came together in cheap motel rooms, Ed telling her it heightened the excitement, the idea of *dirty sex*. She'd been younger then—still working a construction job—and far more naive. She hadn't talked to Ed since that morning-after, farewell phone call. Or seen Marla Jeski again until just now. Seeing the woman sitting there brought back a flood of conflicted emotion that Del wasn't quite prepared for. She hesitated a second longer. Then, the psychic weight of her presence caused Marla to look up and see her standing there. They held each other's gaze across the room—Del trying to decide if it was grief or resentment she saw straining Marla's face. Finally, Marla gave her a slight nod, and Del crossed inside to meet her.

———

Afternoon sun played outside beyond the shaded windows. A lone female server, middle-aged, worked both the table area and the bar. There were no other patrons in the room.

"I appreciate that you came," Marla said, from beneath a stiff upper lip. She gestured Del to the seat across the booth from her.

Up close, Del could see deep lines around Marla's eyes, dark circles where she'd been crying. She slid onto the bench seat as the waitress came by.

"Beer," Del said. "Whatever you have on draft."

It sent the waitress off, and Del turned her attention to Marla. Again they took time to consider each other.

"I'm awfully sorry to hear about Ed," Del said.

It brought a wince of pain to Marla's eyes. Del could see she was working hard at keeping it together.

"You're prettier than I remembered," Marla said. "Ed made you out to be a dalliance. But I always knew it was more than that."

"That was a long time ago."

"Ah! But you still have feelings for him. Wives have a second sense about such things."

"Is that what this is about?"

"I'm sorry. I was hoping my resentment wouldn't show. No, I didn't ask you here to open old wounds."

"Then why did you?"

The waitress came with Del's beer, then went off behind the bar to ring the tab.

Marla swirled her ice idly in the glass, then took a sip.

"How much do you know of Ed's death?"

Del retrieved her beer. "Only what I heard on the news this morning. That he was shot inside a motel room on the south side of town three nights ago."

"And what was your very first reaction?"

"Marla…"

"Go on! Tell me! Tell me honestly that your first thought wasn't that he was cheating on his wife again."

"Marla, I don't..."

"It's okay, really. Why not? Everybody else thinks so. They all know Ed had a problem keeping it in his pants. It was nobody's secret. It's the first thing the department investigators jumped to after his murder. A philandering husband...a cheap roadside motel...the room had been rented by a woman, did you know that? How much more evidence would they possibly need?"

"Did they identify the woman?"

Marla shook her head and took a drink. "She took off. Wouldn't you?" She stopped. "I'm sorry! I didn't mean that."

Del waved it off.

"The little trollop used a fake name on the registry," Marla said. "The husband probably dragged her back home by the hair, if he didn't kill her later and dump her in a ditch."

"What about Ed's partner, Ray Daniels? What does he have to say about it?"

Marla stopped swirling. "He's an *ex*-partner now. Retired two months ago. You know how cops are. He knew about you all that time and the others! How much did he have to say about it then? I tell you, this thing makes me so goddamn mad, I...!" Marla bit her lip to keep from going on. Her hands were shaking.

Del wasn't sure what to say. She took another sip of beer and thought about Ed. She remembered him the way she had known him back then. He was a good guy, a gentleman. A little too serious maybe, but principled in things other than his relationships with women. He was tall, clean-cut, nice looking. He reminded her of the detective Mark Fuhrman from the O. J. Simpson trial. Concerned for his appearance, a certain self-confident set to his mouth all the time.

She had, in truth, seen him once in the past three years. But only from a distance—looking down on him from the eleventh-floor offices of Desert Sands Covert. He was going into the court-house across the street. His partner, Ray Daniels—older and a little shorter—had been one step off his heels. Both men were in suits and ties, reporters crowding their way. Later that same week, she had seen both their pictures in the newspaper and learned they'd been testifying in a high-profile homicide trial. It's what they did. She could still recall the sudden lurch her heart had taken at the sight of him, the warm sensations that filled her down low. Ed Jeski, the cop, had always had that effect on her.

Now he was dead, and Del was improbably sitting across the table from his widow. She said, "Marla … I am sorry, truly. But why am I here?"

Marla moved her hands to her lap to hide the trembling. "I invited you here, Del, to ask if you've talked to Ed recently. I don't mean that in an accusatory way," she added quickly. "I'm asking everyone … anyone … who might have even remotely had the chance to speak to Ed. Someone who might have seen him, bumped into him on the street. To see if he maybe said some-thing, gave some indication. Anything that would explain what he was doing in that motel that night."

"I haven't," Del said, in all honesty. "I've seen his picture in the papers a few times. Wondered how he was doing. How the two of you were doing, actually. But I don't understand. Why the disbe-lief? You said yourself everybody knew Ed slept around."

"Well, you see, that's the thing." Marla took up her glass again in one hand and knocked back the remainder of her drink, then signaled the waitress for another. "Things between Ed and I were going pretty good these past few years, you know? Ed was trying. I mean, *really* trying. I could tell. And, in a way, I have you to thank for it."

"Me?"

"Ironically and bitterly, yes." Marla said. "Ed had more than his share of trysts, to say the least. A long string of them. Some I knew about and some I'm sure I didn't. But, after you … well … it was like … like he'd come to a crossroads. He knew he'd had the best with you and knew there was a decision to be made. So he erred on the side of marriage."

"He called me the following morning to tell me we were through," Del said.

"I know, I was in the room at the time. And after that day, I never once had reason again to suspect Ed might be cheating. He became a straight arrow. And I believe that he's been true." Marla studied her for a reaction, then said, "See, I know what they're all saying. I know what they're thinking. That Ed was just at the wrong end of a jealous husband's gun. And that's what makes this so doubly hard. Why-ever Ed was in that motel that night. Why he was killed and whoever did it … I can't go on living, believing he betrayed me yet again. Not this time. Not after what we'd become to each other these past three years. I need to know the truth of what happened. I need to know that there was some cause that took him to that room. I need to know that he remained faithful! I need …!" Marla's tirade broke. She turned her face away, making no attempt to quell the tears that streamed liberally down her face.

Del studied her a moment, then reached across the table to touch Marla on the back of the hand.

It caught the woman by surprise. She stared down at Del's touch, as if studying something alien. Then brought her other hand to cover hers, and hold it there. The *scorned wife* and the *other woman* holding hands, it seemed.

"Marla," Del said.

The woman's eyes came up to meet hers.

"I wish there was something I could do, something I could say, that would help. I really do. I did love Ed once, it's true. And there are feelings, still, that I can't deny. But I haven't seen or talked to Ed since that morning on the phone. I'm sorry, but that's the truth."

Marla's bitterness gradually gave way to acceptance. She nodded and dropped her head. "I guess that's the answer I actually prefer to hear. I see your picture in the papers. Maybe, down deep, I was just hoping you would know something. It was stupid of me to ask."

Del withdrew her hand. "I'm sorry," she said.

The woman was desperate, maybe even a little crazed in her state of despair.

The waitress delivered Marla's drink, then went off without comment.

Del slid out of the booth, dropping a five on the table to pay for her beer. Looking down at Marla—her sad, mascara-streaked face—Del said, "I know it must have taken a lot of courage for you to ask me here. I'll keep my eyes and ears open. If I find out anything, I'll let you know. Okay?"

Marla nodded. The hands gripping the glass were shaking again.

"Are you going to be all right to drive home?"

Marla waved her off.

Del left her sitting there.

On the sidewalk outside, beneath the shadows of towering office buildings, Del stopped to gather herself. The strange experience had been emotionally draining. What it left behind was a heaviness in her heart that transcended the news of Ed's death. There were feelings of guilt and regret—large and growing larger. And other feelings she couldn't quite put a label on.

She thought of Ed, remembering the times they had spent together. Ed, the cop, who had taught her how to shoot, how to think on her feet, how to take a man down and make it count. She was remembering places he'd taken her, things they'd done, things they'd said. Remembering saying to him in jest one time, "So, tough guy ... you get killed out there, what do you want me to put on your tombstone?"

Ed had said in all seriousness that time, "Just say ... *Here lies Ed Jeski ... justice is served.*"

Putting her head in her hands, Del felt an overwhelming need to cry. She wanted more than anything to give in to it. Instead, she wiped at the wetness in her eyes, straightened her shoulders, and drew a deep breath. *No,* she coached herself. There would be a time for regret. A time to curl into a protective fetal ball and give in to the grief and self-pity and tears. For now ... there were clients waiting.

THREE

IT WAS A LITTLE past four p.m. when Del arrived at the offices of Desert Sands Covert, coming off the elevator to enter through the glass double-doors. The receptionist, Patti, had already gone for the day. Randall was in his office behind his desk. She stepped inside without knocking.

"How did it go with the widow?" he asked.

"I feel sorry for her," Del said. "She's hurting, and there's no one around to make the pain go away."

"And what about you?" Randall said, cocking his head to give her the look she knew to expect. It was a scrutinizing look, one a father might give a daughter whose blouse was too low-cut for a date. But also one a commander might give a young recruit, looking for reassurance of readiness.

"I'll make it," she said.

"Uh-huh." His vote was lacking in confidence. "I hope so. We've got business to conduct." Randall gave a nod, directing her line of sight across the office bullpen area toward the glass-enclosed conference room.

There were five people there, waiting grouped around one end of the long mahogany table, their backs to her, facing windows that were eleven floors above the street. They appeared beguiled by the view of rooftops and by the panoramic view of mountains that framed the Tucson valley.

"Those the clients?"

"If you want to call 'em that," Randall said. "They're migrant farmworkers from the Central Valley of California. Came with the entire family. I tried to talk to them, find out what they want. But they said they would only talk to Señorita Shannon. That's you. Been waiting like that for the past forty minutes. They friends of yours?"

Del shook her head. "Never seen them before in my life."

"Well, they're insistent."

Del studied the gathering behind the glass. They were five sun-baked Mexicans. *Stoop-workers*—the term that came to mind. One was a man approximately forty years of age, dressed in jeans and a flannel shirt and work boots. He had a red bandana tied about his neck; stiff, brush-like black hair. There was a boy, about nine, standing between the chairs next to him. Probably a son. He was wearing an L.A. Dodgers baseball cap. There was an older woman—the matriarch—sitting straight in her chair. She was flanked closely by two younger women, who were reassuring the elder by holding her hands, one on either side, and stroking her arms gently. Del imagined a battered pickup, weaving along the interstate, the five of them crowded into the front seat. Maybe not that exactly, but traveling over many hot and dusty miles to get here. Come—on faith—to the semi-posh investigative offices of Desert Sands Covert. *Imagine.* Asking to talk to her. *Why?*

"Well," Del said, "let's see what they want."

Del led the way into the conference room, Randall on her heels. As they passed through the door, five faces came around to meet her.

"*¡Madre de Dios!*" the old woman exclaimed, and crossed herself. The family came quickly to their feet, the younger women helping the matriarch from her chair.

"Señorita Shannon," the man said. Then, becoming aware of his son, he snatched the ball cap from the boy's head and thrust it into his hands. "Show respect, Gabino," he scolded.

Del was only halfway through the door, stop-stunned by their greeting. "I'm sorry," she said. "Do I know you?"

The five migrants stared back at her, a look of gobsmacked reverence on their faces. It took the man a second. Then, with a slight bow, Juan said, "Señorita. We are honored. I am Juan Lara. This is my family. Son, Gabino. Wife, Elena. Her sister Alma. Also, let me present my mother, Señora Adelina Dueña Lara. We have come to speak to you about our very desperate matter."

"Then perhaps you should sit down," Del said.

As the family re-settled, Del crossed around and took a seat across from them. Randall followed inside taking his place at the head of the table. They sat looking at each other a moment longer.

"Señorita Shannon …," Juan said, hesitant to start. "We have read that you find and recover missing persons."

"It's what our agency specializes in," Del said.

"*Sí,*" Juan said. "And we have need for such service."

Del waited.

"Our brother's daughter, our beloved niece has been taken from us. We pray for you to find her and bring her back."

"Your niece?"

Fumbling inside his pocket, Juan came out with a photograph and handed it across the table to her. "Her name is Aurea. The photo was taken this past year."

Del took it and examined the image. It was that of a little Mexican girl in a white satin dress that was beautifully laced. Her dark bangs were cut straight across her forehead. She had a sweet face, a calm, accepting demeanor. But for the eyes, that were black as coal, and seemed to carry a faraway, sad-for-the-world look in them.

"How old is she?"

"Six years," Juan said. "Almost seven. She is but a child."

"You said she is your brother's daughter. Where is your brother now? Why is he not here?"

Juan threw a look to his wife Elena.

"Tell her, *mi marido*," Elena said. "We have to trust someone."

Juan lowered his head a moment, then lifted worried eyes to Del.

"My brother and his wife were planning to leave Arizona and come to live with us in California. They were seeking a buyer for their small farm. I had arranged for him a job, as a work crew supervisor. One where he could make an okay living and be free of the fear he and his family suffered."

"Fear of what?"

"Of his wife's brother," Juan said hesitantly. "I put my family at risk at the mere mention of his name … Santos de la Cal."

"De la Cal?" Randall said, trying the name on for size. "I've heard of him. He's a reputed drug trafficker in Mexico."

"*Sí*, señor, the *Asesino de Sonora*. The assassin. He has earned his reputation through violence. His death squads are legendary. They patrol the desert and mountain corridors, the *senderos*, between the U.S. border and Cotorra. They bring treachery to the towns and villages, terrorize land owners. They kill anyone who crosses them or stands in their way. "

Del exchanged a look with Randall. The American news stations were buzzing with reports of the widespread violent conflict occurring across Mexico. The cartels and the smugglers were at war with the Mexican army and federal police. Corruption ran rampant along all levels of authority, and the Mexican government itself was said to be on the verge of collapse. In addition, the breakdown had caused small bands of private resistance to spring up—*vigilantes*—adding to the chaos and violence. The Arizona legislature had passed a controversial bill, making it illegal for anyone to be in Arizona without proper citizenship documentation. U.S. border security was on special alert. And the State Department had issued stern warnings to American tourists about travel across the southern border. She had heard about the *senderos* also—the Sonoran corridors of trade that were used to bring drugs across the border into Arizona. It was said that control of the corridors was more valuable—therefore more violently contested—than even the drugs themselves. It was considered that drugs could be manufactured by almost anyone. But he who owned the *senderos*…ah!…owned the market. It made Mexico and, in particular the Sonoran landscape south of the border, an extremely dangerous place to be.

Del gave it some more thought, then said to Juan, "You still haven't told us where your brother is, why he isn't here in person."

"I believe he is dead!" Juan said, no attempt to disguise his bitterness now. "When my brother didn't call to make further plans, or answer when we tried to call, we traveled to their farm in Palo Blanco, just north of the border. There we found the house empty and the melon fields going to waste. My brother would not abandon his crop or his family."

"*¡Mi nieta!*" the old woman suddenly cried, throwing her head back in anguish, her hands coming to rend the material of her bodice. The younger women worked to calm her.

"Our mother is devastated," Juan said by way of apology. "What has happened to her only other son and his wife?"

"So, let me understand," Del said. "You think Santos killed them?"

"Yes, of course! What else? He has somehow discovered my brother's plan to take his family far away, no longer to help with the trafficking. Now he has killed them and stolen our niece, taken her back across the border with him."

"Where exactly?" Del asked.

Juan shrugged. "To Cotorra likely. It is his home."

Del gave it some thought, then said, "I'm sorry, Mr. Lara. I truly am. But isn't this a case for the U.S. and Mexican authorities?"

Juan lowered his eyes; the others looked off.

Randall was the first to catch on. "Del, I think what Señor Lara here doesn't want to say, is that he and his family are not exactly in a position to contact authorities. If you know what I mean? They risk being deported just coming into this state."

"They're illegal?" Del said.

"And, I'm guessing, not overly trustful of the law no matter which side of the border they're on," Randall added.

"My brother and his wife were U.S. citizens," Juan said. "We are all working hard to become so. And the Mexican federal police are extremely corrupt. No one can be trusted. They are paid well by Santos. And are as fearful of his methods as we are."

"But he is *also* the child's uncle," Del said, restating the obvious.

"*Sí*," Juan said. "Aurea is very fond of her uncle Santos. But she needs to be with a real family, with those who will love and care for her. Not in the hands of a seller of drugs. Not in the hands of a murderer. We are willing to pay for your services."

Juan withdrew a large paper bag from between his feet and placed it on the table.

Randall leaned forward and retrieved the sack. He opened it, then gave a low whistle. "Cash!" he said, respect in his voice.

"Thirty-thousand American dollars, señor," Juan Lara said. "It is money that my brother, Benito, and his wife, Yanamaria, sent ahead for safekeeping. Money paid to him by his brother-in-law for things he would rather not have done."

"Drug money?"

Juan nodded.

Del examined the photo of the child again. Then rose and crossed to the window to look out. Beyond the glass, immediately facing, was the Pima County Courthouse. Eleven stories below were the courthouse steps. The sight of them, ever so briefly, took her back into the past. It was the last place she had seen Ed Jeski alive, perhaps six months ago. Taking the steps of the courthouse two at a time. His partner, Ray Daniels, had been with him that time, close behind, news crews following. The memory that washed over her now was not of that day, however. It was one of Ed and she together. The warm sensation of Ed's fingers gently trailing along the curve of her hip, caressing the soft swell of her breast. His hand coming to cup her chin and hold it as he spoke into her eyes. His voice husky, in the whisper of her name, *"Del…"*

"Del!"

At the perimeter of her mind Del realized it was Randall's voice calling to her. She came back into the present. "Sorry, what?"

"I was asking, what do you think?" Randall said.

Del forced her thoughts back to the matter at hand and returned to the table. "I don't know," she said. "There's nothing to actually say the family is missing or that a murder has occurred."

"But it must be so!" Juan insisted.

"This won't be an easy assignment," Randall said, ignoring the migrants and speaking directly to Del. "I could always give it to Willard or Rudy, or I could assign one of them to work with you."

"I prefer to work alone," Del said. "You know that."

Randall waited.

Del studied the photo of the child once more. Then said, "Señor Lara, you came to Desert Sands Covert for help…I can understand that…the firm specializes in confidentiality and in cases where covert measures may be required. What I don't understand is why you asked for me personally?"

Del caught the guarded look that passed between the migrant and his wife. "What?" she asked.

"Tell her, Juan," the wife said. "She needs to know."

"Tell me what?"

Juan drew a deep breath, then let it out. "I didn't want to mention…" He still hesitated, but then said, "Our niece, Aurea. She is…well…a very special child."

"Special how?"

31

"Some would say she has the 'eyes of the cat'. That she has a certain gift of sight for things that have yet to be."

"Are you telling me she's clairvoyant?" Del said, skepticism in her voice.

"You would only have to see this child, señorita. It is the main cause why we believe Santos has taken her. Because my brother and his wife were planning to bring the child to live with us, many hundreds of kilometers away, and deny him access to her visionary abilities."

"Santos uses the girl?" Del said, the idea unthinkable.

"*Sí,*" Juan said, nodding. "He seeks to *see* through her eyes, visions of the future."

"Okay…" Del said.

Her impatience was showing. All she wanted was a straight answer to a simple question.

"You'll pardon me here if I sound a little skeptical, but… I still don't understand what this has to do with me. Why did you ask for me personally?"

"I beg you," Juan said. "Just go to the farm. I believe then you will see for yourself."

Del turned her gaze back to the photograph of the girl and studied the calm intelligent face, the dark eyes looking back at her. She had learned through experience that every client needed to be approached with a healthy amount of skepticism. Clients lie, clients withhold information—it was nothing new. But there was a certain sincerity in the migrant's voice. And, Del had to admit, he had built a case for curiosity. Still…

"It could be dangerous," Randall reminded her again.

He was right. Going after this child would be extremely dangerous. Mexico was a war zone of late. She could well heed the stories of roving patrols and death squads and assassinations. There was also the well-known overlay of Mexican government corruption. There would be no one there she could count on, no one she could trust. She would be wholly on her own and vulnerable. Not to mention, in the final analysis, she would be going there to ostensibly kidnap a child. Assuming Santos had the child and assuming she did somehow manage to steal the girl from beneath his nose and live to tell about it. If caught by authorities, she could spend the rest of her life in a Mexican prison. *Not an attractive proposition.*

What bothered her most, however, Del realized, was the assertion that Santos may have killed his own sister and brother-in-law, primarily because he believed in this child's abilities and because he could not allow the child to be taken from him. Was she to believe the kid was actually psychic? Or was the story more akin to fable? The result of a superstitious people, from a superstitious culture?

The latter seemed more likely.

"So, what do you think?" Randall asked again, pressing for a decision. "Just say the word and we'll walk away."

Del considered it all a moment more, then slipped the picture of the child into her shirt pocket. "Leave the money with Mr. Willingham," Del said. "He'll hold it in trust for you while I go to Palo Blanco and check out what you've told me. That's all I'll agree to do at this point. Once I look into it, I'll let you know whether I'll accept the job or not."

Relief spread across Juan Lara's face; he lowered his head in humility.

Del studied the little migrant, then each of the sad, expectant family members in turn. If there were ulterior motives at play here, evil intentions ... you sure couldn't tell by looking at them.

FOUR

Del left Randall with the migrants, took the elevator to the street, and began to walk. No place in mind, she brushed through crowds of office workers spilling from the government buildings and law offices. They hurried, here, there, to bus stops or parking garages, to cars waiting at the curb. It had been one heck of a day—first the news of Ed's death, then the strange and uncomfortable meeting with his widow, now the idea of a kidnapped child to deal with—she needed time to think.

The walk brought her to Fourth Avenue, where the sidewalks thinned to the occasional passersby. She ignored the window dressings of the smoke shops and used clothing stores, the solicitations from the bums along the curb. And continued on in solitary thought. She considered the circumstances of the child—the six-year-old girl, Aurea—who Juan Lara and his family claimed had some special gift of sight. Could it be? Was it possible? Were there such things as clairvoyant children in the world? Or was it just a case of parents and relatives being quick to assign mysticism to their child's overly active intuition, quick to label their own progeny as *special*?

She thought of Marla—the widow—in such a deepened state of distress that Del had been reluctant to leave her alone in the bar. And she thought—mostly she thought—of Ed.

She had been holding back her anger out of respect for the dead. But now the pressures of her day caught up with her, and she let it out.

Goddamn it, Ed! You fucking louse!

She was surprised by her reaction. But the thing was, if Ed had walked away from her to become faithful to his wife Marla, then cheating on Marla again was like cheating on her. *Wasn't it?* It made his so-called reason for dumping her a lame excuse. Cheating again walked all over the notion that she had once been special to Ed, trounced all over it and left dirty footprints. It tarnished the romanticized memories she held of him. Blackened them and left them feeling cheap. What she'd earlier mistaken for grief, Del now realized, was out-and-out anger.

Sonofabitch!

Damn it, Ed!

The man was dead, and she was cursing him. Would she ever be able to think of him fondly again?

By the time she had circled back to the office, the sun had slipped low, leaving a dark purple blanket across the horizon. Del found her Jeep at the curb and climbed behind the wheel. She headed east on Speedway, not really knowing where she was heading.

At Alvernon, Del spotted a neon sign reading *Bowling Alley*. The parking lot was packed, and Del thought of Ed's ex-partner,

Ray Daniels, remembering that he used to bowl here on Thursday nights.

Del swung the Jeep off into the parking lot and found what might have been the only empty space, far back in the corner where desert scrub came up to meet the blacktop. She collected her Baby Eagle—her nine-millimeter handgun—from beneath the seat, and stuffed it, holster and all, into the waistband at the small of her back. She covered it with her shirttail, then crossed between parked cars to the main entrance, and went inside.

The cop league was into its fourth frame, judging from the overhead score projectors. At the bar, Del ordered a diet cola and sat sipping as she watched teams of cops roll sixteen-pound balls down polished hardwood lanes. The sounds of crashing pins waged war with country music coming from overhead speakers. Ray Daniels and his team were on lane seven—Ray in the process of picking up his spare.

He was a guy in his early fifties, average height, still solid through the shoulders, but with more of a paunch and a little less hair than Del had remembered. It had been, after all, three years since she'd last seen him. He spotted her then and came with a wide grin, up the short set of steps to give her a hug.

"Goddamn, Del! It's been a long time, sweetheart. You're looking damn good, girl. How you doing?"

"I'm doing all right," she said, as Ray parked himself on the stool next to her and motioned the bartender for a beer. "I wanted to come by and say how sorry I am to hear about Ed."

"Jesus! You?" Ray said. "I'm the one should be saying I'm sorry. You and Ed were … well, what can I say … I always thought the two of you would end up together. No disrespect to the dead, but he was a dick for letting you get away."

"Don't get me started," Del said. "How are the others handling it?" She gave a nod to the rest of the team—four cops in team bowling shirts and shoes, down there perched on benches around the scoring desk, drinking beer, and monitoring the action projected onto screens above the lanes.

"Well … you know … it's always tough losing one of your own and all."

Del nodded agreement. There was a quiet moment. Then, she said, "Ray? Let me ask you something. How do you feel about the idea that Ed was killed by a jealous husband?"

"Well, hell! It kills me, you know, it happening like that. I always expected, if one of us bought it, it would be in the line of duty. It's a cheap shot. That's the way it feels."

"So he *was* cheating again?"

Del studied Ray, testing his eyes with hers, but getting pretty much what she'd come to expect—the flat, no-tell affectation that all cops seemed to master the first week at the academy.

Ray brought a hand to rest on Del's shoulder. "Listen, sweetheart. I know it's a tough thing to swallow. But you of all people should know Ed had a taste for … well … for good-looking women. I mean, look at you, you look fantastic. I can't think of a single other reason why he'd have been in that motel."

Del nodded.

Ray's hand remained on her shoulder, it began to knead her flesh softly. "You know … Ed was a lucky man," he said, his eyes taking on a smoky glaze. "Those times I would be out with the two of you, having drinks, watching the two of you together, laughing … well … I gotta tell you, there were many times … many times! … when I wished it was me instead of Ed there next to you."

"Yeah, well …" Del said, not knowing what to say. She put a hand to his, patted it once, then removed it from her shoulder.

"Hey, Ray!" one of the cop buddies called from the lanes. "You're on deck, dick-breath!"

"Sounds like your little friends are calling you to come out and play," Del said.

"Bunch of yahoos," Ray said, "I think a few of them take this game, and themselves, a little too seriously. Know what I mean? Hey, listen, why don't you hang out, have a drink, and watch the action. Maybe you and me can go for something to eat afterwards. Just the two of us. Catch up on old times."

"Thanks," Del said. "But I have to get up early."

"Still running down missing persons?"

Del nodded again.

"I understand. But I guess you've probably heard I'm retired now. Built a cabin up at Summer Haven. Maybe we can head up there together some weekend, get out of the heat."

"Ray, I don't …"

"Yo! Ray! You're up, man!"

"Yeah, yeah!" Daniels called to his teammates.

"I think the Rat Pack is getting impatient," Del said. "Listen, I really have to be going. We'll talk again."

"You think about my offer, okay? I'll stay in touch, promise. Meanwhile, it's great seeing you again. No shit, you look fantastic!" He leaned in and gave her a kiss on the lips. His hand briefly found a place high up her thigh. Then he was off to join his buddies.

Del sat for moment longer, the feel of hands and lips still present. It made her realize how alone she was, how in need of companionship. The knot of despair that had settled in her throat after meeting with Marla was still present, the threat of tears still only a sentimental thought away. A sudden attack of self-consciousness came over her—the feeling that everyone, all the raucous bowlers and the drinkers at the bar, were watching her. She slid off the stool and left the bowling alley. When she reached the Jeep, there was no reason to hold back any longer. In the shadowy corner of the parking lot, Del finally let go. When she'd finished drying her tears, she started the engine and drove back west, the way she'd come.

She felt restless, behind the wheel. Still unsure of where to go or what to do. The idea of going home didn't thrill her. Home was quiet. Home was still and empty. Home was a place with too much time for thinking. *Home carried its own soiled memories.*

Tomorrow would be another day, Del told herself, trying to elevate her mood. Tomorrow she would drive to Palo Blanco to look into Juan Lara's claims. Tomorrow she would investigate the farm, try to find out why he'd been so insistent she do so. Tomorrow she would ask questions around Palo Blanco about Benito and Yanamaria Lara. Ask questions about the child. Tomorrow she would pour herself into the job, and let work be the cure that vanquished thoughts of Ed and Marla. But between now and then, there was *tonight.* And it was shaping up to be a killer. One of those when the hours crept slowly by. When silence droned in your ears. When thoughts of lunacy became endearing in your mind. When sitting alone, a glass in one hand, a bottle in the other, was as much action as you could handle. When alcohol and a father's old beer mug became a needed, albeit fragile, link to sanity.

One of those nights.

For the briefest moment, Del thought about doubling back to the bowling alley and taking Ray Daniels up on his offer of companionship, giving herself over to whatever raw indecencies he had in mind. Be disgusted and angry come morning, but at least make it through the night…

That's when her cell phone rang.

"Del?" a man's voice said softly.

She recognized the voice immediately. It was Frank Falconet, special agent with ATF—Alcohol, Tobacco, Firearms, and Explosives. They had worked together a year ago, going undercover to investigate a religious compound and its leader. Their hit-and-run love affair had lasted throughout the investigation. But their careers, their volatile lifestyles, had brought them to a decision. Del had been the one to break it off, sending Frank away—hurt and dejected—on to his next assignment within the Justice Department and back to Jersey to tie up loose ends with his estranged wife, Jolana. But—man, oh, man!—it had been volcanic while it lasted. His call—his voice, just hearing him!—brought on a sudden yearning, that damn near spun her off the road.

"Frank? Is that you?"

There was a hesitation. Then, "Yeah. How are you doing? Everything okay?"

"God, it's good to hear your voice."

"I wasn't sure you'd want to."

At a loss for words, Del said, "I've missed you."

"Right? It's why I called. I just felt like … well … like I needed to see how you were doing."

"You couldn't have called at a better time. Where are you? Can I see you?"

There was a silence on the line. Then Frank said, "Well, actually, I'm … well … Jolana and I agreed to give it one more try. I'm back home in Cliffside Park."

Del's heart sank. She thought she'd put feelings for Frank behind her—had done a good job of it, until his call. "You called to tell me that?"

"No … I'm not sure why I called, exactly … maybe I shouldn't have … you mad at me?"

What did she say to that? "No …" she said. "Just … I guess I was hoping … I don't know …"

"Actually, things aren't working out with Jolana as well as we'd hoped." Frank sighed. "I don't know where it's all going, where it will all end up, I just … well … I just wanted to hear your voice, see how you were doing."

Del had barely been aware of the road ahead, the traffic signals, reds and greens; traffic starts and stops. She pulled herself out of it, put on a proud face. "You still with ATF?"

"Between assignments."

"How's Darius?"

"He wants me for another job."

That was as much small talk as Del could muster. She felt the need to end the call.

"Del?" Frank said.

"Yeah?"

"I still love you. I'd still like to see if we have a chance?"

The words tore at Del's insides. Frank had made her an offer once before. Not marriage exactly, but the two of them side by side, doing what they both do best. Partners—was the way she'd viewed it. And she had declined, letting reason get in the way of love. "I…I don't know what to say."

"Just say you feel the same way."

There was a long silence that Del didn't quite know how to fill. After a long heart-rending moment. She said, "I think you need to stay with your wife and daughter. I think I need to get on with my life."

"But…"

"Take care of yourself, Frank."

"Del…?"

Del ended the call.

She hadn't realized the tears that had filled her eyes, the large droplets that had streamed down her face. She wiped at them with the back of her hand. Took a tissue from the glove compartment and blew her nose.

Jesus!

The call that had at first promised to buoy her spirits had served only to yank the last emotional support from beneath her. *"God damn it, Frank!"*

She'd crossed halfway home without realizing it. But now, more than ever, the thought of going home, the idea of being alone… *Christ!*

Blowing past cars on Speedway, the cool night breeze rushing through the open sides of the Wrangler, she thought of a man she'd spent the night with more than a year ago. A cowboy named Allen May. Maybe it was the posters she'd been seeing on nearly every light pole—the rodeo in town. Or maybe it was the warm libidinal memory of him, left over from their night of urgent sex, that had occurred in the parking lot of a country bar, on the front seat of his pickup, neon bar signs flashing reds and blues across their naked bodies, a warm summer night's breeze giving its approval. At any rate, she needed someone desperately now. Someone to hold and be held by. Someone to lose herself in, blanket the memory of Ed and Frank and any other man who might be lurking in her subconscious.

Another rodeo poster flashed by.

Del turned sharply at the next corner, headed south, then back east on Broadway. There was a chance … maybe a slim chance …

On a house phone in the lobby of the Embassy Suites, she asked to be put through to one of the guest rooms. When a familiar male voice answered, she almost giggled. "Are you alone?"

Allen May was waiting for her in the open doorway to his room as she came up the stairwell and onto the landing. Looking hunky too, lean and hard, in boots and jeans, no shirt. Below the landing, lights from the swimming pool cast a wavering aquamarine glow across the courtyard.

"Looky-here what the cat drug in," he said.

"You plan on keeping your boots on, cowboy?"

"I've got spurs, if you think I'm gonna need 'em."

Del brushed past him into the room, stripping out of her shirt as she did, pulling the Baby Eagle from her waistband to lay it on the nightstand.

Allen let the door close behind him. He killed the lights at the wall switch, causing the room to fall into murky shadow, then crossed to the sliding door that looked onto the balcony.

"Leave it open," Del said. "There's a nice breeze."

Del finished stripping out of her clothes and crawled naked, hands and knees, onto the bed. She stretched on her side, the curve of her hip angling toward him.

Allen was watching, his back to the open balcony. She could see his outline, tall and lanky, backlit by light from the parking lot.

"You'll pardon me, ma'am, if I take time to look," Allen said. "It's been a while."

"A while since you've seen a girl naked? Or a while since you last seen me?"

"A while since I've been this filled with the spirit of giving."

"Well, you just gonna talk about it? Or you gonna let the spirit move you?"

Allen said, "Ma'am, in case you haven't noticed ... it already has."

They made love in a heated frenzy, each urgent and selfish in their needs. Afterward, there was time for tenderness. They lay in silence for a time, listening to cars moving in both directions on Broadway. Del had her head in the crook of Allen's arm. The desert breeze sang through the open sliding-glass doorway.

"It's been—what—a year? Year and a half?" Del said. "I've thought about you from time to time."

"Yeah? How'd you know where to find me?"

Del lifted her head to give him a look.

"Oh, yeah, I forgot. It's what you do ... you find people."

Allen freed himself, fumbled on the nightstand, and came up with a pack of cigarettes and a lighter. He lit one for them, took a puff, and passed it to her. Del drew in the smoke and blew it out, and the two settled back in together.

"Actually, it wasn't so hard," Del said. "There's posters all over town advertising the rodeo. I figured you had to be here. I took a shot. This is the same hotel you stayed at last time. I spent the night with you here, remember?"

"That was some night, all right. I remember you'd had a bad fight with your daddy earlier. You got a phone call the next morning and ran out without saying much. I figured I'd seen the last of you. Slam-bam, thank-you-cowboy."

Del turned her gaze to the balcony. Out beyond the open doorway, beyond the traffic on Broadway, beyond the expanse of city, lay the cemetery where her father was buried. Next to him, her mother. And up the hill from them, looking out on all creation, Louise Lassiter—Del's teen probation officer and longtime mentor. All of them gone.

Del said, "Yeah, well... shit happens."

"I guess so," Allen said. "You gotta ride the bull you draw."

It was the last that was said for a while. What Del liked about Allen May, he was a man patient in his thought. They could spend time in silence without feeling awkward in each other's presence. Like now, passing the cigarette back and forth between them, the desert breeze ruffling the curtains.

"You know," Del said, "The only time I smoke is when I'm with you. Why is that?"

"Girls already want to be bad," Allen said. "I just give 'em permission."

They finished the smoke, and Allen stubbed the butt out in the ashtray on the bedside table. "So, tell me, what's been going on with you. You still finding missing persons?"

"You must not read the papers much."

"I confess I do, actually. I've seen your picture in just about every paper from Prescott to the border. You're building quite a name for yourself, girl. You must be real proud."

Del squeezed closer, twirling curls in the hair on Allen's chest with one finger. "You'd think!" she said. "Actually I'm feeling a little lost these days. I go home at night, the house is empty. I wake up, it's empty still. Too much quiet time. And then there's my boss, Randall. Keeps telling me I should think about settling down. Sometimes I think he's actually sorry he gave me my job."

"Created a monster, huh?"

"Something like that." Del hesitated. "I lost a friend a couple of nights ago. They say killed by a jealous husband."

Allen lifted his head to look at her, then lay back. "Were you close?"

"At one time. I can't help feeling like ... Jesus! ... I don't know ... like there's something out there I'm missing. Maybe I need to move away from here. Buy a ranch ... something ... get a dog or maybe a horse ... you could teach me how to rope."

"I don't know about roping, sweetheart. I can teach you how not to fall off the dog."

Del gave him a light punch in the midsection. *Cowboy humor.* It was something else she was coming to like about Allen May. He made her feel good. "So, where are you going from here?" she asked.

"Brookings, South Dakota, for the First Chance Bonanza, on to the Brawley Cattle Call, back to Benny Binion, in Vegas. Hopefully get home to Douglas in time for Christmas."

"Makes it hard on a girl who's thinking about her life."

47

"Let me tell you, sweetheart … settling down? … it's not what it's cracked up to be."

Del realized how little she knew about Allen May. She said, "You sound like you've had some experience with it."

"I was married for eleven months, once," Allen said.

"Eleven months? That's all?"

"All it took. Lori Lynn, her name was. Ran off with a feed-grain salesman from Iowa. She got the boy. I got to keep my daddy Buck and a hundred and fifty acres of ostrich ranch."

Del raised herself on one elbow. "You have a son?"

"Allen Junior. We call him Little Buck, cause he's so damn cantankerous, like his grandpa. I see him maybe once a year."

Del settled back in. "Huh! You learn something new every day."

"Yeah, what about you? What about this old friend you were talking about. What's the deal with him?"

"I never said it was a *him*."

"You did. You implied '*he*'. But even if you didn't, you don't seem to be the type to have a lot of girlfriends around."

It was the same thing Randall had said. It caused Del to go back inside herself. She thought of Ed and of Marla Jeski again, and of Ray Daniels, the partner who feels free to put his hands on her. "Well, you're right. It was a man. A cop I used to know." Del sat up, putting her back against the headboard. "I've got to put it out of my mind, though. I'm leaving for Palo Blanco in the morning. There's a child that's been abducted by her uncle. I need to look into it."

"Sounds dangerous," Allen said.

"Could be," Del replied. "If I decide to take the case."

"You know something, girl? You and me are a whole lot alike. There's always one more bull just dying to be rode, one more missing person begging to be found. Ain't neither one of us ready to settle down."

"Really? Maybe I'll prove you wrong sometime. What would you do if you rolled into town someday and found out I was married?"

"I'd excuse myself as the gentleman that I am," Allen said. Then he added, "... and then I'd go behind the barn and shoot myself. Until that time, however, slide back down here and I'll tell you what it's like to ride a two-thousand-pound bull." He lifted the covers for her.

Del threw one leg across Allen and rolled herself into a sitting position on top. She said, "I've got a better idea, cowboy ... why don't you just show me."

FIVE

La Fortaleza sat high atop a rugged plateau on the outskirts of Cotorra, appearing dark and menacing against a pale blue sky. It was a former federal prison, abandoned for a time, but now belonging to the drug trafficker, Santos. A snaking switchback got you there from the main road. There were gun towers at all four corners, razor-wire coiled atop the walls. A second series of shorter stone barriers formed a perimeter around a large, paved paddock, where dozens of vehicles, mostly SUVs, were parked. The wind seemed to course continually through its parapets, singing songs of heartache and despair, whispering laments of the thousands of imprisoned lives once wasted there.

Nesto Para didn't like coming here.

He didn't like being dragged out of bed early or leaving behind the mountain of paperwork and reports that were waiting in his office. And, in particular, he didn't like responding—quick-step—at a moment's notice, like a mere *segundo*. But when Santos de la Cal requested your presence ... well! ... you came, that was all.

It was just past eight a.m. this Friday morning when Nesto arrived by car at the open sally port, to be waved through by an armed guard. Other guards watched from the high gun towers.

A cobblestone drive made a turnabout around a large flowing fountain, the courtyard itself was lush with palms—one of Santos' improvements in the property. There, Nesto parked his government sedan and got out. He stood surveying the enclosed courtyard for a moment—the drab, stone walls, scabbed with browning moss. He took time to consider the dank, musty smell of it ... wondering ... *why?* Why would anyone want to make such a place their home. But then he reminded himself—oh, *sí*—this was Santos he was talking about.

Nesto rang the bell at the tall wooden door and was told by a female voice inside, "*Un momento.*"

¡Perdóname! Nesto thought. He was captain of the federal police, assigned with sixty-two men to the Sonoran sector in Cotorra, being told—so much as hat-in-hand—*to wait?*

His job—at least on the official record—was Mexico's response to the American drug problem. Take back the corridors. Crack down on drug traffic flowing out of Mexico through Sonora. Quell the rising violence brought on by the cartels in their efforts to maintain supremacy over the land. And unearth major drug figures and arrest them. Men such as the one he was coming to visit.

Santos.

Yet here he was—choking on pride and dutifully waiting—complying to this drug lord's summons. *¡Dios mío!* Like he belonged to the man. At what turn in life, Nesto pondered, had it all gone so wrong?

After several long minutes of waiting, hands jammed into his pockets, a housekeeper finally opened the door for him to enter. She led him up a winding stone staircase, through a foyer and into Santos' penthouse suite atop the fortress. Here the amenities changed. Gone was the drab moss-stained stone, gone the musty smell of age. The floors were done in rich Spanish tile; the walls were bright and cleanly plastered. Across the wide-open expanse of luxury living space were a number of plush sofa settings. Mayan artifacts adorned the tables. On the walls hung paintings of sensual, dark-haired Spanish women, their breasts peeking from beneath billowy wraps.

At a sofa grouping, at the far side of the room, sat Santos. He was preoccupied, it seemed, making child's play with his niece—the strange little girl who had been brought into the house only a couple of months earlier. The housekeeper pointed the way for him, and Nesto crossed through to appear before the man, clearing his throat as means of introduction.

Santos continued doting over the child, while Nesto—himself an important man—was made to stand there like a fool.

It was his own fault, Nesto scolded himself privately. He had sold his soul to this man more than four years ago. Partly giving in out of fear for his life and partly conceding to the lure of money. What choice had he really? His excuse—*la plata o tu vida. The silver or your life.* That was the way Nesto looked at it. It was a dangerous position he'd allowed himself to be in. Made even more dangerous, he believed, now, by the strange little girl—*una profeta*, as Santos claimed her to be. Rumored to have the gift of second sight.

Nesto found himself uneasy. The girl was looking at him, staring up from beneath her bangs with dark eyes that were intelligent but somehow sad, never speaking—this child—but possibly seeing things in him that only she could see. And communicating silently with her uncle through those soulful eyes.

Could it be? Nesto wondered. *Could she sense his fears? Could she read the lies that he had rehearsed inside his head?*

Nesto took check of his emotions and waited.

Finally, Santos looked up at him. "Have you ever seen a more beautiful child?"

"No," Nesto said, working hard to not let his irritation show. "She will make a beautiful woman one day, I am sure."

"Yes, she will," Santos said. He nuzzled the girl, then called beyond the room.

"Casta!"

Casta Correa, Nesto remembered.

Santos' mistress appeared in the doorway.

"*¿Qué?*"

She was beautiful, this courtesan. Born of high Spanish blood— blue eyes, light complexion, high cheekbones. Her dark hair was drawn back and collected in a comb at the nape of her neck. She had at one time, before meeting Santos, been a madam to whores, operating a bordello in Hermosillo. Successful in her own right, now she managed Santos' affairs and saw to his baser needs, while her whores saw to the needs of his men just one floor below. Hundreds of men it was rumored.

"Take my niece, would you, *por favor*?" Santos said to his mistress. "It is more than time for her morning meal."

Casta crossed to Santos to receive the girl. "Come," she said.

Aurea held on, clinging tight to Santos' neck.

"Now!" Casta admonished, putting command in her voice.

"Do not scold the child for her feelings, my love. She simply adores her uncle. Don't you, Aurea?" Santos freed himself, saying, "Go on, my little *profeta*. Make sweet daydreams."

Daydreams, Nesto thought. What did such a child dream?

Casta left the room leading the girl by the hand. When the door had fully closed, Santos crossed to the bar and began mixing himself a drink. He didn't offer one to Nesto.

Nesto tried not to fidget as he waited—but did anyway—letting his gaze move about the room for something to do.

On the wall above the bar was a bank of surveillance monitors, something that hadn't been there on previous visits. Playing on them were views of the sally port, views of the yard, the walls, the gun towers. Views of interior hallways in the men's quarters, the floor below. Views of the prison cells in the dungeon far below that.

One cell was occupied this morning, Nesto noticed on one of the monitors. The prisoner, a woman, sat hunkered down in the narrow corner space between a cot and the stone wall. She was attractive—Mexican for sure—and Nesto wondered about her. What had she done to be there? he wanted to ask. And how long would it be before he would wind up there himself? Something he didn't want to ask.

Santos tested his drink with a small sip, then, satisfied, turned with it to the window that looked out onto Cotorra.

"You see that house?" Santos said after a moment, directing Nesto's line of sight with a pointed finger. "At the far end of the main street, just there, at the base of the tailing dams of the copper mine?"

Nesto craned his neck to peer out. From this elevated height, the second story atop the plateau, he could see across all of Cotorra, across rooftops, streets, and roadways, to the sky-high piles of reddish slag discarded from the strip-mining operations. A cloud of red-brown dust hung above the open pit, telling Nesto that the miners were hard at work with their heavy equipment. Now he let his eyes settle on the little house where Santos was pointing. He said, "The one with the sagging rooftop?"

"¡Sí! That is the house I grew up in, Nesto. Did you know that? As a child, when the winds would blow from the west, I would go to sleep with the red dust of copper ore in my nostrils. The copper! Everything was about the copper! While the walls of my house were made of corrugated cardboard. Wild dogs and coyotes would chew their way inside to steal the food from my hand. Sometimes they would take pieces of flesh with them. My sister and I grew up very poor, as do most of the citizens of Mexico. But no more. I have come a long way, Nesto, and I plan to go farther. Control of the entire border, from Matamoros to Tijuana, will one day, soon, be mine. You can place your money on it."

"And I do," Nesto said, nodding.

"You understand, then," Santos said, "why trust is such an important issue with me?" He sipped his drink as he waited for Nesto's reply.

"Sí, I understand," Nesto said. "There is much at stake."

Santos nodded, then turned to Nesto to level his eyes on him. "We will be taking the northeast trail this time through Santiago Canyon. Tonight."

"Of course, I will instruct my men elsewhere," Nesto said, putting as much matter-of-factness into his voice as possible. "But...what of Francisco Estrada? Will his men not be waiting to strike?"

"Estrada's men will not be there."

"Then, you have consulted your niece?"

"I have. And she tells me the way is secure."

Nesto nodded.

"You understand how important this is, do you not? Estrada's rebels have taken a toll on my deliveries. The cartels in Bucaramanga and Cali...they all wait impatiently to see how well I perform. *Estrada!* This humanitarian! He raids my caravans. His efforts mean little to me, but it shakes the confidence of my clients."

Santos took time to sip.

"But now," he continued, "with my niece's gift, I am able to act with a clear vision. This delivery is extremely important. Do you understand?"

Nesto nodded again. "But if I might be so bold, Señor de la Cal...Estrada strikes without warning. No one knows where he lives or where he hides. He is like a phantom, coming and going in shadow. What if he should suddenly change his plans? Surely, it would complicate your efforts."

Santos held his gaze.

Nesto faltered. He could feel sweat trickling down the inside of his shirt beneath his arm. "I am just inquiring," he said, "your opinion."

"It will not happen. Do you not understand? My niece is special. A child of God. She sees what is to *be*, not what mere mortals might plan."

"*Sí*, of course. Will there be anything else?" Nesto asked, anxious to be gone.

Santos shook his head, then corrected himself. "Yes. Make sure not to give orders to your men until it is time for us to leave this evening. And make no mention of it to anyone. In my business, I am never quite certain of who exactly I may trust. You understand what I am saying?"

Nesto confirmed with a slight bow, then turned toward the door. He didn't look back, not even a glance to measure Santos' gaze. Instead, he steeled himself against further scrutiny and made his way off through the penthouse and down the stairs.

Only when he was in his vehicle and heading down the winding switchback did he venture the use of his cell phone. He dialed a number from memory. When the proud voice came on the other end of the line, Nesto said, "Tonight, Señor Estrada … Santiago Canyon. It is confirmed."

SIX

MORNING BROUGHT A RENEWED sense of purpose. Del's night with Allen May had eased some of her pain over Ed Jeski's murder and allowed her to refocus, for now, on the job at hand—the job of investigating Juan Lara's claims about the child, and make a decision whether or not to take the assignment.

She arrived in Palo Blanco shortly after ten a.m. Just a few miles southwest of Bisbee, it was nothing more than a string town on Highway 92. Along the north side of the strand was a quick-stop convenience store, a junkyard advertising pick-and-pull used car parts, a dealership that sold farm equipment, a feed store, a self-serve truck wash. To the south side of the highway, amid the open stretch of desert scrub, lay rectangular patches of furrowed farm fields of melons and beans. Beyond that, no more than half a mile away, was the Mexican border.

Del drove on, watching the numbers on rural mailboxes count down toward the address she was looking for. Cars blew by in the opposing lane. The occasional truck would blast past, buffeting her Jeep with a wall of fast-moving air. Soon, the entrance to the Lara farm appeared before her, on the left, across the highway from a roadside diner.

Del cut the Jeep hard across the highway and into the gravel drive. It led her down and across a parched section of land, then through a sweeping curve toward the farmhouse. A cloud of dust followed, until, at last, she swung the Wrangler into the yard and to a stop near the barn, and killed the engine. She sat for a moment studying the Lara homestead. Furrowed fields—surrounded by desert on all sides—stretched off south toward the border. The soil was parched, irrigation ditches were dry. Rotting melons lay between the rows. Bean vines were burnt brown and weighted to the ground with yellowing pods. A small, tired-looking farm tractor, with a rusty till attachment, sat abandoned off near a pile of creosote brush. In the lower yard, beneath the shade of a desert willow, sat a picnic table. Tall grass had overtaken it from beneath. A weathered hay-barn stood just in front of her. Next to it sat a gray-primered pickup, the passenger door standing ajar, as if its last occupant had left in too much of a hurry to close it. The house was off to the left. It remained quiet, but for the screen door flapping in the on-again, off-again breeze.

Del stepped out onto the hard-packed earth. She removed her aviator sun glasses and hooked them through a belt loop on her jeans. She studied the scene but a moment longer, then closed the door of the Jeep firmly behind her and walked into the melon field, following the furrows out some fifty yards.

It was obvious that the farm had been neglected by its owners for some time. Something that Juan Lara insisted his brother would never do. It made her wonder about the couple, Benito and Yanamaria. Where were they? And could Juan be telling the truth?

Del let her gaze move from the fields to the horizon south, picturing Mexico somewhere out there in the haze. A dust devil kicked up—as if suddenly noticing her there—and spun off in a huff. The farm's proximity to the border was unsettling indeed. Its perimeter lay open, unguarded. Its underbelly exposed to forces—both human and natural—that were largely ruthless and unsympathetic in this part of the world. Del lingered in the field a moment longer, feeling a forlorn sadness for the land, then turned and retraced her steps back into the yard.

Next, she went to the barn and took a peek behind the doors. Shadow and sunlight formed narrow slats across the straw-covered floor. The space inside was barren but for a few old tools that hung from nails on the pine beam supports. The barn and its implements gave off the same lack-of-love loneliness that pervaded the land. Nothing to see, she closed the door and crossed to the pickup.

Inside the open passenger-side door, she found newspapers stacked on the seat. They were outdated sections of various editions. Some were U.S. in origin and printed in English, others were from Mexico printed in Spanish. A pair of small scissors lay nearby. Del lifted a section of paper and held it to the light.

Two rectangular holes had been cut out of the double-page sheet, as if someone had clipped articles or maybe coupons from it.

Del thought of the child, Aurea. The scissors on the seat were of the safety style that children used. If the child had been taken, as Juan Lara had claimed, and taken by her uncle ... would she even understand that she had been abducted?

There were missing persons, Del considered, who were missing for no reasons of their own—those abducted. And, then, there were missing persons who were missing of their own volition. People who wanted to be missing—deadbeat dads, fugitives, people who changed their identities to avoid prosecution or to escape to another life. The child felt like neither of these. All she had was Juan Lara's suspicions. For all she really knew, the child could be with her mother and father this very minute, and all things could be fine.

Del re-folded the sheet of newspaper, laid it back on the stack, and shut the door. Now she turned her attention to the house.

She crossed the yard, and took the three steps up onto the porch. She caught the screen door, mid-swing, in one of its breeze-driven flaps, and wrapped twice on the inner door. As expected, there was no response.

"Hello? Anyone here?" Del called, easing the door open to step inside.

There were dirty dishes in the sink, coffee half-filling a glass pot—mold had formed as a green-gray layer across the surface. "Hello? Anyone?"

Letting the screen door close gently behind her, she made her way across the kitchen and through an arched opening into a living area. There, simple furniture adorned the room—a sofa and recliner, a couple of end tables. It was all grouped around a worn area rug. A small television sported rabbit ears. Over the fireplace were framed photos. Del crossed to the mantel and took one down. In the photo, a humble-looking Hispanic family put their best faces forward—a man, a woman, and little girl. It was Benito and Yanamaria Lara with their daughter Aurea. Other photos, Del recognized were of the brother, Juan Lara, and his wife. And one of the older woman she had met in the office the day before—the Lara family matriarch. It was somewhat heartbreaking, the family love emitting from the gathering of photos. Something Del had never had. She wasn't sure she even had a picture of her late father. And certainly none of the mother she'd never known. Del returned the framed photo to the mantel and moved on inside.

Down the hallway, Del found the first door she came to standing open a crack. She used the toe of her boot to ease it open. There was a large bed, a Bible on the lamp table next to it, a dresser in the corner. A crucifix hung on the wall. There were clothes hanging in an open closet, a pair of work pants across a chair. Not much else. One item that caught her eyes, however, was a purse on the upper shelf. Del took it down and examined it. It was made of cloth and had the name *Yanamaria* spelled out across the front in colorful sequins. This was a family full of pride, she believed, turning it in her hand. A good family. Del returned the purse to the upper shelf and softly closed the door. She moved on down the hallway, to search the remainder of the house.

Midway down the hall was a laundry closet, a washer and dryer behind closed doors. Farther on, on the right, was another room, the door standing open. It was piled with miscellaneous junk—a dismantled sewing machine, a busted recliner, a tricycle with the front wheel missing—the by-products of difficult living and hard times. The entire house had a half-starved aura about it.

Del moved on.

The last room she came too was on the left. The door was closed tight, as though in guardianship of the contents inside.

Something about the stalwart nature of it said ... *You really don't want to see what lies beyond here, do you?*

For one brief moment, Del thought of leaving the room un-inspected. But then considered the child—a little girl, so far, no-where to be seen. She turned the knob quietly and pushed the door inside.

What she saw caused her to step back.

It was the child's bedroom—that part she got right away. There was a small bed with a wooden headboard, a tiny desk where cray-ons and coloring papers were scattered about. The walls were cov-ered with clippings. Newspaper articles, photos, and headlines, ar-ranged in no particular order and held in place by tiny pieces of tape. What was disconcerting about them was ...

The clippings were all of *her—Del Shannon.*

"What the hell?" Del said aloud. She swallowed hard and stepped inside.

The captions, that read in both English and Spanish, were from a variety of newspapers. The photos themselves were familiar. This one ... that one ... another over there. Every damn last photo was of *her!*

Del lifted one of the clippings free and read half-aloud, "*No Place To Run!*" She recognized the article as one that had appeared in the newspapers a couple of years ago. The deadbeat dad, Carl Ray Ellis, who'd disappeared to avoid child support payments. A reporter had snapped the picture in the Pima County Superior Court building as Del led Carl Ray down the hall in cuffs. It had been her very first case.

Del let her gaze move back to the wall, to other news clippings of other cases, recalling the open door of the pickup outside, the stack of newsprint on the front seat, the empty holes in one of the sections of newsprint. It was obviously the work of the child, but...

Del believed she understood now why Juan Lara had asked for her by name. Why he had urged her to come to the farm and see for herself. The clippings... this shrine dedicated to her likeness... had likely been perceived by him and his family as some sort of prophecy. Some psychic vision conjured in the child's gifted little head, and presented as an omen, a prediction of things to come...

A prediction of *her* to come.

"Come on!" Del told herself skeptically. "Do you really want to get into all that?"

Then again, she thought, feeling a chill run down her spine.... *You are here! You have come!*

What did it all mean?

Del wasn't sure exactly what to make of it. Was she supposed to come to the farm, see the child's handiwork, and immediately fall on her knees in praise? Was she to see it as the work of a gifted mind, find faith in it, and make the decision to go searching for the child out of reverence?

Del could admit, it might be a small leap of faith for a God-fearing family like the Laras to see this collection of photos as some message from above. In fact, it had brought them across many miles just to find her and make their appeal.

But wouldn't it be just as easy, maybe more logical, to chalk the whole thing up to idol worship. A young girl sees repeated photos of an adventurous female in the newspapers, she becomes infatuated, romanticizes the images, and she begins clipping them, saving them as cherished mementos. Kind of like collecting *Star Wars* movie posters of Princess Leia. Surely it makes more sense. Still…

She was curious. *Who exactly was this child? What was behind all the hoopla?*

Del lingered a moment longer, feeling a strange foreboding overtake her. It raised goose bumps on her arm, and sent a series of chills rippling down her spine.

She returned the clipping to the wall and left the room.

———

She spent the rest of the afternoon in Palo Blanco. Her cell phone had rung off and on—Randall trying to reach her. She had ignored his calls, picturing him, in frustration, kicking the trash basket around the office and abusing the tired little ficus that stood in the corner next to the water cooler. He would be anxious to hear what she had found, want to know if she'd come to a decision. She wasn't ready to talk to him. Seeing the clippings of herself covering the wall of the child's room had tweaked her interest in the case, but it had not been the hook she was looking for. No, she told herself, curiosity alone wasn't reason enough to run off to Mexico on a doomed mission to kidnap a child from a major drug figure—no matter how special the child might be or how deserving the Lara family.

Del wandered the streets of town, taking time to talk to passersby and meet the merchants in the stores along the drag. Ranchers at the Feed-N-Seed told her, yes, they knew the melon farm down the road—*nice Mexican couple, Benito and Yanamaria Lara. Private. Respectful.* No one had seen or talked to them lately. But, then, no one had reason to—they were quiet folks, mostly stuck to themselves.

And did they know the daughter?

Sure … strange little six-year-old. Watched everything you did and said, but never made a sound.

There was very little any of them could tell her.

Late in the afternoon, Del encountered Tom Sutter, the Cochise County sheriff. He was a big man, with a mild-mannered disposition, wearing an authoritative Stetson, cocked low across his eyes. He was coming out of the convenience store with a Diet Coke and two packages of Twinkies. Del caught him as he was getting into his patrol car.

"Well, hey, Del," Tom said, giving her a smile.

"On the Stake-Out-Diet again, Tom," Del said, indicating his choice of dinner entrées.

"You know how it gets. Still driving the red Wrangler, I see."

Del had met Tom once before. That time more than a year ago when she had dragged Ruben Vazquez in from Benson on a felony warrant. Tom had shown her all respect and had booked the man into custody. She liked him, felt comfortable talking to him.

"So what gives?" he asked. "What brings you to Palo Blanco?"

Del told Tom about Juan Lara and his family, and their request for her to investigate the farm. Had he seen anything suspicious?

"There's been no reports of anything," Tom said. "No complaints filed. You suspect foul play of some kind?"

Out of deference to her clients, Del didn't tell him that the brother believed the Laras had been killed and the daughter kidnapped into Mexico by her uncle. Besides, what did she know really? Only that there was no one home at the farm. She said, "Actually, I don't know what to suspect, I'm just asking around right now."

"Well, it's my experience people come and people go. It's been a rough year for farmers, these parts. You let me know if there's anything I can do."

Sutter slipped behind the wheel, piling his purchases on the seat next to him.

"Take care," Del said.

She remained watching until he had backed out of the space and turned the patrol car out onto the highway heading east.

People come and people go, Del repeated to herself.

It was possible she was dealing with a family who had simply pulled up stakes and moved. But then … it really didn't feel that way.

———

It was well past six p.m. when Del gave up on the people of Palo Blanco and what they did or, mostly, didn't know. With October days getting shorter, the sky had turned dark, the nighttime desert air had grown cool. She put on a denim jacket against the chill and drove back up the highway to the roadside diner. From a booth beside the window, she could see the driveway leading down to the farm. She ordered coffee and a breakfast meal, and sat sipping, picking at her food, studying the darkness that had overtaken the landscape south to the border. She pictured her photos down there on the wall of the child's room. And wondered for the thousandth time … *what's it all about?* Is there really such a thing as clairvoyant children?

By seven, she had eaten her toast and hash browns, but had hardly touched the eggs. The coffee was tasting good. Del realized she hadn't thought about Ed all day. It was the child who dominated her thoughts, the clippings on the wall. There as a decision to be made, whether to take the assignment and go after her, or tell Juan Lara and his family to find someone else.

As she sat sipping, considering the pros and cons, a pair of headlights came up the highway from the east. They slowed at the entrance to the Lara farm, then turned left off the highway, into the drive leading down into the farm—a tan-colored van. Maybe it was her first break, someone who knew the Lara family perhaps. But then a second pair of headlights appeared off to the south, bounding out of the wash and coming along the road between the fields. Del watched as the two vehicles converged in the yard in front of the farmhouse, their headlights crossing momentarily, before going out.

"More coffee?"

The waitress was there and asking.

"What?"

"Coffee?" she repeated, showing Del the pot.

"Okay … sure."

Del had been lost in her head, curious about the evening arrivals. She waited until the waitress had finished pouring and left before turning her gaze back to the farm. The tan-colored van didn't remain in the yard long—ten minutes at the most. Then the headlights came on again, and it made its way back out the drive, turning east along the highway, back the way it had come.

The second vehicle, the one from the desert beyond the farm, remained in darkness.

Del considered the proximity of the Mexican border, remembering what Juan Lara had said about his brother no longer willing to help with the drugs. *Could she have just witnessed an exchange? A meeting between Mexican and American drug partners?*

Something had been bothering her ever since she left the farm. Something sniggly, nagging at her from the back of her mind. It stemmed from the idea that all the photo clippings in the house were of her. Every last one of them. But the sheet of newsprint in the pickup truck had *two* holes cut out of it. *That was it.* Her picture might have appeared once in a given newspaper. But not twice, on two different inside pages—not that she could ever remember. So, what was the second hole? What had been the photo clipped from that adjoining page?

Del withdrew her cell phone from her jacket pocket and dialed Randall.

"The hell you been?" Randall answered, not bothering with hellos. "I've been trying to reach you all day."

"I'm still in Palo Blanco," Del said. "I've been checking out the farm. Everything seems pretty much as our client indicated. The place is abandoned and there's no sign of the Laras or the child."

"Well, I've been thinking," Randall said. "I've decided we're not taking the job after all."

"Actually, I'm starting to think just the opposite, that there might be something to Juan Lara's claims."

"Doesn't matter. I've decided it's too dangerous. You'd need an army to get that child away from de la Cal … if in fact that's where she's at. I'm telling the Lara family to take it up with Mexican authorities."

"Randall, are you still in the office by chance?"

Randall hesitated. "Yeah ... trying to catch up on paperwork ... why?"

"I'm curious about something. Pull up Nexus on the Internet. There's a newspaper article about me I want you to find."

"Now? This minute?"

"Yeah, I'll hold."

"Getting an ego attack, are we? All right, hang on." A touch of irritation was showing in his voice.

Del could hear him moving around in the background, tapping keypads on the computer.

"I'm looking for May tenth, a year ago," she said. "In the *Arizona Republic*. The time I brought back Melissa Cameron, remember?"

"The teen, yeah. Abducted off the street."

"Right, I need you to find that article."

"You're a lot of trouble, you know it?"

She could hear him tapping again.

Del sipped her coffee as she waited, her eyes on the darkness down at the farm. So far as she could tell the second vehicle was still down there.

Several seconds passed, then Randall was back on the line. "Got it," he said. "Now, what is it you want to know?"

"My photo returning Melissa Cameron to her family is on the lower left-hand column of page two. What I want to know is what's on the upper right-hand corner of the opposite sheet ... not on page three ... but opposite on the same signature. Try page nine."

Del waited.

"Okay ... well ... hey! ... whadda ya know! ... It's an article and photo of your old boyfriend, Ed Jeski."

Del's stomach did a sudden flip.

"Ed? Are you sure?"

"I'm looking at it, ain't I? But what's that got to do with …?"

Del ended the call and was on her feet and moving. She pulled a twenty from her pocket and tossed it on the table as she headed for the door. Her phone was ringing again—*Randall.*

She ignored it.

Del raced across the parking lot to her Wrangler, slid behind the wheel, and fired the engine.

All of the clippings she had seen on the wall had been of her. The only other clipping the child had cut from the newspaper was of Ed Jeski! *Why?*

Del urged the Wrangler onto the highway, giving it all the gas she could, then whipped it hard at the entrance to the farm and raced down the gravel drive heading toward the house.

There was a danger involved. Del had previously witnessed what was very likely a drug deal. But whoever was down there, risky or not, knew something about the farm, about the Laras, and quite possibly knew something about Ed. She wanted to know.

It occurred to her that Ed might have been involved in some sort of undercover operation, a task force maybe. But then the department was touting his death as the result of domestic violence, a love triangle. Would they have dirtied his name, brought shame to the department, if he had been killed in the line of duty? Either way, the child had clipped Ed's photo. Del wanted to know why.

She slid the Wrangler to a stop in front of the barn and bailed out, slipping the Baby Eagle out of her waistband and releasing the safety in one smooth motion. She crouched on the hard-pack, keeping the cast iron of the engine block between her and whoever might be out there. So far, she saw no one.

Del let her eyes move about the property. The night was not as dark as it had appeared through the window of the diner. Down here, moonlight cast soft shadows across the yard. The rusted pickup sat undisturbed. The house was still dark, the barn doors still closed. There was no sign of the second vehicle. *Had it slipped in darkness back into the wash and left?*

Del crossed first to the abandoned pickup, keeping the Baby Eagle poised, and peered inside. Moonlight angled in from the driver side window. The section of newsprint, with the holes in it, was still folded and lying on the stack where she had left it. But what she had missed the first time around was one loose clipping lying on the floorboard beneath the seat.

Sure enough, it was the photo of Ed.

It was, remarkably, the way she last remembered seeing him— on the steps of the courthouse, his partner Ray Daniels close behind. *Why would the child do this ?Why would she save clippings of her and at the same time cut a clipping of her ex-lover? How could she possibly connect the two of them? What on earth—or beyond— would inspire her to do so?*

Del folded the clipping and tucked it into the back pocket of her jeans. She studied the yard, the dark fields stretching off toward the border. It was quiet. Almost too quiet. She made her way around the front of the pickup and crossed to the barn. Standing to one side, Baby Eagle poised, she eased open the barn door.

Without warning, an engine roared to life, and a vehicle launched itself toward her. A massive SUV struck the door, splintering it into a shower of wooden pieces. The force threw Del backwards, off her feet, and sent her sprawling, rolling, crab-clawing to safety.

A dark-blue Chevy Blazer powered into the yard. Its large, knobby tires ate at the earth, creating a second shower of dirt and gravel, that pelted her about the face and body. There were two Hispanic males in the front seat—one behind the wheel, fighting against the fishtailing whip of the vehicle, the second man flashing a gun at her from the passenger seat.

Del dove to her right, rolled, and came up behind the bumper of the abandoned pickup. She leveled the Baby Eagle, settled her finger against the trigger. There were no shots fired. Instead, the Blazer gained control and tore off south down the road between the fields.

Del tucked her Baby Eagle away and quickly crossed to the Wrangler. Whoever these men were, whatever their dealings, they were connected to the farm. And, therefore, would be connected to the Laras and possibly to the child. *Were they also connected to Ed?*

Del fired the engine and gunned it. She sped down the road between the melon fields, giving chase.

…forty miles per hour…

…fifty…

Whatever they knew, her aim was to pin them down, at gunpoint if necessary, and get some answers.

She went airborne at the end of the road, off into desert, working power train and steering as she dodged mesquite and palo verde, mowed through cholla and prickly pear.

Up ahead the Chevy Blazer had its lights on now.

They were two rushing figures on a moonlit landscape. A cloud of dust chased them south toward the border.

Del lost sight of the Blazer's taillights, two hundred yards ahead. She picked them up again dipping into, then out of, the dry wash bed.

She followed.

Back onto the desert floor, she bounded hard over downed saguaro carcasses, swerved sharp around stands of mesquite.

Her cell phone was ringing—*Randall.*

Del answered.

"Del, what's going on?" Randall's voice came to her through the phone.

"Not a good time, Randall. I'm right on somebody's ass, headed for the border."

"Somebody? Who?"

"Drug smugglers, maybe. I don't know."

"Smugglers…? Goddamn it! Just come home!"

"I'm right on them… "Shit!" The Jeep bucked hard.

"Del, damn it!"

"I'm sorry, but you're gonna have to hang on, Randall." She was gaining on the Blazer.

Del tucked the phone between her legs to free both hands for the wheel. She could hear Randall's muted voice still coming to her from down below.

"Del? … Del! …"

Del put her foot to the floorboard. The Wrangler's engine responded. She caught up to the Blazer, both vehicles bouncing wildly on the rough terrain, and nudged the bumper with the push-bar on the front.

The Blazer swerved.

She nudged again.

"*Del ... what's going on? Talk to me, now! ... Give it up, sweetheart! ... Del ...?*"

Border wire glinted in the headlights up ahead. The Blazer aimed its nose for it and gave it gas.

Fifty yards ...

Thirty ...

Ten ...

"*Sweetheart, damn it!*"

Twenty feet in front of her the Blazer burst through the strands of border wire.

Del hit the brakes hard and skidded to a stop. A cloud of dust enveloped her. It swirled and played in the fan of headlights, then settled as the Blazer continued on south. The last thing Del saw of the two Hispanic males was the driver's middle finger raised high through the open window as they raced off into the waiting arms of Mexico.

Randall was still with her.

"*Del, what's going on? Talk to me! ... Del! ... Del! Answer me, damn it!*"

Del stepped out of the idling Wrangler, taking the cell phone with her, and crossed around to the hole in the fence line that defined the Arizona/Mexican border. The Blazer's taillights, out there in the distance, bounced and jerked, and then disappeared amid the scrub.

"*Del! Talk to me!*"

Del took time to kick sand at the busted strands of wire, curse God for his lousy sense of timing, curse the fugitives for their damned good luck. She squatted at the line, Randall's voice still coming to her through the phone, and fingered one of the busted strands as she considered the landscape ahead.

The sprawl of Sonoran wasteland before her seemed endless. The angular glare of her headlights cut shadowy stick figures out of saguaro cacti and mesquite. Prickly pear and cholla huddled in dark brooding masses. Cloud-muted moonlight gave a cold, icy feel to the landscape. The night air put a chill down her back.

The child, Del thought. Did she know Ed Jeski? Was there some logical reason for the clippings? *Or was this child something more?*

She was on the precipice of a major decision. She could feel it. Disregard the violence playing out across the border, forget penalties and harsh treatment for carrying a handgun into Mexico. Go after the Blazer. Or…

Turn around. Go home with her tail between her legs. Tell Juan Lara and his family, sorry, but there's nothing I can do?

Who killed Ed Jeski and why?

The question was still with her. And maybe, just maybe, for what reasons only God knew, this strange, special child had the answer.

Standing there, alone in the darkened middle of nowhere, she could hear Randall imploring her through the phone. *"Girl … goddamn it!"*

Del brought the cell phone to her ear.

"Randall …" she said, feeling a certain resolve come over her. "I'm taking the assignment."

"What? Now, listen, Del …"

Del hit the *End* button to kill the call. One more look south and she crossed to the Wrangler, fired the engine, and dropped it into gear.

Back home at his desk, Randall would be throwing a fit, kicking the trash again and wringing the ficus. *"I'm just asking you to take a good look at who you are,"* she heard his voice say inside her head.

"I'm just a girl with a lot of questions," she told herself. "That's all."

And, giving the Wrangler gas, she crossed the border into Mexico.

SEVEN

Nine p.m. and Santos was already into his fourth drink and feeling loose. He was in his boxers, no shirt, slouched deep into the sofa, his feet propped on the coffee table in front of him. He held a Cuban cigar, poised limply between two fingers. From time to time, he would puff on it and blow smoke into the air as he studied his niece on the carpet across from him—the girl preoccupied with crayons and paper. A confident smile would cross his lips whenever he thought of her and how incredibly fortunate he was to have access to her vision.

The information he had planted with Nesto Parra had been leaked to his enemy, Estrada, exactly as he had expected. *So much for trust, ah?* The empty caravan, which he'd sent as a decoy into Santiago Canyon, had been intercepted by Estrada's men, and the ambush that he had prepared for them had caught the marauders totally by surprise. Mata's squad had swept down on them from behind the rocks, guns blazing, killing two and wounding several others. It was a blow to the dogged resistance and, as importantly, a test of Nesto Parra's loyalty … or better yet … lack of it. He now knew for sure where he stood with the chief of police. And for the time being, he would keep that knowledge to himself and use it.

The tests, the diversions—they were all part of Santos' bigger plan.

One week from tonight, he would attempt a border crossing with more drugs than he had ever dared to deliver. It would be—*¡a todo dar!*—the mother of all drug transactions. Arrangements were being made this very minute.

Earlier, at the same time that the ambush was taking place, Paco and Ramón were meeting with the American contact at the farmhouse, the man who would put into play on U.S. streets the product he had to sell him. They were confirming the arrangement. Agreeing on time and place. All that would be left to do would be to finalize the arrival of product from Cali and move it across the border for the exchange. The planned mega-deal would yield millions for Santos and make both the American distributor and the cartels in Cali very … very! … happy.

Paco and Ramón should be finalizing plans just about now, Santos thought, looking at his watch for verification. And the delivery next week was sure to be successful, now that he had full access to his niece—the miracle child who could look into the future.

Santos took another draw on his cigar and studied his niece more intently now, as she deftly worked the crayons across the paper. He was fascinated by the intensity of her concentration.

How remarkable!

Only two nights before, Santos had sat with her on that very same stretch of carpet, maps of the *senderos* spread out before them. He prepped her by saying, "Little one, in a little more than one week from tonight, your Tío Santos will make the most important delivery of his life. Do you understand?"

The child had looked up from the maps to lock her eyes with his—her way of conveying understanding.

He said to her, "Tell me, *profeta*... which is the way to go? Which passage might avoid my enemy Francisco Estrada and his men?"

He directed his niece to the map, offering the girl three possible routes by tracing them one at a time with his finger. "This one?... Or maybe this one here?..."

He waited as the girl considered the choices, wishing then, as he always did, that the child would simply open her mouth and tell him what he needed to know. But, as always, he was forced to rely on their special bond, their divine understanding of each other, for answers.

Aurea pointed with one small finger to the route following the San Pedro River basin through the dry wash to the farm—the same route he had taken to make smaller deliveries in the past.

"Are you sure, little one?" Santos had questioned, wanting to be absolutely sure. "I have used this route many times. What about this way?" He offered another alterative route, tracing it for her to see.

The girl had taken his finger and moved it back across the map to the river passage leading to the farm. Then she had turned her eyes to meet his calmly.

Santos took the look, as he always did, as her silent affirmation.

That had been three nights ago. And so tonight, Santos could sit back and sip his drink, and wait for Paco and Ramón to return from their meeting with the American.

How magnificent, this child, Santos thought again, continuing to study his niece on the floor.

Still, it was frustrating, he had to admit, that she did not speak. Even more maddening at times the games he had to invent to communicate with her.

How much easier it would be, Santos told himself, if she would just speak. How much more assured he could feel.

Why? Why all the silence?

With the buzz of nicotine and alcohol swimming inside his head, Santos decided to ask.

"Aurea?" he said to the girl, getting her attention. "Aurea, child... tell Tío Santos... why it is you do not speak?"

The girl's eyes held on his, never wavering. Her expression was the picture of innocence.

"Can you just this once make language, little one? The doctors say there is no reason why you cannot!"

Aurea's gaze remained fixed.

"Okay, then... confirm for Tío Santos... Has the meeting with the American contact been successful? Are Paco and Ramón on their way back safely? What does your vision tell you, *profeta*? Can you answer me in words?"

Santos waited. Aurea's gaze remained steady.

¡Qué gacho! Santos thought, giving in with a sigh. *Why did things have to be so difficult?*

Aurea was still looking at him, waiting for further questioning.

"All right, my little flower," he said. "You can go back to your pretty pictures. If we must work in silence, so be it. We have much opportunity ahead of us."

Aurea turned her attention back to her drawing.

Santos slumped down farther in his seat and, for the thousandth time since she was but an infant, questioned to himself, *¿Quién y de dónde? Who* is this child? And from *where* in God's heaven did she come?

————

On a mesa overlooking the landscape, Paco Díaz drew the Blazer around to look back from where they had come. The woman had stopped, unwilling to cross the border. But now the headlights of the Jeep were moving again, working their way toward them through the scrub.

"I tried to tell you, *ese!*" Ramón said, his eyes darting nervously from Paco to the headlights on the horizon. "We should have smoked her when we had the chance, man!"

"No!" Paco said. "You saw the porch lights at neighboring farms! Gunfire in the night, it draws curiosity. We could not afford to bring attention to the farm."

"Then what about now? We're here, there is nobody around. I say we make a stand, duel it out with this *mujer*, man, be done with the loco bitch."

The headlights were doggedly persistent, still coming their way. This woman, whoever she was, had come driving into the yard with purpose. She could be law enforcement. She could be a bitter relative or friend of the Lara family. Either way she had appeared in a hurry. Now she was following.

Paco checked his cell phone—hoping for a signal from one side of the border or the other—but got nothing… *nada.* Out there in the night, the woman continued to advance. "No," he said, after a moment's thought. "We keep moving. Estrada and his men could be nearby. Santos will be anxious for our report. Perhaps we will run into one of our own patrols along the way. Then we will have backup."

"Fuck, *ese!*" Ramón said, giving him an exasperated shake of the head.

But it was the last to be said. Paco cut the wheel south and urged the Blazer on toward Cotorra and home.

He kept the gas pedal down, trying to get as much speed as possible on the rough terrain. The Blazer humped and bucked, banged hard, bottoming its suspension. They eased into a shallow wash, followed it for a distance of some fifty yards, until the river bottom became too rough to navigate.

Paco cut the wheel to take them out again, found the slope of the embankment sharply elevated and resistant to their climb. He let the Blazer rock back a bit, giving it distance. Then hit the gas hard, to get a run at it.

With a bone-sickening *snap*, the left front wheel met the incline, cocked, and dug in to the sand. The engine stalled and the night went silent.

"What the fuck?" Ramón said. "Let's go!"

Paco re-cranked the engine and gave it gas. The Blazer tried, spinning its rear wheels in the sand, but failed to budge.

"It's stuck," Paco said. "It won't go."

"See what it is!"

Paco killed the engine again and climbed out.

Ramón slipped out the other side and came around the front of the vehicle to join him.

The left front wheel was folded under the frame; the steering strut was bent and sticking out at an odd angle.

"You broke the fucking axle!" Ramón said. "*¡Pendejo!*"

"I didn't break it!" Paco said, defending his honor. "The axle broke itself!"

He glanced back across the horizon. Out there in the darkness, the woman's headlights continued to advance.

"What do we do now?" Ramón asked.

"All we *can* do. We go on foot, hope we meet our patrols before we run into Estrada or his men."

"I say we split up," Ramón said, "Make it harder for the woman to follow. One of us has to report back to Santos."

Paco thought a moment, then nodded.

"I'll circle east. You go off that way," he said, pointing the way for Ramón. "Just no gunfire. We don't need Estrada coming down on us. *¿Me entiendes?*"

Ramón gave him a look of disgust, but turned and headed off on foot through the desert scrub.

Paco took a last look at the headlights still bearing down on them from the north.

Jesus! Who was this woman?

He turned and headed off quickly in the opposite direction.

———

For more than five minutes of trailing, the Blazer's taillights had remained nowhere to be seen. But, now, Del spotted them, low to the ground, aglow in the depths of the wash, a mere thirty yards ahead. The vehicle had come to a stop.

Del slowed the Jeep, coaching herself to use caution. If one of these men was Santos himself, she would take him at gunpoint to authorities. If these two were simply men of Santos', flunkies doing his bidding, then she would take one or both of them and drill them for answers. Del found the Blazer empty. It was lodged between the banks of the wash. Its headlights were on, the keys still in the ignition, the left front wheel jacked out of shape, abandoned. The males were now on foot and even more dangerous in the dark.

Del climbed the nearby embankment, on hands and knees, to get a better view of what lay beyond. Out toward the south, the full moon had turned the landscape into a milky, murky wonderland. A hundred yards ahead, a rail spur cut a path through the scrub. Beyond that, nothing but the dark silhouettes of cacti and mesquite. All was quiet. Then…

She caught a glimpse of headlights from the corner of her eye, followed by rumbling motor sounds. To the west of her position, a caravan of four SUVs was making its way north. The vehicles neared to within a hundred yards of her, still moving. They stopped suddenly, as if sensing her presence.

Del scampered down the rise and killed the lights on her Jeep, then raced around to kill the lights on the Blazer.

Had they spotted her?

Quickly, she scurried, hands and feet, back up the embankment to peer out at the still waiting vehicles. They could be traffickers. Illegals, maybe? Mexican authorities? The term *roving death squads* entered her mind, and sent a chill down her back. The Sonoran desert, isolated and cold, was no place to be alone—not for a man, definitely not for a woman.

Del waited, hoping and praying, for the vehicles to move off without incident. One of the vehicles turned a spotlight her direction, scanning the scrub for whatever they thought they may have seen or heard.

Damn it!

She ducked her head below the rise, and held her breath, as the beam of light scanned over her in one direction, then back again the other way.

Finally, the light went out and she ventured another look.

The vehicles held a moment longer, then slowly started off through the desert once again. Del continued watching until the taillights were mere dots in the distance. At last, she could let her breath out. She slipped quickly over the rise and down into the wash, turning her thoughts to the Hispanic males once more.

Footprints in the sand led off in opposite directions. Choosing the pair that led more or less straight ahead, she followed on foot, letting the moon guide her way. Unwilling to chance the sound of the engine, or the glare of headlights.

She came out through cactus scrub, stepping onto the rail spur, where the footprints she had been following turned and followed the spur line east. There, she squatted to rest.

The moon was fully awake now. The man's boot heels left clear impressions in the cinder base between the ties. She took only a second to catch her breath, then moved off once more, following the footprints.

She continued for more than a mile, until the spur line came to an end at the darkened outline of a building, sitting silhouetted by the moonlight, some fifty yards ahead.

A warehouse.

Abandoned, from the look of it. It was old and graying and listing toward the tracks. Signage displayed faded images of strawberries and cantaloupe. The panes of glass in the skylights were discolored. Some were broken. A paddock, off the loading dock, had weeds sprouting through the gravel. All was quiet.

Del removed her weapon, the nine-millimeter Baby Eagle, from its holster at the small of her back. She checked the load—fifteen rounds in the magazine—and racked it once to put a round in the chamber. She checked the time on the illuminated dial on her watch, then took a furtive look back to where her Jeep sat waiting. She was well below the Mexican border—nine, maybe ten, miles. She had never felt more alone in her entire life. Still, one of the smugglers was in there, and she wanted to talk to him.

A last look around, and Del moved off down the tracks toward the warehouse.

———

Paco Díaz waited in a crouched position behind a stack of wooden skids and watched as the woman entered through the sliding door off the truck dock, stepping into the packing area at the back. She was moving cautiously—that damned gun of hers held alongside her thigh. She crossed first past the stacks of formed and unformed cardboard fruit cartons. And, then, on past the rows of cold-storage walk-ins, checking each door in turn, clearing each cooler box with her weapon.

He thought of Ramón. They had made the decision to split up, to throw the woman off their trail. Now he wished the two of them had stayed together. Wished the odds of two-to-one were in his favor. He cursed Estrada and his men, wondering how near the marauders might be. He cautioned himself to avoid gunfire at all cost. Avoid any disturbance that might arouse them, alert them to his whereabouts. To be captured by them would not be pleasant. Again, he cursed the woman for her dogged persistence.

Forgoing his gun, Ramón drew a switchblade from his pocket, eased it silently open and checked the cutting edge with his thumb. He turned it slightly, first one way, then the other, letting the cold steel catch light from the skylight above. The knife would have to do, he told himself, reminding himself that he did have the element of surprise on his side. *Use it*, he coached. Wait until the woman was in range, then run the blade deep into soft flesh beneath the ribcage. Paco waited, ducked down behind the skids, knife poised, the sick-sweet smell of rotting fruit filling his nostrils.

The woman continued to come, on toward him, her ears and eyes scanning the darkness. On, past waist-high conveyors. Paco waited, timing her footsteps as she crossed beyond his line of sight, behind the stack of wooden skids where he was hiding.

He counted… *One!* … feeling an odd sexual tension at the thought of the woman here in the dark with him.

Two…

On the count of three, Paco bulled over the heavy stack of skids. He charged from darkness, knife raised, a combatant's scream on his lips, then… *stopped*.

The woman wasn't there.

"How you doing?" Her voice came to him from across his shoulder.

Paco spun in place to see the woman off behind him now. She was sitting on one of the conveyors, legs dangling just above the floor. She held the gun waist high, leveled on him.

"Who are you?" Paco said, working to get the sheepish surprise off his face.

"Just someone you don't want to fuck with, so you can drop the knife," the woman said.

"And if I don't?"

"Then I'll put a bullet in you and leave you to ferment with the rest of the rotten fruit."

Studying the knife in his hand, Paco made rapid calculations about his chances. *How fast could he lunge? How quick could the woman pull the trigger?* He considered some more. Then let the knife clatter to the floor.

"Good decision," the woman said, sliding off the conveyor. "Now the gun."

Paco eased the gun from his waistband and slid it across the floor in her direction, she stopped it with one foot.

Pulling steel cuffs from her back pocket, she said, "Where's your partner?"

Paco shrugged.

The woman cocked the weapon.

"We split up! Shit! Who the hell are you, lady?"

"I'm an investigator out of Tucson."

"This is Mexico. You don't have authority here."

"I don't need authority," she said, "I have the gun." She stooped to collect Paco's weapon from the floor. "And now I have two guns."

Paco stared, mouth open, unable to think of anything to say.

Del eased the hammer down. "Turn around," she said, showing him handcuffs now.

He did as he was instructed, turning away from her, then, in a sudden change, turned back on her.

The last thing Paco saw and felt was the flash of moonlight off cold, hard steel and the heavy thud of her gun against the side of his head.

Paco slumped to the floor—lights out.

———

Del stood looking down at the little man. She had hoped he would go without resisting. But then, that's what you get for hoping. She waited for the stars to clear from his eyes, then she slipped his gun into her waistband, and used the free hand to drag him to his feet.

"Get up, asshole."

She had laid the Baby Eagle—four pounds of brass and steel—up hard against the side of his face. It had dropped him like a rock. Now a large red mouse appeared below his eye. The cuffs were in place, the man's hands secured behind his back. He was a little guy, a good three inches shorter than her.

"Shit, lady! Goddamn!" he said, staggering to his feet.

"I tried to tell you. What's your name?"

"Paco!"

"Well, tell me something, Paco. What was that back there at the farm?"

"Fuck you!" Paco said, then flinched expecting to be hit again.

"My guess is that it was some kind of drug transaction."

"You see any drugs, lady? Any money?"

"Then maybe just a consort, huh? A meeting? Tell me, who killed Benito and Yanamaria Lara?"

The man blinked, the question coming at him from out of the blue.

"Was it you? Your amigo out there? Or was it Santos?"

Paco shrugged. "Maybe they got hold of some bad chili peppers, who knows."

"All right," Del said. "I didn't really expect a confession. So, tell me something else … where is the child, Aurea?"

This question seemed to surprise him even more. He hesitated, but said. "Is that what this is about? You come looking for the kid? Well, forget it, lady. Santos would rather die than give up his niece."

"We'll see. Where can I find him?"

Paco scoffed, and put a cocky grin on his face for her to see.

"All right, if that's your choice. But maybe you'll consider better of it on the ride back to Palo Blanco. I'm sure the Cochise County sheriff will have some questions of his own."

Del gave Paco a push to get him going, then followed close behind keeping the Baby Eagle pressed hard into his back.

They went out past the sorting conveyors. Handcuffed and hurting, her prisoner did his best drag-step gallows march toward the exit. The physical protestations did little to slow their progress. Even less to deter Del's determination.

Through the packing area, Paco continued to grumble. Past the cold-storage walk-ins and the stacks of packing cartons, they arrived at the sliding door where Del had entered.

"Time to hit the trail," Del said to Paco, pushing him out through the open door, "Are you ready for it?"

Headlights suddenly filled the loading dock, pinning Del and Paco to the wall.

"¡Alto!" a Mexican voice commanded.

Shielding her eyes, she could see a half-circle formation of vehicles on the paddock, armed men in shadow behind the lights.

Paco tore loose from her grasp, bolted in three quick strides to the end of the dock and made the leap of desperation, out, across the fence. Still cuffed, he hit the sand, rolled, and came up running.

Three of the men broke formation and gave chase. The night became filled with urgent voices. Three shots rang out, then two more. And then the night was suddenly quiet again.

A slim figure stepped forward out of shadow. The semicircle of headlights cast shadows across his face, revealing a determined expression.

"My name is Del Shannon," Del offered. "I'm a ..."

"*¡Arriba las manos!*" the voice commanded.

They were words she understood all too well.

Del put her hands in the air and dropped the gun.

EIGHT

From an overlook, high above the San Pedro River basin, Francisco Estrada watched through binoculars as his men blindfolded the woman and tied her hands behind her back. She was young, attractive, and carried a gun.

Next to him, watching, was Tomás Villarreal, his second in command. He was a man tortured by the memory of his wife, who had been kidnapped off the streets of Cotorra and believed murdered by Santos. Tomás had joined La Banda, the resistance to Santos, shortly after her disappearance, along with his teenage son Reynaldo. That had been ten months ago.

"What do you want to do with her?" Tomás asked.

Estrada scanned the binoculars across the landscape in a wide, slow arc. The patrol he had spotted earlier, moving north, was now nowhere to be seen. Still, it was somewhere out there. Paco Díaz and the woman had come out of the desert on foot. First Paco, hurrying along the rail line alone, throwing furtive glances over his shoulder. Then the woman—minutes behind, tracking Paco's boot impressions in the soft cinder base between the rails. He had held his breath for the woman, concerned for her, as she entered the warehouse alone.

Estrada said, "Tell the men to bring her in."

"¿*Aquí*, señor?"

"Yes, here. I want to talk to her."

Tomás engaged a handheld radio without further question and quietly issued instructions.

Estrada watched as the men, at the warehouse far below, crowded the woman into the back of the van. And continued watching until the vehicles moved out, then disappeared beyond the rise. Only then did he lower the glasses and let the whole of the Sonoran landscape come back into view.

There, the moon lay a soft blanket before him. But beneath its warmth, Estrada knew, lay the torturous canyons and rutted washes—from Cotorra to the desert, across the San Pedro River basin to the mountains—arteries that served to funnel illicit drugs north, across the border.

Earlier in the evening—acting on a tip from the chief of the federal police—he had ordered his men to converge on Santiago Canyon, hoping to intercept Santos' delivery. What had been planned as a blow to Santos and his operation had proven to be disastrous to his own squad. An ambush. Now he would have to go after Santos with two fewer men and decide what to do about the lying chief of police, Nesto Parra.

"*Padre*? Señor Estrada?"

The inquiry brought Estrada from his thoughts. He turned to find Reynaldo, Tomás' seventeen-year-old son, coming to join them on the ledge. He was a strong and handsome young man—

fiercely loyal to his mother's memory, terminally dedicated to the cause.

"The men have been bandaged and fed," Reynaldo said. "They seem to be doing okay."

Estrada studied the young man. He would make a strong leader one day. He nodded solemnly and said, "And how are you yourself doing, Reynaldo?"

The young man looked at him, his eyes fixed with determination. "You need not concern yourself with me, Señor Estrada," he said. "It is the women I worry most for. The conditions are cramped, the comforts little."

"Francisco," Tomás said, interjecting in a somber tone, calling their leader by his given name. "We have trusted the chief of the federal police one too many times, and it has cost us. Where do we go from here?"

Estrada let his gaze move across the landscape. Amid the scattered porch lights down there in the darkness, he believed he could make out the speck of land that had once been his home. In his mind, he could still see the raging fires that had consumed his house and stables, reducing them to ashes while he watched helplessly. He could still hear the maddening chorus of cries, the plaintive pleadings of his wife and child, still inside the house amid the blaze. *Santos!* Estrada re-avowed to himself. He would fight to the death to destroy this man. Would find a way to lure him from his prison fortress and put an end to his reign of tyranny once and for all. It *had* been sworn; it *would* be done.

Estrada leaned down and picked up a loose pebble. He rolled it between his thumb and forefinger, then hurled it into the void below. He waited for the stone to complete its descent, the sound of it clicking from rock to ledge, until it found the bottom.

"Señor?" Tomás prompted.

Estrada shook his head in despair. "I know that some of the children have taken ill," he said. "And the women have grown tired of sleeping on stone. I will deal with Nesto Parra. Be sure of that, Tomás. And one day when we have ended this scourge, you and your son and the others will return to your homes."

"As will you, Francisco," Tomás said.

Estrada turned his gaze first to Tomás, then to his son standing next him—tall and straight, shoulder to shoulder with his father—then he let his gaze move back to the nighttime panorama. "No," he said. "For me, there will be no return. Have the young woman brought to me when she arrives."

———

In the bedroom, close to midnight, Casta Correa found Santos at the window. She had come with snifters of brandy, dressed in a sheer black negligee, her hair down. Santos was still in his boxers, staring off toward the dark streets of Cotorra. The only sign of life beyond the window came from the glow of work lights at the strip mine far across town. La Fortaleza—the rooms below, as with the town—had slipped into late-night mystery.

"You look so serious, my love. What troubles you so?" Casta said, handing a snifter to Santos and setting her own glass on the window ledge to slip her hands about his waist from behind and pull him to her.

"I am not troubled, Casta, I am impatient. Is my niece sleeping?"

Casta laid her head against his back. "You think too much about the girl." She could feel his warmth against her breasts, could feel the coiled muscles of his abdomen beneath her fingers. "Come to bed with me. The child sleeps soundly."

Santos said nothing but continued to stare off at the rooftops of town.

"Please, my love," Casta said. "I want to look into your eyes as you make love to me."

"I have dreams, Casta."

"Then tell me what you dream, Santos. Make it so I can see it for myself." Casta moved in tight against him, planting kisses along the curve of Santos' neck.

"You know my dreams, Casta. I dream of greatness. Of wealth and power beyond belief. I was born for such things."

"Such confidence," Casta said, cooing the words at him.

"Imagine," he said, "if the entire border, all of it, was within my control. What wealth and prestige would come of it."

"I have imagined," Casta said.

Santos turned himself within her arms to look at her. "Really? You have considered such?"

Casta brought her face to his. "You are a warrior, Santos. If you had lived many years before, you would surely have been a conquistador. I see you astride a mighty black stallion, in your metal-plated armor. Armies behind you, marching on cities of gold."

"Such men were highly regarded."

"They were like kings."

"Hernán Cortés … Francisco Pizarro …" Santos offered, speaking the names with reverence.

"And 'Santos de la Cal!'" Casta added. "You see how easily the name fits among those? They were men with dreams also. They saw mountains and climbed them, encountered civilizations and conquered them."

"You are trying to tell me something, my dear?"

Casta let one hand snake in between them. She slid the palm of it down to the front of his boxers. She felt him, there, beginning to stir. "I'm telling you, Santos, you are more than man enough to do anything, have anything, your heart desires."

"It would mean finding Francisco Estrada, his band of vigilantes, wherever they hide and destroying them. Then it would take waging war on the other corridors … Chihuahua … Sinaloa …" Santos seemed to consider. "It would take guns, of course."

"You have guns."

"And men …"

"You have men."

"It would require boldness and cunning."

Casta brought her lips to his ear, let her teeth find flesh and bite softly. "You are bold as the lion, more sly than the fox," she whispered.

"And, of course, it would take a vision from my niece," Santos said.

Casta stopped nibbling and drew away.

"Your niece!"

"Yes! Why not? Aurea is my eyes, Casta."

"Your eyes!" Casta crossed her arms. Her lips narrowed to a razor-thin line. "You want to believe this little … girl! … has the power to see, when she has not even the power to speak."

"Stick to being the madam of whores, woman. How I choose to run my business is *my* business."

"Your business? Ha! Your business is for a true man. Not a boy who plays with little girls."

"Be careful, mistress!"

"Tell me then, where are Paco and Ramón? Do you see them? No! No! You sent them to meet your American contact on the advice of a child. Should they have not returned by now?"

"Aurea has *seen* their safe passage, Casta! Witnessed it in her mind!"

Casta spat to one side, matching the defiance in Santos' eyes with her own. The static war of wills lasted for several seconds, then a knock at the door broke the standoff. A tentative female voice from the other side, said, "Señor Santos? Señora Casta?"

"Come!" Santos ordered, still drilling back at Casta with his eyes.

A pretty, young Mexican woman, dressed in red garters and stockings, her breasts bare, appeared in the doorway—one of the whores from the rooms below. "You should come quickly," she said, a worried look in her eyes. "It is Ramón!"

Casta crossed her arms, putting a self-satisfied smirk on her face.

Santos shot her another warning, then turned on his heels and headed out the door.

Casta quickly followed.

———

Santos found Ramón in what the men called *Sala Roja*—the red room. It was a lounge, of sorts, made for lasciviousness, where the men gathered to relax and drink amid cantina music and subdued lighting. By now, the room was quiet—the men and whores already off behind closed doors. Ramón was seated on the edge of a chaise, working hard to catch his breath. Santos nodded toward the bar, and the red-gartered whore went off to retrieve a glass of water.

"Take it easy, my friend," Santos said, putting a hand on Ramón's shoulder. "Tell me, what happened?"

Ramón accepted the glass from the girl and gulped half of it down before attempting to speak. "A...a woman...!" he said. "Came after us...we...broke an axle!"

"Woman? Axle? Where is Paco?"

"I don't know, we split up. I have been walking fast...running at times for...for miles...trying to make it back to inform you. I finally hitched a ride in the back of a pig truck."

"Ha!" Casta huffed, seizing the opportunity to prove her point. "A woman? And what vision did your niece have for this?"

"Be quiet, *mujer!*" Santos spat. He admonished her with his eyes, then turned his anger unjustly on the whore who stood with her arms hugged tightly about her bare breasts. "Are you still here? Go! Go on about your filthy business! This is none of your concern!"

The young woman ducked her head and hurried off toward the back.

Santos turned a harsh look back to his mistress for good measure, then brought his attention to Ramón. "This...this woman?" he said, searching Ramón's face for answers. "Who is she?"

Ramón shook his head. "I don't know...truly, Santos. She came out of nowhere! Surprised us at the melon farm! We met with our American contact as planned. There were no complications until…"

"Wait!" Santos said, throwing up a hand to stop him. He was remembering his exact questions he had posed to Aurea. *Which is the way to go, profeta? Which passage might avoid my opponent, Francisco Estrada and his men?* He said, "So, you did, in fact, make safe passage to the farm. The meeting was held?"

"*Sí.*"

"And it was not Estrada who interfered?"

"No," Paco said. "We never encountered Estrada or his men. We traveled along the river corridor, just as you had ordered. Just as Aurea had advised. There was no trouble. The American met our terms, a deal was made, and we scheduled delivery for next Wednesday as planned. Only after our American partner was gone did the woman show. I tried to tell Paco… kill her, man! … now is the chance! But he was afraid the late-night gunfire might draw attention."

Santos made a mental note to be more careful, more complete, with his questions to his niece in the future. But then he turned his gaze to Casta, narrowing his eyes to mere slits. "You see!" he said, forming his voice into a knife with which to stab. "It is… not! … my niece's fault. Her vision is true!"

Santos waited for a response, expecting one.

What he got was another huff of disrespect and a burning look of resentment from her eyes. Casta turned sharply on her heels and stomped off up the stairs.

Santos waited until the door at the top of the landing had closed. Then said, "Wake Mata and the men, Ramón. You must find Paco and this woman, pronto!"

NINE

THE SMELL OF COOK fires greeted Del as she was led blindfolded
up an uneven path and into what she took from her senses to be
an encampment. She could hear the crackle of campfires, feel the
warmth of them on her face, hear the sounds of murmured curiosity from voices all around. *Who is this gringa? Why was she being
brought here?*

Del had some questions of her own, like ... Where is *here*?
What did they plan to do with her? Who were these people—the
voices? And why was she blindfolded?

Lots of questions.

They had taken her gun and the keys to her Jeep, and had
stuffed her into the back seat of a van, pinned shoulder to shoulder between two rank-smelling men. The ride had lasted no more
than thirty minutes. Then she was led stumbling along a rocky
path, urged on by a pair of silent escorts, one at each elbow. Others
followed—she could hear their footfalls. No one spoke.

Del realized from the cooking smells that she was ravenously hungry, and wished she had eaten more of her meal at the diner. Finally, she was brought to a stop—delivered it seemed—vulnerable to eyes that she was not at liberty to see.

"Remove the blindfold and untie her," a man's voice said before her. The command was authoritative but not at all harsh.

Del felt hands fumbling at the knot of her blindfold, others working the ones that secured her hands. And then she was free, rubbing her wrists as her eyes adjusted to the light.

Standing before her was one of the most handsome men Del believed she had ever seen. He was lean and work-strong, average height, maybe forty years old. A light-skinned Latino, reminding Del a little of Jimmy Smits, the actor. His hair was naturally waved and trimmed above his collar. He was wearing khaki pants and a work shirt that fit tight across his chest. He had her gun, the Baby Eagle, stuffed into his belt in front where she could see it. Del found it hard to take her eyes off him, even harder to speak. Until the man himself broke the silence.

"I am Francisco Estrada," he said. "Do not be alarmed."

"Hi," was all Del could think to say.

When at last she could draw her eyes from him, she ventured a look around. They were in an encampment, laid out just inside the open mouth of a large cavern. The cave walls and stone ceiling were worn smooth by water and time. There were cook fires burning. Natural ventilation carried columns of thin smoke up and out through a rock chimney formation. There were crude beds laid out on the ground throughout the cavern. There were uncomfortable looking chairs, woven from saguaro ribs and lashed together with rawhide, tables built of rough-hewn pine. People were gathered in a circle around her—men, women, children. Brown refugee faces stared back at her, curious about this woman, this American, who had been brought among them. A number of the men had guns. A few of the women held soup ladles or serving bowls—her arrival into camp was not something they'd been expecting.

Del brought her eyes back to Francisco Estrada. "Why have you brought me here?"

"Mostly for your own safety," he said, his English good, with only a hint of a Mexican accent. "The roving patrols are out in force tonight. It is not a good time to be exploring the beauties of Sonora."

"Yeah, well … being dropped into this place has left me feeling a little like Alice in Wonderland. Where are we? What are you all doing here?"

"This encampment is our sanctuary," Estrada said. "A place to wage war on our enemy, the motherless animal who has murdered our loved ones and driven us from our homes."

Del threw a glance at the ragtag band of poorly fed and under-equipped rebels. "War against Santos de la Cal?" she affirmed, a measure of skepticism in her voice.

"We are few, it is true. But we have God and righteousness on our side. I have told you our purpose, now tell me yours. What brings a woman alone into Mexico with a gun?"

"It wasn't exactly something I had planned," Del said. "I followed a couple of men who I thought could provide me information on a recent homicide."

"So, you were not sent to oppose the drug trafficking?"

"Drugs? No. I have nothing to do with it. Except that I figured the two men might be smugglers."

Estrada's expression morphed into one of hatred and disgust.

"You figured right. They are part of Santos' crew of killers. You are lucky still to be alive."

"Out of curiosity," Del said. "What happened to the one man I followed, Paco? Where is he now?"

"Paco Díaz? You know him?"

"Only by first name. Is he here?"

"I'm afraid he is no more," Estrada said.

"You killed him?"

"Let's just say he died unexpectedly. The other man, more fortunate, was Ramón Paz. He has escaped us for the moment."

Del took another look around at the circle of tired faces. "So, am I your prisoner or what?" she asked.

Estrada crossed casually to her, coming face to face to study her a moment more. Then he removed her gun from his belt and offered it to her.

"Thank you," Del said, accepting the Baby Eagle and stuffing it into her waistband at the small of her back. "What about my keys?" she asked.

He handed them to her next. "I took the liberty of having your Jeep brought up from the desert."

"Well, that was quite nice of you. So, I'm free to go?"

"Of course. Unless," Estrada said, "you'd like to join me for dinner."

An invitation to dine, on the rocky outcroppings of a mountain range somewhere in Mexico, *charming*, Del thought. But her stomach was growling. She said, "All right … but you won't blindfold me again, will you?"

A smile crossed Estrada's face. "Only if you insist," he said.

After searching the desert for hours, Ramón, Mata, and the men found Paco near the abandoned fruit warehouse. He was lying face down, where he'd been dropped with two bullet wounds in his back. His body had been left to the elements and to scavenging night prowlers that had already begun to feed on his flesh. There was no sign of the mystery woman.

It was Ramón's job to break the difficult news to Santos. He wasn't looking forward to it. He entered La Fortaleza through the courtyard and was met immediately by Santos in the ground-level foyer as he came through the door—he had little time to prepare his speech.

"So? Where is Paco, Ramón? Did you find him? What about the woman? Do you have her?"

Ramón took a deep breath, unsure how to begin. Paco had been a longtime friend to Santos—to him as well—the three of them were close. But Paco had always been Santos' favorite, Ramón believed. And there was something more that made him hesitate.

The man, Santos, had been acting strangely of late. Behaving more like a boss than a friend. Ramón had noticed the change starting sometime around the little girl's arrival. Santos had become more brooding it seemed. More quick to lash out. It had caused Ramón to question his real importance in the Santos hierarchy. Forced him to be more guarded with his words. Conscious of it now, he said, "It's not good, Santos."

"What do you mean *not good*?"

There at the base of the steps leading up to the penthouse, beneath the wagon wheel chandelier hanging from the high ceiling, Ramón decided to give it to him straight. "He's dead," he said.

"Dead? What do you mean, *dead*?"

"We found him near the abandoned fruit-packaging warehouse, shot two times in the back, about a mile from where the two of us split up."

"Shot?"

It took a moment for it to sink in, then Santos' chest began to expand, build pressure like a cooker building steam.

Ramón braced himself for what he knew would come next.

"Ayyyiiiiiiii!"

Santos exploded, giving off an ear-numbing shriek that seemed to shake the wagon wheel overhead and rattle the walls. He grabbed for the nearest object, a stone-carved Mayan figurine that sat on a pedestal near the base of the steps, and hurled it with all his might against the heavy wooden door. The statue crashed and shattered, sending a shower of rock and splinters in all directions. "Who!" Santos bellowed. "Who has done this! Who dares to defy me! Was it the woman who followed you there? Tell me you have her!"

"We did not find her," Ramón said, his eyes downcast.

"I want to know who she is! I want a name, Ramón! So I might carve it into the bullet that will blow her fucking brains out!"

"We don't really know it was the woman, Santos," Ramón argued. "We only found Paco lying face down. It could have been Estrada or someone else who killed him."

"But you said you were followed by this woman. You split up and she went after Ramón?"

"Yes, but…"

"I want to know who she is! I want to know who sent her and why she has come!"

Ramón didn't answer. He studied his leader's eyes. He had witnessed Santos' fiery anger many times before, but he couldn't remember having ever seen the man this flushed with rage. Best to follow his line of thinking, Ramón considered. Best to placate him until they could learn the truth. Ramón said, "Maybe the woman works for Estrada."

He saw immediately it was the wrong thing to say.

Santos' anger built for another explosion.

Ramón added quickly, "Or perhaps she works alone. But truly, Santos, we simply do not know."

It seemed to mollify Santos somewhat, the impending explosion failed to materialize.

Santos turned his gaze on Ramón.

Ramón dared not to look away. "We will do our best to find out who this woman is, I promise you. First thing tomorrow morning, I will have men looking into it."

"Yes! … First thing!" Santos said, fire still smoldering in his eyes. "And while you're at it, Ramón … bring me Nesto Parra. The chief of the federal police and I will need to have a little talk."

———

Estrada watched the woman using her long slender fingers to roll a piece of tortilla and dip it into her broth. She was beautiful beyond words, her eyes intelligent and clear. She seemed to have purpose in every movement. He wondered why it was she had chosen the life she had and felt the need to ask.

Between bites, she told him about her job. She told him about the kidnapped child, who was the niece of Santos. And of the farm and the photo clippings and the chase into Mexico and the close call with the roving patrol. She told him of the child's extended family, migrants, who believed the child a visionary. A clairvoyant. Told him of their desire for her to find this child and return her to them. And she told him of the recent murder of an old friend, a Tucson police officer, who had been gunned down in a motel room. Speaking about it with pain in her voice—pain she could not hide. And she told him about the mystery of the clippings— how *this* and *that* and all these *things* seemed to be somehow, inexplicably, connected.

What about *him?* she had asked. "What drives Francisco Estrada to oppose Santos so?"

Estrada told her—feeling pain of his own—of the loss of his wife and child. Of his home and his feelings of bitterness and rage. Of Tomás Villarreal and his son Reynaldo. Of the wife and mother who had been kidnapped and was believed dead. Similar stories of others. He told her of his running raids on Santos' drug caravans. Of his goal to defy Santos' at every turn. He told her of the hardships they all endured, and of the ambush earlier that night in Santiago Canyon. Of how it had taken its toll on their cause. And he told her—expressing his anger fully now—of his insurmountable frustration with his corrupt government and with his own weak inability to stop the scourge that was upon them all.

The woman listened intently, looking directly at him as he spoke, seemingly unshaken by the rising defiance in his voice. Reflected firelight danced warmly in her ice green eyes. And Estrada felt something stir inside of him that he hadn't felt for such a long, long time. Something he vaguely recognized as ... *life.*

"So, this child ... this little girl," he said. "Is it duty that drives you to find her, or is it because you believe she can look into the stars and tell you who murdered your friend?"

"I don't know," Del said. "Maybe a little of both. On one hand, I picture her sad and alone, in a strange new environment, without her mother and father, wondering why she's been taken away. Feeling un-nurtured and without someone to truly care for her. On the other hand, I can't help wonder why she seems so fixated on me, and on Ed. I don't guess I buy into the whole *hoo-doo* thing, but I do wonder if she's witnessed something, maybe met Ed on some occasion for some reason."

"So you believe this idea of clairvoyance is better saved for fairytales."

"Are you telling me you believe in it?"

Estrada shrugged. "There are many things in the universe we cannot explain."

"Couldn't it all just be a coincidence?"

"Maybe. But if you truly thought so, would you be here now?"

"All right. I have to admit, I am curious. I mean, she's never met me before in her life. I'd like to see this child just once and, straight up, ask her *why?* Why clippings of me? Why the clipping of Ed?"

The conversation found a natural lull, and the woman turned her attention back to the food in front of her. Estrada found himself studying her, wanting to know all there was to know about her. He wanted to reach across the table and take her hand. Wanted to ask, what goes on in that pretty head of yours? What *really*? Tell me all your secrets. But he didn't. Instead, he gave her time to eat, content with studying the lines of her face.

Several moments passed in silence. When she had finished her soup, she laid her spoon aside and looked up at him. "Tell me about Santos," she said.

"It is still your plan to go after this child?"

"I really don't have a plan. I guess that's why I'm asking."

"I'm sure I will live to regret telling you, but … He lives at La Fortaleza in Cotorra, not far from here. It is a former prison, remodeled to suit Santos' needs. It is virtually impenetrable, otherwise we would have long ago attacked and done away with him. He makes sure it is well guarded and rarely leaves the safety of it, except under great secrecy and heavy guard. I can also tell you he is prone to quick bursts of temper and extreme bouts of paranoia. And will not hesitate to kill at the slightest provocation. He believes in God and the power of things beyond this world. And he keeps his men loyal by paying them well, and by providing them with whores supplied by his mistress. What else would you like to know?"

"What about Cotorra? What if I … say … went there as a tourist to check things out? What harm could come of that?"

"Perhaps no harm at all. It is a beautiful city and generally friendly to outsiders. But do not be fooled. Behind every smile are sharp teeth. No one is to be trusted. One slip of the tongue, one question too many, and Santos will know. Word of your arrival has likely already reached his ear."

"All he could possibly know is that a woman followed his men across the border. No one knows me here."

"Still, be forewarned," Estrada said. "Do not underestimate Santos. He seems to have eyes everywhere these days."

"Or one set of eyes who sees all?"

"Ah, still you play the skeptic. Please! Go home. Return to the United States and forget about this child. Whether there is some connection to the murder of your friend or not, it is not worth your life."

The woman turned her gaze away from him now, her mind off in thought. After a moment she brought her eyes back to him. "I have to know what happened to Ed."

"So be it then," Estrada said. "I would do all I can to help you in your pursuit, but I myself cannot go to Cotorra. Like Santos, I must remain in hiding. I will send Reynaldo with you, however, as your guide. He is but a boy but dependable. His face not so well known to Santos or the federal police."

Estrada expected an argument. But the woman nodded instead—perhaps she was starting to understand.

TEN

AT EIGHT THE next morning, Nesto Parra was brought against his protests back to La Fortaleza—Ramón dragging him by the arm through the foyer, past shattered figurine parts, and up the stairs to the penthouse. There he was made to stand and wait yet again, while Ramón took a seat in the corner and watched him suspiciously, one leg draped across the arm of his chair. Oh God! It was about the Santiago Canyon crossing thing last night—Nesto was sure of it.

He had gotten word from one of Estrada's emissaries—a message that said that Santos' caravan had turned out to be a decoy. A ploy that drew Estrada and his men into an ambush. Very clever. Very clever indeed.

But how would Santos have known that Estrada would know to attack?

He had told Nesto which corridor he would use, and he had said that his niece had approved the way. So! There were two possibilities, as Nesto saw it. Either Santos was testing him, testing his

113

loyalty. Or, testing the child. Which one? Was Nesto in deep water? Or was the child's so-called gift to come under scrutiny?

Such a conundrum.

Nesto had decided it was possible, even likely, that the girl was nothing more than an exceptionally intuitive and overly imaginative child. So when push came to shove—*a la hora de la verdad*—blame it on the girl. That's what Nesto would do. And who would Santos believe?

He prayed to God it would be him.

Ramón eyed him from the corner.

Sweat broke out beneath Nesto's arms as he waited … waited …

———

When Santos did arrive, he came in leading his niece by the hand. He escorted her to the sofa and lifted her to a seat on the edge of the cushion. The child was dressed in bib overalls, a yellow cotton shirt, tiny patent leather shoes with turned-down lace socks. Santos was in a silk robe, over cotton pajamas, belted at the waist. He took a seat next to the girl, crossing his legs, and casually adjusted the pleat in the robe. He didn't seem angry … but then with Santos you could never tell. The man could look you in the eyes and smile, as he slit your throat. Santos said nothing, ignoring Nesto's presence as if he were invisible.

Say something, Nesto told himself. *Say anything to break the awful silence.*

"Señor Santos …" he said, getting it started, his voice cracking a little. "*Buenos días.*"

Santos continued to ignore him, choosing to toy with the collar of the girl's shirt instead. Not a good sign.

But now Santos turned his eyes on him.

"Have you seen my man Paco Díaz, Nesto?"

The question came out of the blue, immediate and direct. Santos' eyes were narrowed.

Of the many things Santos could challenge, Nesto considered, why would he ask that? A quick recollection of the shattered figurine he had seen in the foyer came to mind. Nesto glanced at the child, to see her reaction. She sat perched calmly on the edge of the cushion, watching him closely from beneath soft, dark bangs. So odd this child, Nesto thought. How adorably creepy.

"Why … no," Nesto said. "Should I have, señor?"

No response from Santos. Only a further narrowing of the eyes.

Nesto felt sweat break out across his upper lip now. He stole a glance about the room, counting the exits. He imagined in his mind the floor below, where it was rumored that more than a hundred armed men lived with prostitutes.

Santos was letting him stew. *Say something else,* Nesto admonished himself.

But before he could respond, Santos said, "My men inform me, Nesto, that my shipment was attacked in Santiago Canyon. I ask myself … 'How can this be?'"

Nesto wanted to say, *What shipment? The vans were empty, weren't they? A decoy?* But he wasn't supposed to know this, was he?

He said, "You wish me to say that I am aware, Señor de la Cal. But I had no idea. I ordered my men to stay clear of the area. They did as they were instructed."

"Yet, my caravan was struck," Santos said. "Even after I consulted my niece, Aurea, about it. How do you explain this?"

Nesto felt his bladder loosen. "If I may say, señor, perhaps the girl was wrong. Predictions can be such tricky things. Even for a child so remarkable, wouldn't you say?"

Now Santos and the girl were looking at him with something of perplexed expressions, as if he had just said the most ridiculous thing either one of them had ever heard.

Nesto let his eyes run from one to the other. He ventured a glance to Ramón in the corner. The man sat paring his nails with a pocket knife, smiling to himself.

Santos placed his hand on the girl's head and stroked her hair affectionately. "Have I told you that my niece is responsible for saving my life, Nesto?"

Nesto had heard the story from Santos perhaps a dozen times already. Of the Hotel Palmas, in the central part of town. Of the child's birthday celebration. Of how the child had clung to her uncle's neck, that day, as he tried to depart. Fiercely refusing to let him go. How Santos' car had exploded in the parking lot, killing the valet who had been dispatched to retrieve it. How Santos would forever see the child's behavior as proof of some visionary talent. A talent, that if true, had saved Santos' life.

Nesto wanted to bring logic to it. He wanted say to Santos, *But she doesn't speak!* How do you know what she was seeing that day? Could it not have just been an outburst by a strange and temperamental child? He wanted to say, perhaps the girl simply didn't want her favorite uncle to leave? Perhaps she simply didn't want the special occasion to end. Have you thought of these things, *pendejo*?

Nesto wanted to say all these things and more. Instead, he said simply, "I have heard the wondrous story, *sí*."

Santos nodded approvingly. "In my world there are many men who would seek to betray me, Nesto. So you understand why I depend on my niece's visions so."

"She is quite remarkable," Nesto said. It was all he could think to say.

Santos sat forward. Clearing a space on the coffee table before him. He withdrew from his robe pocket what appeared to be a stack of printed photos, and began laying them out, one at a time. "I keep photographs of all the people in my organization and everyone I do business with," Santos said. "Did you know that?"

Nesto felt his bladder threatening to give way. He pressed his legs tightly together to allay the feeling.

"In this way I may communicate with my niece. These five are of a few of my men," Santos said, arranging the photos into a matrix, organizing them three high by three wide, the girl watching. The pictures were upside down to Nesto.

Santos continued placing the photos.

"These two are a couple of my allies," he said, adding them to the matrix. "This one, a photo of my mistress Casta ... beautiful woman, and ... Ah! Would you look at this? I have one of you also, Nesto." Santos held the photo for him to see.

Nesto felt an icy finger drag down his spine, felt his face drain of color. "Why ... yes ... *sí*! So it is."

"I say we place you in the center, Nesto," Santos said, completing the matrix. "In a place of honor."

"That is ... very generous," Nesto said, restraining the nervous half-smile that had formed on his lips. "A true honor."

Santos sat back, recrossing his legs, He reached inside his robe beneath his left arm and withdrew a gun. The gesture was almost casual, as if to get more comfortable, but the weapon he brought out was big and bold and menacing. He laid it on the seat cushion next to him. Then, from the robe pocket, he withdrew a pack of cigarettes and a lighter. He tapped one out, lit it, and blew smoke into the air.

Nesto couldn't take his eyes off the gun.

"There is a game that Aurea and I like to play, Nesto," Santos said.

Nesto felt the cold chill return.

"Would you like to see?" Santos didn't wait for a response this time. He got straight to the game at hand, querying his niece for her attention. "Aurea? Do you see the pictures I have arranged? Pictures of these people?"

The girl turned her gaze to Santos for a moment, then to the photo matrix. Not a word passed her lips.

Nesto continued to sweat. A cold drop of it trickled down his neck and found its way beneath his collar.

"There are people in my business who would seek to do harm to your Tío Santos," Santos said to the girl. "Do you understand? Tell me, little one, who among these do you see?"

The girl looked the photos over, then turned her gaze on Nesto.

Unable to hold it, a hot trickle of urine leaked down the inside of Nesto's leg. He thought he heard Ramón chuckle.

"It is okay, Aurea," Santos said. "Tell Tío Santos. Are there those, among these, of whom your uncle should be concerned?"

The girl looked at Santos, then back to the photos.

"Look carefully, *profeta*. What do you see?"

The girl raised her eyes back to Nesto.

Nesto squirmed, feeling them penetrate his soul. He tried to block his mind, put mental music there to erase all thoughts of his calls to Estrada, his meetings, his long list of rehearsed lies. He knew he was failing badly. Voices of his deceit clamored inside his head, threatening to blurt forth their confessions.

The girl continued to hold him with her gaze. Then, at last, she removed her eyes from him. Reaching inside the bib of her overalls, she withdrew a folded piece of newsprint. She opened it and held it for Santos to see.

"What is this, Aurea?" Santos asked.

The girl placed the newsprint at the center of the matrix, covering Nesto's photo with it.

Setting the cigarette aside, Santos sat forward. "A clipping?"

The girl turned her eyes to her uncle and held his gaze.

The clipping was a photo, laying reversed to Nesto. But he could make out the grainy image of a woman—blond hair, clean good looks. *What was the child trying to say?*

Suddenly, Nesto understood how very dangerous this girl could be. Whether clairvoyant or not, Santos was prepared to take her every gesture as a sign of divine truth. It sent a chill down his spine.

"I don't understand, *niña*," Santos said. "This is merely one of your pretty pictures. Why do you show me this thing?"

The girl held his gaze.

Nesto focus hard on the clipping. It was a picture of a blonde woman, perhaps American, relinquishing a teen to what looked to be a grateful set of parents. The bold caption, in reverse, read: *Desert Sands Covert Returns Teen Unharmed.*

Santos picked up the news clipping and examined it. "This woman?" he queried Aurea. "This is what you see, child? You see this woman?"

"Woman?" Ramón suddenly interjected, rocking himself out of his chair. He came quickly to check it out. "Let me see!"

Santos handed him the clipping. "You think it could be the woman who followed you?"

"I don't know..." Ramón said, taking his time with it, studying the image carefully. "I only got a brief look at her at the farm... she was American... short hair... *sí*..."

Santos, impatient for answers, snatched the clipping back from Ramón and scanned it carefully. "She is some kind of investigator? But... but why, Aurea?" Santos turned the photo clipping to his niece again. "This is the photo clipping you showed me in the yard, several weeks ago, yes? The one I placed in your clothing for safekeeping, the day I came to pick you up? Think carefully, my flower... is this the woman who followed Paco and Ramón?"

The girl made no response. She held Santos with her eyes until at last he turned his attention back to the woman in the photo.

"I... I do not understand, *profeta*," Santos said, continuing to study the photo. "What is it this woman wants? What purpose does she have? Please! Speak to me, child, and tell me what I need to know!" Santos' voice was rising.

Mother of God! Nesto thought.

Now Santos was looking to him for answers. Nesto felt another tiny release of urine and knew he had to get out of there soon.

"Do you know this woman, Nesto?" Santos asked.

"I have never seen her, señor. Truly, I swear." Nesto was suddenly grateful that he could simply tell the truth for once, without

120

feeling the prying eyes of the child upon him. Silently, he thanked God and the Virgin of Guadalupe that the girl had not picked his photo from the lineup. At the same time, he wondered about the woman in the photo, feeling a deep sense of dread for her.

Santos turned his gaze to his niece now, the innocent face still looking at him. A swell of pride ballooned his chest. "Is there any wonder I love this child so?" Now he turned to Ramón. "Ramón!" he commanded. "Make copies of the clipping and put the word on the street. From here to the border. I want to find this woman. I want to know what my niece sees in her."

Ramón hurried out of the room, taking the clipping with him. Nesto swallowed hard, his bladder now on the verge of collapse. "Is there anything else you require, señor?"

Santos didn't respond immediately. Instead, he was absorbed with his niece again, stroking her hair, looking into her eyes with a kind of devout adoration. Without looking up, Santos waved him away with an idle sweep of his hand.

Nesto didn't hesitate. He turned quickly for the door.

"Wait!" Santos suddenly amended, halting Nesto in his tracks.

With his hand on the knob, Nesto's bladder finally let go, his pant leg flooded warm with urine, his face flushed red with shame.

Santos said, "If you see this woman, you will inform me, won't you, Nesto?"

There would be time for embarrassment later on, Nesto told himself. For now, he wanted to put distance between himself and La Fortaleza. His back to Santos, his eyes squeezed shut, Nesto managed a slight nod across his shoulder. Then pushed quickly out the door and was gone.

ELEVEN

THEY LEFT THE ENCAMPMENT late morning—Del and her young escort, Reynaldo—coming out of the rugged, mountainous terrain onto paved federal highway heading west. They were both quiet at first, content with the breeze rushing through the open sides of the Jeep. Occasionally, Del would become aware of Reynaldo looking at her. More than looking, actually—privately consuming her with his eyes.

He seemed to be particularly fixated on her face and lips, but sometimes his eyes would stray to trail the line of her breasts down to the curve of her hip. When she would glance at him, he would look quickly away.

Del was used to the ogling. She got it routinely from men. But they *were* men, and they mostly didn't look away. She'd get a come-on smile, maybe even a come-hither toss of the head. But Reynaldo was not yet a man. He was on the doorstep of burgeoning manhood for sure—tall and handsome, his long black hair rich and flowing. Still, despite his attempts at manliness, there was boyishness in his voice, angst and uncertainty in his eyes. Could she blame his infatuation really? She was a full-grown woman, mature and self-assured. And she was, quite possibly, the first blonde he'd ever actually been this close to. Breaking the ice, Del said, "So, you grew up in Cotorra?"

"Yes," Reynaldo replied politely.

"You speak English very well."

"My mother was a journalist. She insisted I learn both languages."

"I'm sorry about your mother, Reynaldo. I know how lonely that can feel."

"You have lost a mother?"

Del took her eyes from the road long enough to look at him. "I didn't get to know my mother. I met her once and only had one glimpse of her before she died. We never got to say … things … to each other."

Reynaldo lowered his gaze, this time in obvious sadness.

"Tell me about your school," Del said.

And so the conversation began in earnest this time, Del leading Reynaldo with questions. What grade was he in? Did he play sports? Did he miss his friends?

He answered politely in English, throwing smiles her way as he named the school he had once attended, the soccer team on which he had played. How he had made the game-winning score to take the Sonora state championship. He told her of Saturday nights, of social gatherings of classmates, of fiestas in the market square. It carried them the better part of the way to Cotorra.

"He likes you, you know," Reynaldo unexpectedly declared.

"Who?" Del asked.

"Señor Estrada."

Del felt herself blush, something she wasn't accustomed to doing. She fumbled with some kind of response. Something that came out like "Oh" or "Ah" … then nothing else.

She was picturing *Francisco*—couldn't think of him as Estrada—still the most ruggedly handsome man she could ever imagine. Earlier, he had walked her to her Wrangler. Reynaldo was already in the passenger seat, waiting. Francisco had taken her hand to warn her once again of the dangers, reminding her to take Reynaldo's lead, reassuring her that, while the boy was young, he was smart and knew the streets of Cotorra. He had held her hand much longer, it seemed, than necessary to effect a proper goodbye. At one point, Del believed, he was on the verge of leaning in to give her a kiss. She had felt a powerful magnetic pull—the urge to do so herself. For one brief moment, she felt moved to offer her lips to him—this near stranger. But, then, Reynaldo was there and watching them, like a test monitor watches his class. The moment passed—they had allowed it to pass—and Del had slipped behind the wheel and driven away.

She was seeing him now in her mind's eye, as she had seen him this morning in her rearview mirror—alone on the trail, hands jammed into his pockets. She wished, for just a moment, that he had kissed her. Wished that she had kissed him back.

"You like him too," Reynaldo was saying.

She had been off in fantasyland, his voice brought her back to the present. "He's very…" she had to search for a word … "*determined*."

"But you like him … I can tell." He was showing her his boyish grin now.

"Sure, I admire him. You do too, don't you?"

"I think you more than admire. But, yes, he is my leader. I respect him very much."

"Why do you think that is?" Del said, feeling like a school teacher, coaxing introspection from her student.

Reynaldo seemed to think about it. "Because..." he said, something dark crossing his face. "Because he burns with a passion to kill Santos. As do I!"

It was sad, Del thought, such venom coming from such a young man. But it was not by choice. It was the lot he had been handed.

"Perhaps it will all be over one day," she said. Though she didn't necessarily believe it herself.

They drove on down the federal highway, the sun nearly directly overhead now.

It was afternoon when they reached Cotorra, the town coming into view across a small rise.

"Is that our destination?" Del asked.

"Cotorra," Reynaldo said, with a certain pride. "Pull over here and I will show it to you."

Del slid the Wrangler off onto a pullout in a cloud of dust. From the overlook, she could see across a wide valley. The town—made up of stucco buildings and clapboard houses—lay in the sway between the hillsides. Dominating the landscape to the west was a copper mine. Red slag, stripped from the ground and plowed into tailing dams, encroached on the backyards of houses and back lots of businesses, pushing into, and sometimes over, the mile-long chain link fence that had been constructed to keep it contained.

"That's the market square," Reynaldo said, directing Del's line of sight to the center of town, where main boulevards intersected in the heart of the commercial district.

"It looks peaceful enough," Del said.

"It would be, but for him," Reynaldo said, pointing her now toward the eastern edge of town, where a massive, gray stone fortress sat atop a plateau, looking down onto the city.

"Santos?" Del asked.

"La Fortaleza," Reynaldo said, giving it a nod, his face full of dread. "He hides there like the coward he is."

Del considered the fortress for a long moment, then let her gaze run back across rooftops to the town itself. While the streets seemed quiet enough, there was a palpable air of menace that hung about the place. A dark foreboding. It reminded Del of old westerns where the stranger arrives to quiet, dust-blown streets, residents quickly scurrying fearfully ahead of the new arrival, eyes peering from behind locked doors. Maybe it was her imagination getting the better of her. Maybe it was the dark brooding fortress itself, projecting its shadow across the land. She thought, for one moment, she heard Francisco's voice on the sudden inexplicable rise of wind, warning her—*go home*. It gave Del a chill, and she wondered for the briefest of moments—had she made a mistake coming to Mexico?

"It feels … *dangerous*," Del said, choosing the word carefully.

"Believe your gut, señora," Reynaldo said. "It tells it like it is."

"Maybe I should go into town alone. Can you find your way back to the encampment?"

"My father says I should stay with you. It is Señor Estrada's wish."

Del gave Reynaldo a smile. "Then I'm happy to have you with me."

Del slipped the Wrangler into gear, and together they drove down into the heart of town.

———

Nesto Parra was still feeling shaken from his earlier visit to La Fortaleza. It had been a close call with the child. She had not fingered him for death this time, but what about the next visit or the visit after that. It would only be a matter of time before she did, Nesto believed. All it would take would be for Santos to merely *read* something into the girl's behavior, and Nesto would be at the end of a rope, a gun, or something worse. Nesto knew he was expected to take some action now, re-demonstrate to Santos that he was still in the game and working on his behalf. But he also wanted to know more about this child, about this idea of her having special powers. Only in knowing could he ever hope to avoid the axe that Santos continuously held poised above his head.

Nesto showered at the men's barracks that adjoined his office, then slipped into a fresh suit and tie. Still dealing with his shame, he buried the urine-soaked pants deep in the trash dumpster behind the building, covering them with paper and refuse, then went back inside to attend to official business.

He first typed an arrest order for a pharmacy owner and his two sons—reported conspirators to the drug trade. The arrest held little validity, in fact, but was something to demonstrate the power of his office, its judicious efforts to stem the flow of narcotics in the area. Then he called a briefing with his men. He laid out their instructions for the day, stressing that he would be out of touch during this time. But he felt no need to explain his plans or justify his temporary absence from the office—he didn't have to, he was the boss. He dispatched them to their duties, urging diligence in their cause. It was a dirty business, playing both ends against the middle. No matter. To Nesto it had become a matter of life or death.

His life or death.

Once his men were on their way—official business taken care of—Nesto got behind the wheel of his government sedan and drove south out of Cotorra along the federal highway. He had heard about a woman, named Quinia, who lived in the town of Magdalena, some eighty kilometers away. The woman, an American citizen living in Mexico, was reported to be studied in the ways of the mystics. Some referred to her as *la bruja*—the witch. Others just called her the crazy old woman who lived at the end of the road. Either way, Nesto wanted to talk to her. He had to find out, once and for all, if the child could truly be psychic. Could she see through his deceptions? Or could he relax in her presence and continue his charade of serving the law while helping Santos to break it?

Nesto leaned back in his seat, tried to forget about Santos and the child for a while. But the drumming of his fingers on the wheel said he was in for a journey of anxious anticipation.

———

Del and Reynaldo came into the center of town by way of the main boulevard—Calle Mercado. There were people on the street, more than it had initially appeared from their vantage on the overlook. Matronly Mexican women milled along the sidewalk, dressed in layers of clothing. They browsed the canopied fruit and vegetable stands, shopping bags filled with daily needs. Men in heavy work clothes stood along the store fronts, others in shadows of open doorways. A simple village, full of simple people. Yet, Reynaldo had told her not to take it all for granted. It put Del's warning system on high alert, her nerves on edge.

They mixed and mingled, and perused the offerings of the street vendors. All in an effort to seem casual. Fit in, as the tourists that they were.

Her initiation into life on the streets of Cotorra came within the first half-hour of being in town. At precisely two o'clock, a heavily armed federal assault team, suited with body armor and wearing knit stocking masks to disguise their identities, roared into the market square in a squadron of open-bed vehicles. They quickly deployed and laid siege to a small *farmacia*, midway down the street. With automatic weapons locked and loaded, they kicked in through the front door and rushed the establishment with shouts and deafening reports from their weapons. Screams filled the street, as pedestrians fled down the sidewalk or took cover behind parked cars. Del and Reynaldo were no more than twenty yards away. They found an open doorway and ducked inside for safety.

At the pharmacy, there continued shouting and commanding and the sounds of glass breaking and merchandise tumbling. Then, in moments, the police were back out, dragging an elderly man, the business owner, and his two sons into the street. There followed a great fanfare of pushing and shoving and waving of official-looking papers, as the three men were forced into the back of the waiting vehicles.

Women family members spilled from the pharmacy onto the sidewalk, issuing tearful protest amid tormented cries, despairing sobs. Their anguish could be heard for blocks around. The storm troopers quickly piled back into the vehicles and, as quickly as they had arrived, roared off down Calle Mercado and were gone.

The street stood hushed for a time. Only the whimpering sobs of the terrified townsfolk could be heard.

"Wow!" Del said, feeling somewhat breathless. "What was that all about?"

"What you just witnessed, señora, was a theatre production. A show for the people's benefit," Reynaldo replied.

"What do you mean?"

"What I mean is, someone must pay the price for the illusion of justice. A price to make the chief of the federal police look like he is doing his job."

"Those people are innocent? They're the police! That's outrageous!"

"Yes! But they are not the ones *you* must be afraid of. You see those?"

Reynaldo pointed Del toward a group men in satin jackets, gathered near the vegetable stand at the far side of the market square.

"They look kinda like the men I followed across the border."

"One, possibly," Reynaldo said. "The others are his friends. They all belong to Santos. See how they swagger, how they watch the streets with interest? Later, perhaps within a day or two, these men will find a federal officer on his own and gun him down. Another show for the people's benefit, to state who is actually in charge. Tit for tat. The citizens must believe the authorities are battling to stop Santos. Santos must make sure they believe he is unstoppable. It goes on like this forever. Both sides know, and accept, that there is no better purpose for the violence."

Del studied the men in the satin jackets. It was true, from a distance, one of the men looked as if he could be Ramón Paz. But she couldn't say for sure. The others were reasonable replicas. "I don't think it would be such a good idea for them to get a serious look at me," Del said.

"Now I think you're getting the picture, señorita," Reynaldo said, taking her by the arm to turn her down a side street, away from the market square. "This way."

"Where are we going?" Del asked. "I could use something to eat."

"First, we'll find you a place to stay," Reynaldo said. "We'll avoid the streets and wait for sundown."

"What happens at sundown?"

Reynaldo gave her a look as if she'd just asked the most stupid question of all time.

"At sundown," he said. "Santos' men become preoccupied with their whores."

———

In the town of Magdalena, Nesto asked about the woman Quinia, and was directed to a dirt drive that led off into the scrub. A small rock house sat far back amid the growth. There was smoke curling from the chimney, cooking smells wafting on the breeze. A natural spring gurgled from the hillside, and was channeled with tiles into a holding tank.

Nesto thought once to turn around and go home. But then decided to buck himself up and knock on the door. Several minutes passed, then a woman appeared in the doorway. She was a *gringa*, as Nesto had been told to expect—in her sixties perhaps, hair graying. She was wearing a woven poncho over her clothing. Her pale blue eyes seemed to give off their own light.

"*Perdón*, señora," Nesto said. "I am looking for the woman who goes by the name of Quinia."

"That's me," she said, in her calm and friendly voice.

"*Muy bien*. My name is Nesto Parra. I am a commander with the federal police in Cotorra."

"You don't wear a uniform," she said, as an observation, not as a challenge.

"I am with AFI, señora. … the *Agencia Federal de Investigación*," he said. "We often work in plain clothes. I apologize for my intrusion, but I had not planned ahead of time to come."

The woman held the door open for him. Nesto stepped inside.

Closing the door behind him, the woman crossed past Nesto to take a seat in a rocking chair near the hearth. She picked up her knitting and began to purl.

Nesto let his eyes adjust to the dim light. There were oil lamps burning, macramé hangings on the wall, hollowed-out gourd pots sitting on the table. In the fireplace, a kettle dangled from a hook above the fire. There was nothing electric that he could see. Nesto spotted a hardback chair against the wall. "May I sit?" he inquired.

The woman gestured to a spot at the hearth, and Nesto pulled up a seat across from her.

"I would offer you some tea," the woman said, "but I just put the water on to boil."

"Gracias, no, I have recently had something." Nesto paused to gather his thoughts, then said, "I am told, señora … the reason being that I have come … that you are … how should I say? … acquainted with things of a mystical nature."

"You think I'm a witch?" the woman said.

"I would not presume such," Nesto said.

"But you came because of what you have heard."

"I admit, señora, I have followed the rumors to your doorstep. Please, do not be offended."

"It's all right, Mr. Parra. It's what the locals have chosen to consider me. But only natural, I suppose. A strange, aging woman, living alone in a hovel here in Mexico. They say things like … 'Aye, the crazy old devil woman, she is in concert with the afterlife.'" Now she took time to study him. "What is it that you want?"

Nesto gathered himself. "There is a child … I don't know how to put it … a very strange child who …"

"Who is said to be clairvoyant?" the woman said, matter of fact.

"Yes, *sí*, but …"

"And you want to know should you believe?"

Nesto waited, saying nothing, questions running through his mind.

"Señor Parra, I hope I don't come as a disappointment to you, but I have no magical powers, no ability to conjure curses, no mystic insights. Quite the contrary. I studied and taught paranormal psychology at the University of New Mexico for more than thirty years. In part, that's where this reputation for being a witch comes from. And, in part, it comes from just being old and alone. I came to Mexico to get away from the fast pace of life in the States."

"I'm sorry, señora. It was not my intention to …" Nesto found himself at a loss for further explanation.

Quinia came to his rescue. "Not to worry, sir. It's simply that people love to pass rumors and judgment. But that's my story, and what you came for is to learn about the child. So, tell me about her, Mr. Parra. And please don't fret on my account."

Nesto nodded and sat up straighter in his chair. "Sí … she is a six-year-old girl, the niece of a colleague. She is extremely intelligent, this little one, and …"

"And seems to intuit outcomes before they happen?"

"That is this child, sí," Nesto said. "I have so many questions."

"Or fears, Mr. Parra?"

Nesto understood now that he was dealing with a person of considerable intuition of her own. "I wonder, at times," Nesto said with a nod, "can she see inside my soul? Know my darkest truths? The child is very strange."

"So you harbor secrets?"

Hanging his head, Nesto said, "I must confess, señora, I live with much dishonor, it is true. And, I suppose, yes, I have come seeking some measure of absolution for my guilt." He looked at her now. "But there is also a side of me that wants to understand. *Who* is this child? Could it be that God sends such children into the world?"

Quinia observed him carefully.

"Perhaps you're not ready for the answer, Mr. Parra."

"Please, if only for my family's sake."

The woman took up a poker and stirred the fire. "There is a belief," she said, "among new age thinkers, that there are children being born this very moment throughout the world. Children with a more evolved sense of … universe … let's say … than the rest of us, you and I."

"Yes?"

"They are extremely bright, these children. They seem to exhibit an acute awareness. One of my programs at the university sought to evaluate these kids. They are referred to as *Indigo Children*."

"Indigo?"

"Named for the aura they give off. It is proposed that these children are the next generation in the evolution of mankind. The last and final phase in our development before we become one with the source."

"God?"

"If you so choose."

Nesto swallowed hard. "I wish to say the child is insightful, yes. But she never speaks. I am told by choice."

"But she is very observant. Watchful."

"*¡Sí!* But does this mean she is a visionary?"

"What is her name?"

"Aurea," Nesto said.

"Aurea," the woman said, repeating the name aloud and nodding as if it explained everything. "All I can tell you, Mr. Parra, is that these children are quite remarkable. It sounds like Aurea could very well be one of them."

The woman rose, letting Nesto ponder the idea while she used a can to water African violets in a pot on the shelf. When she was once again seated, she said. "We ran batteries of tests on children just like the child you describe. I wish I could tell you, yes, that these children are prophets … sent to us for what reason only God would know … but nothing is for certain. As scientists we deal in statistics and norms. These children seem to do better than other children in any battery of tests."

"So, you are telling me you don't believe in psychic children?" Nesto said again, wanting definite assurance.

"I said I have no proof. Only empirical evidence."

"Oh," Nesto said, feeling let down. He wasn't sure what *empirical* meant.

Sensing his disappointment, the woman said, "If it makes you feel any better, Mr. Parra, there are many mysteries that lie beyond the understanding of modern academia. Perhaps this is one of them. You'll have to decide for yourself."

Nesto nodded. He remained seated for a moment, considering if there was anything more to say, then rose reluctantly and gave the woman a slight bow as way of thanks, and turned toward the door.

"I wish you luck," the woman said.

His hand on the knob, Nesto paused. "*Por favor*, señora," he said, turning to her again. "One more question only, if I may."

"Yes?"

"This indigo light you speak of," Nesto said. "Is it something you can see?"

TWELVE

DEL CHECKED INTO a hotel one block off Calle Mercado. It was the kind you might see in an old movie, where the keys are kept in slots behind the desk, and the innkeeper watches patrons with a suspicious eye. She was shown to her room on the second floor. The furnishings were old, the water barely warm, and the sheets were something less than white. Still, it beat sleeping on the ground in the encampment.

She rested until after five p.m.—eyes closed but not sleeping— thinking about Francisco, the La Banda leader who railed against Santos, the government, and the absence of law. She then showered and changed into a blouse she had bought from a street vendor outside the entrance to the hotel—a white peasant blouse. One with lace trim and a neckline that hung slightly off the shoulders. She put it on over a pair of clean jeans that she dug from the work duffel bag she kept in the Jeep. She refilled her pockets, slipping the clipping of Ed into her hip pocket. Tucked the Baby Eagle into her waistband at the back, covering it with the tail of the blouse. Then checked her look in the mirror.

Kazow! So much for incognito.

Okay, so … she figured there wasn't much she could do to keep from being noticed. So she decided to work on her story—a tourist on vacation, a woman looking for a little time alone, a boyfriend, call him Bob, who had dumped her for his ex. Now, heartbroken and in despair, she just *needed to be alone.* She recited her delivery to the mirror, until she could tell the story and make it sound convincing.

Just past dusk, she came down. Reynaldo, her scout, was waiting for her on the sidewalk in front of the building, where he spent the afternoon keeping an eye out. Together they made their way over to Calle Mercado in search of someplace to eat. The Wrangler was still parked near the market square. Clouds had moved in, occasional raindrops spotted the sidewalk as they walked. There were far fewer people on the streets. The gang of men—Santos' henchmen—was gone, as Reynaldo had predicted.

"I should probably call my boss," Del told Reynaldo. "He worries about me like an overprotective grandmother."

Del pulled her cell phone from a hip pocket and dialed. True to form, Randall answered on the first ring. "Goddamn it, Del. Where the hell are you?"

She had been avoiding the call. The last time she had talked to him was just before she crossed the border. That had been nearly twenty-four hours ago. His last words had been to not do anything foolish. Well, she had already crossed that line it seemed. So now she would have to sit through a protracted rationale of why listening to *him* in all future endeavors would be her best course of action. And hear all the reasons why she should just get her ass back home. Now!

Del said to Randall, trying to make a joke of it, "Notice how nobody says hello anymore?"

"Don't try to blow this off! Jesus! I've been worried sick about you, sweetheart."

"I'm fine, I'm in Cotorra, Mexico, Randall. I'm walking and talking, so if I lose you I'll call you back."

"The hell is going on?"

"I've found out that Santos lives in this kind of prison here. I believe it's where he's taken the child. I can see the place from here. Ugly as hell. A fortress."

Del threw a smile at Reynaldo, to let him know she was still aware of him there at her side.

"Del, honey," Randall said into the phone. "Forget about the girl. Turn your Jeep around and come home."

"I don't know, Randall. I've had time to give it some thought. If someone doesn't get this child out, she'll spend her entire life with Santos, questioning every single minute of her life about her parents, and wondering where they are and why they haven't come for her. Not remembering much of them, mind you, but believing every single day that they abandoned her. Trust me, Randall, I know of what I speak."

Randall said, "Del, honey…" then stopped, at loss for a solid argument.

Randall was aware of her story, her own sad tale of how she had been taken away from her mother in infancy—kidnapped, as it were—by her father. The result being she had questioned her mother's love for her entire young life. The emotional pain that she'd endured, the scars that it had left behind—well, it was something she would not wish on any other child.

She had to admit to herself, though, that perhaps her motives were not all about the girl. There was still the issue of Ed's death and his unlikely link to the girl through her clippings. There was still the curiosity of the child's purported gift and whether she might know something important. And then there was just the goddamn unfairness of it all.

Del said, "Look, I know it's dangerous here and the truth is I don't know if there is anything I can do about the girl. I may just stick around a bit and see what happens."

"Shit is what happens," Randall said. "You told me so yourself. I prefer you come home."

"I'll think about it," Del said.

Del heard a sigh of exasperation on the other end of the phone. Randall said, "All right! Just promise me you'll be careful."

"I will. I have my first-class guide to look out for me." Del turned a smile on Reynaldo, and got his boyish grin in return.

"Guide?"

"I'll call you back later this evening, when I have more time to talk."

Del ended the call.

"He worries like a mother bear," Del said to Reynaldo.

"He likes you too," Reynaldo said "The rain is picking up a bit. You still hungry?"

"Starving."

"There are several restaurants in this next block. One is very busy with mine workers this time of evening. We can get lost among the crowd."

"You're the man. So long as they serve food," Del said.

Reynaldo gave her a smile, turning his collar to the increasing drizzle. He headed them for a place called Miguel's.

———

What took Nesto Parra to Miguel's was the need for a strong drink. His trip to see *la bruja* had been less than reassuring. He had gone hoping to discover some kind of truth about the girl. Either be convinced that she was psychic or once and for all have the idea dispelled.

Neither had happened.

What he got were stories of *indigo children* and statistical analysis—kids as lab rats. It all went to simply raise more speculation on his part about the truth of paranormal phenomenon. Nesto took a seat at the bar and ordered a shot and a beer.

As he sat sipping, he noticed, behind the bar, a photocopy of the news clipping that the child had presented to Santos. Word had already reached the streets—the woman's photo perhaps in every business establishment in town. The owner, Miguel, came by to check on him.

"*Por favor*, Miguel," Nesto said, gesturing to the photocopy. "Could I have a look?"

Miguel was an obese man, labored by his weight. He moved heavily to retrieve the photo and hand it to Nesto. "You know this muchacha?" he questioned.

Nesto feigned ignorance and shook his head. "No, I'm merely curious," he said, taking the photo and sipping his beer as he studied it carefully for the first time. *Hmmm, the woman was very attractive.*

"We have been instructed to inform Santos pronto if we see her," Miguel said. "And there will be a handsome reward. But don't get any big ideas, señor. In Miguel's, all rewards go to Miguel, eh?" He gave Nesto only a second more with the photo then snatched it away.

"It is your establishment," Nesto said. "You make the rules."

Miguel returned the photocopy to its place behind the bar and went off to serve the other patrons.

With his shot and beer in hand, Nesto turned on his barstool to face the window. He let his gaze move beyond the glass to the street outside, feeling a dark sense of dread fall over him.

According to the child's prophecy—if you were inclined to call it that—the American woman was someone Santos should fear. Did that mean the woman would be coming soon to Cotorra? And coming to—what?—defy Santos? *Impossible.* And *if*—God forbid—he should encounter the woman, what then? Would he run to Santos with the news? Or would he warn the woman and condemn himself to death? Nesto wasn't sure. Because, if by some miracle the woman did show, well! …

He downed his shot and chased it with his beer, still troubling over the child and the idea of mystic revelations.

———

At exactly 5:55 p.m., well into his second drink, Nesto became a believer in all things paranormal. The day shift from the mine had let out and the cantina had filled with men in heavy work clothes. They were crowded into the bar on either side of him and grouped around tables scattered about the room. At first, he considered that his eyes were playing tricks on him, that it was all in his imagination. Or maybe fueled by alcohol, some delusional, psychotropic episode. He rubbed his knuckles hard into his eyes to clear the image, then opened them again.

"Mother of God! It's her!" Nesto murmured. *The woman from the photo!*

She had just come through the door, along with a young Mexican boy, who looked familiar, but whom Nesto couldn't place. They crossed together past the bar, to take a booth in the far back corner away from the crowd. She was wearing tight jeans and a white peasant blouse off the shoulder—a standout amid the dusty workmen.

Miguel, the bar owner, had seen her too.

Nesto thought of the photocopy behind the bar and wished for just one moment that he could wiggle his nose and make the woman disappear. Blink his eyes and erase Miguel's memory of her too. By such magic, he wouldn't have to worry. He could sit back and have another drink and pretend the attractive blonde waving to Miguel for service was just any other tourist. Or, maybe, any other apparition.

Miguel had his eyes glued to the woman and her companion. He acknowledged her request, then threw a quick look to Nesto as a warning. *"I saw her first,"* was what the look said.

Nesto avoided his eyes, pretending preoccupation with his napkin that had suddenly become marvelously fascinating.

Miguel waddled around the end of the bar, menu in hand, to take the woman's order—breathing hard with each labored step.

Nesto angled himself on the barstool so he could watch without appearing to do so.

Miguel waited, as the American woman and her young companion shared the menu. From time to time, she would mouth something to Miguel in Spanish, check for agreement from the young man with her, and Miguel would nod his head.

On one occasion, the woman glanced across her menu toward the bar, catching Nesto's eyes.

Nesto looked away.

They made eye contact a second time, as Miguel turned away to fill their orders. This time Nesto tried holding her gaze. He was imagining that if he stared long enough and hard enough the woman would feel his warning and get the hell out. That would solve a lot of problems. At least for him.

But not this woman.

She held his gaze until Nesto himself was forced to look away.

¡Suavecita! Nesto thought. Very cool, this woman. Calm, collected—confidently aware of her surroundings. As he continued to study her, Miguel came to retrieve a bottle of Tecate beer and a Coke from the cooler behind the bar. He threw Nesto another warning glance.

Nesto watched as Miguel delivered the drinks to the table, then went off toward the pay phone in the back, dialing a number and cupping the receiver as he spoke quietly into it. He wanted to warn the woman. He wanted to rush to her, tell her to take the boy and *get out quick* before it was too late. But he couldn't. To do so with Miguel watching would seal his fate with Santos. *¡Madre de Dios!* Could he just stand by and watch it happen?

Miguel was back behind the bar again, whistling a merry tune now. The young man at the table had gotten up and left for the men's room in the back.

Minutes past. Nesto debated with himself.

Soon a car appeared at the curb on the opposite side of the street. Nesto watched as an hombre in a satin windbreaker stepped into the street. It was Ramón Paz. He closed the car door and leaned back against it to light a cigarette, turning his collar against the drizzle as he eyed the cantina and smoked. Soon another car rolled up, and now two more men piled out to join him. One was Mata, the huge bull with the pocked face. Nesto felt a chill run down his spine. Words passed between Ramón and Mata. Now glances were running toward the cantina, nods being exchanged.

Nesto knew this was the moment of truth. He could remain quiet and forever be damned, or he could act now and risk the wrath of Santos. Without further hesitation, he brought his hand around and swept his shot glass off the bar and into his own lap. Tequila splashed down the front of his clothing—ruining his second pair of slacks for the day. The shot glass shattered with a crash on the hardwood flooring. "*¡Buey torpe!*" Nesto bellowed, directing his outburst toward the worker nearest him at the bar—calling him a clumsy ox and slapping him hard across the shoulder.

Eyes raised from their drinks. The man looked over, a surprised and puzzled look on his face.

Nesto came to his feet, brushing tequila from his pant leg and issuing more insults.

"Perhaps you do not know who you are dealing with, señor! Would you like to consider an apology? Or would you like to spend the night in jail?"

The man raised his palms to Nesto as if to suggest his innocence.

Nesto grabbed the worker by the wrist and wrenched him off the stool. He used his weight to pin him hard against the bar rail, rob him of air and protest. He spun him, then, out into the middle of the room, amid the tables, issuing more obscenities in the process.

"Is this the kind of establishment you wish to provide, Miguel!" Nesto bellowed, getting the bar owner involved. "I will have you shut down instantly!"

It brought Miguel quickly around the end of the bar, waddling fast to save his place of business. "I am so sorry, Señor Parra! Is this man a disturbance?"

In the street, Ramón took a final drag on his cigarette and crushed it beneath his boot.

Inside, Nesto went for the grand finale.

Grabbing the Mexican worker by the lapels, he threw him hard against a table, sending the man sprawling, the table toppling to crash at the feet of the American woman sitting in the booth. He used the moment to throw her a quick, purposeful glance, holding it just long enough to make it register. Then turned back to the worker to tower over him with fists clenched.

Miguel came quickly to Nesto's aid. "You've had enough, *muchacho*," he said to the worker. "Time to go!" He grappled the man beneath the arms, lifted him, and manhandled him toward the exit.

Nesto followed, guiding and shoving both men to keep them moving.

In the street, Ramón had joined forces with Mata and the other man to cross now, shoulder to shoulder, toward the cantina.

Nesto timed his exit with their approach.

As the men stepped onto the curb, Nesto ushered Miguel and the little worker through the exit, saying, "No more for you!" rushing them, using Miguel's weight and momentum to carry them across the sidewalk just in time. The moving body mass struck the three approaching men with force and sent the entire crowd sprawling, legs and elbows, into the street—Miguel's huge weight taking down even the large bull, Mata.

Nesto came quickly to his feet and began attending to Santos' men, bustling about them, dusting them, but generally stalling them for time.

As the moment of chaos past, the men freed themselves of Nesto's attentions and turned back toward the cantina.

Nesto threw a look inside. *It was up to the woman now.*

———

Del had seen the two cars arrive at the curb and felt an immediate sense of trepidation. But then the disturbance had begun, capturing her attention along with everyone else's in the bar.

The heavyset man in the suit with the pencil-thin mustache, sitting at the bar, had been oddly observing her all along. She had seen him tip his own shot glass to cause a mess. Then watched him provoke an intentional confrontation with the Mexican worker on the barstool next to him.

What was it all about?

The question remained there, while the man in the suit fanned the flames of conflict into a full-blown conflagration. Then, without a word, he had suddenly met her eyes—a quick but purposeful glance. *Was he trying to tell her something?*

The man had continued his ruse, ushering the bartender and the worker through the door, orchestrating calamity in the street with the arriving trio.

147

Now the arrivals were picking themselves up outside, and gathering their composure, while the suited man continued to impede their progress by overly attending to them. Only then did Del recognize one of the men as Ramón.

Reynaldo was still in the bathroom.

Del slid from the booth and rushed quickly into the narrow hallway leading to the back. Reynaldo was just coming out of the men's room, still adjusting his fly. "Come on!" she said, grabbing Reynaldo by the arm and turning him. He threw a quick glance toward the front, but didn't hesitate.

Together they fled down the back hallway, through a swinging door, and into the kitchen. They bolted through an aisle between stainless steel preparation tables, blowing past startled kitchen help, banging over stacks of metal mixing bowls with a crash. There was shouting inside the main bar area now. Neither looked back. They burst through the rear door and into the alley.

Scattered raindrops met them, the early evening sky turned dark with threatening clouds.

"This way!" Del said.

They bolted east over potholes, past parked cars and garbage dumpsters.

At the corner, they turned south down a side street, each stride putting distance between them and the cantina, but also putting them farther from the hotel and the possible safety of it. "We need to get to my Wrangler," Del said.

They took another street east again, panting hard with exertion. The rain that had been but a drizzle when they first stepped into the alley was picking up force, pelting them and soaking their clothing.

A couple of blocks down, they cut back toward Calle Mercado and the market square. Del prayed the Wrangler would still be waiting at the curb. Getting to it safely was perhaps their only chance.

But what if Ramón had already spotted their vehicle with the Arizona plates?

He would recognize it from the night before and have men waiting.

Breathless, Del slowed, bringing Reynaldo to a fast walk with her. "I think we lost them," she said, venturing a glance over her shoulder. "But we have to keep moving, get back to the vehicle."

Reynaldo had said nothing throughout the ordeal. His eyes were wide, his face red from exertion. "They could have others," he said now.

Del nodded. "I know ... come on, let's keep moving."

They continued on steadily in the direction of the market square. The rain was increasing in intensity, coming hard now, soaking them through and chilling them to the bone. Del could feel her teeth chattering as she hurried herself and Reynaldo along the street.

They arrived at the market square, coming at it from the back side. The street was empty, the produce stands abandoned to the lateness of the day and to the rain that was beginning to rage out of control. Del took Reynaldo by the hand, and led him inside one of the empty produce stalls, ducking beneath its canopy top, to escape the downpour. Together, they crawled on hands and knees beneath one of the slanted produce tables. There they hunkered down, out of the rain and out of sight, peeking out at the street and the whole of the market square from between the wooden slats.

"Do you see them?" Reynaldo asked.

What Del could see was her Jeep—thankfully—where she had parked it. It was on a side street a block away, but near the intersection. Their panicked flight had circled them to end up some four blocks from Miguel's Cantina. Ramón and his men were nowhere in sight.

"I don't see anyone," Del said. "But that doesn't mean they're not there. They could be calling for reinforcements. Soon the whole block could be filled with Santos' men."

"What should we do?" Reynaldo queried. His teeth were chattering. He was definitely frightened.

"What I don't understand," Del said, "is how they knew we were in Cotorra. It was almost as if they were coming specifically to get us. And the man at the bar … the one with the mustache. How did he know to warn us?"

"I don't know," Reynaldo said. "All I know is that Santos has eyes everywhere."

Eyes, Del thought. It brought to mind the child, Aurea, and the photo clippings on the wall. If she wasn't careful, she was going to start believing the child was actually psychic.

"Should we make a run for it?" Reynaldo asked. "Your vehicle is just a block away."

Del sat shivering in the wet, chilled clothing, calculating their odds of making it there without being seen. Rain roared against the canopy overhead, making it difficult to think. She was coming to understand Francisco's warnings. In the current climate of drug warfare, Mexico was indeed a dangerous place. It held within its menace a rare complexity. Malice could come cloaked in a smile. And aid could come with a stranger's glance. Both were hard to recognize, even harder to trust.

She wondered, once again, how Ramón knew to look for her at the cantina. Wondered who the man in the suit was and how he knew to warn her. And *why would he*? What motive would he have to do so? She was a stranger to this land and to these people. Yet everyone seemed to know her, seemed to be savvy to her purpose. Yet…

It was all too puzzling, and for now beyond the reach of answers.

"We can't stay here," Del said. "And I don't trust going back to the hotel. I guess we have to chance getting to the Jeep."

"Let's do it then," Reynaldo said.

Checking the streets in all directions, Del crawled out from beneath the produce table first. The pouring rain flooded her eyes, making it hard to see.

Reynaldo crawled out behind her.

"Stay close," she said, slipping the Baby Eagle from her rear waistband.

Hand in hand, they led off up the street, hugging close to the produce stalls. Up ahead, the Wrangler appeared unguarded. As they reached the end of the market square, they stopped with their backs to the wall of a building. The rain poured down around them. It streamed into their eyes, obscuring their vision and drowning out all sound. The Wrangler sat just down from the intersection on the opposite side of the street.

"What do you think?" Reynaldo asked.

"It's now or never," Del said.

With that, they dashed quickly across the street. Del readied the key for the ignition as they ran.

They reached the curb without incident. Then, in the instant before they reached the Wrangler, a man stepped from a doorway to block their path. He wore heavy jackboots, was massively built. His jet-black hair and bandito mustache dripped wet with rain. His face was pocked, his skin oily. His lips were thick and bulbous, like two bruised halves of a pear. Del recognized him as one of the two men who had joined up with Ramón in the street outside the cantina. He stood, offering her a gold-toothed grin.

Del froze in her tracks. Reynaldo backed away.

"Step aside," Del said, bringing the Baby Eagle up to level on his middle.

The man said nothing. He continued to grin.

"Comprende?" Del said. "Step away!"

Hurried footsteps suddenly rushed them from behind.

Before Del could flinch, arms were thrown tightly around her, and the Baby Eagle was wrenched from her hand.

Reynaldo, younger and quicker, managed to dodge their grasp. He faked a move, then fled in the other direction.

"Go! Run …!" Del called after him.

A burlap sack was quickly skinned down over her head. The rough fabric abraded her skin and muffled her cries. The sickly sweet smell of old earth and produce filled her nose. She could see no more.

In bundled darkness, Del heard a vehicle rush to a stop at the curb. The sound of a van's doors sliding open came next. Then she was swept from her feet and tossed, free fall, to land on the hard ribbed flooring of the vehicle. The air punched out of her as she hit the flooring hard. The van's doors were slammed shut and engine revved. They were moving, gathering speed.

Inside the bag, Del tried in vain to wriggle free. The burlap was soaked through with rain, it was cold against her skin. The nearness of it made it hard to breathe. Del squirmed and twisted, kicked blindly at the space around her. From outside the bag, a swift sharp punch landed in her midsection, forcing the air from her in a heavy rush. It ended her efforts at freedom.

Del lay back, resigned to her fate for now.

The last thing she had seen of Reynaldo was the young man's back as he fled for his life. One of the men had given chase. Had he made it?

Del said a quick prayer for the boy, prayed that he had been shrewd enough to elude capture. No one but him knew where she was, that she'd been captured. She could disappear from the face of the earth and the only thing that would happen was that it would leave Randall scratching his head and fretting. Reynaldo was her only hope.

Please God, let him have escaped! Get word to Francisco, was all that she could think.

THIRTEEN

FROM HIS GLASS-ENCLOSED office at Desert Sands Covert, Randall could look out past the reception desk and into the foyer where elevators came and went. His receptionist, Patty, had gone home for the evening. Rudy and Willard, his other two investigators, rarely made appearances in the office. So, Randall was alone and feeling the need to stay busy. He pushed paperwork to one side of his desk, then pushed it back. He tapped a pen to chase the silence, and grumbled to himself about people and things and life in general. He was anxious for Del to call back. From time to time, he would dial her cell number and let it ring...

Eight ... nine ... ten times ...

No answer.

It was going on eight p.m.—nearly three hours since he'd last talked to her.

Had something happened?

More likely—Randall wanted to tell himself—she got caught up over dinner with *the guide*, whoever that might be, and lost track of time. Or she had gone back to her room and fallen asleep without remembering to call. Then again, knowing his best investigator, she had decided to go after the child this very night. Do it suddenly on impulse. Do it against his best advice. She had determination, this girl, and an annoying little streak of careless confidence that caused her to take unnecessary risks. It was a combination of traits that worked well for investigators in his business. But it worried Randall fiercely with Del.

Randall continued to wait, drumming his fingers for something to do. Go easy on her when she does call, he admonished himself. Push too hard and she would dig her heels in just to make a point. Just get her back here—that was the goal.

Randall tapped the pencil some more, then rocked back in his chair and crossed his arms. Maybe she was already on her way back—that was another comforting thought—maybe she was crossing the border this very minute…

———

At a little before nine, the elevator light came on out in the hallway, and the doors to one of the two elevators slid open. Randall's heart leaped at the idea that it might be Del returning. Instead, a man stepped out. He was dressed in a colorful cabana shirt and baggy Bermuda shorts in robin's egg blue. He wore sandals over black nylon socks, looking like he'd just got off a tour bus from Tampa.

He was smoking a cigar despite state law, and Randall recognized him now as Ray Daniels, the retired cop and former street partner of Ed Jeski. He watched as the man oriented himself, found the glass entrance to Desert Sands, and came to push his way inside. Randall met him halfway to the reception desk.

"Nice digs you got here," Ray said, scanning the office space with appreciation. "If I'd known private practice was so lucrative, maybe I would have taken it up while I still had some sand in my shorts." He reached his hand out for Randall to shake.

Randall had only met the man once, maybe twice, before. He wasn't really sure if he liked Ray Daniels all that much. He was a little too verbose for Randall's taste. But he was a former cop and therefore entitled to professional courtesy. He accepted Daniels' hand and shook it limply. He said, "What I hear of you retired cops is that *sand* is about all you have left in your shorts."

"Don't let the beachwear fool you, my friend. This old dog has plenty going on. Count on it."

Randall hated this kind of locker-room banter. But when he was with one of the boys—meaning another kind of cop—he felt a certain obligation to keep up appearances. He said, "What brings you downtown?"

"Actually," Ray said, "I was looking for that sweetheart investigator you keep on your staff. I saw her a couple of nights ago and we agreed to get together. She around?"

"Del? She's out on a job."

"Well, damn," Ray said. "I was hoping to catch her."

He took a drag on his cigar for pause, blew smoke into the air. "She came by the bowling alley two nights ago, asking about Ed, how he died and all. Seemed pretty broken up about it, the poor kid. Thought I might take her out for dinner, cheer her up a little. "

"It hurt her some," Randall said. "But, like I said, she's not here."

"Out running down missing persons? What's she working on these days?"

"Nothing special. Just a kid, taken by her uncle."

"Lot of that going around … sick fucks … she be back anytime soon?"

"I don't know," Randall said. "I talked to her a couple of hours ago, she was across the border."

A crease ran across Ray Daniels' brow. "Mexico?"

"Yeah, why?"

"Nothing … it's just … well … I mean Mexico, Jesus! … It's no place for a woman to be working alone. There are wars going on over the drug corridors. Murders. Assassinations. Used to be a nice getaway, Sonora. Things are pretty ugly down there now I hear." He took a puff on his cigar. "A kid, huh?"

"That's right," Randall said.

"Huh, I don't remember hearing anything about a kid in the papers."

"You wouldn't, it's complicated," Randall said, then to change the subject, gestured to Daniels' cigar. "You mind? It's a smoke-free building."

"What? This?"

Randall waited.

Ray Daniels grimaced, lifted one foot, and snubbed the cigar out on the sole of his sandal. He ignored the ashes that fell to the carpet, but palmed the butt and slipped it into his shirt pocket.

"There," he said. "Do the right thing, right?"

Several moments passed where neither of them said anything. Then Daniels said, "Well, I guess if she's not here …"

"I'll tell her you stopped by," Randall said, something to get the man moving.

"Yeah, I'll see you around."

Daniels threw Randall a limp-hand salute, then turned and headed toward the door.

Randall waited until he had reached the elevator and stepped inside, then returned to his office and dialed Del's number again.

There was no answer.

———

Santos witnessed the arrival of his new female prisoner, following her across the series of video surveillance monitors as Mata led her through the dungeon corridors two floors below. He watched as she was dumped, wet and struggling inside a bag, onto the cot in one of the cells. Watched as she kicked her way free of the bag and rolled quickly to a crouched position on the floor, claws bared, ready for a fight. *Impressive.* Watched as Mata turned the key in the lock to seal her inside.

Done.

She was the woman from the clipping all right—more attractive in real life than in the photo, even rain-soaked as she was. Santos felt a wave of mixed pride and anxiety wash over him. Who was this woman? What did she want? Why had she come to Cotorra? What vision had Aurea actually seen?

If only he could ask his niece and get an answer.

Santos turned his gaze to one of the other monitors. His other captive, the woman journalist, was watching the arrival of the new guest from the adjoining cell, her face filling the small window in her cell door. This one had been here a while, serving as late-night entertainment for Mata and a few of the guards. Maybe it was time to dispose of her. Then again, maybe use her to find out what the American investigator was doing here.

Mata came into the penthouse. "You want me to bring the woman to you now?"

Santos took a second to respond, still studying the woman on the video monitor. She was prowling about her cell like a caged cat now.

"No ... not just yet," he said. "I want to give her the opportunity to see what lies ahead for her at La Fortaleza and have time to consider her fate."

This news caused Mata to brighten, show Santos his gold-toothed grin.

"Don't be so anxious, my big friend. Treat the woman respectfully, but, if you must, give her a show that will bring terror to her dreams."

Mata seemed to understand and accept the challenge as a token offering to appease him for now. He nodded dutifully and left the room.

The men he had to deal with, Santos thought, shaking his head.

He crossed to the wet bar and withdrew a cigar from the humidor. He struck fire to it and huffed it to life.

The bank of video monitors was located above and behind the bar. Santos leaned in on his elbows and studied the woman in her cell more closely now. She had given up on prowling. Now she was stretched catlike on the cot. Santos got a mild erection.

"I have a number of questions for you, señorita," Santos said to the monitor. "What happens next will depend on your answers."

FOURTEEN

"*You are wondering where you are.*"

The female voice came to Del seemingly from thin air. She eased onto her elbows on the narrow cot, her ears tuned to the muted darkness. She knew she was somewhere in the bowels of La Fortaleza—cold and dank. A heavy wooden door, bolted tight, was the only entrance to her cell. A small, barred window in the door let in an angled strip of light from the hallway. There were questionable dark stains on the rough concrete floor. The smell of sodden earth all around. She waited for the voice to repeat itself. When it didn't, she asked, "Who's there?"

The voice spoke to her again. "You are wet and cold. You wonder, does anyone know you are here? Will anyone come to help?"

Del turned her eyes to the wall. "Where are you?"

"Down here," the voice said. "Near the floor."

Del dropped to her knees and found the voice above the first row of stones. The aging mortar, crumbling and dry, had been dislodged to open a narrow crack between the stones. She put her face to the opening and peered into the adjoining cell. One eye looked back at her.

"See me? I'm looking right at you," the eye said.

"Who are you?" Del asked.

"I am Liana Villarreal. I watched them bring you in earlier this evening. I am surprised they haven't yet tried something with you. You are very pretty."

"They've assaulted you?"

"The big mongo, Mata ... he is the one you have to watch out for. I scratch his eyes, kick and gouge. He brings others now to hold me down. They each take their turns."

"I'm not going to let that happen," Del said.

"You say that now," Liana replied. "You wait."

"I know this is La Fortaleza," Del said, letting her gaze move away from the hole long enough to consider the cell once more. "But where exactly are we?"

"We are in hell," Liana said. "You see by the defiance in the stone walls, the blood and urine stains on the floor."

"How long have you been here?" Del asked.

"Nine months, two weeks, five days," Liana said. The eye diverted momentarily, then returned to the opening. "I am, what I suppose you would call, a political prisoner. I write as a freelance journalist for *La Verdad,* a very controversial newspaper here in northern Mexico. I write about the drug violence. I suppose I write too much and too well. I was stolen off the street by Mata, coming home from my office of work. They did it, I know, to silence me and as a warning to others. They could have killed me ... preferable that they had. Now they hold me only for Mata's pleasure and the pleasure of the men, the animals he keeps around him.

My husband and son…" She took a moment to swallow her pain. "I have no idea what has become of them. Mata tells me they are dead. But I do not believe it."

"Wait!" Del said. "Your name, Villarreal! You're the woman they spoke of."

"Who speaks of me?" Liana's interest piqued.

"The men in the encampment. I have seen your husband and son."

"Tomás? Reynaldo? Do not tease, God in heaven!"

"No. They're alive. I have seen them. Reynaldo escorted me to Cotorra," Del said. "They are with a resistance, fighting to stop Santos. They believe that you are dead also. Your husband and son fight to avenge your death."

"Reynaldo is in Cotorra?" Tears filled the woman's eye looking back through the crack between the stones. She blinked, sending a stream down her cheek. "Tell me, *por favor*, how my son is doing?"

"He was with me when I was abducted," Del said. "But he got away. I am sure of it."

"My Reynaldo."

"He's a very handsome young man," Del said.

"*Bastardos!*" the woman cried out. "If I were to have but one chance, I would gouge the eyes from Santos de la Cal, leave him blind and begging for assistance in the streets! Right after I kill the animal Mata and watch him die in pain!" She took a moment, running the back of her hand across her eyes to wipe the tears. Then said, "I am sorry."

"It's okay. We're going to get out of here. We'll see you reunited with your husband and son. I promise."

"If only it could be so."

There was silence between them for a moment. Del said, "I'd like to see you. Move back so I can take a look."

Liana slid herself backwards across the cell floor, then called toward the opening, "How is this?"

Del adjusted her eye closer to the hole. She could see a softly built Hispanic woman with long, straight, dark hair. She had a proud face, possibly beautiful behind the darkly ringed eyes, the tired slump of her shoulders. Del could see she was wasting away in this place.

Now the woman slid close again. "Not very pretty, I know."

"Just hang in there," Del said.

"So, what about you?" Liana asked. "What cardinal sin have you committed that would bring you to this hell?"

"The sin of miscalculation. My name is Del Shannon. I work for an investigative agency out of Tucson. I followed a couple of men across the border, hoping to ask them some questions. They are Santos' men. One was Paco Díaz, the other Ramón Paz."

"Paco? Ramón?"

"You know them?"

"I know them," there was a tone of disgust in her voice. "When you grow up in Cotorra you know everyone. I wish I had come from someplace far away from here. These men are demons! And I wish them all to hell!"

"Well," Del said. "I'm guessing Paco is already on his way... he's dead."

"Good! I hope he burns for eternity." Liana took a moment, then said, "Why did you want to talk to these two?"

"An old friend of mine was murdered a week ago in Tucson. He was a cop... here, I have a photo."

Del reached to her hip pocket for the clipping—it was gone. "I thought I had it right here…" *Mata,* she now remembered. Before tossing her onto the bunk, he had patted her down and run his hands into her pockets, groping her ass and between her legs in the process. His hands—the putty-like feel of them—had sickened her. She had not realized when he had taken the news clipping. "Sorry, I guess they have it now," Del said.

"I bet your man was very handsome," Liana said.

Del nodded. "There's this farmhouse on the border in Palo Blanco, Arizona, where a little girl lives. She is the niece of Santos. The family believes that Santos has kidnapped her. I was hired to find her and return her to them. You haven't seen her, have you?"

"I see only these four walls," Liana said. "But I tell you, if she is with Santos, she will never see her family again. And what about your murdered friend? What does he have to do with it?"

"I don't know," Del said. "It's completely impossible, but the two things seem to be somehow connected. The little girl is said to be clairvoyant. She is believed to have a gift for seeing things before they happen. She clips photos from newspapers and saves them. She has many of me and, for some reason, she has also clipped a photo of Ed. I've never seen this girl before in my life. You see why it's so puzzling?"

"It makes you curious, and so you come out of duty, but, also, because you think to yourself, maybe this child has some vision for the person who killed your friend."

"Actually, I'm more inclined to believe that Ed was somehow connected to Santos. Maybe he went to the farm asking questions… he is a cop. Maybe he saw the girl clipping photos from the paper and showed her his picture. Then, maybe, he saw my photo and pointed it out as someone else he knows. Christ, I don't know!"

"If your friend was investigating Santos, I can tell you without being psychic who killed him."

Actually, the thought had crossed Del's mind. Maybe Ed had gotten caught up in some investigation that led him to the farm. Santos found out and had Ed murdered. That simple. But then what was Ed doing in a motel on South Sixth? Why was he there with a woman, unless... like they say... he was fooling around? It just didn't make sense. Del said, "I don't know why I care so much. It's been three years since I last saw him."

"Because you loved him, and love doesn't stop just because you are apart," Liana said.

"Is it that obvious?"

"You call this man a friend, but the sadness in your voice tells me he was so much more."

The woman had a simple but clear way of looking at things. She was insightful, perhaps in the same way as the child. Maybe it was that all people were clairvoyant in some way. Maybe that which is labeled extrasensory perception is nothing more than simple intuition at work.

It really didn't matter, did it? Del considered. In the end, the kid either knew something, or she didn't. Ed either fucked around on his wife, or he didn't. That was the simple truth of it. You could get overly caught up in the *why* of things. She'd been hired to find the child and return her to her family. That was another simple truth. But look at her now.

Del took a moment to consider her situation again, inspect the stone cold resistance of her surroundings. "I guess this is home for a while," she said through the opening.

"Yes. Just pray that God has some special purpose for you."

"Why is that?"

"Because, otherwise..." Liana said. "You end up like me."

FIFTEEN

DEL LAY ON HER back, muted in darkness. The mattress on the anchored steel cot was lumpy and smelled of sweat and urine. She was in that murky half-world between sleep and consciousness. With too much time on her hands and nothing to do but think.

Let's hope God has some purpose for you! Liana's warning echoed in her mind.

Funny where life took you, Del thought.

Randall, with his motherly nagging, had given her this job. Now he wanted to take it away from her because he thought she was too impetuous. Or maybe because she was a girl.

Not much argument against it just now.

Actually, Ed, you could say—remembering him now, the way he looked in a suit and tie, collar loosened, shoulder rig bulging beneath his left arm—was the one who had brought her to this end. He had taught her how to fire a weapon, how to take a man down. If he hadn't done so, would she be here now?

Blame it on the dead guy.

She thought of Marla—the brooding widow. And Ray Daniels—the not-so-brooding cop. It seemed like weeks since she'd last spoken to either one of them. But it had only been two nights ago. Time was like that.

She thought of Francisco Estrada—the handsome rebel, the passion he exuded when he spoke of bringing Santos down. Had Reynaldo gotten back to him? And, if so, what, if anything, would he, could he, do?

All the mindless thinking.

It brought her full circle to the cowboy, Allen May. They had met in a country bar the night of her father's death, a little over a year ago. They'd engaged in sweaty sex on the front seat of his pickup with the light of flashing neon beer signs highlighting their naked bodies. She had spent the night in his hotel room, waking to the news of her father's accident...

Suicide?

Their getting together again this time—had it been two nights ago already?—had been passionate, as well as therapeutic. She realized, lying there in the dark, her eyes closed, she could call Allen May to mind and get a tingly feeling down deep inside. Feel her head swim, picturing him on the bed in just his cowboy hat and boots. Then... she realized she could get that same feeling picturing Francisco... or picturing Ed.

She had to stop thinking about it.

She held on to the image of Francisco—naked—replacing Alan May on the bed. No cowboy hat and boots... just lean hard muscle... shirtless, brown... looking up at her with smoldering eyes.

Was she having feelings for him?

168

Randall was back inside her head, coming in uninvited to spoil her fun. *"Look at you, girl!"* he was saying. *"You need to get hold of yourself and not in the pleasurable way you're doing right now."*

Del withdrew the hand that had somehow found its way between her legs and placed it behind her head to keep it out of trouble. It was the isolation that was doing it to her, she understood. The confinement and the fear.

And time...

Christ! Del thought.

Time!

It seemed to stretch off into eternity with nothing to do but *wait.* Wait for what?

Sleep, she told herself.

On the dark side of wakefulness, she dreamed of running through the streets of Tucson on the heels of male teenage friends... *Jimmy Samone... Angel Padilla... the Tucson night jaundiced beneath yellow, sodium-vapor streetlights. She could smell backseat vinyl, taste the brine of young sweat on bare skin.*

Tweaking toward consciousness, she thought: How are you going to get yourself out of this?

Drifting, she dreamed. *"The hell you want to know about your mother for? She's a liar and a whore, and that's all you need to know!"* Her father's voice as clear as day.

Liana had asked: Who would be looking for her? Would anybody come?

"Goddamn it! She's my mother, Roy! I've got a right to know!"

Thinking—or was she dreaming... *"I'm going after my mother! She may be sick and dying."*

Would she have made different choices if her mother had been in her life?

"*Come on … just break the lock.*" Jimmy Samone's voice.

If you could go back in time and change any one single thing—she thought or maybe dreamed—would it change the outcome of your life? If so, what would that one thing be?

Police sirens … dogs barking …

If she hadn't been caught that night, then she wouldn't have met Louise Lassiter, her probation officer. And if she hadn't met Louise, her life may never have been turned around.

See how it works?

Pop … pop … pop … half-silhouettes down range … dirty gym mats … *clean sheets …*

What if Ed Jeski had been an insurance salesman instead of a cop?

Neon.

Vacancy.

There! There! Oh, God, don't stop!

What if Ed had not been married?

Banging!

The door.

Marla Jeski.

Angry!

Shouting!

Dreaming …

Or was she thinking …

WAKE UP!

A shrill cry brought her fully alert. Del sprang off the cot and to her feet.

Scuffling sounds were coming from Liana's cell next to her. Loud cursing.

Del dropped to her knees and put her eye close to the hole in the wall. She could see legs only, four sets of them, engaged in a kind of awkward dance. Liana's legs were flailing, kicking. The other legs—those of three men—struggled to subdue her. One, she knew to be Mata, by the heavy jackboots he wore.

"¡*Hijoputa!*" Del heard Liana cry.

"Stop it, goddamn it!" Del screamed through the opening in the stone.

Now Liana was spun around and pinned, her backside to her assailants. Her cries became muted, as she was forced forward across the end bed rail, her dress bunched above her hips, her face pushed into the mattress. Mata took a structural stance behind her, his jackboots spread wide.

"Stop it, goddamn it! Leave her alone!"

Del pounded the unforgiving stone with her fists, feeling nausea overtake her.

She pounded harder. Again. And again…

"Stop it! Stop it!"

One by one, the figures took their turns. When finished, they took turns again, only this time brutalizing Liana by throwing hard fists into her face and stomach. Liana's cries ebbed into silence.

Del slumped down against the wall, tears filling her eyes and overflowing to stream down her cheeks. They had assaulted Liana before, she'd been told. But this time had been overtly brutal. It was a show, she realized. Directed by Santos. He was giving her a glimpse of the horrors that awaited her. Seeking to break her down mentally and emotionally, by filling her dreams with terror, and rob her of her will.

It was working. Feeling helpless and lost, Del crossed back to the cot and buried her face in the smelly mattress. Soon would come her interrogation. And when the inquisition was through … the questioning run its course …

It would be her turn across the rail.

SIXTEEN

"HOW ARE YOU DOING?" Del asked through the crack in the stone.

The men had come and gone. Liana was on the far side of her cell, crouched in the narrow space between the wall and her cot, her knees hugged to her chest, her face buried between them.

The assault had taken it out of her, and Del wondered how much more the woman could endure.

"Liana?" Del urged.

It took a moment for Liana to respond. But then she lifted her face toward the sound of Del's voice and shook her head—*not good.*

"I'm sorry, Liana! God! I wish there was something I could do."

"There is nothing you can do," Liana said. "There is nothing anyone can do. I tell myself, get used to it."

"It's not something you should ever have to get used to," Del said. "I know things are bleak. But your husband is out there fighting for you. So is your son."

"They don't even know I'm alive. And besides … why would Tomás want me now? Why would any man? I am soiled goods."

"Your husband loves you, Liana. There will come an end to this someday, I promise."

Liana buried her face again, the conversation over.

Del turned away from the crack in the wall.

"Del…?"

Liana's voice pulled her back to the opening.

"Yes?"

"No matter what," Liana said, "You are my sister, yes? *¡Mi hermana por siempre!* Don't forget, okay? Forever!"

"Okay," Del said, feeling touched by the offer of sisterhood. She had no sister of her own and few, if any, real female friends—as Randall had not so subtly pointed out. There had been Louise. But she had been older—a mentor, more like a mother figure. This idea of sisterhood was something of a first for her. It brought rise to an unfamiliar stirring of emotion.

Del moved away from the crack in the wall and returned to a seat on her cot.

Mata appeared at the small window in her cell door, his broad, oily pocked face filling the opening. He remained, watching and salivating. She had the impression he was touching himself, lusting for the chance to repeat his performance with her. His eyes were red and watery with drunken anticipation. If he had not made his move as yet, Del understood, it was only because Santos had forbidden it—*for now*. But there would come a time when lust would overpower his sense of duty, and she would have to deal with this animal *mano a mano*.

Del glared back, holding the man with her eyes. After a moment he relented with a sneer and lumbered off down the corridor.

Del lay back and draped a forearm over her eyes. Her head was pounding. Her stomach was growling. *Food!* she thought. That was another pleasure Santos would withhold in order to break her down. Consider it a test of survival, she told herself—a way of thinking of it. Otherwise she was just another victim, as Liana had said.

Lying there, trying to ignore the empty pit in her stomach, she thought of home and of Randall, of warm showers and cold beer. She thought of Friday nights and lovers, of fate and choices. She thought of Louise Lassiter, her old probation officer and mentor. *"You see, Del,"* something Louise was prone to say. *"The thing about the Devil, sweetie… is the Devil knows how to wait."* The Devil in this case was Santos.

Del tossed and turned throughout the night. From time to time she would awake to find Mata leering again through the window opening.

She managed some sleep… but with one eye open.

———

Del awoke to the rattle of a key in the lock and the throw of the heavy-metal deadbolt. She'd made it through the night, and morning had arrived. But now the door was swinging open and there was Mata, filling it.

"What do you want?" she asked, rolling quickly to her feet, fists clenched, nails digging into the palms of her hands.

Now another figure entered the cell, pushing past the bull to take her by the arm. It was Ramón Paz.

"Santos wants to see you," he said.

"You go," Del said. "I'll follow you."

"Del?" Liana was calling to her through the hole in the wall, concern registering in her voice.

"It's all right, Liana."

"Just come," Ramón said. He nodded Mata out ahead of them, then gave Del a shove to get her going.

They passed through a labyrinth of stone corridors, Del taking in as much of her surroundings as possible, memorizing exits, weighing options that were few. Eventually, they came to a stairway that led upward. Three flights later they were on a landing at a doorway that opened into posh living quarters. Ramón gave her a shove inside. And led her, wrists pinned, into the spacious penthouse, past the bar where a bank of surveillance monitors showed views of the fortress and the dungeon below. Del recognized her cell, and the one just next to it. She could see Liana sitting on her cot, wide-eyed, wringing her hands.

At one of the sofas, a man, possibly in his early forties, sat waiting. He was dressed for introductions in a silk suit and tie. He had his legs crossed casually, an amber-colored morning drink in hand. A nine-millimeter handgun lay on the seat cushion next to him. Not bad looking, but with cold, calculating eyes.

So this was Santos, Del thought.

"So, Miss Del Shannon..." he said, as they approached.

It caught her by surprise, *Santos knew her name.* She thought of her wallet, her driver's license, but realized it was still in her duffel, back at the hotel.

"How was your stay? Did you sleep well?"

"It's not the Hilton," Del said. "What about you? How do you sleep at night?"

Santos smiled to himself and took a sip from his drink, a practiced gesture.

"What is it you want?" Del said. "Why am I here?"

"Yes, why *are* you here?" Santos said. "That is what I would like to know."

"I'm here on vacation," Del said, giving her rehearsed line a shot.

Ramón stepped forward and backhanded Del across the mouth. She felt her lip slip, and tasted the blood that flooded into her mouth.

"You'll want to consider your answers carefully," Santos said. "Let me ask again. Why are you here?"

Del shrugged.

This time the slap came from Mata, on the opposite cheek. It rattled her eyes in the sockets and sent stars spinning through her head.

"You followed my men, Paco and Ramón, across the border. Now Paco is dead, and I ask myself … why? What is it that brings this pretty *investigator* from *Desert Sands Covert* to Cotorra?"

He knew her name, now he knew her company. How did the man become so informed? For one brief moment, Del thought of the child, but then dismissed the idea as quickly as it came. She said, "I didn't kill Paco, if that's what you're thinking."

"Then who did?"

"Someone else, I suppose."

Santos studied her a moment. "Perhaps another line of questioning," he said.

Reaching into his shirt pocket, he withdrew a piece of newsprint and laid it on the coffee table in front of her. It was the clipping of

Ed that Mata had taken from her pocket the night before. Something else for him to fish with.

"Where did this come from?" Santos inquired.

"From a newspaper, I'd say."

Ramón cocked his arm to strike her again.

She flinched.

Santos held him off with a hand.

"I'll ask again … Where did this come from?"

"I found it at the farm where your boys were doing their thing," she said. "One of the men in the photo is a friend of mine."

"A friend?" Santos said, suspicion crossing his face. "Then this is one of my niece's clippings."

"It is, and that's exactly why I'm here." Del retrieved the clipping from the table and held it up for Santos to see. "This man…" she said, pointing out Ed in the photo, "was a friend of mine. A week ago he was murdered. I want to know who did it."

"You are telling me this is why you are here?" Santos said, distrust in his voice.

Del nodded.

"And what makes you think I would know anything about it?"

"Because your niece … the little girl you believe to be clairvoyant … clipped this from the newspaper. If she's truly special, I want to know why she did."

"You seem to know much of my niece. Who exactly are you? And who sent you here?"

"I told you. I found the clipping, then followed your men hoping to find out who the girl was and why she had clipped a photo of my dead friend."

"But that doesn't answer who you are and why you were at the farm in the first place. And it doesn't explain how you come to know of my niece. Tell me!"

Until now, Del had no specific evidence that Santos had kidnapped the girl, only Juan Lara's suspicions. She decided to take a stab in the dark. She said, "If you want to know so bad, why don't you just ask Aurea. She's here, isn't she?"

Santos jaw tightened, his face flushed red with rage.

"Oh, I forgot," Del said. "You can't ask her … she doesn't speak."

"What is your business with my niece!"

"How do you communicate with her, Santos?" Del said, on something of a roll now. "Do you ask questions and assign whatever answer suits your needs?"

"Aurea and I are of one mind!" Santos screamed. His voice was shrill, his fists and jaw were clenched. "I know what she sees, and she sees what I need to know!"

Del had him on the ropes and she liked the idea of keeping him there. "Then show her to me," she challenged. "Bring her here and ask her why I've come. Asked her why she clipped this photo … and while you're at it … ask her who killed my friend."

"You mock my niece and accuse me of killing a man I have never met!"

"It's not the child I mock. It's you!"

She had pushed it further than she dared. Del waited for the explosion that never came. Instead, a dark shadow spread across Santos' face. "Very well! I will give you that chance to meet my niece. And you will see her, as I do, as the miracle that she is. And then we will see just why you have come to Cotorra … Casta!" Santos bellowed beyond the room.

179

A woman, beautiful and mature, appeared in the doorway. "Bring my niece to me!"

Del waited, returning Santos' glare. A long minute passed, then the courtesan returned with the child. She was adorably neat, wearing a red and white striped shirt above blue corduroy pants, little running shoes on her feet.

"Come sit with me," Santos said, tucking the handgun into his belt and patting the seat cushion next to him.

Casta sent the girl in motion and Aurea came to slip in beside Santos on the sofa. Her eyes were locked on Del.

Del had not been wholly sure of just how she might react if she ever got the chance to meet this child. She hadn't been convinced that she would get around to stealing this child away from Santos, even though she'd been hired to do so. The forces that had brought Del here, to this place and time, across the table from Santos and the girl, had been largely driven by emotion over Ed's death. And curiosity—the puzzling nature of the clippings of her on the wall. But now, looking at this girl, this child with the sad, innocent eyes beneath squared-off bangs...

She knew.

Special or not, if she ever got the chance... she would get this kid the hell out of here!

"Do you recognize this woman, Aurea?" Santos inquired of his niece.

Aurea had been watching Del with dark, penetrating eyes. Now she turned those eyes to Santos and held his gaze.

"She is the woman from your clipping, *sí*?"

Aurea continued to lock Santos in her gaze.

Now Del understood how Santos knew so much about her. The child had retained one of the clippings. Very likely the one that was represented by the second hole on the news page on the front seat of the truck. *No special vision required.*

Santos was still leading the child. "Is this the same woman who followed Paco and Ramón, the woman you warned me was coming? Tell me, *profeta*, why has she come?"

Santos waited expectantly. Aurea turned her eyes back to Del.

"It's okay, *profeta*," Santos urged. "The woman cannot hurt you."

Aurea's eyes held on Del.

"Look at me, child," Santos said, coaxing the girl's face back to him. "You love your uncle very much, don't you? Tell me what you know of this woman."

"Leave the girl alone," Del said. "Can't you see she's just a child? She can't tell you anything."

Santos looked up.

"It is no matter," he said. "No one understands Aurea more than I." Now he turned to Mata. "Take the woman back to her cell. I will deal with her later."

Mata took Del fiercely by the arm, seemingly delighted for the opportunity. He dragged her roughly, past Santos and the child, out past the courtesan who had been watching from the doorway, arms folded.

Minutes later, she was tossed unceremoniously onto her bunk once again.

Mata stood over her, ideas flitting through his mind. With a lick of his lips, he left the cell and rebolted the door.

Del rolled onto her stomach and lay staring down at the stains on the concrete floor. It was going to be a long incarceration.

Afternoon rolled around, and Del still hadn't called. Randall took a walk to the newsstand on the corner. It had been almost twenty-four hours since he last talked to her. She had said she would call when she got back to the hotel, but she hadn't. He had tried calling her, no answer. He called at daybreak, no luck again. By afternoon, he was sure—call it fatherly instinct—something bad had happened.

One option, Randall considered, would be to contact Mexican authorities, maybe the American embassy there. But tell them what? Who in Mexico could be trusted anyway? He picked up a copy of *La Verdad*—a Mexican newspaper sold at Tucson newsstands—on an outside chance that it might report any happenings across the border. Maybe something involving an American woman, for instance. Standing on the sidewalk, he rifled the pages searching for something, anything. But the print was in Spanish and the pages were clogged with photos of drug arrests by Mexican authorities and retaliatory assassinations in response by the drug cartels. Disheartened, Randall closed the newspaper, and crossed the street, heading toward McGuff's, a familiar cop bar located below street level on Pennington. He thought there would be a few off-duty cops there who could offer some advice. And if not, well, he told himself, he could use a drink.

Randall took the steps down to the entrance, then stopped with one hand on the door handle.

Inside, beyond the glass, Ray Daniels sat at the bar. He had his shoulders hunched over a shot and beer.

Shit! Randall said to himself, the very last guy he wanted to see. But he pushed on inside and approached Daniels from behind. "This seat taken?"

Daniels looked up at him through bloodshot eyes, nodded Randall to the stool next to him.

"What brings you down from your glass menagerie?"

"Same as you. I could use a drink." Randall slid onto the stool and waved to the bartender. "Beer, Jimmy, and another for Mr. Daniels."

Jimmy went to work on his order.

"You're a good man," Daniels said. "But, actually, I was hoping you were going to tell me that sweetheart investigator of yours had come home and was waiting for me at my place in leather garters."

"Maybe we could skip the locker room banter," Randall said. "Del's a good kid, almost like a daughter to me."

"Come on, don't tell me you've never thought about hitting that at least once."

"I just don't want to hear it, all right!"

"Okay, okay," Daniels said. "You know you really ought to start thinking about retirement. What are you now sixty, sixty-one?" He finished off his beer and accepted the fresh one Jimmy delivered.

Randall took time to sip his. "Listen," he finally asked, "you're former law enforcement, what can you tell me about what's going on across the border?"

"If you'd have asked me six months ago, maybe I'd have something to say. But I'm retired and don't know shit."

"I'm just trying to figure out what to do. I haven't heard from Del since late yesterday."

"And you think our girl got her pretty little tit in a Mexican wringer?"

"Hell, I don't know," Randall said. "I just need to do something, you know? Find out if she's okay."

Daniels stopped drinking and gave Randall a thorough look. "You're serious, aren't you? You're worried."

"She told me she'd call, and she didn't."

"Well, I wouldn't worry too much. She'll probably come dragging back with a couple Mexican hickeys on her neck. Listen, why don't you and me head over to the Foxy Lady, have a couple strippers do a face dance for us. Take your mind off things."

"You really are retired," Randall said. "You got nothing better to do?"

Daniels tossed back a shot of whiskey and chased it with his beer.

"My friend, I drink, chase pussy, and bowl on Thursday nights. What else is there that's worth doing?"

"Well, I can't just sit here," Randall said. "I've got to do something." He took a long slug off his beer, then slipped off the stool.

"Come on, jeez-peez, I'd like to see the woman back here, too. But what the fuck can I do? I mean, really?"

"I don't know," Randall said. "When I figure it out, I'll let you know."

Randall left McGuff's and headed back to the office. The truth was, Daniels was right, what could he, or anyone, really do but wait?

Still, the man was an ass, just the same.

SEVENTEEN

THEY WERE SPEAKING THROUGH the crack between the stones again, Liana wanting to know what had transpired with Santos.

"He wanted to know why I'm here," Del said.

"Yes? What did you tell him?"

"I didn't tell him anything. Once he gets what he wants out of me, I'm dead. He won't need me anymore."

"Did you get to see the child?"

"Yeah, he brought her in, more to show her off than anything. You should see this little girl. She has these big intelligent brown eyes. But there's a sadness behind them that I can't seem to get over."

"You think she is the God-child they claim her to be?"

"You sound like the girl's family. No, I think she's just shy and insecure and needs somebody to hold her and make her feel safe."

"I think that person is *you*," Liana said.

"Oh, no! I'm not ready for that kind of responsibility. But I have to admit, the girl has a way of getting to you all right."

It was true. Seeing the child, the innocence in her, had made Del aware of feelings she never knew she had—maternal feelings.

"So, what now?" Liana asked. "What will Santos do?"

"I don't…" Del suddenly stopped.

"Is he watching again?" Liana asked, her tone changing to one of fear and concern.

"Yes."

He was. Mata was back at the opening again, leering in at her.

"The pig," Liana said. "I tell you, if I ever get the chance, I will kill him without hesitation or guilt. With pride even!"

Del kept her eye on Mata, until at last he moved away from the opening. "I'm hoping Santos can keep him on a leash, while he figures out what to do with me."

"You better hope it is one big leash. Sooner or later, he will become tired of waiting. Santos is the boss, but Mata is an animal that goes with his instincts."

Del withdrew herself from the opening between the stones and made her way back to her bunk. If Liana was right, Mata would sooner or later make a move on her. Her only hope was that Santos had a change of heart and let her go. But then how did a man with no heart have a change of one? No, Del thought, laying her head back and closing her eyes…

She'd be better off placing her bets on the psychic child.

———

Darkness allowed Nesto to slip back to the government building unseen.

After his charade at the cantina, he had called his wife on his cell phone and told her to take the kids and go to her sister's house in Hermosillo. *Don't ask questions,* Nesto had told her. *Stay there! Speak to no one! He would call.*

That being done, he placed himself in hiding, in a Port-a-Potty, at a vacant construction site not far from the tailing dams of the mine. He made sure to have a bottle with him, and hit it liberally as he sat and thought.

Helping the woman at the cantina had signed his death warrant—this he knew for sure. *And to what end?* She had been captured anyway, and was either dead by now or in Santos' prison getting who knew what done to her. *And Nesto himself was now a dead man.*

He understood—having given the alcohol time to burn reason into his brain—that he couldn't stay in the toilet forever, and that there was no future in hiding or in running. Sooner or later, Santos would find him, no matter where he hid or how far or fast he might run. Time was running out, and there was really only one answer. So Nesto decided it must be done. Place his soul in the hands of God first, then finish with it all.

Nesto closed himself inside his office and locked the door, fumbling around in darkness until he found the gooseneck lamp on his desk and turned it on. The lamp threw a circle of light on his desk, enough to see by without banging into things. He sat his current bottle of tequila on the desk and removed his coat and tossed it over a chair. He stripped out of his shoulder rig and piled the gun and holster on the desk next to the bottle. He worked fingers into his tie to loosen it, undid the top button of his shirt. Now he took up the framed photo of his family from the credenza and placed it in the center of his desk where he could look at it. Not until he'd finished these rituals did he settle into his chair and prop his feet up.

¡Híjole! he told himself, feeling a weariness in his bones. *You have done it this time, Nesto Parra! You have openly defied Santos. Now your life is worth nothing.*

Nesto removed his service revolver from its holster and laid it across his lap. He retrieved the bottle of tequila, uncapped it, and put it to his mouth. He tipped it sharply and drank, studying the framed photograph of his family before him as the fiery liquid burned its way down.

There was a scolding look on his wife's face, seeming to say *shame on you, Nesto. We trusted you, Poppi.* Her name was Maria. She had fattened up over the years, but Nesto still saw her the way she had been when they were first married—beautiful and soft in Spanish ways, faithful as the day is long. That had been thirty years ago. Thinking of her now brought on a flood of guilt. He had dishonored her in so many ways—giving into the seductive lure of the bordellos, and to Santos, trading his good name for some meager measure of fortune.

Nesto took another slug of tequila.

Mis hijos, he lamented to himself—six strong boys. The oldest a man now himself. And what about Tino, the youngest? Would life without a father wipe the playful grin from his face? Also, little Día, his only daughter. She was but six years old, the same age as Santos' strange little niece. Who would protect her honor when the male dogs came sniffing at the door?

Nesto tipped the bottle up and took another long swallow, nearly draining it to the bottom. The liquid touched off tears in his eyes and set off white hot pain in his stomach.

No matter now, he told himself, and finished what was left.

Nesto turned the framed photo facedown, unable to take the weight of his family's scrutiny any longer. He thought of his career—that had *mostly* been one of honor, had it not? Twenty-six years of service to his government. He'd received commendations, taken numerous advancements in rank. Still, here he was, beneath the boot heel of the most dangerous man in Sonora. He was stuck, plain and simple.

So, say your prayers, *miserable wretch.*

Nesto tossed the empty bottle into the wastebasket and gathered his service revolver from his lap. "Please, find forgiveness for all my earthly sins," he murmured offering his plea for atonement up to God. "Watch over my family... *poor, poor familia.* And, God... please tell them I'm sorry."

Nesto wiped the tears from his eyes and straightened himself in his seat. He brought the barrel of the revolver up and placed the muzzle inside his mouth. He cocked it, remembering Mamá now. Seeing her soft sweet face looking down at him from heaven.

Nesto closed his eyes, swallowed hard, and turned his focus to the finger that was wrapped around the trigger.

Slowly, hand shaking, he began to squeeze...

"It's tough playing both sides of the law, isn't it, Nesto?"

Nesto bolted upright, out of his seat, his heart close to climbing from his chest. "God? Is that you!" he said to the shadows beyond the circle of light.

"You flatter me," a male voice said.

"Señor Estrada?" Nesto thought he recognized the voice now.

A hand moved in shadow to the light switch and flipped it on.

Nesto blinked back the flood of light that filled the office. Estrada was sitting in a straight-back chair, tipped back against the wall.

"What are you doing here, señor?"

Estrada rocked forward to sit straight. "I had come to tell you what a slimy little weasel you are, and to thrash you," he said. "But I see now you are prepared to be your own executioner."

Nesto became aware of the gun, still cocked and waving in his trembling hand. He quickly eased the hammer down and tossed the weapon back on the desk as if ridding himself of something vile. "You shouldn't be here," he said. "Santos or his men could be on their way this very minute. If he finds you, he will surely kill you, along with me."

"I would welcome a visit from Santos," Estrada said. "Welcome to meet him outside the protective confines of his fortress."

Nesto swallowed hard. "I know you wish to retaliate for my deceit, señor … Santiago Canyon … the decoy vans … the ambush … but I'm afraid it is too late for that. There is nothing you can do to me that is worse than the fate I face."

"I see that."

"No, really you don't, señor. I have openly defied Santos. He will not be satisfied with simply taking my life. No, that I deserve, clearly. But before Santos would let me die in peace, he would pleasure himself to my long and excruciating torture. I am a weak man, as you can see. I have no stomach for my own pain."

"Then you have nothing to lose if I ask for your help."

"Help?"

"The woman. The American investigator."

"You know this woman? But how … oh, wait …" he said. "The boy that was with her at the cantina …"

"He is the son of Tomás Villarreal. He said he didn't recognize you at first, but later remembered you as the chief of the federal police."

"The boy made it away safely?"

Estrada nodded. "I understand you helped them to escape."

"Yes, but to no avail. Santos has the woman. I fear for her safety."

"That is why I need your help, Nesto. I am going after her."

"To La Fortaleza? Oh, señor, I would advise against it, truly. Santos has more than a hundred men inside the fortress. Not to mention his strange little niece who will likely foretell your coming before you even think it in your mind. She is the one who proclaimed to Santos the arrival of this woman. He was waiting for her, had her picture on the streets, even before she first set foot in Cotorra."

Estrada seemed to give this some thought. "I have to do this, Nesto. I won't risk the lives of the others in my company, that's why I have come to you. I will go alone if necessary."

"Señor, you don't even know if she is alive. Santos may already have killed her."

"I have to take the chance, Nesto. You helped the woman once. There is no reason not to help again."

Nesto relented with a sigh. There was logic in the man's words. He nodded weakly. "When, señor?"

"Tonight," Estrada said, rising from his chair. "Prepare your men and meet me at the base of the plateau in one hour."

"I will do my best," Nesto said, though his heart wasn't in it.

Estrada gave him a last, long hard look, then slipped quickly out.

Nesto stood staring at the open doorway, his portal to the afterlife. It occurred to him that he could always warn Santos. Use this opportunity to re-bargain for his life, maybe even get back into Santos' good graces.

Nesto closed his eyes.

When he opened them, the framed photo of his family was standing upright on the desk facing him again.

Had Estrada righted it before he left?

He didn't think so. And couldn't remember having done so himself.

But there they were—nine expectant faces, to include his own, looking back at him.

¡Pues! "What was there to lose?" Nesto told his image in the portrait. "You are a dead man as it is, my friend."

With trembling hands, Nesto picked up the phone and dialed.

EIGHTEEN

WELL PAST THE CHILD'S bedtime, Casta Correa found Santos trying to get his niece to talk. They were in the girl's bedroom, Aurea in pajamas, sitting with her feet dangling from the edge of the bed. Santos was on his knees in front of her. He had the photo of the American woman in his hand and was showing it. "Speak to me, Aurea. Do you understand how important it is we communicate? This woman you have seen, why has she come?"

"You are wasting your time!" Casta said, not trying to disguise her disgust with the matter.

Ignoring her, Santos continued to prod his niece. "I need eyes, *profeta*. Your vision. But how am I to know what is right if you do not talk?"

"Can't you see she can't help you?"

"Just open your mouth, little one. Tell me what you see."

Casta crossed to a chair and began collecting the girl's discarded clothing and stuffing it into a hamper that sat against the wall. "Why don't you try placing words in the girl's mouth, then nod her head for her. It would be just as dependable." She drew open the drawer of the child's play-desk and raked scissors, clipping clutter, and crayons brusquely inside. "I don't know why I put up with this."

"Because I require it of you, that is why," Santos said, over his shoulder, still focused on his niece. "Please, *profeta*. All I need is for you to speak, some little word."

Nothing.

"Agghh!" Santos said, giving up and coming to his feet. "Why this child does not speak is a mystery."

"Are you that blind, Santos? She knows nothing of your business, nothing of the *senderos*, and nothing of this woman. She is but a child. A simple … ordinary … child. And you have brought her into our lives, and for what? So you can feel powerful?"

Santos crossed the room in three quick strides and backhanded Casta across the mouth. The slap smacked loudly and spun stars in her head. When her surprise dwindled she touched at her lip to find blood. Casta spat in Santos' face.

This time, he brought a closed fist around in an arc. It connected hard with the side of her face. She felt her legs buckle. She folded to her knees.

Santos left her, without amends, turning on his heels, out the door.

Blood ran in a crimson river from her nose. Casta mopped at it with a hand, doing more to spread the oily flow than to stop it.

When she looked up, Aurea was staring at her.

"What are you looking at?" Casta said.

———

Del lay on the cot with nothing more to do than wait. From time to time, Mata continued to appear at the cell door. He would fill the small window opening with his face and leer at her for a time. Most recently he had taken to bringing a bottle of tequila with him, that he would sip from as he watched. After a while, he would go away, only to return again later and leer and sip some more.

Lying there, Del wondered where all this might end. Would Santos have her killed if he found he had no use for her? Would he try to keep her alive as a playmate for Mata and his guards, as he had done with Liana?

Who knew?

What she did know was that she had few options for escaping. And, sooner or later, the bull Mata would grow impatient. When that happened, Del believed, not even Santos could stop him.

Del closed her eyes and tried to sleep.

Sometime later—she didn't know how long—Del was nudged from her dreams by the sound of a key in the lock. And then, before she could react, the door slammed back against its hinges.

There was Mata.

He was wearing a canvas car coat over a sweat-stained muscle shirt, jackboots to mid-calf. His dark eyes were watery, red-veined, and dreamy from the alcohol. The bottle of tequila he clutched in his right hand was near empty.

"Santos wouldn't like you being here," Del said, a weak attempt to forestall him, she knew.

Mata swayed drunkenly. He tipped the bottle up and took a swig. He studied her long and hard, before tossing it aside. It struck the stone wall and shattered, sending a shower of glass shards across the floor.

Del took an involuntary step backwards and felt the back of her knees make contact with the steel frame of the cot.

"What is happening?" Liana's plaintive voice came to her from the crack between the stones.

"Santos won't be happy," Del said to Mata again.

It caused him to grin, his big lips wet with desire.

"Leave her alone!" Liana cried through the opening.

Del quickly weighed her options.

Finding only one, she lowered her shoulder and charged headlong, giving a combatant's yell and as much driving force as she could muster.

It was like running into a brick wall.

Mata staggered back only a step, then stabilized.

Del raised a fist. But before she could use it, Mata grabbed a handful of her hair and jerked. Her head came up hard, her neck wrenched in pain.

He held her there, forcing her to look straight into his eyes.

She could smell the alcohol on his breath and what passed for rotting cabbage. Del tried a kick that missed its mark. She tried to claw at his bloodshot eyes.

Mata wrenched her up tighter, the pain in her scalp immense, and brought his oily face close to hers.

Del spat in Mata's eye.

Mata drew her back by the hair, and without warning, brought his fist up hard into Del's stomach. She felt the air punch out of her, felt pain explode inside of her. Her eyes rolled back in their sockets. She fought to keep from blacking out.

Mata closed in tight again. His tongue snaked out to taste the flesh at the crook of her neck. Del felt a wave of sickness wash

196

through her. Her head was growing light, the fight draining out of her.

Liana's pleas faded to some distant whisper, prophecies from the past.

When he was finished tasting, Mata brought one fat hand to cover her face, then he dropped his shoulder and shoved, putting his weight into it, sending Del backwards off her feet.

She landed hard on the cot, her head banging off the stone wall behind her. Stars danced wildly in her eyes. Waves of blackness flooded in.

Now he was on her, straddling her, pinning her hands above her with one thick paw. With his other hand he began working at the snap of her jeans ... then the zipper ... now he was dragging at her pants, forcing them down toward her knees.

Del strained against him with all her might. She managed to get one hand free. With it, she raked her nails down the side of his face, digging flesh where she could find it.

Mata ignored whatever pain she might have inflicted, and with his paw, swatted her hand away, as if it were a troublesome gnat. He then went to work on his own clothing, freeing his belt from the rolls of fat around his middle.

Del fought back with her one good hand, swinging it wildly as she could. She dug her nails into his neck this time. He slapped her hard across the face.

Bells rang inside her head. Her arms flailed helplessly now, searching desperately for something—anything—she could grab on to, to keep from going under.

Her hand landed on the flap of Mata's coat pocket.

Mata unzipped his pants.

Del's head swam.

She was aware of something hard and heavy inside the jacket pocket. Del willed her fingers beneath the flap, wriggled them inside.

Mata moved to get his knees between Del's legs, began forcing them apart.

Del found the thing inside.

It felt cold ... hard ... *familiar* ...

Her gun! The Baby Eagle! That he'd taken from her.

Mata positioned himself, preparing to grunt his way inside her.

Del came out with the weapon and brought it in a swift arc, to smash it against the side of Mata's head. He rocked back, bewilderment and surprise on his face, only partially dazed from the impact.

Del jammed the muzzle hard up under his chin, bringing awareness to his expression now.

"Get off me now!" she said.

Mata slid back a bit. Then changed direction and came at her again.

In one powerful swing, Del brought the butt of the Baby Eagle down hard on the bridge of Mata's nose. She heard the bone crunch, saw the gush of blood in time to turn her face from it.

Mata's eyes rolled. He slumped back.

Del brought the Baby Eagle around, this time in a vicious home-run swing that landed hard against the side of Mata's head.

His body went completely limp.

She finished the job by shoving him backwards off her to the floor.

"What is happening? God, tell me!" Liana's voice came from the opening between the stones.

Del eased herself into a sitting position, feeling lightning bolts of pain in her ribs and in her head. She still had the Baby Eagle tight in her grasp.

"I'm okay!" she called out.

Behind the wall, Liana sniffed out a cry of relief. "*¡Dios mío!*"

Del could picture Liana crossing herself, her face turned toward the heavens. Del stood, testing her legs to make sure they were weight-worthy. She was still somewhat wobbly. "We have to get out of here," she told Liana.

Del pulled her pants up, snapped and zipped them. She stepped over Mata and crossed to the opening between the stones. One frightened eye was looking back at her.

"Go to the door!" she said.

"Where is Mata?"

"He's out. Just go, quickly."

Del was on her feet and moving now. She grabbed the ring of keys that was still dangling from the lock. Securing the cell behind her—Mata still inside on the floor—she moved into the hallway and unlocked the adjoining cell. Liana fell outward into Del's arms.

Del held her tight, the two rocking in a slow, lullaby embrace.

"I was so scared for you," Liana said. "What happened?"

"I'll tell you later. We have to move quickly." Del tossed the keys aside and took Liana by the hand.

At the door to Del's cell, Liana faltered. "*¡Hijo de puta! ¡Vete y chinga a tu madre!*" she cried to the closed cell door, where Mata lay inside. She spat at it for good measure.

"Come on!" Del said, pulling her toward freedom.

"You should have killed him!"

"We can't chance the sound of gunfire," she said.

Del dragged Liana away, and the two set off down the corridor. Hand in hand, they raced through a labyrinth of interconnecting hallways, past the stone stairway leading up to the penthouse, until, at last, they came to a closed door. There they stopped.

Del ran her hand along the jamb. She could feel cool night air penetrating though.

"It leads outside," she said.

"Then let's go!" Liana said.

"Not yet, take this."

She handed Liana the gun.

"I want you to wait right here for me," she said. "Promise me you'll wait."

"But where are you going?" There was panic in Liana's eyes.

"I'm not leaving without Aurea," she said. "Give me five minutes."

"Del, no!"

"Just stay right here!"

Del didn't wait for protests. Within seconds, she was at the steps leading up and climbing fast toward the penthouse.

———

Estrada squatted in shadow at the base of the plateau. The moon was up and full, casting silhouettes out of prickly pair and creosote scrub. He checked his watch—an hour and fifteen minutes had passed since he had spoken to Nesto Parra. The man and his army should have been there by now.

There was little time to waste. Santos could have already dealt with Del Shannon by now, have her body dumped in the desert somewhere. Francisco didn't think so. He could concentrate very hard and believe that he could feel her, feel her heart beating in rhythm with his own. She was alive.

He had only just met the girl, but felt there was something going on between them. What, exactly, he wasn't sure, but something personal and on the verge of intimacy. Francisco checked his watch again. Nesto Parra, apparently, wasn't coming.

Perhaps, he considered, it was better that the Federales didn't show. Perhaps a man working alone, using stealth and guile, would have a better chance at freeing her than a full-on assault. The odds against success were impossibly huge either way. The fortress was formidable, and Santos' guards would be many.

Estrada eased himself out of shadow. He took one last look at the switchback leading up. There were no headlights in the darkness, no sounds of vehicles heading his way. Convinced the cavalry was not about to show, he began his way up the hillside, sticking close to rocky outcroppings and below the cover of darkness.

———

Del moved fast through the penthouse, the room dark and quiet. On the surveillance monitors above the bar, Del could see Liana prancing nervously at the exit, the Baby Eagle clutched tightly in both hands. On another, a couple of men lounged, somewhere in the bowels of the fortress with women on their arms. In an outdoor view, a guard paced casually in a tower above the sally port. Beyond that, La Fortaleza was mostly in a state of slumber.

Thank you, God! Del thought to herself.

She moved quickly to the hallway, where the matron, Casta, had appeared with the child. On tiptoes, she continued on at a silent pace. She considered doorways as she passed. It made her think of a story she'd once read about a slave who was given a chance to choose from a series of three doors. He was told that two of the doors would lead to sudden death, only one of the doors would lead to freedom. It was kind of like that now. *Which way might bring her death? Which way might lead to the child?*

She studied each doorway in turn. Then, acting on impulse, decided on the door at the end of the hall. Slowly she made her way there. The door was closed. Del turned the knob and eased it open.

Aurea—the child with a gift for surprising—was waiting for her, it seemed, on the edge of the bed.

How impossibly so?

She was fully dressed, a colorful lunch pail held protectively in her lap. Sitting, as if waiting for a bus. Del stepped into the room and knelt down in front of her.

"Do you know why I am here?" Del asked, her voice a whisper.

Aurea said nothing, but held Del with her eyes.

"Would you like to go home?" she asked

Aurea gave her a nod.

"Then that's where we're going," The girl was remarkable, even in her silence. But there was no time to consider her now. "Come on," she said. "Let's go."

Aurea slipped off the bed and took Del's hand.

When Del turned with her toward the door, Casta Correa stood blocking the opening, her arms crossed.

"I'm taking her with me," Del said. "I'm really hoping you won't try to stop me."

Casta glared at her, hip cocked. Then, without a word, she stepped back and gave them room to pass.

"Bless you!"

"Just make sure you never return, either of you," Casta said.

"That's the plan."

Not taking any more time for pleasantries, Del led Aurea past her and into the hall.

She could still feel the matron's eyes following them. She wasn't sure of the woman's motives for letting them go, but she was thanking God right now that she had done so. She kept Aurea moving, the child's little legs peddling fast to keep up. The taste of impending freedom was sweet in Del's mouth. But all that changed as they entered the penthouse and she spotted the surveillance monitors.

"*Oh, no …!*" she said, beneath her breath.

Liana no longer appeared on the screen in the corridor near the exit. Instead she appeared on a different monitor, the one showing the view of the hallway outside Del's cell. She was bent over, Del's gun in one hand, collecting the key ring from the floor where Del had tossed it.

Shit!

Now Liana was moving to the cell where Mata lay inside.

"Liana, no!" Del blurted out. And, sweeping Aurea into her arms, she began to run.

NINETEEN

AT THE TOP OF the switchback, Estrada ventured a look across the outer perimeter wall. Beyond it was a wide paved paddock, where vehicles—SUVs and cargo vans—were parked at varying angles. Moonlight glinted off chrome and finish. The fortress itself was buttoned down for the night. The iron gate to the sally port—the only conceivable entrance to the fortress—was closed. A single guard, smoking a cigarette, stood in front of it, an automatic assault rifle strung casually across his shoulder.

High above the entrance, in a gun tower, another guard stood watch. From time to time he would pace, observing first the courtyard inside the compound, then across to peer onto the paddock area below, scan the switchback leading up from the bottom of the plateau.

He had to somehow get beyond the gate. To do so, he would have to eliminate first the guard out front, then climb his way to the gun tower and do the same with the guard stationed there. Estrada checked his weapons. He had a handgun that he believed he shouldn't use unless he had to. And a knife, strapped beneath his pant leg—the blade eight inches long and serrated. This would have to do—*mano a mano* and quietly.

Estrada skirted the perimeter wall for a short distance, bent low, coming up to peer over the wall, again, at the gate guard's flank. He then slipped his knife free of its sheath, took the blade between his teeth, and did a belly roll across the wall, dropping into shadow on the other side.

The gate guard hadn't moved. Above, the tower guard continued to pace quietly.

Estrada waited, watching, as the gate guard shifted back and forth on his feet. Occasionally he would draw on his cigarette, then turn his head away to blow smoke into the air. He was no more than twenty-five feet away.

Estrada timed his move for the next time the guard exhaled, then went for it. He crossed the distance fast, coming up on the man from behind.

Surprise registered on the guard's face, only an instant before Estrada seized the man by the hair and swiped the knife cleanly across his throat.

The guard gurgled once, then slumped into Estrada's arms.

Estrada lowered him to the ground quietly. He wiped blood from his knife on the man's clothing, then slipped it back into its sheath beneath his pant leg.

Above, all remained quiet. Estrada studied the wall. It was a good forty feet high. Controls for the gate would likely be located there. The only choice was for him to get there somehow. He ran his fingers over the wall, searched out a crack from which to make his first hold, then began to climb—stone by stone.

Del reached the corridor, breathless, still carrying Aurea, to find Liana in front of the cell, the door open. She was standing back from it, the gun extended in both hands. Inside the cell, Mata was regaining consciousness and starting to move. Dazed disbelief registered on his face at the sight of Liana with the gun pointed at him. Now he hastened his struggle to find his feet.

"Liana, no!" Del cried. She slipped Aurea quickly to the floor and charged forward.

Liana squeezed the trigger.

Del reached the gun in time to wrench it from Liana's hand, but not before it went off, sending the errant shot pinging off the walls.

The resultant boom echoed through the corridors.

Mata stumbled his way upright, stood waving on his feet, then started forward.

Del kicked the door shut and turned the key in the lock, just in time.

Mata let out an coyote howl and slammed his fists against the door.

"Nooooo!" Liana cried. She put her face in her hands and sank heavily to her knees. "You should have let me kill him," she sobbed.

"I didn't want the shots to arouse the guards. Now we really have to get the hell out of here!"

She dragged Liana to her feet, found Aurea where she'd left her, the yellow pail still dangling at her side. She swept the child into her arms and gave Liana a tug to get her moving. Together, the three of them hastened off down the corridor once again.

"This is the girl?" Liana said, seemingly aware of the child for the first time.

"This is Aurea."

Somewhere above them, an alarm began to sound. Bells and sirens issued a mighty protest.

"Let's get out of here!"

Del broke into a run, leading Liana with her.

Within seconds, they were back at the exit, questioning what might be waiting for them beyond.

———

Estrada heard the alarms as he reached the top of the wall. Automatic security lights suddenly flooded the courtyard. The guard came alert and readied his weapon.

At first, it wasn't clear if he had somehow tripped the alarm himself, or whether the wailing signaled some other calamity that might have arisen somewhere inside the fortress. He knew he had to move quickly either way.

Estrada rolled himself atop the wall and came to a crouched position.

The alarms continued to wail, filling the world with a kind of dizzying madness. From inside, could be heard the sounds of men shouting. The guard paced quickly from one corner of the tower to the other, his eyes scanning the well-lighted courtyard below.

He was less than fifteen feet from Estrada, but a good six inches taller and more muscular. Estrada's only chance, he knew, would be to strike hard and fast while the man's attention was still on the grounds. He slipped his knife again from its scabbard, readied himself, then rushed the gun tower.

Sensing movement, the guard suddenly turned his gun toward him.

———

In the corridor, at the exit door, Del put her ear to the cool metal surface and listened for sounds from the other side. Beyond, the chaos seemed even more intensified.

"I'm not sure what's out there," Del said.

"Let's just go!" Liana said. She pranced nervously, throwing anxious glances down the corridor behind them.

Del handed Aurea off to Liana. Then, positioning the Baby Eagle in front of her, she eased open the door. Blinding light struck her face and flooded into the narrow corridor.

They were off to the side of a wide central courtyard, lit up beneath security lights like a football stadium at game time. Down and off to her right was a sally port, the main, gated entrance to La Fortaleza. A walkway led from the exit out to a wide cobblestone turnaround. In the center was a large fountain, spewing light-sparkled water. And waiting on the far side of the turnaround, facing the fortress, was Del's Wrangler.

"Oh, my God! My Jeep!" Del said. "Thank heavens, it's there!"

"For once they do something bad in reverse," Liana said. She was peering across Del's shoulder into the light.

The prison fortress was now coming alive. A man appeared on a balcony off to Del's left. He was fastening his trousers, tucking in his shirt. Their eyes met momentarily, then he turned hastily back inside, shouting orders in Spanish.

"Now, we really—really!—need to get out of here!" Del said.

A meek whine emitted from the child, the sirens and wildly rushing chaos making her fearful.

"Please go!" Liana said.

Del pushed out into the courtyard and headed quickly down the walkway. Liana was right behind her, carrying Aurea in her arms. Together they raced across the cobblestone turnaround, past the fountain, to reach the Wrangler.

"What about keys?" Liana cried.

Del quickly fished beneath the front wheel well, retrieved a magnetic keyholder, and extracted a spare ignition key. "I always knew this would come in handy someday."

"Today, I think this is *someday!*" Liana said.

The sound of hurried boot steps could be heard coming from down an open portico.

Del took Aurea, lifted her across the driver seat, and slid in beside her. Liana raced around and leaped in through the passenger side door to perch on the edge of her seat, eyes darting between La Fortaleza and the exit.

Del cranked the engine and jammed the Wrangler into gear.

With an urge from the nighttime breeze, they circled the turnabout with tires squealing. She pointed the Jeep toward the exit, then just as quickly slammed the brakes and brought them to a stop.

"What! Why are we stopping?"

"The gate to the sally port," Del said, her voice barely carrying above the shrill cry of the sirens.

"So, ram it! Mother of God, get us out of here!"

"It's too heavy," Del said, shaking her head. "We'll end up like a big metal door knocker."

"What then, Del? Do something!"

Men were piling out of the portico and into the courtyard. One by one, they took up positions with rifles. And began to fire.

Gunshots whizzed above their heads.

"There's no place to go!" Del said.

"God, don't let me die! Not now!" Liana prayed to the heavens.

Suddenly from above, as if by divine intervention, a burst of automatic weapon fire sprayed the portico, scattering the gunmen and sending them running. Del looked to see a familiar figure there. He had the tower guard in a chokehold, using the man's own arm to guide the weapon. Now the knife appeared and found its way to the guard's throat. The guard's lips mimed a cry, beneath the chaos of the alarms. Estrada let go, stripping the weapon away in the process, and the man sank out of sight inside the tower.

"Francisco!" Del cried.

Estrada gave her a quick wave, then directed the weapon and laid down another hail of cover fire.

"So this is your man?" Liana said. "I believe I am liking him already."

Her man, Del thought. It was a momentary consideration amid the chaos. She gave him a return wave. "The gate!" she called.

In an instant, the heavy wooden gate began to move, lumbering its way slowly upward.

Shots pinged around them. Estrada laid down another burst of gunfire.

"Let's get out of here!" Del said.

She floored the accelerator and dropped the clutch. The wide tires dug in and the Wrangler leapt forward. They gained speed, bearing down on the gate.

It rose … *crankity crankity* …

Del said a silent prayer as they bore down on it and cleared the trailing edge by only inches.

Now, outside the fortress and blocked from gunfire by the walls, she slid the Wrangler to a stop.

Francisco appeared on the wall above. He tossed the weapon over the side and began climbing down. Halfway, he let go and dropped the remaining distance to the ground, sticking his landing like an jungle cat. "*Buenos días*, señora, señorita," he said, still in his crouch.

"This is no time for flirtations, Ricky Ricardo," Del said. "Get in! Hurry!"

Francisco grabbed up the weapon and vaulted into the opening behind the seats.

Del floored it, and they were off.

They sped across the paddock, past vehicles parked along the perimeter wall. Behind them, a cadre of Santos' guards filed out through the sally port. Some dropped to a kneeling position and began popping off rounds, while others quickly spread to the vehicles and began cranking the engines. Some thirty yards ahead appeared the opening in the wall, leading to the switchback.

"Through there," Estrada said, across the seat. Then, "Hello little one," he said to Aurea, giving the child's hair a tousle.

"You are our savior," Liana said.

"And you must be Liana Villarreal," he said.

"But how did you know?"

"Because I know two people who will be very happy to know you are alive. I am greatly relieved."

Liana gave him a broad smile.

Her man, Del thought.

The Wrangler bucked over bumps in the road. In the rearview mirror, Del could see vehicles spilling onto the switchback. Riflemen took up positions along the perimeter wall and began firing. Shots pinged off nearby rocks and zipped past them through the brush. She caught a glimpse of Francisco in the mirror, moonlight softening his rugged face. There were things she wanted to say— words brought on by admiration welling up inside her.

Now was not the time.

She said instead, "How are we doing?"

"From what I can see," Francisco said, catching Del's eyes in the rearview mirror, "we're doing just fine."

———

Nesto saw a pair of headlights descending fast down the switchback. He put his field glasses on them. "Impossible!" he said to himself. "Completely impossible!" It was a red Jeep Wrangler, the American woman driving fast. Two other shadowy faces flanked her. One was Estrada himself. Another, the woman prisoner he had witnessed on monitors in Santos' penthouse. And ... *look at that!* he told himself, seeing the top of a small head, barely visible above the dash ... they had the child.

He had arrived late, admittedly, after struggling too long with the decision to come. But he was here now, and he was going to have to follow through on his commitment.

His initial sense of relief at seeing the Jeep coming, and knowing he would not have to wage a full-on assault on La Fortaleza, was being quickly replaced by a dire uneasiness over the two vehicles that were in pursuit. The escapees had the girl, and Santos was not going to take that lightly. *How far? To what ends of the earth would Santos go to get her back?*

His question was answered, when he moved the glasses farther up the switchback and saw even more vehicles filing out. Five—count them—six, maybe more. The wave of apprehension that washed through him sunk him low inside his skin. His knees became weak, the hand holding the field glasses heavy.

¡Madre de Dios! Nesto crossed himself in prayer.

The fleeing escapees were still coming. Now was the time to take a stand.

Nesto steeled himself. "*¡Preparen!*" he called to his squad.

Scattered among the rocks were twenty-five of his officers, silhouettes in the night. All that he had been able to gather on such short notice.

They readied their weapons.

Nesto waited, watching through the field glasses as both the Wrangler and its pursuers continued down the slope.

His men were no match for Santos and his army. In a one-on-one fight—*say it, you know it's true*—they would lose. "*¡Apunten!*" he commanded next, telling his men to aim.

The Wrangler was nearly at the bottom of the plateau now, the occupants bouncing on the seats. Nesto gave it another second, then gave the order to fire … "*¡Fuego!*"

The squad let loose with their automatic weapons, spraying the hillside above the Wrangler with bullets. It caused the pursuit vehicles to slow. Another round of fire, and the vehicles skidded to a stop in unison. The armed occupants bailed for cover among the rocks and scrub.

Now they were returning fire.

Nesto moved to the protection of an outcropping of rocks, as the Wrangler came off the switchback onto paved road. It skidded to a stop just in front of him.

"Thanks for helping, Nesto," Estrada said, calling to him over the spatter of gunfire. "This is Del Shannon. Also Liana Villarreal. I believe you know Santos' niece."

Nesto nodded to the women, getting nods and smiles in return. He avoided eye contact with the child. "I am happy to see you both free, señoras. But you must not hesitate, my men will not be able to hold Santos back for long. You must go, get away, pronto."

"What about you, Nesto? Will you be okay?" Del asked.

Nesto finally ventured a glance at the child. She was sitting between the two women, her face calm amid the calamity. "Perhaps my welfare no longer matters, señora."

"You know the caverns in the San Pedro Mountains to the east," Francisco said. "If you have nowhere else to go, you and your family can join us there."

Nesto wanted to say, *Should I be so lucky as to live through the night, señor.* Instead, he simply nodded.

Bullets pinged off rocks just above their heads.

"We need to be going," Del said.

Nesto waved them off.

The Wrangler sped away. He watched them all the way to where the road intersected with the highway heading east, nothing more than taillights in the darkness, then they were gone.

Nesto turned his attention back to his squad. They were putting up a valiant effort.

On the hillside above, Santos' men reorganized. Now the response was overwhelming. Bullets zinged off rocks and ripped through underbrush. More vehicles, more men, appeared at the top of the switchback. The roar of gunfire in the night became deafening.

"*¡Listos!*" Nesto called, reminding his men to stay with the fight. Then he crossed to his government sedan and slid behind the wheel.

Guilt lay heavy on Nesto's heart as he abandoned the scene, leaving his men to whatever fate might hold for them. In his rearview mirror, he could see the firefight continuing. It was no matter. His squad would soon begin unraveling. First, a few would pull back, then others would follow. And when the opposing force of gunfire became too great, they would drop their weapons and flee into the desert. He was sure of it.

Nesto couldn't blame them. And he reminded himself to no longer blame himself. There was nothing he could do personally. Nothing more he could offer as chief of the *Policía Federal*.

Turning his mirror down so that he would not have to witness the final breakdown of authority, Nesto left by the way of Calle Mercado, heading back into the center of town.

TWENTY

On the outskirts of town, Del pulled the Jeep to a stop on the plateau overlooking the city—the same plateau where she had first glimpsed Cotorra. From there, she and the others could see La Fortaleza and the switchback leading down to the road. The fire line put up by the federal police had broken down, and now pursuing vehicles were filing onto the highway, spreading out in different directions to search for them.

"We can't stay in the open for long," Francisco said. He was peering over Del's shoulder from the space behind the seat. "And I don't think you should risk trying to make the border tonight. I suggest we head for the encampment and give the *senderos* time to cool down."

"I want to see my husband and son," Liana added. Tears of joy and fear streaked her face.

Del turned her attention to Aurea on the seat next to her. She gave the child's hair a stroke. "You okay, sweetie?"

Aurea said nothing, but curled up on the seat to lay her head in Del's lap.

"That's a good girl," Del said, giving her head a pat. "We'll be where you can sleep soon," To the others, she said, "I agree. We'll head for the encampment."

Del cut the steering wheel toward the highway and gunned the engine. Within minutes they were skirting the eastern mountains, away from their pursuers.

————

Ramón left the men to their search for the American woman and her allies and returned to La Fortaleza. In the penthouse he found Santos admonishing Mata, reading him the riot act for allowing the woman to escape with his niece. He was using the words *puta* and *American whore* to refer to the woman.

"You are a fool!" Santos was saying. "Letting this *mujer* get the best of you! How can I possibly tolerate such incompetence? Get out of my sight before I have you stripped and beaten!"

Hangdogged, Mata made his way off. Ramón stepped in to take his place.

"I am surrounded by fools," Santos said, crossing to the sofa.

He was dressed in his silk bathrobe, his nine-millimeter handgun in one hand, a bottle of tequila in the other. He took a seat, laying the handgun across his lap, and took up a remote that operated the video surveillance system. The smell of gun smoke lay throughout the penthouse.

"The patrols are searching for the woman and your niece," Ramón said, hoping to give the man something positive to chew on.

Santos ignored him and began operating buttons on the remote, replaying scenes of the earlier events on the video monitors.

Ramón waited, saying nothing. The gunfire from the switchback had long gone silent, the searchers were now combing the corridors, the secret routes leading to the border.

Santos remained fixated on his replays. He was wanting to know, Ramón knew instinctively, *why? How could this have happened? What deception may have played out?*

It seemed obvious to him. You didn't need a visionary child to know that the woman had come to Cotorra specifically to recover the girl. *Why* and *who sent her* was anybody's guess. Perhaps she had come—as she had stated—because she was looking for information about a friend of hers who had been murdered. If so, then why her interest in Santos' niece? What information could the child possibly give? *Unless…*

Unless she also thought the child was a visionary.

Ramón had never really bought into the idea of the girl being gifted. To him, she was just strange and maybe a little bit off. He went along with Santos' affections for her, his lopsided trust, simply to appease the man. Life was just easier at La Fortaleza when Santos was pleased. It was that simple. So Ramón played along, and let Santos do what Santos does.

Waiting was also part of pleasing.

Ramón watched Santos with his video replays for a moment longer. When his impatience began to grow thin, he said, "Santos, the outlying patrols have been alerted. I have everyone on the lookout. We will find the woman and get your niece back."

Santos took a swig of tequila, but said nothing.

"We don't believe they have crossed the border," Ramón tried again. "Wherever the woman and your niece are hiding, we will find them."

Santos continued to study the action playing out across the monitors. From time to time, he would pause one of the scenes to let another catch up in real time. Then he would hit the play button and watch the rest of the scene unfold.

What Ramón could gather from the scrolling videos was that the American woman, Del Shannon, had somehow gotten the best of Mata. One monitor had shown her in her cell, standing over his unconscious bulk. Another monitor showed her outside the adjoining cell, aiding the female journalist to escape. On yet another, the two women were stealthily navigating through the lower corridors. Now the American woman, alone again, was on the screen, crossing right through Santos' penthouse—these very quarters—like she owned the place! *One cool bitch!* Ramón thought. Now she was down the hallway, entering the bedroom where Santos' niece slept.

The woman had a set of *cojones* for sure, only doors away from Santos' room where he made love to his mistress.

It was getting to Santos, Ramón could see, watching the videos. The audacity of this female. The man's jaw was clenching and unclenching. His hand clutching the bottle of tequila had tightened into a sinewy claw.

Ramón waited, still looking for a way to ease Santos' tension—a way to please and return the man to reason.

Finally, Santos decided to share his thoughts. Without removing his eyes from the monitors, he said, "I don't have to tell you, Ramón, how much I want to find this woman. How badly I want to rip her heart from her chest. The shipment, our largest ever, is scheduled for tomorrow night. And now I find myself without my niece's counsel. Do you understand what that means, how much we would risk? Can you comprehend how important it is to find her?"

"And we will! Not to worry!" Ramón said, trying to make his assurances seem as reasonable as possible.

Santos nodded. He was still studying the replays. In this most recent view, the woman was in the child's bedroom, preparing to take her away.

"You can leave me now," Santos said with a wave.

Ramón turned to go, bored with the videos and happy to get on with his life.

"No, wait!" Santos suddenly said, stopping Ramón only inches from freedom.

"What is it?" Ramón asked, taking a few steps back into the room, somewhat perturbed by Santos' sudden change of heart.

Santos sat forward on the sofa studying one of the monitors closely. Something had caught his eye. Something of specific interest apparently. Now he was backing the video up to take a better look.

Ramón tried to follow the action on the video, one showing a view of the hallway leading to the child's room. *What was so damned important?* Santos already knew the girl was gone, didn't he?

Ramón waited.

Suddenly, Santos became volatile. Ramón knew the look—the sharp narrowing of the eyes, the rage-building swell of his chest, the sinewy tendons that sprang up along his forearms. "Bring me my mistress!" he demanded. "Wake her if she is sleeping!"

Ramón hesitated—this couldn't be good. He could think of nothing more to please or mollify Santos in his given state of agitation.

"Go!" Santos cracked, turning on him with a venomous look.

Ramón hesitated no more. He strode quickly across the room and down the long hallway to the master suite. He didn't bother to knock. He pulled the door open without notice and found Casta Correa sitting in a chair beside the bed.

She was dressed in a flowing evening gown, three-quarters of a bottle of tequila into a weepy-eyed drunk.

"Santos wishes to see you!" he said.

Casta didn't move at first.

"You need to come with me now!"

Slowly, Casta managed her way to her feet, stumbling a bit on unsteady legs.

"Santos wants to see *me*? Really?" she said. "Why? So he can weep into my bosom, decry the loss of his precious little niece?"

She knocked back a swig of tequila.

"You have to come," Ramón said, crossing to her to take her by the arm.

Casta stumbled. Ramón caught her in his arms.

They were face to face now. Her lips close to his. He could smell the liquor on her breath, the perfume in her hair.

"I've always liked you, Ramón," Casta said in a slurred, sultry voice. "I believe you know that?" She teased his cheek with the tip of her nose.

Ramón could feel her breath warm against his face, feel the fullness of her mature, voluptuous body pressed against his own. She brought her fingers to stroke along the curve of his jawline. Her touch was like that of silk.

"In so many ways, you're so much more of a man than Santos," she whispered. "Forget about him. Take me yourself, Ramón. Here! Beneath the man's own nose."

Ramón's body—God help him!—responded. There was no hiding his desire. He wanted with all his might to throw her back across the bed and take her—this beautiful, drunken bitch, this madam of whores, who had learned since the age of twelve the forbidden secrets for igniting a man's passions.

But to do so would be suicide.

Ramón felt her hand between his legs now. He wanted to cry out.

With all the willpower he could muster, Ramón bit his lip and pushed the woman away.

"Ramón," Casta cooed. She reached for him again.

Ramón grabbed her by the arm and twisted her around. "Come on!" he said. "Santos wants to see you now!"

Casta dropped her act and, in a tempestuous display of annoyance, allowed him to lead her away.

When they arrived back at the penthouse, Santos was still fixated on his monitors.

Ramón steadied Casta on her feet before Santos and stepped away. He was sweating profusely, he realized, and mopped his forehead while he had a chance.

They waited.

Whatever this was about, Ramón knew, it couldn't be good.

Finally, Santos said "Come!" His eyes were still fixed on the monitors.

Casta, sobering a bit and wary now, stepped closer. "What is it, Santos?" Her voice—the one that moments ago had been so guttural and seductive—had now become that of an innocent ten-year-old. "I was just going to bed. Why do you ask for me?"

"My niece has been taken from me," he said. He let the statement hang in the air.

"Yes, I heard, but I am sure you will find her. She will be returned."

"My enemies have conspired against me, Casta."

Casta straightened a little. "I don't know what you mean, my love. Please, come to bed."

"Would you not like to know who my enemies are?"

"It is late. Let us make love."

Santos cut her off. He repeated, more forcefully this time. "Are you *sure* ... you would not like ... to know who my enemies are, first?"

"If ... if I must," Casta said, her face a worried mask of uncertainty now.

"Then I will show you, my mistress."

Santos clicked the remote, and Del Shannon appeared on one of the monitors. It was the earlier scene from the lower corridor. "There is one of my enemies!" he said, his voice calm at this point.

Ramón suddenly knew where this was headed. He wanted to look away, but couldn't.

Santos clicked the remote again.

This time, Francisco Estrada appeared on one of the courtyard surveillance monitors. He was atop the tower, in the process of overcoming and subduing the guard positioned there.

"This one is another one of my enemies!" Santos said, his voice beginning to rise.

"Santos, please," Casta attempted.

Ramón's stomach tightened.

"And … this! … is yet another of my enemies!" Santos said, a grinding anger in the set of his jaw.

"Santos, I …" The mistress's protest froze at the tip of her tongue.

On one of the monitors, Casta herself appeared, vaguely visible in the shadowy depths of the long hallway. She stood just inside the doorway to the child's room. Seconds passed with nothing, no movement. Then, on the video, she stepped back into the hallway with a gesture. Del Shannon appeared in the hallway next to her, coming out of the child's bedroom, leading Aurea by the hand. They came out, down the hallway, and into the camera. Casta, in the background, did nothing … she merely *watched* them go.

Ramón closed his eyes.

This beautiful courtesan, this exquisite, stupid, fucking whore, had defied Santos. She had willingly allowed the American woman to escape with his niece. Out of jealousy, perhaps.

The room itself seemed to catch its breath. Silence lay thick and heavy about the room.

Ramón reluctantly reopened his eyes.

Santos was staring at his mistress, waiting for an explanation.

There was none forthcoming.

Casta's lips began to quiver. Her face took on the simpering, pleading look of a child. She said nothing, but the tears and the pleading outreached hands said it all.

Ramón wanted desperately to interject. Wanted to offer something, anything, that would save this beautifully seductive creature.

He could think of nothing to say. Nothing he could do to settle the look of hatred that now burned in Santos' eyes.

Casta opened her mouth as if trying to form some prayer, some plea for forgiveness.

But before she could make a sound, before the words could form on her lips...

Santos lifted the nine-millimeter from his lap and shot Casta— *once!*—between the eyes.

Ramón's breath caught in his throat.

The wound—the small round hole centered on her forehead— seemed, at first, to have no effect, except to widen her eyes. The pleading expression was gone, replaced by a look of ultimate surprise. It remained frozen there, as if to be memorialized for all time. Then it faded, and a quiet mask of innocence took over. Her legs buckled, and the mistress dropped heavily to the floor.

The room was silent. A thin cloud of gun smoke, and the acrid smell of it, hung in the air. It remained for a moment, then slowly drifted off toward the open balcony.

Santos took a casual sip of tequila.

Ramón swallowed the lump that had caught in his throat. When he could once again breathe, he said, "Mother of God... Santos!"

Santos appeared unmoved. "There are things I must tolerate, Ramón," he said, taking another sip from his drink. "Disloyalty is not one of them. Take her with you when you go."

Ramón hesitated but gathered himself and crossed to the lifeless body. He managed to heft the dead weight of her across his shoulder—a seductively packaged sack of grain. Then he took a last look at the monitor that was still freeze-framed on the moment of truth. He stole a glance at Santos—the man idly swirling the tequila inside the bottle before taking another drink—unremorseful.

Ramón turned with the body toward the exit.

"Ramón!" Santos called to him.

It stopped him in his tracks.

"Next find me Nesto Parra."

———

Del followed the reach of the headlights through turns until they were well into the mountains east of town. The night air at the higher elevation had turned cold, bringing a chill through the open sides of the Jeep. The Wrangler bumped and fought against ruts and ridges in the road. Steadily, they climbed to the top of the ridge.

At the encampment, they were waved through a narrow gap in the rocks by armed sentries. Del glimpsed Liana, across the seat from her. She was leaned up over the dash, anxious, expectant at the thought of being reunited with her husband and son. Francisco was steadfast, but looking cramped in the space behind the seats. Aurea had fallen asleep in Del's lap.

Together they rolled into camp, to be greeted by a throng of Estrada's followers. There were cheers and cries of victory—"*¡Viva Estrada! ¡Viva México!*" The intonations caught on, and morphed into a rhythmic chant.

Liana was the first out of the Jeep, leaping to the ground even before the Wrangler had come to a complete stop. Through the gathering that had come to greet them, her husband, Tomás, appeared. When he saw his wife, his face drained of color.

"Tomás?" Liana said, hesitantly.

Slowly a smile found its way to his face, touching off a waterfall of tears and hysterical laughter.

Reynaldo appeared now amid the crowd. "*¿Mamá?*" he cried. His hands were encumbered by firewood. He immediately dropped the load and ran to his mother, landing on her in a fierce embrace.

Tomás finally found his legs. Retrieving a blanket from the hands of one of the women, he rushed to his wife and son. Spreading the blanket wide, he hugged them into a family embrace, drawing them close beneath the cover. Together they rocked and swayed, filling the hushed space with murmured intimacies. When, at last, they were able to dry their tears, they separated from the crowd and drifted off to be alone.

"There is still a God," Francisco said.

Del glanced at him across the back of the seat. There was wetness in his eyes. Tears had formed in hers. "We need to make it so they can return home without fear," she said.

"Indeed!" Francisco was nodding. Then his face took on a grim, determined expression. "Adriano!" he called across the gathering.

One of the men reported promptly.

"Go back into the city. Keep me advised of Santos' movements."

The man went off without hesitation.

"He's a good man," Francisco said. "He is not known to Santos. He will be able to move among the townspeople without notice."

Some of the women came to greet them now. Del noticed a pretty young girl, no more than a teen, scurry forth to be among the front line of attention. She pressed close to Francisco's side of the Jeep, fawning youthfully, flattering him with her eyes, longing to be noticed.

"Celia," Francisco said to her. "Take the child and find a warm bed for her."

The girl seemed both thrilled to be of service and reluctant to leave his side.

Del assisted the girl, offering Aurea across the seat. She was sleepy-eyed and docile, and allowed herself to be gathered and passed into Celia's waiting arms.

Celia went off with her, tending to her as a mother might.

"I think you've got a fan in that one," Del said.

"Celia? She has lost her father, has only her mother. She needs someone to guide her."

"Yeah, well, I think you better watch yourself," Del said, giving him a knowing smile.

Francisco clambered out from behind the seats and offered Del a gentlemanly hand.

She took it and stepped out.

They were escorted by the remaining women to seats before the campfire. Blankets were brought and draped about their shoulders. They were each handed bowls of stew. "*¡Coman! ¡Coman!*" the women urged—admonishments to *eat*.

The fire was warming, the stew filling. The tiny encampment gave off an air of tranquility. A false illusion, perhaps. Santos and his death squads were out there, somewhere in the darkness, prowling the night to find them. Still, the fire and the peacefulness of the encampment was a welcome diversion.

Del took her time eating. She intentionally tried thinking of nothing. For soon, she knew, it would all have to change again. She would have to plan how to get the child back across the border. How to protect her, and herself, once they got there.

Francisco seemed to be savoring the respite, too. Between bites, he quietly regaled the others gathered around the fire with the story of their harrowing escape from La Fortaleza. He discounted his own role—being the gentleman—giving all credit for courage and heroism to her, Liana, and Aurea.

Every ear seemed to hang on his words.

Later, when they had finished eating, Celia brought Aurea to Del. She had been fed and was awake now, fussing somewhat to sleep.

"I'll take her," Francisco said, bringing a light to Celia's eyes. "I am known to have a way with little ones."

Celia folded Aurea into Francisco's arms, and found the nearest seat next to him on the ground. She threw occasional glances toward Del, presumably weighing the competition. Del would give her a smile, and the girl would look away, returning her eyes to her leader and doing all she could to avoid a swoon.

Francisco nestled Aurea close, pulling his blanket about her shoulders to keep away the chill. He closed his eyes and rocked gently. Softly, he began to sing.

A quiet serenity fell about the campsite. Other members of the camp gathered around to listen. His voice was soft and clear. A Spanish lullaby filtered through the star-filled night.

This is what I'm talking about, Randall's voice said inside Del's head.

She felt a sudden wave of guilt and melancholy overtake her. A sudden longing hit her that she couldn't quite put a name to. Was this a man she could spend her life with? This strong, defiant rebel, who wages war while singing to children? Could they have the kind of relationship that Randall would approve?

Del let herself be lulled into tranquility.

Aurea's eyes fluttered, then slowly shut.

One by one, the women drifted away to attend to chores. The last one to leave was Celia. She gathered Aurea from Francisco's arms, and carried her off to a bed inside the cavern.

Del and Francisco were alone now.

"It's peaceful here," Del said. "You have a beautiful voice."

Francisco drew in a long breath of night air. "My mother used to sing to me as a child. I still remember all the songs, all the lyrics. It was such a peaceful time in Sonora. Sadly, now peace comes with such a price. Someday, perhaps…"

He let the thought go unfinished. He rose and extended his hand to her, offering her space beneath his blanket.

Del allowed herself be pulled to her feet and cradled beneath the warmth of his arm.

"Let's take a walk," he said,

He led her down a path through the trees to a rocky outcropping that looked westward across the valley.

"It's beautiful," Del said, taking in the lights of Cotorra far below. The vastness of the Sonoran landscape lay before them.

"It was this very spot," Francisco said, "where I first saw you."

"Here?" Del said.

"Through field glasses, at the fruit warehouse, just there." He pointed to a distant spot amid the smattering of lights. "I said to myself then, I *like* this woman."

"You actually said that?" Del said, putting a bit of skepticism in her voice.

"Well, perhaps only to myself."

"And you decided you liked me by ... what? ... the way I walked?"

"You walk very nice, that is for sure. But no! Mostly it was the way you handled yourself. A girl with a gun can be very alluring to a man."

"That seems like such a long time ago, but it's only been a few days," Del said, her mood darkening a bit with the memory of all that had transpired.

Francisco had no reply. He drew her closer, his arm around her shoulder beneath the blanket.

They stood that way, in the muted darkness beneath the stars, neither of them speaking for the longest time. Her eyes were on the sparkling panorama, but her mind was on the man next to her. She felt safe with him, at peace in his arms.

As if sensing her thoughts, Francisco said, "The stillness of the night ... the beauty of the lights below ... it can all be very deceptive. Nothing has changed, you understand."

"With Santos?"

He nodded.

"I know," she said, lowering her gaze. "I'll be leaving first thing in the morning."

"You will take the child with you?"

It was Del's turn to nod. "She belongs with family. Real family, not living in some drug fortress."

"I don't want you to go," Francisco said.

His admission caught her by surprise.

Del was aware of her feelings for him, but had believed Francisco to be a man consumed by the loss of his wife and child. She'd only vaguely been aware of his attraction to her. *Was there room in his life for her? Was there room in her life for him?* Del turned her gaze from the vista to look at him, take in the strong profile of his face silhouetted in moonlight. She said, "I have to. I have a job to complete. A responsibility to Aurea's family and to my firm."

Francisco continued to gaze at the faraway lights below, perhaps struggling with demons, remembering things from the past that he would be better off not remembering.

"We would be magnificent together," he said.

Del tried to imagine a life with this man. On one hand, he brought feelings to life that she hadn't felt since … well … since Ed. Warm feelings. Tender feelings. Feelings of peace and tranquility. It brought to mind Mexican villas, with long shaded verandas, ristras drying in the sun, warm desert breezes, children playing in the yard.

"We come from two different worlds, you know." It was a declaration as opposed to a question.

Francisco turned his eyes toward her now. He took her face in his hands, coaxing her closer.

She allowed whatever came next. And what came was their lips seeking each other.

They found and joined. New worlds unfolded. A blinding urgency overtook her.

Del freed her arms from the blanket and wrapped them hard about Francisco's neck.

He pulled her tight against him. Their mouths and minds worked and moved. Until, at last, he slipped her grasp and quickly spread the blanket on the ground.

He lowered himself onto it, beckoning her to join him.

Del laid herself down into his embrace.

He drew the corners of the blanket across them.

"I get lonely sometimes," Del said.

"A woman as beautiful as you … that is such a crime."

Del put her lips to his ear. "Then arrest me," she whispered.

TWENTY-ONE

NESTO RETURNED TO HIS office to collect his personal belongings. From a small safe in the wall behind the credenza, he withdrew several stacks of bills. More than 380,000 Mexican pesos, or nearly 30,000 U.S. dollars. It was all that was left of the many payoffs he had accepted from Santos. The money had improved his lifestyle greatly and that of his family. It allowed for luxuries—cars and housing, fine clothing for his children, jewelry for his wife. And of course ... *women*. There had been many women of the night for him. Touching the stacks of bills made him feel dirty. But he would need it for travel. Need it to build a new life. A more simple life. Free from greed and envy. Free from guilt and shame.

Where he was heading, he did not know. All he knew was that he needed to put great distance between himself and Sonora. Great distance between himself and Santos de la Cal. South America might be good—Brazil perhaps. He could send for his family once he had made accommodations.

Nesto stuffed the money into a canvas bag along with the family photo from his desk. He considered important papers, but told himself, *What does it matter?* There was little time, and he knew it.

One last look around, and Nesto left the office by way of the back door. He hurried quickly across the parking lot, found his government sedan, and fumbled his key in the door lock. His hands and brow were slick with sweat.

As he reached for the door handle to open it, he thought he heard someone call his name. Or ... not so much call it, as whisper it ... *Nessss ... toooo!*

Nesto turned in place. There was nothing there. Only the desert breeze playing tricks on a worried mind. A nervous grin formed at the corners of his mouth.

Nesto turned to his vehicle, the key still in the lock.

Nessss ... toooo! It was louder this time.

"Who is there?" he called to the wind, searching the darkness with his eyes.

No response.

Nesto turned quickly to his car. He managed to lift the handle, break the door from its seal, and spring it open. The door made its arc, no more than four to five inches, when it stopped abruptly.

Unable to turn his head, Nesto slowly shifted his eyes to see the hand that held it.

"Going somewhere?"

Nesto recognized the voice. He squeezed his eyes shut. "Ramón?" he said. "What are you doing here?"

Ramón said nothing, but stepped away.

Nesto had to will his body to turn, force his eyes to open and see.

It was Ramón, all right. And beside him, *Mata*. The sight of this one sent a chill down Nesto's spine. Then he saw the baseball bat held close along Mata's leg, and his insides turned into slag.

"I ... I was just ..." Nesto offered.

"Just what?' Ramón queried.

"Just ..." Nesto had no words for him. His mouth had suddenly gone dry.

Ramón gave a nod to Mata.

The bat flashed in a swift low arc and struck Nesto hard across the shins. The pain was immense. He lost control of the bag he was holding, thought to scream, then realized he already had. His howl cut through the night like a coyote's plaintive cry. His legs folded and he went down.

"*¡Por favor!*" he managed to say, offering his appeal to Ramón.

There was no bargaining. Ramón nodded and the bat came at him in another vicious arc. It struck him on the left arm, just below the elbow, and Nesto felt and heard the bone snap. Once again, a long, anguished howl escaped his lips.

Nesto closed his eyes, and waited for the next blow to come.

He didn't have long to wait. But this time, when it did, he didn't feel the pain. Instead, his world went thankfully black.

———

Nesto awoke to the feel of cold concrete against his back, and a dull ache inside his head. He tried opening his eyes, and was met by the harsh glare of light from a bare bulb overhead. He tried to move and felt his left knee cry out in pain. His left arm lay limp at his side, purple and swollen. He used his other arm to try to lift himself up.

Slowly, carefully, he managed to raise himself.

He was in La Fortaleza—of that he was sure. Probably somewhere in the lower dungeon. He recognized it by the dank, mossy smell and the hard, unyielding resistance in the stone floor. There was shadowy darkness all around. On the walls he could make out the outlines of various implements hanging from hooks—a tool room of sorts.

Nesto blinked to get a better look.

"So nice of you to join us, Nesto!" It was Santos' voice this time—steel-edged and mocking.

Nesto raised himself further on his one good arm to see Santos looking down at him from shadow.

"I ..." Nesto began, thinking to provide explanation. But the act of speaking brought on the raging pain in his skull. He tried again. "I ... I was ..."

"You were what, Nesto?" Santos prodded.

"I ... I was ... just ..."

"Get him up!" Santos ordered.

Ramón appeared, as did Mata. Together they hoisted him up and into a straight-back chair. His broken arm cried in pain. Immediately they went to work, binding his waist and ankles to keep him upright. The chair was then scooted up to a metal table, as if they were seating him for dinner.

Nesto didn't smell frijoles cooking. There was no *carne* on the grill.

Instead of a knife and fork or a napkin beneath his chin, two pools of super glue were squeezed onto the metal surface before him. His arms were roughly stretched—even the broken one—and the palms of his hands were pressed firmly into the pools. Nesto tried to lift them free of the sticky goo. But Ramón held one tight; Mata held the other.

When the glue had set, they released their grip on him. His palms were adhered tightly to the table top. Only his fingers were free to wiggle.

"Where is my niece, Nesto?" Santos asked. His voice was calm at this point, almost loving, Nesto thought.

"Santos … I …"

The *whirring* sound of a power tool suddenly drowned Nesto's protest. Ramón reached across the table with a cordless drill and ran the bit through the back of Nesto's left hand. It made a thick, wet slogging sound as it bored through flesh and bone, then whirred again, slinging pulp, as it was withdrawn.

Nesto felt his entire body convulse in knotted pain. He clenched his teeth tight, holding back a cry. But when he could hold it no more, he opened his mouth and howled. The banshee wail lasted for what seemed an eternity, then morphed into a breathless struggle for air. Tears filled his eyes and streamed unashamedly down his face.

"Where is the American woman? Where is Francisco Estrada? And *where*!" Santos said with emphasis. "Is my fucking niece!"

"I … I don't know, Señor Santos!" Nesto pleaded. "I was … I was forced only to do my duty. Required only to help them in their escape!"

A second time, the drill whined. A second time the bit bored into Nesto's flesh at the back of his hand. A second time he howled until his voice gave out.

Santos gave him a minute to catch his breath.

"Do you wish to continue? Or would you prefer to tell me where they have gone?"

It had taken all of Nesto's courage to help Estrada and the woman. In doing so he had redeemed his pride, restored his honor. He had sworn before God and the smiling photo-faces of his family that he would never betray his office again. Now he wished he could go back in time and give himself another life entirely. "I … I don't … know …"

"I see," Santos said.

Once again, Nesto heard the whine of the drill, once more heard his own banshee cry.

Darkness overtook him again.

"Don't pass out on me, Nesto!"

Santos was slapping him about the face.

Nesto realized he had been out for … *how long?*

He wasn't sure. A second? An hour? There was no way to tell.

He had endured three holes through the back of his hands, before blessed nothingness rushed in to take him away. Now, slowly, the world in all its depravity and pain was returning to remind him of his fears. They had wrapped his wounds with oily shop rags, tying them off to slow the bleeding, prolong his agony. Stiff shards of pain, jagged and raw, ran through him. His mouth was dry. His limbs had turned to mush.

"Water …" Nesto muttered. "A drink, *por favor!*"

"Tell me where I can find my niece, Nesto, and you shall have all the water you can drink." Santos was cooing the words at him again.

"What … what was the question?" Nesto asked, certain he should remember.

"WHERE IS MY FUCKING NIECE?"

Santos was all but screaming now. *What happened to the love?*

Nesto closed his eyes—all he really wanted to do was go back to that dark place of forgiveness.

"Open your eyes, Nesto … Open them!"

Santos slapped Nesto on each side of his face.

Nesto managed to open his eyes again.

"Where is my niece and the American woman? No one crossed the border tonight. Where are they hiding?"

So tired, Nesto thought.

Ramón came around the table to appear in front of him. This time, instead of driving the drill through one of his hands, he leaned across the table and drove the whirring tip of the bit into his shoulder. It met with bone in a grinding growl, and the pain this time seemed to reach his brain like a storm of flying glass. Nesto screamed long and hard, then worked to find his voice. "No more!" he blubbered. "Mother of God!"

Ramón touched the tip of the bit to Nesto's cheekbone just below his left eye.

"I will give you one last chance," Santos said. "Tell me where they are hiding, or I will have Ramón drill your sockets hollow. Do you understand?"

Eyes! Nesto thought. *They were windows to the soul, were they not?*

The image that this new threat—that of the drill sinking sickly into the soft, wet pulp of his eyeballs—seemed more terrifying somehow than everything he had endured thus far. Nesto's stomach heaved. Heaved again. Then he vomited.

"Sonofabitch!" Ramón cried, as a violent spray of bile hit the top of the table, splashed, and chased him back a step.

"Are we there yet?" Santos inquired.

Nesto thought of his children—*¡Madre de Dios!*—his wife.

Slowly, painfully, he raised his head to Santos and nodded once. "The caverns…" he managed to mutter. "San Pedro Mountains… to the east."

Nesto closed his eyes and felt himself drop, free-fall, into a deep, dark, bottomless well of shame.

It was done, he noted—his road to hell at its end.

"Kill me! *¡Dios, por favor!*" he whispered.

TWENTY-TWO

MORNING CAME TO THE overlook.

Del awoke to the sound of urgent voices. She was cradled in Francisco's arms beneath the blanket. Tomás was calling to them, "*Get up! Hurry!*" jolting them out of their dreams.

"Francisco! Señorita Shannon!"

Francisco was first on his feet. Del joined him, slipping into jeans and buttoning her blouse in the dawning light.

"Adriano has returned from town ..." Tomás said, out of breath and gasping for air.

"Slow down, my friend," Francisco said. "What is it?"

"The chief of police ... Nesto Parra ..." he said now through hurried gasps. "He has been found hanging in the market square. He is dead. Santos' men are on their way!"

"Wake the others," Francisco ordered. "There is no time to break camp. We leave now!"

Tomás didn't hesitate. He turned up the path, calling to the others as he went.

Francisco reached a hand to Del, where she sat slipping into her boots. "Santos got to Nesto. Come! We must hurry!"

Del finished tying her laces and allowed Francisco to pull her to her feet.

The scene in the encampment was one of chaos, men and women collecting whatever they could grab in haste—blankets, cooking utensils. The children were being corralled and herded quickly toward the vehicles, a panicked migration.

Francisco stopped Tomás on his way, "You know where to go, we have discussed it before. I will be right behind you."

Tomás didn't hesitate. He gathered his wife and son, and began herding the remaining followers out of the camp. "Quickly!" he urged the others. "Take only what you can carry!"

Del crossed to where one of the women had finished dressing Aurea.

Liana broke ranks and ran to her. She threw her arms tightly about Del's neck. "¡Mi hermana por siempre! Don't forget, okay?"

"Sisters forever! I'll remember," Del said.

Liana hugged her tight, then with a quick kiss on the cheek she raced off to join her husband.

"We must hurry also," Francisco said to her. "You will come with us, yes? With me?"

The urge to follow was strong. After making love the night before, Del had lain awake in Francisco's arms, listening to his gentle breathing. Her mind had played with dreams of them together— romantic dreams filled with Mexican villas by the sea.

"I want to," she said. "But I can't. I have to get Aurea back home to her family."

She saw the crestfallen look that crossed Francisco's face. It caused her own heart to break.

"Take the fork in the road to the east," he said, giving in to reason. "It will lead you down the back side of the mountain. Then follow your instincts north, and you'll find the border. Please, be careful!"

"I'll be okay," Del said. "Go!"

Francisco kissed her long and hard. "¡Ve con Dios!" he said, and turned to go.

"Francisco?"

He stopped, met her eyes with his.

"It doesn't mean it has to be forever," she said.

Francisco studied her a second longer. "I would lay down my life for you! Right here!" he said.

And Del believed he would if it came to that.

"Go," she said. "You must."

Their eyes held. And then he turned and left.

A stab of heartbreak struck Del. The camp became eerily quiet as the vehicles, one by one, spun out of their spaces and were gone.

Del became aware of a presence beside her. Aurea had come to stand with her, share in her loss and grief.

"That's right, sweetie," Del said. "It hurts to be alone. But we have to be going, too."

Without further delay, Del swept Aurea into her arms and headed toward the Wrangler.

———

The cook fires were still smoldering when Ramón, Mata, and a full cadre of men reached the encampment. There were beds abandoned in haste, food uneaten at the tables. How long ago, how many of them, Ramón wanted to know?

Perhaps thirty minutes; three dozen or more.

"Look around!" he commanded the others.

The men spread out through the encampment, Mata taking the lead.

Ramón waded through the spoils, dreading what he would have to tell Santos—that they had arrived too late. That his niece and the American woman had escaped yet again.

It wouldn't be pretty.

Ramón kicked his way past artifacts—mixing bowls and the like, clothing, blankets—to come to one small rumple of bedding. Beneath a ragged quilt, he spotted a yellow lunch pail. He opened it and found crayons and pencils, a pair of child's scissors. He recognized it as belonging to Aurea. Ramón collected it, rehearsing in his head how he would present it all to Santos.

Mata was returning now with the men—some of them carrying minor treasures they had collected. "*¡No están aquí!*" Mata reported. "We find nothing to say where they have gone."

Ramón nodded. He turned the lunch pail in his hands, trying to decide whether or not to take it with him.

"Do we follow the woman or go after Estrada?" Mata asked.

Ramón turned his gaze north, toward the border. He had come to the same conclusion, that the woman and child had likely separated from the group. But he was thinking now of the drug delivery. A shipment of cocaine would arrive from Cali later this day. It was far more important than this one child, he believed. Even if it was Santos' niece. He considered the yellow pail once more, then tossed it aside. No need to provide Santos with proof of their failure. No need to add sentimentality to the shower of sparks that would set Santos off.

"*Vámonos*," he said, to Mata. "We return to La Fortaleza."

TWENTY-THREE

RANDALL HAD BECOME A complete basket case. Throughout the early morning and pushing on toward noon, he had continued to pace. Patti, the receptionist, had tried to settle him down by bringing him hot coffee. The caffeine only served to spike his nerves and set him further on edge. Now they were into the lunch hour, and still no call from Del. Randall finally decided to stop pacing and take action.

He called Ray Daniels, the retired cop.

He still didn't like Daniels all that much. But decided, aside from being something of a prick, he was once an accomplished officer of the law, and a friend to Del. He could handle himself if the need arose. And if he could shed some daylight on Del's status, ease Randall's worried mind, then the prick was worth putting up with for a time. Randall dialed his number and waited as the phone began to ring.

"The fuck! What time is it?" Daniels said. His voice was thick with morning sludge.

"It's afternoon," Randall said. "Normal work time to us humans. Maybe you've forgotten how that is?"

"What can I do for you?" Daniels said.

"I need someone to go to Cotorra."

"Mexico? Shit! Don't you have investigators to do that kind of thing?"

"Rudy's in Ohio on a fugitive warrant. Willard's working a case up in Portland. You're still a cop at heart. What do you say?"

There was a long pause. Finally, Daniels said, "This about our girl?"

"You said you were pretty fond of her," Randall said. "I'll pay you time-and-a-half and travel."

"When's the last time you heard from her?"

"Going on three days."

"Fuck!" Daniels said. "Can I at least shit and shower first?"

"Just make it snappy. Come by the office, I'll lay it out for you."

Randall ended the call.

———

Del crossed the border, heading north, in the same spot where she had crossed, chasing south after Paco and Ramón. The flight to escape Santos' men had gone without incident. She was back on American soil. She could breathe easier now.

The Lara farm lay just ahead. The sun-parched fields and the sad little house and barn were quiet. "Are you happy to be home?" Del asked, gazing across the seat to Aurea.

The girl pulled herself up and craned her neck above the dash to see out. She turned her eyes on Del, a worried, apprehensive look on her face.

"It's okay, we're not staying. We'll only stop long enough to pick up some of your things, then we'll spend the night at my place in Tucson. We'll be safe there."

It seemed to satisfy the girl. She sat back without further consideration.

Del slipped the Wrangler back into gear, and pointed it up the road between the fields. They had come full circle, back to where it all began.

———

The house was untouched since Del had last seen it. Musty and quiet. The phone had been disconnected, but the electricity and water were still working. With the frantic escape from La Fortaleza, the heady exhilaration of freedom, the blissful night with Francisco on the overlook, and the, once again, urgent race for the border earlier this morning, Del realized she had barely had time to consider the consequences of all that had happened. Now, being here, back in the farmhouse where the chase had begun, she was suddenly struck with a chill of anxiety. She had actually stolen Santos' niece from under his very nose—the proverbial goose that lays the golden eggs—and the giant would want her back.

A sudden image of Nesto Parra hanging in the village square came to her. She moved quickly now, wanting to collect just the necessities and get out. She hurried Aurea through the living area and into the hall.

In the junk room, she found a small suitcase and took it with them to Aurea's bedroom. The clippings of Del still covered the wall—her own image looking back at her from two dozen locations. It gave her a familiar chill, and served as a reminder of why she had gone to Mexico in the first place. It had been about curiosity over the child's so-called gift. But also out of interest in the clippings of her, and the clipping of Ed. She recalled that *all* she had ever really wanted was the chance to ask Aurea *why?* Now she had the child with her, and there was no time for questions.

Del laid the suitcase open across the bed, and began gathering various articles of Aurea's clothing from the dresser and placing them inside—a change of shirts, pants, underwear and socks, pajamas. Aurea helped by arranging the items hurriedly, seemingly aware of the need to make haste.

Outwardly the child seemed to be taking it all in stride. But Del guessed that somewhere inside that quiet little head, the child felt frightened and alone. She'd been taken from her home, her parents... Del suddenly wondered, *Did she know her parents were dead? Had she witnessed the murders in person? Or...* if you believed in such a thing... *had she witnessed it inside her head?* Del hoped the girl—this precious little child—had been spared that much torment, at least.

When the suitcase was full, Del knelt down in front of Aurea, placed her hands on the girl's small shoulders. "You know you must go away, don't you, sweetie?" she said.

Aurea said nothing.

"And your Mommy and Daddy won't be coming back."

Aurea turned her eyes to Del's, a sense of knowing already present in her gaze.

"You miss them, don't you?"

Aurea held her eyes.

Del felt a stab of heartbreak. "You're such a good little girl. I just want to hug you to pieces." And she did, giving Aurea a long, tight squeeze. "We have to hurry now."

Aurea turned her eyes to the wall of clippings and pointed a finger at them.

"What? You want to take the clippings, too?"

Aurea brought her eyes back to Del by way of confirmation.

"All right, you've got it," Del said. "The clippings go with us too."

Del began pulling clippings from the wall. She still had that uneasy feeling, seeing her own face looking back at her from so many places. When all the wall clippings had been collected, she stuffed them into an inside pocket of the suitcase. "I have one more for good measure," she said, fishing inside her hip pocket to come out with the clipping of Ed on the courthouse steps. She placed it with the others. "There, I think that's all of them."

Del zipped the suitcase closed and hefted it off the bed. "Ready?" She gathered Aurea by the hand, and together they made their way outside.

As they reached the porch, a Cochise County sheriff's vehicle came rolling down the drive. Sheriff Tom Sutter was behind the wheel. Less than a week ago she had talked to him outside the convenience store up the road. She hadn't had much to tell him at the time. His appearance surprised her now.

Del crossed down into the yard to greet him, trailing Aurea by the hand.

"I saw the Wrangler and thought it might be you," he said, stepping out to greet her. "How the hell you doing, Del?"

"I suppose all right," she said, greeting him with an encumbered hug—the suitcase still in one hand, Aurea's hand in the other. "I just came back from across the border."

"You say! Nasty place, Mexico, these days. I saw you last week, up the highway. You were asking about this farm and the family. Isn't that the little Lara girl you've got there with you?"

"This is Aurea," Del said. "She was kidnapped by her uncle and taken to Mexico. That's why I went down there. To get her back."

"Shy little thing," Tom said. He gave Aurea's head a stroke.

Aurea clung close to Del's leg, unwilling to look at him.

"She's been through a lot," Del said.

"Kidnapped, huh? I've come by the place a few times since I saw you last. The melon fields are all gone to hell. You find out where the girl's parents are?"

Del urged Aurea toward the Wrangler. "You go on, sweetie. I'll be right there." She waited until Aurea had climbed into the passenger seat and sat back.

"Benito and Yanamaria, I believe they're dead, Tom. I didn't know any of this when I saw you last. But I've been getting an education. I plan to call Aurea's extended family to come get her. But I'm taking her home with me in the meantime. You may want to keep an eye out here … Aurea's uncle is Santos de la Cal."

Tom gave out a long, low whistle. "De la Cal? You're kidding?"

"I wish I were."

"You think he killed the kid's parents?"

"I'm pretty sure," Del said. "He took their daughter. I had to snatch her from under his nose. He might come looking for her. I know that he's used the wash south of the melon fields to cross the border on other occasions. He may just do so again."

"Santos de la Cal, huh?" Sutter tipped his Stetson back on his head. "It'd be worth a chance to take that guy out of commission. Ninety percent of the crime I see here in my county is drug related. I'm betting the Border Patrol wouldn't mind getting a crack at him either. I'll notify them to keep their eyes open."

"I was hoping you'd say that."

"You hear anything, you be sure to let us know."

"I will, Tom. Thanks."

Tom Sutter reset his hat and turned to go.

"Oh, something else..." Del said, stopping him.

"What is it?"

"Just something I've been thinking to ask you. Did you ever know a man named Ed Jeski, a cop from Tucson?"

Sutter shook his head. "Never had the privilege. But I read about him in the newspapers. Got himself shot and killed a week or so ago, didn't he?"

Del nodded. "You ever worked with him on anything? Ever have occasion to see him in Palo Blanco, here at the farm, maybe?"

"No... can't say I ever did. Why?"

Del shook it off. "Nothing. I just thought he might have been involved with the Laras in some way."

"I guess I can't help you." Sutter studied her a moment. "This Jeski mean something to you?"

Del nodded.

"Well, I'm real sorry to hear about his death."

"Yeah. Thanks, Tom."

Sutter gave Del's shoulder a squeeze, then turned toward his patrol car. "It's always good to see you, Del," he said. Then he was behind the wheel, starting the engine.

Del watched as the patrol car circled the yard and made its way out and up the gravel drive. When it made the turn onto the highway and disappeared, the quiet stillness re-pervaded the farm. With it came Del's sense of foreboding. She remained in the yard for a moment longer. Thoughts of Tom, of Ed, and of the strange little girl who awaited her in the car, played together in her mind. A desert breeze lifted her hair as she turned her gaze to Mexico. *Somewhere out there is a man who wants to kill me,* she thought. *Somewhere out there is a man who wants to love me.* Would either one come to pass?

Del coaxed herself back to the moment to find Aurea watching her from the passenger seat. "It's time we get going, isn't it, sweetie?" She tossed the suitcase into the back of the Wrangler and climbed behind the wheel.

She had given it a shot, asking Tom Sutter about Ed. But now the mystery of his murder would have to wait. She had a child to look after ... and the farm was not the safest place to be.

––––––

It was a little after two o'clock when Daniels came off the elevator and into the offices of Desert Sands Covert.

"Fucking traffic," Daniels said, pushing through the glass double doors. "You'd think the snowbirds arrived early this year." He threw a glance at Patti behind the reception desk. "How you doin', hon?" He came on past and into the bullpen area of the office.

Randall was waiting for him.

"Thanks for coming. I'd do this myself, but my knees, I don't get around as quickly as I used to."

"You're keeping me from my very serious leisure," Daniels said. "So what's this about our girl?"

Randall laid it out for him, relating the story of the kidnapped child and events that led to Del going into Mexico.

"You say this kid ... how old again?"

"Six, we're told," Randall said.

"Six! Fuck! Still in diapers. And you say she's the niece of Santos de la Cal?"

"That's also what we're told."

"And that our girl has gone down to Mexico to get the kid and bring her back?"

"Against my better judgment, yeah."

Daniels shook his head. "Jesus-fucking-Christ!"

"So, you know the guy?" Randall asked.

"Know him? How could I not know him ... know of him ... he's the Sonoran *Asesino*, for Godsake. Christ! Aside from the cartel bosses themselves, he's considered to be one of the most violent drug figures in Mexico. He controls every square inch of the Sonoran border on the Mexican side and is responsible for more drugs entering this country then any five other traffickers. The hell she want to go get mixed up in shit like that for?"

"She's a tough kid, figures she can handle herself."

"Handle! Christ almighty!"

"I know, I know! Just tell me you can help, all right?"

Daniels shook his head in disgust again. "This is going to cost you, you know." He retrieved a cigar butt from his pocket, struck a match to it, and puffed it to life, blowing smoke into the air.

Randall guessed, now that he was asking for something, the guy felt free to take liberties. He ignored the smoke and said, "Whatever it takes."

"All right. I'll start by making some calls and let you know what I find out."

"I appreciate it," Randall said.

Daniels, still shaking his head, turned to go.

Just then, the elevator dinged and Del stepped out, leading a child by the hand.

"Well, I'll be ..." Daniels' jaw went slack. The cigar slipped from his mouth, and he had to grab to catch it, juggle it like a hot potato, before regaining his composure.

"Del!" Randall called. He felt a huge weight suddenly lift off his shoulders.

Del spotted them, threw them a wave, and started through the glass doors. Aurea balked, fearful of these strangers, or maybe just apprehensive of all the formidable glass and chrome.

Patti said, "He's going to be happy you're back. We all are." She gave Aurea a little finger wave and a smile.

"Thanks, Patti, " Del said. "I'll go on in now."

Randall watched her cross inside, hardly able to control his excitement. He wanted to race across the room and throw his arms around her. Instead, he waited, a foolish grin on his face, his mind reciting silent prayers of thanks.

"Damn, Del," he said, as she crossed to give him a hug. "I can't tell you how good it is to see you. I've been worried sick."

"It's been a trip," Del said, feeling happy to be back among friends. To Ray Daniels she said, "Hey, Ray. It's a surprise seeing here."

Daniels leaned in and gave her a peck on the cheek. "Your boss here called me. I was just about to come looking for you. But ... well, hell ... it looks like you found your way home. Who's this little thing you got here?" Daniels nodded to the child now.

"This little lady is Aurea," Del said. "Say hello to Mr. Willingham and Mr. Daniels."

Aurea clung to Del's leg, eyes downcast.

"Hey, kiddo," Randall said, wiggling his fingers at her.

"Doesn't talk much," Daniels said.

"She's being shy," Del said.

"So, you stole the kid from de la Cal?" Daniels asked.

"You could say that. She belongs with family who will care for her."

Daniels let out a long low whistle. "You got guts, girl. I'll give you that."

"I still can't believe it," Randall said, shaking his head in disbelief. "You want me to notify the Lara family to come get the kid?"

Del shook her head. "I'll call them tomorrow to make the arrangements. Right now I just want to get home to a hot bath and a warm meal."

"You think that's wise?" Randall asked. "I mean, this de la Cal ... he can't be a real happy camper right about now. Maybe you should hole up in a hotel for a while. We could get some security over to keep an eye on you."

"Randall's right," Daniels said. "There's always my cabin up at Summerhaven. Makes for a great hideout. I could come up and check on you."

"I appreciate the offer, Ray, but I'd really rather just go home."

"You're one tough cookie. Let me give you some directions, just in case you change your mind."

Against her objections, Daniels found a notepad on a nearby desk and began jotting.

"Is there anything you need from me?" Randall asked.

"What I could really use is a cell phone," Del said. "I lost mine to some big asshole in Mexico."

Randall unholstered his phone from his belt and handed it to her. "You need to reach me, I'll be in the office late, or you can catch me at home."

"Thanks," Del said. She took the phone and slipped it onto her belt.

"We've got a helluva lot to talk about, you know," Randall said, more gruff than he meant to sound.

"I know. I'll fill you in when I get the chance."

Daniels came with directions. He handed them to her, saying, "You think about it hard. We could spend some quality time reminiscing about Ed."

"Thanks, Ray. I'll think about. It is good to be back." She pried Aurea loose from her leg. "Let's go, sweetheart." And then she was off.

The two men watched her go—out past the reception desk with a wave goodbye to Patti, then into the elevator and gone.

Daniels gave a puff on his cigar. "My oh my, one determined young lady."

"Too determined for her own good," Randall said.

"Uh-huh." Daniels cigar slid to the other corner of his mouth. "So, I guess you don't need me after all."

"I'd be glad to pay you for the time it took you to come up here."

Daniels removed the cigar from his mouth altogether. "Forget it," he said. "Consider it enough that our girl is back and safe, am I right?" He put the cigar back in his mouth, and strolled out of the office.

Randall waited until Daniels had reached the elevators in the foyer beyond the glass doors, and then he crossed to the reception desk where Patti was sitting, legs crossed beneath a short skirt. "You're a woman, Patti... give me your honest opinion... what do you think of a guy like that?"

Patti scrunched her face up and made a shivering gesture.

"Yeah... me too," Randall said.

TWENTY-FOUR

Back at La Fortaleza, Santos reacted pretty much the way Ramón had expected. He exploded into one of his volcanic rages, wanting to know why Ramón couldn't get just one thing right?

Ramón defended himself by telling Santos of the encampment that had been abandoned in haste. Someone obviously tipping them off. Of signs that the child had, in fact, been there—not mentioning the lunch pail directly. And his belief that the woman had made it back across the border with his niece.

Santos picked up the nearest artifact, another Mayan figurine, and hurled it. Then he shoved over the heavy stand that it had been sitting on. For good measure, he spat at the wall.

"Do you want us to cross the border to look for her?" Ramón offered.

Santos paced, grumbling to himself.

"Don't forget, we have product coming from Cali today," Ramón urged, feeling the need to remind his leader.

The mention of business got Santos' attention.

"Do we proceed with the scheduled delivery?" Ramón asked.

Santos indulged in more private consideration, then said, "I'll let you know."

That was it? *I'll let you know?* Ramón thought.

It was all he would get for the time being.

It was a little after three p.m. when the drugs arrived from Cali. *¡Híjole! Wow!* Ramón thought, seeing the bundles stacked high in the back of the cargo van that brought them. It filled more space than he had imagined—twenty-two hundred pounds of refined Colombian.

The street value was estimated at eighty million dollars. The American contact would pay twenty million at wholesale. This belonged to the cartel. Santos' cut, for his role in getting the goods to market, would be just under five million—his biggest take yet. And, of course, Ramón was looking forward to a healthy paycheck as well.

The delivery vehicle that Santos had chosen was a black Hummer H2, equipped with four-wheel drive. *Lots of muscle, low visibility*, Ramón considered with a nod of approval. It sat angled against the perimeter wall with the other SUVs. Its back seat had been removed to offer more cargo space. Its windows were tinted dark.

"Get it transferred," Santos ordered.

Ramón supervised the task until all of the bundles had been loaded into the Hummer and the rear door slammed shut. Then he sent the cargo van on its way. "We have a little over an hour before dusk," he said, looking at his watch. "You never said, Santos ... Do we make the delivery tonight or reschedule with our contact?"

Santos turned his back on him and walked off a few steps. He stood looking off toward the border in thought. "We make it," he said finally. "But I will have to call and let you know what time."

"Call? Are you going somewhere?"

Santos offered no reply but turned on his heels and trekked off toward the vehicles. He called to the crew of men standing around, singling four of them out. "You, you, you, and you ... Come with me! ... Mata, you drive!" he said, making it five. "We take two vehicles."

Ramón had to run to catch up. "But, Santos? Where are you going? What about the drugs? The delivery? Which corridor should I take?"

They had reached the line of vehicles. Santos slid into the passenger seat of the lead SUV without further direction. Mata was already behind the wheel. The four others piled into the second vehicle. The engines were started. "I will call you once I have Aurea's counsel available to me," Santos said, then closed the door.

That was all Ramón would get from him for now. Soon the two vehicles were departing off the paddock and heading down the switchback. He was going after his niece.

Ramón wheeled and kicked the Hummer's rear tire. *Santos and his fucking little prophet,* he grumbled. He was putting their futures on hold to get her back.

Finally, Ramón turned to the remaining crew in disgust. "Put the Hummer inside the sally port and lock it down. We wait for Santos to call."

———

It was good to be home. Newspapers had piled up on the stoop at Del's house. Advertisements were stuffed inside the screen door. The flowers in the planters beneath the windows had all gone to hell.

Del unlocked the door and pushed inside. Hot, stale air greeted them.

"It's a little stuffy," she said to Aurea. "You want to bring the newspapers?"

Aurea picked up one of the rolled newspapers and cradled it in her arms. Del loaded Aurea's arms full. Then she led them inside, bringing the girl's suitcase with her.

"This is it. Not much to brag about, but I think we'll be safe here. And we should be able to find something simple to eat until I have a chance to get to the grocery."

Del set the suitcase inside the bedroom door, then went about the room opening blinds and curtains to chase the gloom. Aurea dumped the armload of newspapers on the sofa, crawled up next to them, and sat back. "You want to make clippings, while I fix us something to eat?" Del crossed to a hall table. "Let's see ... I've got some scissors, someplace ..." She fished through a drawer and came out with a pair. "You must be hungry, right?"

With Aurea occupied, Del went off into the back, still talking through the open doorway.

"My duffel is still back at the hotel in Cotorra. I don't have a billfold or driver's license. I've been wearing the same clothes for days. I must smell like wet puppies."

Del found a bathrobe hanging on a hook in the bathroom. She slipped the Baby Eagle from her waistband and laid it on the narrow shelf above the sink. Placed the cell phone next to it. She undressed and put the robe on. Now she rifled the pockets of her jeans, emptying keys onto the shelf, along with the directions Ray Daniels had written out for her.

"You like soup? I think I still have soup and maybe crackers."

She took her clothes—jeans, blouse, underwear, bra—to the laundry room off the hall and tossed them into the washer. She poured in detergent and set the wash cycle. Aurea was still on the sofa with her scissors.

"It's always so quiet here. We could turn the TV on."

She was making small talk. Something she felt compelled to do to bring life to the empty space and make Aurea feel at home. "My father used to supply all the noise in this house. He would have the television going 'round the clock. And, if not, he'd be yelling at the top of his lungs about one thing or another."

Del rejoined Aurea. She was still on the sofa, flipping pages in the newspaper, looking perhaps for just the right photo to clip.

Del went on into the kitchen.

"How's bean soup sound?" she said, fishing a can from the cupboard, then searched the drawer for the opener.

Aurea said nothing, but continued to peruse the papers.

Del watched her through the open doorway as she put the soup on and adjusted the burner beneath it. Then she went back into the living room to be with her. The child looked up momentarily, as she parked herself on the arm of the sofa, then continued paging through the newsprint.

On one of the inside pages, a photo of Ed Jeski appeared: *Distinguished Tucson Police Officer Killed in Southside Motel*. It was from the previous week, an article relating the details of his murder, perhaps outlining his many years of meritorious service.

The photo was a good one—a dead ringer for the one of him crossing up the steps of the courthouse. Del expected Aurea to pause on the photo, recognize it, and start clipping. Instead, she glossed past it without reaction, turned the page, and continued her search.

Why hadn't she recognized Ed? One more mystery to ponder.

The soup had begun to boil.

Del left the ever-puzzling little girl to her quiet pursuit. She set place settings for both of them, then called Aurea to the table. They ate in silence for a time. There was only ice water to drink.

"I plan to call your uncle Juan to come get you tomorrow," Del finally said. "Would that okay?"

Aurea pointed one small finger at Del.

"Me? No, sweetie, you can't stay with me. You need a real family to care for you."

The child had no response. She seemed neither disappointed nor relieved. Simply accepting of the fact.

Del thought of Santos. Would he truly risk the border to get his niece back? *Of course, he would.* Would Tom Sutter and his deputies spot him as he crossed? *She wasn't sure.* In fact, she doubted it. But Santos had no easy way of knowing where she lived—her address was unlisted.

As she continued to sip her soup, she thought about Francisco. Would she ever see him again?

"*It doesn't have to be forever,*" she remembered saying.

His words, "*I would lay down my life for you.*" Love didn't come much more giving than that.

Del ate quietly, studying Aurea as she spooned soup into her small mouth.

The afternoon passed in relative quiet…

Santos and his men reached the border just before dusk. They came out of the wash onto American soil, stopping amid dense desert foliage to wait. From where they sat, they could see off past the melon fields to the farmhouse. A porch light was burning in the late afternoon. The house looked quiet. There was no vehicle in the yard. Beyond, the town of Palo Blanco sat quiet—the sun lowering behind the string of commercial buildings along the strip.

"We wait here for darkness," Santos said to Mata.

As they sat and waited, a vehicle appeared, working its way through the scrub, in the near distance off to their right. Mata straightened in his seat, bringing his hand to the MAC-10 automatic weapon that lay across his lap. In the second vehicle, the four men—equally suited for violence—came to their ready.

"Sit tight," Santos said to Mata, signaling the others to do so with a wave of his hand.

The vehicle came closer. There was no mistaking the green and white emblem on the door panel, the U.S. Border Patrol, Department of Justice, Customs, and Naturalization. It bumped its way through the scrub, occupants scanning the desert for activity.

"They expecting us," Mata said.

"No matter. We are prepared."

The vehicle passed without incident and disappeared off into the distance.

On the highway, a short time later, a white sedan appeared. A gold shield on the door panel proclaimed it to be a Cochise County sheriff's vehicle. It slowed for a moment, near the end of the gravel drive, surveying the farm. It remained for no more than a moment, then made its way off, toward the center of town.

They continued to wait.

When dusk had settled over the fields, Santos said. "It's time to go."

Slowly, they moved off through the scrub, to the road between the fields. The second vehicle followed.

"It looks like no one is home," Mata said, as they reached the farmhouse, slowing to observe more closely. "Where to now?"

Santos considered the quiet little house. "Take me to Tucson," he said.

———

By the time Del and Aurea had finished eating, and then clearing and washing the dishes, the sun had gone down and shadowy darkness filled the house. Del turned on lamps and returned Aurea to the sofa where she could sift through newspapers while Del drew a bath.

When she returned to the living room, Aurea had curled up, sleepy-eyed, onto a cushion. *Jesus,* Del thought, the poor kid was tired.

"Don't fall asleep yet, sweetie. Let's get you a nice hot bath. It'll make us both feel better. You okay taking one with me?"

Aurea said nothing.

"Come on. Let's do it."

Aurea allowed Del to slide her off the sofa without a fuss and lead her down the hall to the bath.

Del stripped them both of their clothing, and climbed with the girl into the tub.

Her ribs were still sore from Mata's attack, her body achy from sleeping on the ground. The hot water on her skin, the sweet fragrance of lavender scented bath salts, was like heaven. She sat with Aurea between her legs, luxuriating in the sensation. Occasionally she would scoop handfuls of warm, soapy water across Aurea's bare shoulders. Aurea seemed to enjoy it. She relaxed and laid her head back against Del's breasts and let her administer to her. From time to time, Del would replenish the bath with hot water.

It seemed odd, Del noted—strangely and wonderfully so—having a helpless little person to care for. It brought on a melancholy that Del wasn't sure how to label. Call it maternal instincts. Or call it what you want. The warm and fuzzy feelings carried her into the evening.

They remained in the comfort of the bath for as long as they could. In the end, Aurea began to nod.

"Had enough?" Del asked.

She didn't have to wait for an answer. Aurea scrabbled to her feet. Del helped her out and onto the bath mat, and used a large fluffy towel to dry her off. She gave her a hug and kiss when she had finished. Then she wrapped her in the towel and took a brush to her hair. She finished by pushing the bangs back to reveal a face that was way too adorable for words.

Standing naked before the mirror, Del went to work on herself. She brushed her own hair, studying her reflection in the mirror. There were tiny lines at the corners of her eyes that had disturbingly appeared within just the past few days. A large, purpling bruise showed on her ribs.

Maybe Randall was right. Maybe this job, this way of life was ...

No, don't go there, Del warned herself, soon you'll be thinking about having a kid of your own.

That idea turned her thoughts to Francisco. She wondered how he was doing. *Had they found safe quarters? Was he alone? Did he miss her?*

In the hallway, the dryer buzzed, pulling her from her thoughts. She retrieved her clothes and folded them onto the dresser in the master bedroom. She retrieved the Baby Eagle, the cell phone, and the former contents from her pockets, and piled them next to the clothes. Then she dressed Aurea in pajamas from her suitcase and tucked her into bed.

"We're safe here," she whispered with a kiss.

Aurea's eyes dropped and within seconds the child was asleep.

Del was right behind her. She curled naked atop the covers next to her. And quickly drifted off.

TWENTY-FIVE

RANDALL WAS ALONE IN the office—the clock on the wall showing a little past eight-thirty—when the elevator in the hallway dinged open. Four Mexicans came into the foyer, one of them the size of a house. At first, he thought they might be more of the Lara family coming to collect the girl or check on her status. But then on closer inspection—the darting eyes, the aggressive posturing—he knew that wasn't the case.

It took them a minute to get their bearings, then seeing him through the glass double doors, they came to push their way inside.

"Can I help you fellows?" Randall said, meeting them just inside the doorway.

"That depends, señor," one of them said. "Is this Desert Sands Covert?"

Randall threw a glance at the lettering on the glass doors, and took it as a rhetorical question. He brought his eyes back to look them over.

The one who had posed the question was a small man with wavy hair. He spoke pretty good English. The others were in muscle shirts and bandanas and the like, sporting hand-inked prison tats on their forearms and biceps. The big one, arms bulging from his cut-off T-shirt, stood cracking his knuckles. Randall didn't like the looks of it.

"Who's asking?" he said.

A couple of the men took a step forward.

"We are looking for the female investigator, *viejo*."

"You must have the wrong business. Let me just make a quick call, and I'll see if I can get somebody to help you out."

Randall turned toward his office, rehearsing *9-1-1* in his head and picturing the handgun he kept in his lower desk drawer. What he had to do was get to it ...

A rush of footsteps caught up to him. Then a blow to his kidneys shot a fiery shard of pain through his back. His knees buckled. His eyes rolled back in his head. Before he knew it, he was on the floor, his forehead smacking hard against the tile. Sparks flashed behind his eyes. Then there was darkness.

It seemed like a very long time before consciousness returned. It had probably only been a moment. Randall tried to open his eyes and found new waves of pain racking his skull. He tried to remember where he was. Thought he recalled someone asking him a question.

When at last he opened his eyes, he was looking into a pair of heavy jackboots, the big man standing over him.

Randall managed to roll onto his back. His vision was blurry, but he could make out faces in the halo glow of ceiling light. A slightly taller, more elegant man, not one of the original four, was looking down at him.

"*Buenos días,*" the man said, his accent rich.

"I ... I know you," Randall managed to say. He could taste blood in his mouth. "Seen ... your picture ..." He waved his finger in the air to help the words along. "... in the newspapers."

"Then you know me as someone not to be fucked with, señor," Santos said. "Where is the American woman who works here?" Santos showed him a photo clipping of Del, the tagline *Del Shannon of Desert Sands Covert.*

"This ... this is a non-smoking building," Randall said, not sure why he said it.

The big bull stepped forward again, and Randall caught a glimpse of boot leather before the air punched out of him and he felt his rib crack. White-hot pain seared his side. He let out a long coyote howl. His vision blurred.

"Get him up!" Santos said.

Hands came to gather him and lift him into a nearby chair. He was having trouble breathing, difficulty focusing.

Santos started walking about the bullpen. He lifted nameplates from the desks, to read them out loud ... "Willard Hoffman," he said ... "Rudy Lawson ..."

A mewling sound escaped Randall's lips.

Santos reached the third and last desk. "Del Shannon," Santos read. "Could this be our woman?"

"I don't have any women investigators," Randall said.

He braced himself for another blow.

It didn't come.

Santos nodded toward the file cabinets, and the wavy-haired Mexican quickly crossed and started pulling out file drawers and scavenging through them, carelessly discarding files that didn't appeal to him.

"You're wasting your time," Randall said. "There's no women here … just men …"

Before Randall could finish his protest, the wavy-haired Mexican came up with something. It was Del's personnel file, her employment photo clipped to the top right corner.

The man handed the file to Santos.

"Ms. Del Shannon …" A smile spread across Santos' face as he read. "Fifteen-twenty West Mission Road."

"That's an old file," Randall said. "I don't think she lives there anymore."

"I can appreciate your loyalty. But your lies are not to be believed." Santos gave a nod, and the big man in the jackboots stepped forward.

He raised one large fist—giving Randall a chance to see it coming—then drove it hard into Randall's face.

Once again, the lights went out.

––––––

A phone … *ringing … ringing … ringing …*

Del's dreamless sleep was cut short and she bolted upright in bed. It was Randall's cell phone. It took a minute to locate the device next to the stack of freshly laundered clothing on the dresser. By the time she reached it, Aurea was starting to rouse.

"Hello?" she said into it, already feeling her anxiety rise.

"Get out!" a voice said on the line.

"Randall?" His voice was raspy, but Del recognized it nonetheless.

"Just get out now!"

"What's wrong?"

"Santos was here! He's on his way! I didn't tell 'em anything, I swear, Del!"

"You sound hurt, Randall. I'll come to you."

"No! I'm okay! Just get your ass out of the house now!"

Randall coughed into the phone.

"Have you called 911?"

"The cleaning people found me. I'll be all right. Just go!"

"I'm leaving!" Del said. "Just get Emergency Medical there, now. I'll call you later."

"Watch your ass!" Randall said.

Del hung up the phone.

Aurea had come out from under the covers to sit on the end of the bed.

"We have to be going again, sweetie. I'm sorry!"

Del grabbed the nearest clothes she could find, the freshly washed stack in front of her, and hurriedly slipped them on. She tucked the Baby Eagle into the waistband, along with the cell phone, and stuffed Ray's directions to the cabin into her pocket. Then she gathered Aurea's suitcase, and Aurea herself, and headed for the door.

Outside the night was black as pitch. There were no vehicles in sight, no sounds. Del raced with Aurea and the suitcase to the Wrangler. She fired the engine and spun the wheels in the gravel drive getting out of there.

She kept her eyes trained on the rearview mirror. When they had reached the lights of town, only then did she allow herself to breathe.

"That was another close one," Del said.

Aurea was hanging on to the armrest, a veteran escapee by now.

Del fished the directions to Ray's cabin from her pocket. His cell number was scribbled below. She punched in numbers with her thumb, keeping one eye on the road ahead.

"Ray?" she said, when he answered. "I think I'll take you up on your offer."

———

The door gave easily under Mata's boot, and the men stormed inside. When the way was clear, Santos stepped in behind them.

There were lights still burning, bedcovers rumpled. But no one there. They had missed the woman once more, and by only minutes, it appeared. *Did she still have his niece?*

Mata called to him from the living room. "Santos!"

On the sofa, where Mata directed his attention, was a stack of newspapers. A pair of scissors next to them. Aurea had been here, it was true, and the woman still had her. Only, this time, there was no clue to where she might be headed.

"What do we do now?" Mata asked.

Santos thought about his niece some more. It would take time to find her now. The drugs had already been sent from Cali, and the cartel would be wanting their money. To delay the delivery would not sit well with them. Then again, to make the delivery without his niece's counsel would be risky. Santos felt forced to decide. "Contact

Ramón," he said. "Tell him to use the San Pedro River corridor. We will meet him at the farm."

Mata and the men went off to execute the orders.

Santos remained behind. He surveyed the woman's living quarters, the simple nature of her life. She had caused him to make the delivery without his niece's advice. But as soon as it was through, he would track this Del Shannon—this woman with the luck of a thousand charms—to the ends of the earth if necessary and kill her. *That* he vowed!

Santos took out his cell phone and dialed a number. When the voice came on the line, he said, "Midnight, at the farmhouse ... we are on."

———

Throughout the evening, Ramón used the penthouse as a place to wait. He helped himself to Santos' liquor and one of his cigars ... *Why not?* ... Santos wasn't around and his mistress was at the bottom of a dry well, on an abandoned property outside of town.

He was feeling anxious. Worried for their business and for their lives. The cartel in Cali didn't have much patience for those who dallied in their responsibilities, or delayed completion of delivery though indecision. Both of which Santos was doing right now.

The Hummer H2 was sitting idle, inside the sally port, loaded to the wheel wells with precious cargo. He didn't like what was happening. Word of the murder of the chief of the federal police had reached the media, it would bring additional government pressure, serving to make their job tougher, and further give the bosses in Cali something to raise an eyebrow about. *Where was*

Santos?—Cali would want to know. *Why hadn't the delivery taken place? And ... Where is our fucking money?*

Ramón surely didn't want to be the one to tell them Santos was off chasing across the United States in search of his niece, while the multimillion dollars' worth of product that they'd been entrusted with was sitting idle, still in Cotorra, at this late hour.

And why was that? He would have to explain ... *Well, see, it is because Santos relies on a child to make his decisions, and she can't be found just now.*

Might as well shoot himself and get it over with, Ramón concluded.

It occurred to him—sitting in Santos' spot on the sofa—that he had never personally bought into the child's psychic ability. It was something that Santos believed. But his attitude had always been, if it made Santos happy, then thank your lucky stars. Keeping Santos happy was a necessary part of life. But had the girl's advice actually aided them in their deliveries?

Ramón didn't think so.

On any given occasion, you took your chances—that's what he believed. So far, with more than seventeen deliveries to their credit, they had been smart, that's all. And maybe a little bit lucky.

But now, this business of Santos running off to look for his niece, at such a critical juncture ... well ... it made Ramón question the man's leadership.

If there was any sign of sixth sense at work here, any visions of the future, Ramón was the one experiencing it now. And what the second sight was telling him was ... *Be careful, ese! Something doesn't feel right! This is not going to be a good night!* Still, he waited.

What else was he to do?

Around nine o'clock, the phone finally rang. It brought Ramón out of the nap he'd fallen into. He came quickly to his feet. His first thought—spawned by the nightmare he'd been having—was that it was the cartel calling.

But, no ... it was still too soon for that.

Ramón checked the caller ID on his cell phone and saw that it was Santos.

"*Hola* ..." he said into it, anxious for some word.

It was Mata.

"Santos says the farmhouse, midnight." Mata started to hang up.

"Wait ..." Ramón said, halting him. "Has Santos recovered his niece? Which *sendero* should I use?"

"Oh, yeah," Mata said. "He says, come the river way."

A little important thing like that.

Mata hung up, leaving Ramón holding the phone.

More like *holding the bag* was the way it felt.

Faced with the critical task ahead, he too was suddenly anxious to know the child's mind. Maybe he had come to believe in psychic children after all. Ramón closed the phone and slipped it into his pocket. He would take Santos' orders this one last time, he concluded. But when this delivery was through, he was seriously going to think about another line of work.

———

Del found the Catalina Highway, and within thirty minutes was winding past Windy Vista, on her way to Summerhaven. Ray had scolded her, telling her he was glad she'd come to her senses, and that he was there at the cabin now. He'd leave the porch light on for her.

She wasn't altogether happy about having to share the space with him. She'd have to put up with his come-ons, his innuendos, and of course his roving hands. But she had to admit, she liked the idea of having a man around. Someone experienced with a gun, who could serve as backup. The near encounter with Santos had spooked her a little. It really had been a close one.

The road wound through forests of tall ponderosa pines, the night pitch black beyond her headlights. She was familiar with the mountain community. There were ski slopes on one side of the mountain, and on the other, nestled in the gap, an alpine-like village of restaurants, cabin rentals, and craft shops. Only a few years earlier the village had been wiped out by wildfires. But it was slowly making a revival. Most of the cabins and cottages had been rebuilt. The lodge was under reconstruction.

Del passed on through the village, following Ray's directions, to where the road narrowed and the population thinned to near nothing. Soon a gravel road appeared in her headlights, leading back into the trees. It was deserted and dark beneath the heavy pine canopy. The porch light was on as he had promised—a dull yellow beacon, amid the darkness, that somehow felt welcoming. Del pulled the Wrangler to a stop in front of the porch with the motor running.

Ray's sedan sat off to the right of the porch. At the side of the cabin, she noticed a second vehicle parked in the shadowy recesses of a car port. She killed the engine and headlights, and sat there for a moment, taking in the silence. After a second, Ray appeared in the doorway, stepping out to give her a wave.

"You remember Mr. Daniels, don't you?" Del said to Aurea. "He's going to help us out, okay?"

Aurea craned her neck above the dash to get a look, then sat back without further interest.

Del slid out of the Wrangler, gathering Aurea's suitcase from the back, and crossed around to help her out and up the steps. As they crossed the wooden porch, Ray came to put his arm around Del's shoulder—a protective, if not intimate, gesture. "I'm really happy you decided to come by," he said, guiding her through the door into the cabin.

Aurea followed alongside.

The place was bigger than Del had expected. Nicely decorated. It had a new-home smell to it. A comfortable looking sofa sat before a wide stone fireplace. There were wood logs and kindling already stacked and ready to make a fire. *Romantic* would have been the word for it if these were other circumstances—if she were meeting Francisco for a weekend getaway. If there was champagne sitting chilled in a bucket, strawberries decadently arranged in a bowl.

"It's nice, Ray."

"Call it home if you want to."

It would be tempting, Del thought, to think of this as a vacation getaway. But it was a hideout, nothing more, she reminded herself. And temporary at best.

"Santos and his men came to the house," she said. "They did a number on Randall first. Aurea and I just barely got out in time."

"That right?" Daniels said, his face expressing concern. "You'll be safe here. Nobody knows about this place 'cept a few close friends."

Del allowed Ray to take Aurea's bag and lead them into a spare bedroom. "You and the girl can stay in here. Doing my best to be the gentleman." He added, "I'll sleep in the other room."

The room wasn't bad, Del decided. The bed was a double, made up pleasantly enough with a ruffled bedspread and pillow shams. There was a nightstand with a lamp, a bookshelf with a small TV. She was hoping she could count on Ray not to try anything.

"You get the kid to bed, then come on out," Ray said. "You could probably use a drink. You can bring me up to date on Santos and tell me all about this mess."

"All right," she said. Truth was, the idea of a stiff drink sounded good.

Del waited until Ray had left the room, then turned to Aurea. "You crawl up in bed, sweetie. I'll come back in a few minutes and tuck you in, okay?"

Aurea said nothing, but did as she was instructed, climbing under the covers, already in her pajamas.

Del gave her a pat and went out to talk to Ray.

Ray Daniels had already started a fire in the fireplace. He had drinks poured and waiting. He offered her one—a brandy—as she came into the room. He showed her to a place on the sofa.

Del took a seat and sipped the drink to calm herself down.

Ray poked at the fire, then came to sit next to her. Placing the bottle on the table, he sat close, putting an arm across the back of the sofa.

"I have to thank you, Ray," Del said. "I wasn't sure exactly where to go this time."

"Well, you should know you can always count on me. You and me go way back, don't we?"

"I guess."

"So, this Santos wants his niece back, huh?"

Del took another sip. The warmth from the fire and brandy was allowing her to relax. It felt good. She had been under near constant pressure for close to a week. For the first time she was able to let her guard down. "Santos has this notion," she said, "that he can't make a drug delivery without consulting Aurea first. He believes she possesses some kind of clairvoyant ability."

"That right? Does she ... I mean ... you know ... possess some kind of whatever?"

"I don't know," Del said, watching the fire dance. "I suppose I believe she's extremely bright and intuitive. She doesn't speak, so it tends to lend an air of mystery to her."

"She's a mute," Ray said, as if that explained it all.

"No, see, that's the other thing," Del said, shaking her head. "Supposedly there's no reason why she can't talk. She simply chooses not to do so."

"Strange," Ray said. He knocked back his brandy and poured himself another from the bottle. After another hit, he said, "So, you still pining over Ed?"

Del gave it some thought. Then shrugged. "I really thought that his murder was somehow connected to everything that was going on at the farm, but I guess I was wrong. Which is another reason to doubt Aurea's ability."

Ray's hand found a place on Del's leg.

"Maybe you need to get over Ed," he said. "I know it's hard. But you're young, life is short."

The hand began idly stroking, up and down her thigh. Each stroke chanced higher.

Del took Ray's hand and moved it away. "It's going to take some time, Ray."

"All right," he said, raising his hands in innocence. "I'm a patient man. I just want you to know, however, that old Ray is around if you should start feeling the lonelies at night." He knocked back the rest of his drink, then stood and crossed to a coat rack near the door and began slipping his arms into the jacket that had been hanging there.

"Are you going somewhere?" Del asked, surprised by the sudden reversal.

Ray crossed to the mantel and began loading his pockets—keys, billfold, some loose change. "I've got a little business to attend to."

"Business? It's awfully late for business, isn't it?"

"You know how these things are," he said, brushing it off with a slight smile, making it seem casual. "But don't worry now. I'll be back in a few hours. You go ahead and get some sleep. I'll try not to wake you when I get back. You'll be safe here."

Then Ray was at the door.

"But…"

Daniels waved his goodbye across his shoulder and left, closing the door in his wake.

Del sat alone before the fire. She wasn't sure how to feel.

Abandoned? Glad? Suspicious?

She remained there for time, thoughts of Santos and Francisco running through her head. She thought of Ed and Aurea, and the clippings that seemingly connected her murdered lover to the farm. She thought of Daniels, going out at such a late hour of the night. It all seemed such a mystery. When she had finished off her drink, she went back into the spare bedroom to check on the miracle child.

———

Del found Aurea lying on her back, hands behind her head, staring up at the ceiling. She slipped the Baby Eagle from her waistband and laid it on the bookshelf next to the TV. She settled on the edge of bed next to the girl and brushed her hair from her eyes.

"Are you thinking about things, sweetie?"

Aurea continued to stare at the ceiling.

"I know, there's been a lot going on. It causes me to think, too."

Del studied the girl closely. The suitcase still sat on the end of the bed. If there was ever going to be a right time to ask Aurea about the clippings, now was that time. Del turned the suitcase toward her, unzipped it, and removed the stack of news clippings from the inside pocket. She perused them casually—photos of herself with various captions coming and going from view.

Aurea remained unmoved.

"I really like your collection," Del said, by way of leading into it. "Can I ask you something, sweetie?" She gave it a moment, then said, "Why did you make all these clippings of me? Can you tell me?"

Aurea's eyes came to meet hers. She said nothing.

"We didn't know each other before, did we?"

No response.

"What caused you to clip these particular photos from the newspapers?"

Aurea only looked at her.

"Why did you save them and place them on your wall?"

Nothing.

Del's frustration mounted. Her original decision to pursue Aurea had been in large part out of curiosity about the girl. Puzzlement over the clippings of her and the one of Ed. Her goal had been to find Aurea and simply ask the girl *why?* Why me? Why Ed? Why the clippings? But if Aurea decided never to speak, how was she to ever learn the truth? She could imagine now some of Santos' frustrations with his niece. It was maddening, trying to unlock secrets in the head of a child who never spoke. "You're not going to tell me, sweetie?"

Aurea lifted one small finger and pointed it at her.

"What? Me? Are you trying to say? You saw me?... Where? ...How?"

Aurea turned her eyes to the bookshelf. Del followed them there, to the television set that sat on the middle shelf.

"You saw me on television? Is that what you're trying to say?"

Aurea turned her gaze back to Del by way of confirmation.

Del remembered that she had once been on television briefly, the day she returned the kidnapped girl Melissa Cameron to her parents. A television news crew had been there along with newspaper reporters to capture the joyous event.

"So, you saw me on television and that's why you began cutting clippings of me."

Aurea held Del's eyes with hers.

So there was nothing mystical about it. No prophetic visions. No clairvoyant insights. Just a child who had seen her on TV, saw her pictures later in the newspapers, and decided to collect them.

But then, what about the clipping of Ed?

Del rifled through the stack of clippings and came out with the photo of Ed on the courthouse steps. She considered it a moment, seeing Ed, once again, on the steps with his partner Ray. She turned the clipping so Aurea could see it. "Sweetie…"she said. "You see this man right here?" Del placed a finger on Ed's image. "Did you make this clipping because you had seen him before also?"

Aurea glanced at the photo. She didn't raise her eyes to Del this time. Instead she continued to stare at the photo.

"Did you know this man? Had you seen him before?"

Aurea turned her gaze to Del. She could see in her eyes that she had not.

"Are you sure? Look closely."

Aurea studied the clipping for a second, then brought her eyes back to Del.

"Did you know that this man and I were friends?" Del asked.

Aurea said nothing.

"So … you never saw him before?"

Aurea only looked at her.

"Then … I don't understand, sweetie," Del said, confused again. "You made your clippings of me because you had seen me on TV. Why did you clip this photo of my friend if you had never seen him before?"

Aurea said nothing, but continued holding Del with her eyes.

Finally, Del said, "All right! I give. I guess it's just going to have to be one of those secrets of the universe."

Del started to rise. Aurea put a hand on her arm to stop her.

"What?" Del asked. "What is it, sweetie?"

Aurea took the clipping from her, touched one small finger to the image and turned it for Del to see.

Instead of pointing to Ed Jeski in the photo, however, Aurea's finger was poised above the image of Ray Daniels.

"What? This man?" Del said, bringing her own finger to join with Aurea's to identify Ray in the picture. "This man here is why you made the clipping? You know him? You saw him before?"

Aurea brought her eyes to hers, and this time Del could read the positive affirmation in them.

"You know him? ... How? ... He came to the farm?"

Aurea held her gaze.

"Listen to me, sweetie! This is very important!" Del said, needing to be perfectly clear. "*This* man ... the man who is letting us stay in this cabin ... he has been to the farm? To your house? You have seen him before today?"

Aurea held Del's gaze. The answer in her eyes was so clear that Del wondered why she hadn't thought to consider it before. The child had clipped the photo because of Ray. Not because of Ed.

She felt her heart skip a beat.

"I'm really sorry you had to hear that!" a voice said.

Del spun in place to see Ray Daniels standing in the doorway.

"Ray? I thought you left?"

"Came back for my cell phone," he said, raising his left hand to show it to her.

"How ... how long have you been standing there?"

"Long enough for the kid to spill the beans."

"She didn't say anything really," Del said. "I'm not sure what she means."

"Del, Del, Del ..." Daniels said, shaking his head. "I know you to be way smarter than that."

Del threw a look at the Baby Eagle lying on the bookshelf next to the TV.

Daniels caught her glance and stepped quickly inside to collect it before she could move. He turned with it, to point it at her. "I was really hoping it wouldn't come to this, you know. I mean ... I was truly hoping I could conclude my business peacefully and come back to you. Hoping you and I could pick up where we left off ... or should I say ... where you and Ed left off. I hadn't figured the little mute to be a snitch."

Del kicked herself inside. She had been so caught up in believing that Ed was the reason Aurea had made the clipping that she had totally ignored the other person in the photo. *Ray!* She had let heartbreak get in the way of good thinking. "I guess your late-night business is to meet Santos for a delivery. Am I right?"

"You put me in a very awkward predicament, Del. It's a true crisis of conscience. See, I really do like you. I didn't want it to come to this."

"I suppose you thought the same about Ed?" Del said.

Daniels lowered his gaze. "Ed was a friend, but ... well, you know ... a real Boy Scout. Mister Straight-Fucking-Arrow! I tried to offer him a cut. He didn't bite. Tried to get me to turn myself in."

"There was never any woman in the motel, was there? You set Ed up so his death would look like something easily explainable, rather than having authorities look deeper into things. You killed him to protect your interests in the drug trade."

"I do miss old Ed," Ray said. "I suppose the same way I'm surely going to miss you."

His eyes narrowed. Daniels flipped open the cell phone and hit the speed dial.

Del pulled Aurea into her lap, comforted her, while Daniels placed his call.

"Just checking to make sure everything's still clear at the farm." Daniels held Del with his eyes and with the gun as he spoke into the phone. Del could vaguely hear Santos on the other end.

"Good! I've also got a little special gift for you," he added. "Actually, two gifts…"

He listened.

"No, I won't tell you what it is just now. Save it for a surprise. But I guarantee you're gonna love it."

Daniels flipped the cell phone closed.

"So, what now?" Del asked.

"Now we go for a little ride," he said, waving her toward the doorway with the muzzle of the gun. "Get the suitcase, and bring Miss Chatty Cathy with you."

Del did as she was told. She set Aurea on her feet and gathered the suitcase, then moved off with Aurea in tow ahead of the gun.

Daniels escorted them outside and to the vehicle parked in shadow beneath the carport. Up close, Del could see, now, that it was the tan van she had witnessed arriving at the farm to meet up with Paco and Ramón—the night she'd chased them into Mexico. Ray Daniels *was* Santos' American contact, his partner in the U.S. And it had been just that—Ed's discovery of it—that had gotten him killed.

Ray poked her toward the driver's side. "Get behind the wheel," he said.

Del slid in, pitching the suitcase in back and pulling Aurea across her to sit her on the front seat next to her.

Ray slipped through the cargo door behind her, dragging a heavy duffel bag off the floorboards to put it on the seat next to him.

Del eyed the stuffed duffel in the mirror. "Tell me something, Ray," she said. "Where's a retired cop like you get the kind of money it takes to make a major drug buy?"

"Let's just say, my twenty-some years on the force have allowed me access to all kinds of people."

"Do your bowling partners know?" Del said.

"That's the one problem with you, Del. You've always been something of a smartass. So just shut up and drive."

Del started the van and put them on the road back down the mountain—her own gun, the Baby Eagle, trained on her the entire time.

Daniels was returning them to the man they had just escaped...

Returning them to Santos.

TWENTY-SIX

Francisco Estrada sat staring into the flames of the campfire, his hands cupped around a mug of coffee. He felt tired. Tired of running like a frightened sheep. Tired of living like a dog. And his people—brave souls that they were—were at their end as well. Gone was the steel in the men's arms and legs. Gone, the softness in their women's touch. They were all bent to the breaking point, their resolve all but used up. And the children ... *Dios!* ... the light in their little faces had grown dim, their spirits had dulled.

Santos had done this to them all. And now he had come between him and Del—possibly the only woman other than his wife that he believed he could truly say he loved. He had told her he would lay down his life for her. And he had meant it.

Santos!

He was behind Del's leaving. Her sense of duty to make the child free of him, her dedication to returning her to her family and making her safe—these things were her reasons for going. And, once again, he could blame the drug trafficker, a man in league with the devil, for ruining any chance he might ever have at happiness. He wished to vow, once again, to end Sonora of this inhuman scourge. Uphold his vow to the woman he loved. *But how could he?* His resistance was all but spent.

"Francisco?"

Tomás, his second, appeared next to him at the fire. His voice soft, polite, respectful of the peace and quiet.

Estrada turned his gaze to him. He could see in the man's eyes the same weariness as his own.

"The encampment is set," Tomás said. "Our people are settled. However, blankets and bedding … much was left behind in haste … the women have little to prepare to eat."

Francisco nodded. He patted the seat next to him. "Sit, Tomás. I have something to discuss."

Tomás perched himself on the edge of the log.

Estrada turned his gaze back to the fire. "Our people have reached their end," he said. "I believe it is time for us to leave Sonora and find new homes elsewhere in Mexico or perhaps beyond."

The pronouncement took Tomás by surprise. His face dropped. He said nothing at first. Then said, "But Francisco, this is our home. What about our vow to oppose Santos to our death?"

"We are *already* dead, my friend. Do you not see that? Our dream of living free has become hopeless."

"You say you wish us to be free, but will we ever be free of memories? I have my wife back, yes, by the grace of God. Yours will never return, nor will many others. And I cannot forget the torture Santos has put my family through."

"I am no longer fit to command, Tomás. We have exhausted the bulk of our resources and we are no closer to victory than the day we began. If anything, Santos grows more powerful by the day."

Tomás seemed to consider. "It is the American woman, isn't it? Del Shannon, who troubles your heart so?"

Francisco thought about it. He could picture this woman so clearly in his mind, that if he were asked to paint a picture of her from memory, it would be a masterpiece—from the ice-green eyes to the fast-sloping curves of her body. Her appearance into his life had swelled new hope in him for the future. *But now what future was there?*

"I miss my life," Francisco said. "I miss my work. I miss the sound of the heavy equipment in the pit. I still have comrades at the mine. I miss them, too. Though, I must say, I have found no better friend than you. And I miss my wife and child. Del Shannon … this beautiful Anglo … so full of life. I have tried to imagine her as my future. As another chance at marriage and children."

"She is still there," Tomás offered. "Maybe a country away. But still there. I think she feels for you, too. There is still hope."

"No. I don't think so, Tomás. We had our moment. But today I can see the nature of her. She is committed to her life. Her career. Her duty. How could I spoil such a beautiful thing with talk of contentment? My only hope, tonight, is that I should one day get the chance to free her of Santos' quest for revenge. *This* I would do in a heartbeat."

Tomás nodded his understanding.

With nothing left to say, they sat in silence now, the fire crackling before them.

One of his scouts came off the trail and into the encampment. He had raced hard, was out of breath, and gasping for words. "Señor Estrada … Señor Villarreal …"

The man who approached was named, appropriately so, Gregorio—*The Watchful.* He was one of Estrada's most trusted scouts, with a seemingly innate knack for being able to observe without being observed. Estrada looked him over. He was painfully thin, like the others. But, still, he came with his chest out, proud to be of service.

"Catch your breath, my friend," Estrada said, waving him to a place near the fire.

"It is Santos," Gregorio said between gasps. "He has left the protection of La Fortaleza and crossed the border into the U.S."

"*¿En serio?* Are you serious? How long ago?"

"Near dusk. I wanted to return with news as soon as possible. But I was pinned down by roving patrols along the border. Much later, after dark, Ramón Paz also crossed in a very large vehicle. I believe he was making a delivery."

Tomás said, "Francisco, this might be the chance we have waited for. Santos is outside the protection of his home."

"You have read my mind, Tomás." Estrada turned his gaze back to the fire—embers crackled, flames flicked, shadows danced about. It brought back memories of the raging conflagration that had consumed his home with his wife and child inside. It brought distant echoes of their plaintive cries, drumbeats of violence in the night. "If Santos has left his fortress," he said, "it is because of his niece. Not the delivery. Which means he has found her, and Del Shannon in the process. She is in trouble, Tomás. I can feel it in my soul."

"Tell us what to do, my friend," Tomás said. "We are with you."

Estrada took another moment to consider. He thought of Del. She was a strong woman, but, then, so had been his wife. Coming quickly to his feet, he said, "¡*Ándele!* Get me twenty of our strongest men, Tomás. Quickly! Preferably those who have also worked at the copper mine like me."

"The miners, señor? But why the miners?"

"Tonight, amigo," Estrada said. "We go back to work."

TWENTY-SEVEN

THEY ARRIVED AT THE farm a few minutes before midnight. Del pulled the van to a stop and put it in park, leaving the engine to idle. The porch light was burning at the kitchen entrance, as she had left it, shedding a yellow pallor across the yard. There were no vehicles, no sign of Santos or his men anywhere.

Daniels leaned through between the seats to get a better look through the windshield.

Before them, the melon fields also lay silent. Farther out, the desert remained still, only shadowy outlines of tall saguaros could be seen, standing like brooding sentries guarding the land.

"Kill the lights," he said.

Del did as she was instructed.

"He's supposed to meet us," Daniels said.

"Maybe he decided to forget the whole thing."

"You don't forget twenty million dollars," Daniels said, coveting the duffel closer to his side.

They sat for what seemed an interminable length of time in shadowy porch light. Daniels kept Del's Baby Eagle pointed at her.

"The fuck is he?" Daniels said, scanning the desert south, throwing occasional glances back toward the highway.

"He's just making sure you weren't followed. Santos is a cautious man. I wouldn't worry too much. He guesses you have his niece."

"Yeah, well, I don't like it."

"We can always leave."

"And you can always just shut the fuck up!"

They continued waiting, neither of them saying anything now.

More time passed. Daniels became more agitated by the minute. Then a spotlight flashed in the desert to the south. A second later, it flashed again.

"The fuck? You think that's them?"

"He wants you to come to him," Del said. "Like I said, Santos is a cautious man. He's also like a child, he wants everything his way."

Daniels gestured them forward with the gun. "All right, just take it slow, until we can see what this is all about."

Del put the van in gear and pointed it down the road between the fields. When she reached the end, she turned off into the desert, working the nose of the van around stands of mesquite, prickly pear, and cholla. She continued on toward the spot where they'd seen the flash of light, then drew them to a stop on a flat patch of landscape near the wash.

The desert was dark, only a wedge of scrub was visible in the headlights.

"The sonofabitch!" Daniels said. "I'm the one with the money, he should be coming to me."

"The border is less than a hundred yards or so away," Del said. "He's sticking close to it in case something goes down."

"Why should anything go down?" Daniels said. It wasn't a rhetorical question, Daniels was looking at her, wanting to know.

"This kind of thing comes with risk. You of all people should know that, Ray. You don't have to go through with this. There's still time to turn around."

"What? And go back so you can have me hanged for murder?"

"Do you really believe you're going to just go off and live happily ever after?"

"Stop talking!"

"Look at you, Ray. You're a nervous wreck! Maybe you're not cut out for drug smuggling."

Daniels jabbed the muzzle of the Baby Eagle into the soft flesh behind Del's ear. "I just don't like being this close to the fucking border, all right! Now, put the goddamned thing in gear and let's get this over with!"

Del eased the shift lever down and edged them forward through the scrub.

They'd gone no more than thirty yards farther, when Mata stepped into the glare of her headlights and raised his hand.

———

Tom Sutter was on duty that evening, patrolling the highway from the east, down through the heart of town and back out. He was feeling unreasonably anxious and not sure why. There was a creepy-crawly sensation along his spine that came to him at times for no damned good reason. Other than to suggest that all was maybe not right somewhere in the world.

He believed it had something to do with a built-in radar, an innate sixth sense for danger. It had proven itself right, one time, long ago, while on patrol as a young sheriff's deputy. That night, not knowing what to make of his unusual anxiety, he had gone into an all-night convenience store for a cup of coffee, and stepped squarely into a robbery in progress. Before he'd recognized the cost of his mistake, he had taken a bullet in the left side and another in the hand. The perpetrators had run off, fortunately not staying to finish the job. But from that night forward, he promised himself daily ... *if you feel the creepy-crawlies again, pay attention to them.*

He was feeling them now.

Sutter turned back up the highway and made a pass by the Lara farm. The tingling sensation seemed to grow stronger as he approached.

And there it was—the reason for his uneasiness—a vehicle down there in the desert past the melon fields, a large shadowy silhouette of a man in the headlights.

"Thank you, creepy-crawly!" he said to himself and quickly killed his headlights.

He remained on the shoulder of the highway, watching as more shadowy figures appeared. He queued his radio once and said into it, "Dispatch?"

"Dispatch," the radio squawked in response.

"Maggie," Sutter said. "Get me some backup out to the Lara farm, pronto ... lots of it. Oh, and notify the Border Patrol, will you? We got something going on over here, and I'm not quite sure what to make of it."

Sutter ended his call and sat back to wait for backup.

"Come on, boys," Sutter murmured to himself. "We may not have all night."

———

Del watched through the windshield, as Santos stepped into the headlights alongside Mata. He had his weapon in hand, held close to his side. Others came to take up positions on both his flanks. They were armed with automatic weapons. One was Ramón Paz, Del recognized.

Aurea stirred on the seat next to her.

"It's okay, sweetie. Everything is going to be all right."

"Kill the engine," Daniels said from over Del's shoulder. "Leave the keys in the ignition."

Del did as she was told.

Daniels slid open the cargo door, shifted the gun to his left hand and gathered the ponderous duffel bag. "Let's go, you first," he said. " Take the kid out with you through the driver's side and don't do anything foolish. I'm right behind you."

Del pulled Aurea across the seat to her, opened the door, and stepped out with her in her arms onto hard-packed desert.

Daniels eased out through the cargo door, the duffel with him, and pressed in tight against her from behind. He pushed the gun into her back. "Be cool. We'll take this nice and easy."

They were looking across the splay of headlights at Santos and his men.

"This *is* a welcome surprise, Señor Daniels," Santos said. "My niece and the very elusive Del Shannon."

"I told you you'd love it," Daniels said.

"Send them to me," Santos instructed.

"You have the drugs?" Daniels asked.

Santos gestured with his chin.

In the weak outer castings of light, a black Hummer and two other vehicles—SUVs—could be seen lined up, one behind the other, down inside the wash. Their noses were pointed south toward the border.

"It's there, as agreed," Santos said. "Now send the woman and the child to me."

"How come the Hummer's facing south? I thought we agreed to make the exchange at the farm?" Daniels said.

"Just send the woman and child to me."

"Ray..." Del cautioned beneath her breath. "He's not going to let you go."

"Shut up!" Daniels said, close to her ear, digging the gun harder into her back.

"You've become a liability to Santos. Don't you understand that? He suspects you might have killed Ed, because you're with me and I was quizzing him about it. He can't trust now how many others might have the same suspicions."

"I've come this far. Now take the kid and get the fuck out there!"

There was no listening to reason. Del hesitated but shifted Aurea on her hip and stepped out into the light. It was not a good situation for sure. There seemed to be few if any options.

"That's far enough," Santos said, when she was some four to five feet away.

"Santos..." Del said, attempting an appeal.

"Put my niece down!"

Once again, Del hesitated, but set Aurea on her feet.

"Aurea, come to Tío Santos," Santos called.

Aurea didn't move.

"Come, child," he said.

Still she didn't move.

Ramón, frustrated, came forward to grab Aurea by the hand and drag her off.

"Jesus Christ!" Daniels said. "Can we just get this over with?"

Santos turned his attention to Daniels. "Do you have the money?"

Still behind the open van door for safety, Daniels hefted the duffel for him to see.

"Very well," Santos said, and without warning, lifted his gun and fired. The sound of it boomed across the desert floor like monsoon thunder. The bullet punched through sheet metal and struck Daniels somewhere in the midsection. He cried out, sagged, and crumpled to the ground.

Aurea broke free of Ramón and fled back to the safety of Del, grabbing her around the thighs to hold on tight.

"You didn't have to do that," Del said.

"I no longer needed him," Santos said. "Besides, now I have both the drugs and the money. You see how it works?" Santos nodded a silent order, and Mata crossed to Ray's lifeless body lying in the open doorway to the van. The Baby Eagle was still in Ray's hand. He retrieved it, gathered the duffel, and returned to Santos with the spoils.

Santos accepted the gun—Del's Baby Eagle—stuffing it into his waistband in front. He waved Mata away with the duffel. "Put the money in the Hummer with the drugs," he said. "While I finish up one last piece of business."

Del understood all too well what the *one last* piece of business was to be.

"You've got the money and the drugs," she said. "Let me take Aurea and leave. It's obvious she doesn't want to go with you."

"Send her to me!"

"I don't think so," Del said.

Santos raised his gun to her. "Send her!" he repeated.

"She's afraid, can't you see that?"

"Come, Aurea!" Santos commanded.

Aurea held on tight.

"Go on, sweetie," Del said, relenting and separating herself from Aurea. "Go with Tío Santos. It will be all right."

Her words were meant to comfort the child. They sounded false to Del's ear—nothing whatsoever was going to be all right. Del would meet her end here, on this blasted patch of desert. And Aurea would return with Santos to live her life inside a fortress. Del urged Aurea away, and the child, reluctantly but obediently, left her side and crossed to stand near her uncle.

"Such a fine child she is," Santos said. "Now, it is time to say *adiós*, Ms. Del Shannon."

Santos leveled the gun.

Del braced herself for the inevitable.

"*Noooooooooooo!!!!*"

A sudden shriek filled the air and echoed across the landscape. It had come from Aurea.

Santos held his fire, dumbstruck by the child's sudden willingness to speak.

Aurea broke ranks and ran to Del's embrace. Del swept her into her arms and held her close.

Everyone—the men, Santos, Del herself—was staring at the child.

"Aurea!" Santos said, dumbfounded. "You...you speak! I...I don't understand, child. You used your voice! How is it so?"

Aurea said nothing.

"Her wishes are obvious, Santos. Let her go with me."

Santos was still off his mark. He seemed uncertain what to do. "Come..." he said. It was a tentative command. "Come with your Uncle Santos. We can talk together, as I have always wished."

Aurea said nothing, but burrowed tighter into Del's embrace.

"Speak to me, child! *¡Por favor!* Tell me in words that you wish to come with your uncle."

Again, Aurea said nothing.

"What do you want to do, sweetie?" Del said.

In a tiny but affirmative voice, Aurea said, "I want to go home!"

"I guess she only speaks to me," Del said to Santos.

Santos spun on his heels in a display of ultimate frustration. He chewed his lower lip. Then, suddenly, he turned back again and strode quickly to the two of them, to come face to face with Del. "I am taking my niece with me!"

"She still won't talk to you," Del said. "Isn't that clear?"

"Aurea, my child..." Santos said, appealing to the girl in a whimpering tone. "You speak to this woman...this...this stranger. Why, then, will you not speak to me, your flesh and blood?"

Nothing. Aurea kept her face buried in Del's shoulder.

"You are my family, my love, *profeta*. I need you."

"She's not going to talk to you," Del said. "She's decided she'd rather stay with me."

Santos shrieked. He brought the gun to Del's forehead. "Tell her to speak to me!"

"She won't!" Del said.

"Tell her!"

Del showed him a defiant chin.

"Then prepare to die with her in your arms!" Santos said. He cocked his wrist higher, pressed the muzzle of his gun harder.

Aurea raised her face now. "No, don't!" she said simply.

Santos' jaw tightened. Indecision played behind his eyes. Then his demeanor suddenly transformed, as a new idea took hold. He cocked his head slightly and appraised Del from the corner of his eye. "Of course... why did I not see it before?" he said. "The clipping... her insistence to spare you... she thinks of you as a surrogate... a mother to care for her."

"Haven't you already tried that with your mistress?" Del said.

"Casta?" Santos shook his head. "Aurea never did feel for my concubine as she clearly feels for you." He was nodding now, affirming his new insight. "*¡Sí!* The answer is clear. You both will come with me! You will serve as *niñera* to my niece. She will speak to you. And you will speak to me on her behalf."

"Back to the dungeon?" Del said. "I don't think so."

"We will make accommodations... besides..." Santos said, applying greater force to the muzzle of the gun. "I am not asking!"

"What if I just said I won't go?"

"Then we go back to my original plan."

Del had to admit that, while it wasn't the best offer she'd had all day, it beat the hell out of a bullet to the brain. "All right," she said. "You haven't given me many choices."

"I never do," Santos said.

He removed the gun from her forehead and waved her toward the waiting vehicles.

Del moved off toward the wash, with Aurea in her arms. Santos and his men fell in behind her.

"Boss!" One of the men, suddenly called out, pointing off in the direction of the farm. There was a plaintive urgency to his voice.

In unison, they turned to see what had caught the man's attention.

From the gravel drive back at the farm, a squadron of County Sheriff and Border Patrol vehicles flooded past the house and were filing onto the road leading between the fields, racing fast. They fanned out quickly when they hit the open desert, their headlights strafing the darkness as they scurried to take up flanking positions.

"¡*Vámonos!*" Santos ordered, snatching Aurea from Del's grasp, and beginning to move, pushing her ahead of him and the child.

They broke into a run for the vehicles.

Some of the men held position, turning their weapons on the fast-approaching vehicles, laying down cover in a crescendo of gunfire.

Del reached the wash ahead of Santos. She slipped on the steep incline, landed hard on her rump, and slid the last six or eight feet down the steep slope to the sandy bottom. Santos came right behind her, quick-stepping down the incline, Aurea in his arms. He snatched Del to her feet and sent her moving again.

Mata caught up to them at the lead SUV. He tossed the money duffel across the seat to the passenger side, then clambered behind the wheel.

Santos shoved Del into the back seat, and piled in next to her, emptying Aurea onto the seat between them. "Go!" he ordered.

Mata cranked the engine.

Del threw a glance back over her shoulder.

On the desert floor above, Santos' men had begun to receive counterfire from authorities. They held their line as best they could, but fell back quickly when the fire power overwhelmed them. They slipped over the embankment and into the wash. One by one, they took up positions behind the Hummer and second SUV and continued to return fire.

Bullets pinged off metal, zipped through the surrounding brush, and *plogged* heavily into the soft sandy soil of the wash embankments.

Del pulled Aurea beneath her arm and covered her.

Mata stomped the gas. The tires spun freely in the sand at first, then grabbed to launch them forward.

Adrenaline was pumping hard through Del's veins, her heart was hammering. In seconds they were closing fast on the border.

Santos turned in his seat to peer out through the back. Del could see her Baby Eagle peeking out from his waistband. If only she could reach it somehow, she could end his escape and bring this thing to an end.

They were bounding through the wash, gaining speed now ... *twenty-five miles per hour ... thirty ...* Up ahead, the head-lights glinted off the strands of border wire that spanned the wash. By the time Tom Sutter and his deputies could manage to overtake the fire line, Del knew, Santos would be long gone into Mexico.

Thirty yards… twenty…

They closed on the wire.

Del's heart sank low inside her chest. All hope drained from her. Then…

In the wash, just ahead of them, a pair of headlights suddenly flared to life. They filled the SUV and the surrounding wash with a blinding, white-hot light.

Mata threw a hand to his eyes and hit the brakes hard. The SUV slid sideways in the sand, straightened a bit, and skidded some more.

In back, Del, Aurea, and Santos were all thrown hard into the seatback.

The SUV came to rest with the high, blinding headlights still glaring in on them.

Santos was the first to recover. He pulled himself up and took a look across the front seatback, palm raised against the glare.

"*¿Qué es?*" he cried.

Del was thinking the same thing—*What in the hell was it?*

Light continued to flood in.

She shaded her eyes with one hand. Behind the brilliant glare, she could make out the shadowy hulk of something monstrous and immovable. Something made of steel. *Oh, my God!* she said to herself. It was a giant earth mover. And possibly the largest one she'd ever seen.

"*Francisco,*" she murmured to herself.

TWENTY-EIGHT

Sheriff Tom Sutter saw the powerful lights come on in front
of the fleeing vehicle to halt it in its tracks. He called to his men to
cease fire. The assailants in the wash had stopped firing also, turning in awe to see what the bright invading light was all about.

What the hell was it? *Who* the hell was it?

As he watched, a synchronous roar of diesel engines suddenly
filled the night. *Revving and growling.* More headlights flared.
Heavy equipment appeared amid the desert scrub and began
moving, inching forward to form a wide, semicircular barricade,
to block egress into Mexico. In the adjoining headlights he could
see the invaders more clearly now—earth movers, road graders,
ore haulers, bulldozers, front loaders, and the like. Their diesel engines growled. Their hydraulics hissed and spat. Their headlights
washed the desert white with light, leaving no more secrets, and
allowing no place to run or hide.

In the lead SUV, the one blocked by the giant earth mover, Sutter could see three silhouetted figures. One of the figures in the

back seat, he believed, was Del Shannon. The other two—a male also in the back seat could be Santos de la Cal himself. The hulking figure behind the wheel, he could only guess, was maybe Santos' bodyguard. And somewhere, possibly ducked down below the seat, was very likely the Lara girl that Del had had with her earlier. He called to his men to hold their positions.

Now he raised his eyes to the formation of heavy equipment. Whoever they were, these monstrous interlopers from across the border, they had blocked the path of escape. And they now stood in rigid resistance to anyone who might try to cross.

Wh*at now?* Sutter thought to himself. *Somebody needs to make the first move.*

———

Del shielded her eyes and tried to see beyond the glare of light. The heavy equipment continued to rev and growl in a menacing show of solidarity. She wasn't totally sure who these men were or why they had appeared in the nick of time—but she had a pretty good idea.

Santos twisted in his seat, first one way and then the other, uncertain of what to do. "Get us out of here! ¡*Ándele!*" he cried, punching the back of Mata's seat to get him moving.

Mata threw the SUV into reverse and began backing up the wash.

They got as far as where the second SUV and the Hummer sat. Once again, their escape was blocked. Mata tried cutting the wheel hard and taking them up the embankment. That effort, too, was thwarted by the steepness of the incline.

"Give it up, Santos," Del told him. "You're trapped."

Santos ignored the warning. He powered his window down and began shouting orders to his men. "*¡Muévanse!*" he cried. "*¡Muévanse! ¡Ándele! ¡Ándele!*"

A couple of the men clambered behind the wheels of the Hummer and SUV, and cranked the engines.

Del watched as they began to back quickly up the wash. Mata followed suit, chasing in reverse.

To the rear, the sheriff's deputies and Border Patrol spread their ranks to try to thwart their efforts. They were holding their fire, Del realized, out of concerns for her and the child in the back seat.

"They're not going to let you get away," Del said, her voice breaking as they hit a rut hard and bounced.

"Shut up!" Santos screeched.

The men outside the vehicles had taken to firing again, running alongside the reversing vehicles for cover. Santos stuck his gun out the window and fired off a couple of rounds. The Baby Eagle, stuck in his waistband, made a brief appearance. Del thought to grab for it. Then he was rotating again, and her weapon was lost once more in the folds of his clothing.

Just give me one chance ... Del prayed.

On the desert floor, the authorities dodged for cover.

An egress appeared farther up along the wash, where the embankment became shallow. All three vehicles aimed for it. It looked for all the world like they might reach it and escape through the vent into the desert. Then, from the formation, one of the pieces of heavy equipment—a monster-sized bulldozer—revved its engine and broke ranks. It charged forward, gaining speed. Its caterpillar tracks churned, spewing a rooster tail of sand and dirt into the air.

In the headlights of the other equipment, Del could now see past the wide steel blade, past the steel mesh of the operator's cage, to the man behind the controls. *It was Francisco*—the man with a knack for appearing in the nick of time. He was smiling a devilish smile. His eyes were narrowed as he bore down on the fleeing vehicles.

"*Estrada!*" she heard Santos murmur in realization.

"Bless your handsome little heart," Del said, beneath her breath.

The other men saw the bulldozer, too.

The drivers of the trailing vehicles suddenly stopped in midretreat, forcing Mata to hit the brakes again.

"Why are we stopping?" Santos cried. "*¡Muévete! ¡Muévete! ¡Ándele!*"

The caterpillar churned forward, aiming itself directly for the trailing vehicles. Its steel tracks clickity-clacked. Its diesel engine roared. Thick black smoke belched from the overhead exhaust. The smell of diesel fuel filled the air.

With a cowardly cry, Mata abandoned his post, bailing out through the driver door to leave Santos to his own defense.

"Mata ... *¡Alto!*" Santos cried, issuing his protest.

The big bull didn't hesitate long enough to hear it. He made the embankment and was halfway up the side when a single shot from Santos' gun struck him square in the back and brought him down. The big bull sagged to his knees, pitched forward, then rolled the remaining distance into the wash.

Santos' men on the ground turned their weapons to the rapidly advancing bulldozer. Bullets sparked off the huge steel blade and pinged off the steel mesh of the operator's cabin. It raced, faster ... faster ... angling itself directly for them. The blade dropped with a thud. It bit hard into the earth and began to plow. The engine groaned. Sand, rock, and cactus met with powerful hydraulics and mass momentum. A rolling wave of sand and debris built before it, amassing quickly into a giant wave.

Cries of defeat came from the cadre of men on the ground as they pitched their weapons and fled toward the opposite embankment.

Del drew a deep breath and held it.

The bulldozer and its earthen tsunami reached the wash and plowed in.

A wave of sand and debris engulfed the Hummer and SUV. It spilled outward and buried the men who had failed to reach the top. Momentum carried the massive dozer off the embankment. It seemed to hang momentarily in thin air, then slam down atop the Hummer to bury itself to the nose in the opposite embankment. The engine coughed and died.

Del let her breath out, and the night became suddenly quiet.

Santos' face was an ashen mask.

"It's just you and me and the child," she said. "Are you going to give it up?"

Santos sat frozen with indecision for a moment. Then his survival instincts kicked in.

He grabbed Aurea, pulling her into his lap, and put the gun to her head.

Del threw a glance over her shoulder. Sheriff's deputies and Border Patrol agents were closing in. Seeing him with the child, the gun to her head, they halted their advance.

"You won't get away with it," she said, attempting reason.

"We'll see!" Santos said.

Santos sprung open the door and stepped into the gap, taking Aurea with him, displaying his weapon at the side of her head, and using her as a human shield.

"Back away or the child dies!" he called, as the men closed in.

A voice from a bullhorn said, "Put the girl down and drop the gun."

Del recognized the voice as Sheriff Tom Sutter.

"I won't go down alone," Santos said. "Clear a path or I will put a bullet in her little fucking brain."

Reluctantly the authorities fell back.

Santos stood straighter now, more confident, his chest puffed with bravado, his expression filled with defiance. It appeared he would waltz right back across the border with the gun to his niece's head.

Not on your life, Del said to herself, spotting the grip of the Baby Eagle, now clearly visible, beyond the open door, in the waistband of Santos' pants.

It was now or never.

In a swift move, Del slid across the seat and grabbed the gun, jerking it from his waistband to shove the muzzle hard into his gut.

Santos went rigid with recognition.

"Give me Aurea and drop the gun, asshole!"

Santos' countenance sagged. But he held on. "You wouldn't!"

"If you don't drop the gun and give me that little girl, right now! I will splatter your guts all over American soil! No question!"

Santos hesitated only a second more, then tossed the gun aside and raised his one free hand.

Aurea squirmed free and slid back inside into Del's waiting arms.

Del received her, giving the girl a powerful hug, keeping the Baby Eagle trained on Santos' middle.

"It's all right, sweetie! It's over!" she said. "We can go home now."

———

Tom Sutter holstered his weapon and gave the signal for his men to move in.

"Check the man in the bulldozer," he added. There'd been no movement from the cab.

Deputies and Border Patrol Agents rushed into the wash. They swarmed over Santos, throwing him spread-eagle across the front of the vehicle, pinning him, patting him down and generally taking the welcome opportunity to rough him up a little.

Two of the deputies rushed to the bulldozer and began climbing its outrigging to get to the cab. They kicked and banged their way through the battered steel mesh. Then went to work to remove the man from behind the controls—he was comatose and unmoving.

At the SUV, both Border Patrol agents and sheriff's deputies vied to cuff Santos and read him his rights.

Sutter, conscious of his age, gingerly quick-stepped his way down into the wash and crossed to the SUV where its rear door still hung open and the woman and child remained in the back seat. "You're somethin' else," he said, poking his head inside. Light from the heavy equipment headlamps still filled the interior. He could see Del, strongly embracing the child, her cheeks streaked with tears. "Are you all right?"

Del nodded, still holding on to the girl tightly.

"I don't suppose you know anything about these Mexican handymen who showed up to thwart what otherwise might have been a disastrous outcome?"

"That's Francisco Estrada. He's..." She suddenly turned her face on Sutter in awareness. "Is he ...?"

Sutter turned his eyes from hers.

"What?" Del said.

"The men are checking on him now."

Del clawed her way to the door opening, calling ahead of her. "Francisco!"

Sutter blocked her exit.

"Let me go, Tom!"

"It may not be good, Del."

"Just get out of my way!"

Reluctantly, Sutter stepped aside. And Del slipped out with the child on her hip. She rushed quickly, then broke into a dead run. Aurea clung tightly to her neck.

Sutter tipped his Stetson back on his head. The danger might be over, he considered. But he feared the heartache had only just begun.

————

Del found Francisco on the ground where the men had put him. They were kneeling over him, working at clothing and buttons. A plume of bright red blood had spread across the front of his shirt.

Del sat Aurea aside and dropped down next to him, taking his hand in hers.

"I'm here!" she said.

Francisco opened weak eyes to her.

"*Mi amor*," he said.

"One of the bullets made it through the steel mesh," one of the deputies said. "We have emergency medical units on the way." They were tearing at shirttails and packing the wound to slow the bleeding.

"Give us a minute, will you?" Del said to the deputies.

They finished packing the wound as best they could, then rose and drifted off a few steps.

Del leaned in close. "That was a crazy stunt you pulled back there."

Francisco tried a smile. "I am known for my crazy stunts. I wanted to see you again." His voice was weak and fading.

"Try not to talk. You're going to be all right."

Francisco shook his head. "Remember what I told you?"

Del thought back to their last moments on the mountain. "You said you would lay down your life for me."

Francisco nodded and closed his eyes.

"Francisco…"

He opened his eyes to her once more.

"Francisco … I …"

His eyes slid closed, and this time his hand went limp in hers.

"Francisco?… Francisco!" Del cried.

He was gone.

Tears let go in a torrent. Then grief racked her chest. Del dropped her head to his shoulder and sobbed.

One of the deputies came to her, put a hand on her shoulder. "No!"

"There's nothing you can do," he said.

He put his hands beneath her arms now, urging her away.

"Just leave us!" she said bitterly, shrugging him away.

"Come on," the other deputy urged his partner. The two drifted off, respectfully leaving Del with her grief and guilt.

Del held Francisco tightly in her arms. Only when she became aware of Aurea at her side, one arm around her shoulder, did she lift her eyes. "I'm sorry, honey. Sorry you have to see this."

Aurea leaned in close. Del took her into her embrace and hugged her tight. "He was a good man," she told Aurea. "He deserved much better."

Aurea gave her a nod of understanding.

———

The night was filled with red and blue twirling lights. A coroner's van had arrived. Francisco's body was covered and carted away.

Santos sat in the back of a patrol car, face sullen and indifferent. Eventually, he too was removed from the scene. Del watched his vehicle pass. She held Santos in her gaze—anger and resentment boiling inside her.

Tom Sutter appeared. "You want me to arrange a car for you back home to Tucson?"

"No," Del said, a light shake of the head. She had a Kleenex to her nose. She made a final wipe with it, then said, "I'm going to stay at the farmhouse with Aurea. It will be her last chance to feel at home again. I'll take the van if that's okay with you."

"Sure," he said. "I'll need a statement from you. But all that can wait until you're ready."

Del nodded. There was a knot in her chest, the weight of grief dragging her down. She had lost a former lover to violence only a week ago. Now she had lost a man she had only known a few days, but believed she'd fallen in love with. She wasn't sure if she was grieving for her loss or grieving for Francisco's loss—the man who had fought so hard to find peace and freedom, but who didn't live to see peace restored. Perhaps he had found another kind of peace, however—if there truly was a God and heaven. She wanted to believe.

Del collected herself. She took Aurea by the hand and led her out of the wash.

On the desert floor, reaching all the way to the road between the fields, the night was a dizzying sea of official vehicles. She crossed back to where the van still sat with its driver's door and cargo door standing open. Daniels' body was nowhere to be found. The coroner's people must have already gathered it and transported it away. There was nothing left but the van itself and long-reaching streamers of crime-scene tape.

"Climb in, sweetie," Del said, helping Aurea up onto the running board and into the seat, feeling a weariness in her arms and legs and mind.

The child was tired, too, Del realized. *Exhausted.* And rightfully so. But she managed her way across and into the passenger seat. Del slid behind the wheel. The keys were still in the ignition where Ray had instructed her to leave them.

She took one last look at the scene before her. *It was over*, she told herself. But somehow it didn't feel that way. It didn't feel as if it were over. The whole affair lacked ...

Closure.

Maybe it was the loss of Francisco that left her feeling that way. Or, maybe, she just felt cheated. Wasn't that what Ray had once said about Ed's death? "... *Happening like that, it feels like a cheap shot.*"

Maybe that was it.

Francisco had been killed by a random bullet ... *that was a cheap shot.*

Santos being hauled off to a jail, rather than going down hard ... *that was a cheap shot.*

And Ray Daniels—most of all, Ray Daniels—her never having had the chance to wipe the smug look off his face ... *That! That was a cheap shot.*

Del turned her eyes from the brightly lit crime scene, gave a last look to Aurea on the seat next to her, put the van in gear, and headed back to the farm.

TWENTY-NINE

CREWS ARRIVED IN THE early morning to begin digging out the buried Hummer with the drugs inside and recover the bodies of the Mexican henchmen—Ramón Paz among them. The wash, south of the farm, was crawling with digging equipment and workers. K-9 officers prowled the melon fields with cadaver dogs, searching for the possible remains of Benito and Yanamaria Lara. Del sat at the kitchen table with the cell phone to her ear. She was talking to Randall. "How are you feeling?" she asked.

"A couple of broken ribs, a mild concussion, a few cuts and bruises. Urgent care!" he said, as if it were a dirty word. "They taped me up, gave me some painkillers, and sent me home. I'm back in the office this morning."

"You need to be in bed."

"Patti's here. She's a good kid. Remind me to give her a raise."

Del heard Patti say in background, "I heard that, Randall, and I'm holding you to it."

"She cares about you, Randall. We all do."

"What about you, kiddo? How you doing?"

It was a tough question. Del had slept very little the night before—residual adrenaline coursing through her veins. This morning she felt hung over from it. Limbs weighty, her mind dull. Aurea seemed none the worse for wear. She had gone straight to her room and pulled the covers over her head, somewhat cranky by then. But by morning she seemed fresh as a daisy, sitting on the kitchen floor next to Del with crayons and paper. The resilience of youth, Del figured.

The feeling that had haunted her the night before, that idea of being cheated, was still with her this morning. There was no closure, she had decided. Maybe there never was. Maybe the idea of closure was just a myth.

She said to Randall, "Numb. I feel numb."

"You need some time off, Del. Find a beach somewhere and chill out."

"I'd go crazy on a beach," she said. "I don't know what I need."

"You still at the farm?"

"For now," Del said. "I spoke to Juan Lara. They're going to collect Aurea here. Pack up some of her things to take with them."

"So we're done?"

"You can take the money to the bank, if that's what you're asking."

"Thirty thousand in cash? I'm not sure how to deposit it without raising some eyebrows."

"Use it for beer money and tip change," Del said. "It should last you a good long time."

"Not the way I've been drinking lately. You just about gave me a heart attack this time out, you know that?"

"I'll try to be a good girl for a while."

"I'll believe it when I see it. So, when you heading home?"

"Probably later today."

"Probably? I thought you said it was all wrapped up?"

"Yeah, it is," Del said, not sure why she felt uncertain about it. "I'll be home late today. I have to recover my Wrangler from up at Summerhaven. Just take care of yourself in the meantime, okay?"

Randall grunted his reply.

Del closed the phone to end the call.

Aurea was looking up at her from her seat on the floor.

"What?" Del said.

The child looked away.

Del smiled, in spite of her mood. It made her think of Francisco, the courageous resistance leader who sang to children. She had said to him on parting... *It doesn't have to be forever!* He had said to her, *I would lay down my life for you.* And he had. Would they have had a chance at a lasting relationship, had things worked out a little differently?

Del rose with her cup and crossed to the screen door. In the fields the K-9 cadaver dogs pawed at the barren earth. Heavy equipment worked mechanically in the wash to free the vehicles and bodies from the sand. There were maybe twenty personnel from various agencies milling around the scene.

Maybe not, Del thought.

Beyond the powerful physical attraction she had to Francisco, the effervescing fountain of mutual admiration and respect they had for each other, there would have been obstacles to overcome. Geographical boundaries was one. Where would they have lived?

Would she have had to go to Mexico to be with him? Would he have left his homeland to be with her?

Funny how you could say... *I would lay down my life for you.* But consider relocation, a change of lifestyle, and... well, suddenly things weren't so easy. And there would have been cultural differences as well. The callused-hand vigilante was a man who longed for peace in his life. A steady job—perhaps back at the mines. A stable home and family. He would have needed children. Lots of them. Offspring were the ultimate goal for a man like Francisco. Progeny.

Would she have conceded to such a life?

Del didn't think so.

She'd had her dreams of such, for sure—the romanticized fantasy of the Spanish villa, desert breeze wafting across the veranda, children playing in the yard...

But, see, that was the thing.

In the dream—

She'd come to realize this as she lay awake in the dark the night before.

—the children were not her own.

As beautiful as the idea of children playing in the yard was, as appealing the concept... the children she had pictured had not been hers.

Francisco's perhaps. Another woman's, maybe.

Just... *not hers.*

So there it was in a nutshell. Francisco would have wanted children; Del would not have been ready for them. End of story.

Did that mean she couldn't love him?

She decided the answer to this was *no*. In the same way she'd continued to love Ed—a man she could never claim as her own. She would love Francisco and mourn his loss for many months to come. And, in the end, she would buck up—closure or no closure—and move on with her life alone.

For now, at least.

Del turned away from the screen and returned to Aurea, where she sat working with paper and crayons on the floor. She was adorable, Del had to admit. And she couldn't avoid the stab of heartache the sight of her brought. "Your Uncle Juan and Tía Elena are on their way. They'll be here to take you home with them. Will that be okay?"

Aurea nodded. She'd gone back to being the silent type.

Del smiled. "You're a good kid," she said. "You saved my life last night."

She brushed the baby-fine hair that hung across Aurea's eyes and left her to her solitary pursuit of drawing.

From the yard outside, the sound of a car engine could be heard approaching. Del set her coffee cup aside and crossed back to the screen door. A sheriff's vehicle was pulling into the yard. It was Tom Sutter. She stepped onto the porch to wait for him.

"Del," he said, touching the brim of his hat as he came up the steps.

"Morning, Tom." There was little enthusiasm in her voice.

"I thought I'd check on you, see how you're doing."

"I'll live, I guess." She thought she must look like hell to him—pale pallor, puffy eyes.

"The Lara kid?" he said, peering through the screen to where she played on the floor.

"She's remarkable," Del said. "I wish I had her resilience. Her extended family is coming to get her."

"Well, you did a courageous thing last night. I wanted to let you know my department and the Border Patrol ... well ... we're all real grateful."

She wanted to say, *It was nothing*. But didn't have it in her.

Sutter said, "Oh, I also wanted to let you know ..." He lowered his voice a bit, out of respect for the child. "The K-9s have hit on two bodies in the melon field out there. I suspect we know who they'll prove to be. We'll match the gun Santos was carrying to the ballistic samples we recover. I'm sure it will be a match. That should seal the deal on Santos."

Del nodded. Somehow it didn't feel like a victory. "It's sad," Del said.

"Well, we all do what we can. He'll be going in for his arraignment later this morning. We'll have plenty to hold him. But I still need a statement from you."

"I'll stop by later, after I see Aurea off," Del said.

Tom gave her a nod. "Well ... you have a good day," he said, and turned back down the steps and to the patrol car.

"Thanks, Tom," Del said.

He threw a wave over his shoulder and slid behind the wheel.

Del remained on the porch, watching as he wheeled the patrol car around into the drive and headed off toward the highway.

The farm seemed a lonely place now, despite the action still going on in the fields. A sudden pang of remorse struck Del and she felt like she wanted to cry.

No, don't, she told herself ...

You have a little girl to make ready for family.

———

The Lara family arrived at the farmhouse late afternoon. The women—the older matron, Adelina Dueña, and Juan's wife, Elena—quickly went to work in the kitchen packing dishes and the like. Juan Lara set about readying Benito's gray pickup, while, back in the bedroom, Del helped Aurea pack her clothing into a box that Juan Lara had thought to bring.

While the adults took care of business, Gabino, Juan's son, played outside in the yard, pitching rocks into the dried-out melon fields, as far as he could throw them. The crime scene workers had departed. As for Aurea herself, she was back to saying nothing.

By three o'clock, the pickup was ready and loaded with boxes. It was decided that the grandmother would ride with Juan's wife in the vehicle they had arrived in, while Aurea and Gabino—the children—would ride in the pickup with Juan. The stack of newspapers and scissors, which had been on the front seat of the pickup all this time, were left there as something to occupy Aurea on the long drive ahead. All that remained to be packed were the remainder of Aurea's clothes and personal effects.

"You really did save my life last night, sweetie," Del said, "Speaking up the way you did. It was very brave of you."

They were alone in the tiny bedroom, a clothing box open on the bed. Aurea's suitcase open next to it. Aurea folded a shirt and placed it in the box.

"Don't you have anything else to say?"

The bedroom felt empty now. Gone were the clippings on the wall, gone were the bed sheets and pillows. Aurea gave no reply, but continued working, being fastidious with the way she folded and placed her clothing in the box.

"Well, I want to thank you just the same," Del said, keeping the one-sided conversation going. "Are you going to miss your Tío Santos?"

Aurea shook her head *no*.

"So, you're okay with going to live with your Uncle Juan and Aunt Elena?"

This time she nodded *yes*.

Del left it at that. There were things she would still love to ask Aurea. Things she would like to say, just to get her to talk. But Aurea had spoken when it counted most of all. She had kept Santos from blowing her brains out. So, if the kid decided she wanted to go back to being quiet, so be it. It was okay with her.

"How we doing, ladies? We just about ready?" Juan Lara was at the door, inquiring.

"Just a few things left," Del said, placing the last of the clothing in the box.

Juan stepped inside, his eyes immediately going to the empty wall where the photo clippings had once been. "We cannot thank you enough, señorita," Juan said, turning his attention to her now. "Bringing Aurea back to us, it is the answer to our prayers."

"Are you sure the pickup will make the trip?"

Juan shrugged. "The tires will need air, I will get some at the nearest gas station. The battery is strong. The engine is … well, okay, not so good … but I believe good enough." Juan turned his eyes back to the empty wall again. "I am sorry," he said. "But all the clippings our niece made of you, her predictions of your coming, her vision of you as her *salvadora*, I get goose bumps just remembering."

"Well, I wouldn't put much faith in prophecies," Del said. "She had reasons for clipping the photos of me."

"You don't believe she has visions?"

"I believe her visions are that of every child. Gumdrops and lollipops."

"She saw you and you came," Juan said.

"I suppose I have to give you that," Del said. She closed the flaps on the box of clothing and passed it off to Juan—her way of saying, I don't want to talk about it anymore.

Juan accepted the box, but turned his eyes to Aurea now, who was sitting on the end of the bed, stoic as ever. "She still not talking, huh?"

"She'll talk when she has something to say. I wouldn't push it."

"Well, perhaps some time soon maybe."

"We still have her pencils and crayons to pack," Del said. "I'll finish in here with the suitcase. Why don't we meet you outside?"

Juan gave one last reverent look at the empty wall, then went off with the box of clothing.

Del and Aurea were alone again.

"You're going to miss your mama and papa, aren't you, sweetie?"

Aurea said nothing. Del knelt in front of her.

"I want to show you something," she said, turning her left wrist to display the back of it. "You see this little tattoo? It's a tiny little moon, exactly like one my mother sewed on my pajamas long before I was old enough to remember. I grew up with my father, missing my mother. So I put it there to remind me of her every day. A keepsake. You understand?"

Aurea reached one small finger to touch the image on Del's wrist.

"You like it?"

Aurea raised her eyes to Del.

"Good, because I think you need something to remember your mother by, too."

Del produced a handbag from under the bed—the purse from the master bedroom closet that she had found on her first visit to the farm. The one that had the name *Yanamaria* spelled out in colorful sequins.

"This belonged to your mother, sweetie. And if you take very special care of it, it will one day mean a lot to you. It will be your very own keepsake."

Aurea reached with her finger, this time to trace the outline of the name.

"You understand, don't you?" Del said, once more marveling at the child's remarkable intellect, and perhaps a little relieved that the child was not the clairvoyant that her family believed her to be. "What do you say we pack your pencils and crayons in it for now?"

Aurea nodded.

Del raked the items off the desk and into the bag. When she finished she placed the purse inside the suitcase and zipped it shut. "I'm going to miss you, sweetie. What do you say we become sisters at heart. I'll be the big sister and you can be the little one. I'll come to visit you from time to time. Would you like that?"

Aurea put her arms around Del's neck and hugged her tight.

Del returned the embrace. "I love you, sweetie. You bring out the best in me." Her voice cracked a little, tears welled in her eyes.

They held each other for a long moment, then reluctantly pulled apart.

"I guess it's time to go," Del said, coming to her feet. She hefted the suitcase and led Aurea out through the house and onto the porch.

Juan Lara was waiting, the others were already in the car.

Del handed Juan the suitcase, lifted Aurea into her arms, and gave her a hug and kiss. Then handed her off. Parting *was*, as they say, such sweet sorrow. Del forced down the lump in her throat.

"I can't tell you how much we appreciate you bringing Aurea back to us," Juan said.

"I'm happy I could do so," Del said. "Just drive carefully. I'll stay behind and make sure everything is closed up tight."

"No!" Aurea said suddenly, launching herself out of Juan's embrace and into Del's arms to grapple her about the neck.

"She speaks!" Juan said. "Is it so?"

"Yes, she's spoken to me before," Del said.

Juan continued to gape in amazement.

"It's okay, sweetie," Del said, patting her on the back. "I'll stay in touch, I promise."

"No! You go!" Aurea said, holding tight to Del.

"I can't go with you. You know that," Del said. "Please, go with Uncle Juan."

"No! You go!" Aurea pushed Del away now, urging her to leave.

"What? You want me to go? You don't want me to stay at the farm?"

"Go!" Aurea said.

"I don't understand," Del said to Juan. "She's seems to want me to leave immediately."

Juan shrugged. He sat the suitcase down and took Aurea from her.

"Go! Go!" Aurea continued to insist. Her eyes held a look of terror.

"Don't be afraid," she said, trying to calm the child. "I'll be okay. The good policemen have your Uncle Santos, everything will be all right."

Del tried to hug her.

"No! Go!" Aurea said, pushing Del toward the van parked in the yard.

"I don't understand the child either," Juan said.

"I don't know. Maybe she's experiencing some kind of post-traumatic insecurity," Del said, thinking that it must be some irrational fear left over from their recent ordeal. Aurea had, after all, witnessed Santos make a threat on both their lives and nearly carry it out. Was she afraid that Santos could still return?

"Maybe she's having a vision," Juan said.

They were back to the prophecy thing again. What exactly was Del to say?

Just then her cell phone rang.

Del ignored it for a moment, studied Aurea's eyes that were wide with fear.

Two more rings, and she answered it.

"Hello?"

"Del!" It was Tom Sutter.

"What is it?"

"Well … I don't know how to tell you this, but … Santos has escaped."

Del's stomach did a flip. She turned her eyes to Aurea, all the questions she'd ever had flooding back on her now.

"How?" she said into the phone.

"We were transporting him to his arraignment when he overtook the guards. He shot one of my deputies and got away. He's probably long gone across the border by now. I don't know how in the hell this could have happened. We're conducting a full-out manhunt, but I felt you should know just in case. You still at the farm?"

"I'm sending Aurea off with her family now. I plan to leave as soon as they are on their way."

"Good," Sutter said. "I really don't think he'd chance going back there. However, I guess you never know."

No, you never do, Del said to herself. She was still studying Aurea. The child with the curious knack for predicting danger.

She said, "I appreciate the call, Tom. Thanks."

"Let me know if you see anything."

"I will," she said. *But not before I get that bastard,* she was saying inside her head.

Del flipped the phone closed. Aurea had settled back in Juan Lara's arms.

Del said, "I understand now, sweetie. I'll be leaving the farm immediately. I'll be okay. I promise you."

It seemed to satisfy the girl.

She reached out and gave Del a casual goodbye hug now.

Juan repositioned Aurea on his hip, collected the suitcase at his side, and made his way with her to the pickup.

Del watched as Juan loaded her inside, then give a wave as he pulled away. The truck found formation with the other vehicle and together they drove off toward the highway.

Del remained on the porch until they were out of sight, trying to comprehend what had just happened. Had Aurea actually seen some vision of Del being in jeopardy by remaining at the farm? Had she witnessed in her mind Santos' escape from the guards?

Either way, the truth of it was that Santos was on the loose and Del knew exactly where he'd go first. He would return here, to this farmhouse, seeking his niece or seeking revenge. And when he did, she vowed…

She would be waiting.

THIRTY

Nighttime arrived and the farm fell into darkness. There was no sign of Santos, yet.

Del still questioned Aurea's outburst—but with a newfound respect for the girl. Be it psychic insight or intuitive premonition, the child had wanted to warn her—*Santos was coming.*

Del was convinced of it either way.

She made preparations, placing a chair with its back to the wall where she could see across the living room to the open doorway leading in from the kitchen. The Baby Eagle lay in her lap, safety off, magazine full, a round primed into the chamber. The porch light was off. The van was parked in front, where Santos could see and recognize it, and know she was there.

He would come in off the porch—the way she imagined it—the screen door would creak on rusty hinges. He would make his way on tiptoe across the kitchen tile, gun poised. He'd pass into the living room on his way to the hallway that led to the bedrooms. She would stop him before he got that far.

She would say, *"Santos!"* in maybe a soft, cool voice.

It would stop him in his tracks.

She would give him time to see the Baby Eagle pointed straight at his heart, let the smugness drain from his face. Watch him ponder a moment, then lunge in sudden desperation to bring his weapon up.

And she would shoot the *motherfucker* where he stood.

It was all a fantasy, she knew. But entertaining nonetheless. It would go down however it would go down.

The minutes ticked by slowly.

The darkness beyond the doorway deepened.

Going on ten, she thought she heard a noise from somewhere out in the yard. She braced herself. Took up the Baby Eagle. Quietness returned. The clock on the mantle ticked in rhythm with her heart. *Seconds passed ... More ...*

Another muted sound came from beyond the door.

Del readied the gun.

RINNNNGGGGG!!!!

The cell phone jolted Del to the edge of her seat.

Frantically, she searched to recover it.

Somewhere outside, a tree limb scraped against the side of the house; the porch railing creaked.

RINNNNGGGGG!!!!

"Goddamn it!"

Del found the phone between her hip and the padding of the chair.

RINNNNGGGGG!!!!

She flipped it open.

"WHAT!" she said into it, a little too harshly.

"Not much of a greeting," Tom Sutter said.

"Now's not a good time, Tom. Santos is here!" She had the Baby Eagle trained on the open doorway, her senses on high alert.

"Well, that's a little odd," he said. "See, we picked up Santos two miles east of Douglas, just minutes ago. He was trying to make his way back across the border."

There was silence on the line, silence throughout the house.

"Del?" Sutter said.

"I … I don't understand," Del said.

"What's not to understand? I just thought you'd want to know the Border Patrol has him in custody. He's being transported to a federal facility. This time he's not going anywhere."

More silence. Del studied the dark, open doorway.

"I thought you'd be overjoyed," Sutter said.

"I'm … just, still a little upset over last night, is all."

"Well, I'm real sorry about your Mexican friend. But we got the bastard responsible."

"Yeah … I'm happy, Tom … that's good."

"You get a good night's sleep. I'll talk to you tomorrow."

Del let the line go dead without goodbyes. She stood staring at the dark, beyond the open doorway. Aurea had tried to warn her of Santos, but Santos had been making his way to the border, not back toward the farmhouse. It didn't make any sense. Then again, it only made sense if you believed in psychic children.

Jesus! Del thought. The idea could drive you crazy.

Del moved carefully to the open doorway, checked the kitchen, then checked the porch. She crossed to the window and peered out into the yard. The yard was empty. The field were empty. The moon lay a soft blanket across the desert floor. There was nothing to be seen or heard.

Del took a deep breath and let it out. She lowered the gun.

She had been primed and ready for a fight. So convinced by Aurea, and by the earlier call from Sutter, that Santos would return to the farm. But he hadn't. She could let her guard down, and go home. *A nice thought*—not as fulfilling as her fantasy of filling Santos full of holes. But a *nice thought*, nonetheless.

Del turned back inside, turned off lights, and began closing things up. The idea of finally going home, now, was powerful in her mind. She gathered the keys for the van, checked the safety on her weapon, tucked it back into her waistband. Then made her way out through the kitchen. Closing the door behind her, she crossed to the van and slipped behind the wheel. She cranked the engine...

"And where do you think you're going!" a voice said, from the seat behind her.

Del's heart gave a leap, she stiffened in place. She could feel the point of something sharp digging into the soft flesh at her neck. Slowly she lifted her eyes to the mirror.

"Ray!" Del said.

It was Ray Daniels—inexplicably and impossibly so.

His shirt was covered in dried blood, but he was alive and well. His right hand held a sharp stick, pressed tight against her jugular. His eyes held hers in the mirror.

"Pass that little gun of yours across the seat. Easy..." he said, jabbing the point of the stick harder against her skin. "Nice and slow."

Del slipped the Baby Eagle from her waistband and passed it to him.

Daniels grabbed the gun and tossed the stick over his shoulder into the cargo area.

"Drive," he said, pressing the gun to the side of her head now.

"Where to?"

"Down there into the desert."

Del's mind flashed to Aurea's warning, to the fear and terror in the little girl's eyes. *Had this been her warning after all?*

"What are you going to do, Ray?" she said.

"What I should have done in the first place. Drive!"

Del put the van in gear and started forward. She took them through the yard and onto the road between the fields. "Why are we going down there? I would think you'd want to get out of here."

"Oh, I'll get out all right. Once I finish this."

"Won't it seem a little strange, authorities finding me down here in the desert?"

"They'll just think you were somehow involved in all this drug mess. Somebody got to you to shut you up, keep you from testifying against Santos."

"But I'm in your van."

"Your Jeep is back at my cabin. You came for a visit and borrowed my van. I didn't know what for at the time, but can now obviously speculate you must have been tied up with the drug trade somehow."

Del continued down the dirt road, to where it turned out into the open desert.

"Keep going," Daniels said. "I'll tell you when to stop."

"How did you manage, Ray? I thought you were dead."

"I crawled off during all the commotion, been hiding out in the scrub since last night."

She met his eyes in the mirror.

"What?" he said, seeing the way she was looking at him. "You thought the coroner's folks took me away, didn't you?"

It was true. In her grief over Francisco last night, Del had given no more thought to Daniels, other than to believe some of the authorities on the scene had dealt with the body. She said, "I told everyone about your involvement."

"No, you didn't," Daniels said. "I saw the way you looked when you came out of the wash with the kid last night. You were a ghost, moving in slow motion. You haven't left the house all day. With you gone, it's like I was never here."

Del turned her eyes back to the darkness ahead. As she wove the van through the desert scrub, she thought of what Ray had just said. It was true, she had not said a word to anyone about his involvement. She had assumed the authorities had found his body, taken it away, and would be saving questions about him for when she came in to make her statement. All the grief, all the heartbreak, and all the concern for the child had left her in a fog. She had not been focused on her duty, her professionalism in her job. And now it had left her vulnerable to one last threat.

Del pulled the van into the wide open patch of desert where they had met with Santos the night before.

"This is far enough," Daniels said.

Del stopped the van and killed the engine.

"So what now, Ray? You going to shoot me in the back of the head with my own gun?"

"That would be too civilized, considering what you've cost me. Get out!"

Daniels slid open the cargo door and waited for her.

Del opened the driver's door and stepped out.

"Go around and open up the back."

Del complied.

Daniels slammed the side doors shut and followed with the gun.

"Open the doors and crawl up in there."

Del opened the double doors in back and climbed inside the carpeted cargo hold. She turned on her knees to face him.

"That gas can there," Daniels said, gesturing to a red plastic container strapped in behind the rear wheel well. "Take it out."

"You going to burn my body, Ray? They'll still identify me. You're an ex-cop, you know that."

"It'll slow them down. Give me time to get back to the cabin, put in a call to your boss, say how worried I am about our little girl. Borrowed my van the night before and hasn't returned."

"Sounds like you've thought it all out. Have you saved some of those illicit funds for your retirement?"

"Enough to put me on an island, far, far away," Daniels said. "Now get the can!"

Del unstrapped the gas can and removed the cap.

"Pour it on."

"Ray…"

"Pour!"

Reluctantly Del began to douse her clothing with gasoline. Harsh fumes rose up to choke her throat, burn her eyes.

"Make sure you get it on real good. Pour the rest on the floorboard."

Using her left hand to maneuver the can, Del soaked her clothing down the right side, then poured the remainder over the carpet around her.

"I never would have suspected you of this, Ray." Del's hope of appeal was fading fast.

"Shut up!"

"Maybe we could team up, you and me! You've always wanted that."

"You say that now." Daniels kept the gun trained on her with his right hand, with his left he reached into his pocket and came out with a Bic lighter.

"At least have the decency to kill me first."

"I'll think about it, sit back."

Del inched her way backwards, her hand suddenly coming to rest on a familiar object. It was the long, pointed stick that Ray had discarded across the seat.

Ray flicked the lighter, keeping the gun pointed at her. It sparked but failed to light.

"Don't do it, Ray."

He flicked again. Once again, the lighter failed.

Now he swapped hands, fumbling the gun into his left, the Bic into his right to get a better strike.

Del seized her chance. With all the force she could muster, she launched herself out toward him, stick in hand, a banshee cry on her lips.

Daniels looked up in surprise as she landed on him, brought the stick around in a swift arc, and drove it into his throat at the side.

The gun dropped from his hand; he was still holding the lighter.

Del grabbed the gun and rolled with it.

Daniels staggered toward the open doors of the van. He turned to her now, mewling sounds gurgling from his throat, blood gushing from the wound in his neck.

On her back now, Del pointed the Baby Eagle up at him, using her left, dry hand. Extended it as far away from her saturated clothing as possible.

Daniels' eyes were wide and wild. He flicked the Bic once, and this time got a flame.

"Don't do it, Ray!"

He stepped toward her with the fire.

Del hesitated no more. She said a prayer that the muzzle flash would not set off the gasoline and squeezed the trigger.

The bullet struck Daniels in the chest, rocked him backwards.

She fired again.

A third time.

Her clothing had not ignited.

Daniels stumbled backwards with the burning lighter. The back of his knees struck the rear bumper and he pitched backwards into the open cargo hold. The lighter dropped. The gasoline-soaked carpet flashed. A giant fire ball erupted with a *whoosh*.

Del scrambled backward to escape the flash.

Fire engulfed the van. Ray Daniels thrashed about, then went still. Thick clouds of black smoke rolled upward toward the sky.

Del dropped back onto the cool night earth and gazed without seeing at the star-filled sky. Ray Daniels—Ed's killer—was dead.

Now! she had closure.

THIRTY-ONE

FOUR DAYS LATER—IT WAS a Monday now—Del returned to the office. Randall was hobbling around, his ribs still on the mend. Patti was fretting over him, bringing coffee, scolding him frequently to sit down, take it easy. Rudy, one of the other investigators, stopped by the office to see how Randall was doing. Randall handed him a case file and sent him back out the door. He wasn't so quick to put Del back to work.

"I think you need to take a couple of weeks off," Randall told her.

Del was at her desk, looking over a missing persons file, a cold case she had been considering for some time. She was only half-listening to Randall, her thoughts still held captive by the traumatic events of the past week.

She had come close to dying—on more than one occasion—in the past days. The close encounter with the gasoline, the Bic lighter that had thankfully been stubborn in its reluctance to light, had taken its toll on her nerves, left her shaky and indecisive. Ray

Daniels' fiery, gruesome end had served to punctuate that realization and drive the trauma home. She had been lucky this time out. Maybe Randall was right.

"Vacation? Is that *with pay*?" Del said, without looking up from the file.

"With pay ... with bonus ... whatever you need, sweetheart. You've earned it."

A couple of weeks didn't sound bad actually; she had a lot to think about. She was still sad over Ed's death, still reeling from the loss of Francisco—just when they were becoming close and intimate. But she would mend in time, she knew. She would hike up her skirt and get on with life. She had learned how to do that, having dealt with the traumatic loss of both parents, as well as that of her longtime friend and mentor Louise Lassiter.

She *was* thankful for certain things, however.

Liana had made it free and was now reunited with her husband and son. Santos was in custody and facing a lifetime of incarceration. And Aurea had been brought back from Mexico and placed with her extended family. A family, Del believed, who would nurture and support her ...

How was she taking it?

Juan Lara had called earlier in the morning to say that they had arrived in Fresno safely and that Aurea was doing well. She had begun to talk a little and was finding Gabino to be a source of comic relief.

It was welcome news. Maybe, one day, Aurea would come to speak openly; maybe her life would turn out all right.

As for Del's vacillating belief in the child as psychic visionary? Well, she'd come to terms with that as well. She'd decided, whatever went on in Aurea's sweet little head was okay with her. As mysterious and awesome as it was, she would leave it to the psychologists and new age thinkers to figure out. Give *them* something to do. She was just happy the child had come into her life and that perhaps she would have future opportunities to see her and spend time with her. Big sister—little sister. *Sisters at heart,* as Del had said. It was a good thing.

So, all things considered, the case of the missing child had found its way to a satisfactory end. And Ed's killer had been brought to ultimate justice.

There was just one thing left to do.

———

The Congress Hotel was pretty much as always—dark and quiet after the noon lunch crowd. Del sat in the same place where she had met with Marla Jeski just over a week ago. This time she arrived ahead of Marla to wait, taking a seat on the opposite side of the booth facing the entrance. She had a draft beer in front of her. The same waitress was on duty behind the bar.

After a time, Marla Jeski appeared in the doorway. She spotted Del, but stood with her back stiff until Del waved her over. This afternoon she was wearing a stylish, lightweight blazer, in red, over an expensive silk blouse. Her hair was crisp from a recent trip to the stylist. She was looking a little less wrung out than she had on their previous meeting. Still, there was a perpetual weariness about her that Del thought came from maybe always trying to look so perfect.

Del pointed Marla to the seat opposite her.

"I got your message to come," Marla said. "You didn't say what you had to tell me."

Del detected an air of coolness still with her. And who could blame her. Marla was the scorned wife; Del was the cookie on the side. Marla owed her nothing.

"You haven't seen the newspapers this morning?"

"I've come to avoid them," Marla said.

Del caught the waitress on the fly and ordered a drink for Marla. She gave it a minute, giving her beer a sip, while she thought about how to start. When she sat the mug down, Marla was looking at her, seemingly expecting the worst.

"Ed wasn't cheating," Del said, deciding to just hit her with the best part first.

Marla's breath caught in her throat. Her face tried to brighten, but fell short as Del believed it might be accustomed to doing.

"Truthfully?" Marla said.

Del nodded.

"But ... how ... why ...?"

"This is the part that's hard to say," Del said, allowing a slight hesitation. "It was Ed's partner, Ray Daniels."

"Ray? But ...?" Questions crisscrossed Marla's face. She came just short of stammering. "I ... I don't understand?"

The waitress arrived with Marla's drink, a Seven and Seven. Marla accepted it quickly and took a drink.

Del waited for Marla to gather herself, then began.

She told her of the drug dealings at the border. Of Santos de la Cal and the child. Of Ray's involvement in the smuggling. She told her how Ed had found out about it. How Ray had tried to buy his silence. How Ed had stood on his ethics, planning to turn

Ray in. How the seedy hotel and the mystery woman were all a setup—a plot Ray had used to portray Ed as a philanderer, thereby eliminating him, ensuring his silence, and deterring police from looking closer into other motives. Daniels had almost gotten away with murder.

When she finished Del sat back and waited for a response.

"This…this little girl…was the one who brought it into the open?" Marla asked, seemingly baffled by the child and her insights.

"She's a pretty remarkable kid," Del said.

"So…Ed really wasn't cheating, after all?" She still seemed reluctant to believe.

"No," Del said. "In fact, he was just trying to do the right thing."

Marla looked off in thought.

She would be replaying history in her mind now, Del believed. Going over every event in her head to see if all the pieces of the puzzle truly fit. When she had reasoned enough, she looked back at Del. "You found all this out."

"With the help of a six-year-old, yes."

Marla took another large sip of her drink, not quite finishing it off.

"I guess I owe you quite a bit."

"You don't owe me anything," Del said. "I wanted justice for Ed as much as you."

Now Marla drained her glass empty. "I…I guess there's nothing left to say then."

There was actually something Del wanted to say. She wanted to say to Marla how she had never really meant to hurt her. How she was sorry for Ed, sorry for her. She wanted to say she deeply regretted their past, all this, and more. But she decided it was well enough to end things here. Ed was gone, and he wouldn't be coming back. Del said, "I guess not."

Marla hesitated, then slid wearily out of the booth to stand. "Well ... I guess I'll be going now." Marla gave Del one last soulful look—one filled with a mixture of pain and perhaps pity.

Del wasn't sure how to take it; she said nothing.

Marla turned to go, then stopped. She turned back to Del.

"Maybe I'm wrong for asking," she said, with a casual shrug. "But ... do you think you'd like to get together for a dinner sometime? ... I mean ... I'd like to hear about the child."

Del thought of Randall—his admonishments about her personal life. She said, "Yeah ... I'd think like that."

Marla showed her what passed for a smile.

Del nodded her away, and Marla turned and left the bar.

Del sat alone now, in the shaded darkness of the bar. Maybe she and Marla would get together for dinner; maybe they wouldn't. Either way she was satisfied that they had made their peace with each other.

Del turned her thoughts away from the events of the past now—away from Ed and Marla and Francisco and the child.

When the waitress came by, she ordered another beer. *Why not? She deserved it.*

She wondered about the two weeks' vacation she now had. Where she might go. What she might do.

She thought of Allen May—the cowboy who made her laugh. Where did he say he was heading? South Dakota?

She'd never been that far north ... never roped a calf ... never ridden a dog.

When the waitress delivered her beer, she paused long enough to ask, "What you smiling about, hon?"

Del didn't answer. She just continued to smile.

It was okay being Del Shannon ... *life was good.*

THE END

© Lesley Bohm

ABOUT THE AUTHOR

Darrell James lives in Arizona. His stories have appeared in numerous mystery magazines and book anthologies and have garnered a number of awards; his latest story appears in the MWA Lee Child anthology *Vengeance*. His debut novel, *Nazareth Child*, the first in the Del Shannon series, was the winner of the 2012 Left Coast Crime Eureka Award for best first novel and nominated for both the Anthony and Macavity Awards.

Please visit him online at www.darrelljames.com.